POSTERITY
A Trilogy

Published by Indies United Publishing House, LLC
First Edition published March 2024

Edited by Shaylin Gandhi

Cover art designed by Amrita Raja

ISBN: 978-1-64456-710-4 [Paperback]
ISBN: 978-1-64456-711-1 [ePub]

Library of Congress Control Number: 2024902253

INDIES UNITED PUBLISHING HOUSE, LLC
P.O. BOX 3071
QUINCY, IL 62305-3071
www.indiesunited.net

Acknowledgments

Writing Privilege was a surprise to me, and so was writing Skingrafters. But not this final piece of the WP Saga. No, I've known for decades now that I wanted to write this book. In here, you'll find the closing chapter of a series that serves as an unapologetic celebration of the strong women who've taught me everything I know. It's appropriate that it took over 350,000 words to do them justice.

Monali Krishnan: The love of my life, who gives me strength, intelligence, and resolve that WP never could.

To the mom and four sisters who taught me that vulnerability is strength and kindness is the great equalizer: thank you.

And finally, to the aunties: There are so many of you that to list you all would be ridiculous. You are my "second moms" who raised me to believe that strong women will save the world.

POSTERITY

A Trilogy

Bharat Krishnan

INDIES UNITED PUBLISHING HOUSE, LLC

PURPOSE

"Freeing yourself was one thing; claiming ownership of that freed self was another."
– Toni Morrison

Chapter One

January 7, 2028

Therese Johnson didn't mind the cold, thin morning air of Albuquerque as long as she woke up wrapped in the warmth of her husband. Her routine involved waking every day about five minutes before her cell phone alarm rang. That way, she could turn it off before its ringing woke Russell. Despite her best efforts, though, he whispered to her groggily as she made her way to their connected bathroom.

"'Iz Saturday," he mumbled. "Come back to bed, Madame Mayor."

She smiled as his strong frame and sinewy fingers stretched out from the bed to touch her raven hair, which was as messy and tangled as her life before she'd had a chance to put a hair straightener to it. And Albuquerque was the hair straightener that'd given her life structure and order again after New York.

"Work never ends," she cooed in his ear, looking back and kissing his lips softly before entering the bathroom to start her morning routine. She left door open as she applied makeup to mask her crow's feet and popped a pill for her arthritis. Through the doorway, she saw Russell hogging the covers to himself now that she'd left their bed. She smiled, taking the opportunity to apply her dark red lipstick more fully in order to accentuate her smile—a smile she'd fought long and hard to reclaim.

What a journey it's been.

It'd been over two years since the city had elected her mayor, a fantastical idea borne out of a night of drinking too much red wine with her former boss, Alicia Wright. She'd been a babysitter when she'd first moved to New Mexico, before even President Begaye had been elected, and Alicia had been working out of the then-Senator's Albuquerque office. Therese's schedule had become crazier after Alicia had moved herself to DC to become the White House Press Secretary but left her kids here so they could remain in school with their friends and away from the bloodlust of the Capitol. And when the Mayor's seat had opened up, to her surprise, Alicia had said she'd discussed the issue with the State Democratic Party and wanted Therese to run.

I guess I'm doing a pretty damn good job, too.

She knew Jerome would be proud of her. Both Jeromes, for that had been her husband's name as well. Finally, after years of therapy and finding a doting husband and satisfying career, she could admit that to herself.

Jerome would've wanted me to not just live, but thrive. And she was.

Since she'd taken office in January 2026, she'd personally monitored the city's approach to WP legalization. Crime was down, jobs were up, and Intel had just committed to building a new WP refinery station in Rio Rancho, a $1.5 billion investment that put her on POLITICO's list of top American mayors. Not that she cared much about her press, but she knew it helped with raising the community's profile.

President Begaye's landmark legislation had established a process for refining the drug and imposed strict penalties for buying it unrefined, and that had presented all sorts of issues only compounded by the fact that the global war for WP had ended less than six months ago in total disaster. SCOTUS had delivered the war effort a fatal blow last July when the nine Justices ruled the WP Force illegal. And as soldiers had come home, many of them had turned to unrefined WP to cope with their PTSD. On top of what Lucas Brooks had done—that joke of a president—there'd been no other recourse for America than to lick its wounds, tuck its tail, and pretend the new world order was what it had always wanted.

Therese's hands balled into fists at her side as she exited the bathroom and saw Brooks's face on her TV. Russell had decided to get up.

"Go back to bed," she said. She put her clothes on and pretended not to hear as the local news discussed Brooks's funeral. She'd forgotten it was today.

At least the whole world now knows what a piece of shit he was. She'd been taught not to speak ill of the dead, but in his case, she would make an exception.

Still draped in their comforter, Russell rolled over to paw at her as she sat on the bed to put her pants on. His fingers brushing against her bare thigh sent a thrill up her body. The fact that he slept without a shirt on helped, too.

"I've got something more fun than work in mind for us this morning."

His voice changed her world, focused it. She sighed with contentment now, a relief from the last twenty-plus years. Even before Jerome's murder, before her husband's heart attack, she'd only ever sighed with frustration and fear in her throat. It had clawed at her insides. Paralyzed her. But now—she could breathe! And the best part about it was she didn't feel even a little bit guilty about it.

I am enough. She spent the first moments of every morning wishing she was dreaming, that she'd died in her sleep and gone home to her son. But then she realized it wasn't her time yet and committed to honoring Jerome by living her life to the fullest. The hole in her heart would never heal, and she wouldn't want it to. But through years of therapy and self-love, she'd understood after fifty-three years that the missing parts of your life could ache a little less through public service.

Zipping her pants up and draping a scarf around her neck, she gave Russell another peck on the lips. "Wasn't last night enough?"

"Oh, with you I'm insatiable," he said, grinning ear-to-ear like some dumb teenager.

"Sleep in. Like you said, it's Saturday. I know how hard you've been working to close this Intel deal."

They were a power couple. Her in the Mayor's office, and him at Intel leading their Department of Governmental Affairs. Before that, he'd done research for the Democratic Senatorial Campaign

Committee (DSCC) in DC.

"Have Luke push your schedule back a couple hours," he said, referring to her assistant.

"What are we gonna do after the first five minutes?" Therese joked, prompting him to grab her legs and pull her back onto the bed. She screamed in surprise as she fell, but as always, he was there to catch her. Leaning over her body, he let his cornrows brush against her face. She wrapped her arms around his neck and they kissed as if it was their first time. She took in his raw scent and gasped when his mouth went to her neck.

"Baby, I gotta go..."

His fingers fidgeted with her skirt, and that was when she heard a knock at the door.

"Saved by the bell," Russell said, stopping and getting up to throw on a shirt to go with his sweatpants.

"In a minute," Therese shouted. Running back to the bathroom to brush her hair, she promised Russell they'd finish tonight and then opened the door. "Good morning, Luke."

"Ma'am, I'm sorry for bothering you." He nodded at Russell before finding something fascinating on his shoes to stare at.

"What's up?"

"Two big issues, ma'am."

"Luke," she interrupted him. "It's been two years. Therese is fine, or Madame Mayor if you can't stand my name."

"Yes, ma'am," he said. She rolled her eyes as Russell chuckled behind her. "Two things."

"Give me a minute," Therese said. Turning to face her husband, she asked him to try and enjoy his day off.

"Oh, I'mma enjoy myself fully," Russell said. "The Indiana Jones trilogy just came to Netflix."

She kissed her fingers and touched the bedside photo of her son, then walked out with Luke.

"You said two things?" Therese sat passenger side as Luke drove them away from her house on the Westside, mere feet from the Rio Grande.

"Chief Justice Swindell finally died."

Therese closed her eyes and said a prayer. "When?"

"I heard it from Alicia this morning. The press will probably have it within the hour."

"Glioblastoma is a death sentence. Send flowers to his wife, would you?"

"Of course."

"And the other thing?"

Luke bit his lip as he merged onto I-25 North. "The other thing is a bigger problem for us."

"Where are we going? This isn't the way to the office?"

"We're going to the Sandoval County Jail."

Therese frowned. "Luke, how many times do I have to tell you? I can't get one of your friends out of a DUI. At this point, I think it's cheaper to just find better friends."

"That's not what it is," he said. "A homeless vet was caught breaking into a city reserve last night."

Therese closed her eyes again, but this time she didn't say a prayer so much as some four-letter words. "He was looking for unrefined WP?"

"Yes, ma'am."

"And he got some?"

"No," Luke said. "Cops picked him up before he could use it."

"Thank God for that."

"Ma'am, we don't have to go there today. His arraignment isn't until tomorrow."

"No," she said. "I made a promise when I was elected that I'd speak to all these poor souls, and I intend on keeping my word."

They drove in silence the rest of the way, Therese's leg moving up and down like a piston as the car navigated through morning traffic.

⸺⚫————————⚫⸺

The big block letters in silver, announcing the SANDOVAL COUNTY DETENTION CENTER against the adobe brick walls, made the jail look almost appealing, like a summer camp. Sheriff Ritter was there to greet them as soon as they parked near the back entrance and entered.

"We appreciate the cloak-and-dagger approach," Ritter said.

"Yeah," Therese muttered, "can't have the press snapping a photo of us together."

While she'd been elected with 63% of the vote, Sandoval County was a little more accommodating to Republicans. Ritter was proof of that, and he'd just as soon shoot himself in the foot than risk a photo of them together in an election year.

"You've got ten minutes," Ritter grunted. "His lawyer's already seen him and I don't need the guy getting any more face time before his arraignment."

"County attorney?" Luke asked.

"The finest representation the taxpayers can provide," Ritter said. The scowl on his face could've had its own zip code.

"Luke, wait in the car, please."

Opening the door to a holding cell, the sheriff waved Therese in and then left with Luke.

She almost cried just looking at the prisoner handcuffed at the metal table, sitting as if he'd made peace with his lot in life ages ago. With his scrawny frame and short hair, he was the spitting image of what her son would've looked like if he was still alive. She opened her mouth, Jerome's name on her tongue, before closing it again.

"Thank you for seeing me, ma'am."

Shaking her head, she walked to his side and lay her hand on his, squeezing it. "What's your name, and why are you here?"

He gave her an answer she'd heard a hundred times over the last seven years. WP legalization hadn't changed anything. The GOP had won back Congress in 2022 and passed all sorts of liability protections that limited its distribution, that established differences between refined and unrefined WP. Everyone had come together to agree that the stuff Jerome had used, unrefined WP, was still illegal. And if you were caught with it? Mandatory minimums, just like cocaine.

Taking WP to a refinery station was no problem if you were rich. Too bad if you weren't. And even now, after years of research, security devices still couldn't detect subtle differences between refined and unrefined WP. It had become such a problem that most government buildings (including the White House) didn't even allow staffers to wear WP.

Fucking politicians.

The prisoner's name was Justin. He'd served on the WP Force in Rwanda, but when the shit had hit the fan in 2024, he'd gotten discharged and sent home with a pat on the back and a TBI. The VA had messed up his healthcare and he hadn't been able to see a therapist for weeks upon returning to Albuquerque. When he'd finally gotten an appointment, his anger had grown to such lengths that he'd decided to skip his meetings. The military had tried setting him up with a job, but he hadn't lasted long with his anger issues. He'd lost a girlfriend, an apartment. He'd been on the streets for six months when he'd finally been arrested.

Thank God he wasn't killed.

Each state treated the possession of unrefined WP differently, through a patchwork set of loosely defined laws. Democrats had won back Congress in 2024, but still, no major reforms had happened on WP legalization since then. Corporations, small businesses, schools, hospitals—they all operated as flexibly as they wanted, depending on local regulations and the whims of their senior leadership.

Are we really running the country like this? Cops were given free rein to act with deadly intent to bring down anyone they suspected of holding unrefined WP. They pulled cars over habitually to check. And, of course, those cars just happened to be driven by nonwhites. Then the cops could confiscate the drugs and sell them back to the government or a private buyer. It was a great income stream for underfunded police stations, and political leadership was generally happy to look the other way and pat themselves on the back for the added funds (delivered back to taxpayers in the form of tax cuts if you lived in a red state or teacher salaries if you lived in a blue state). Either way, no one was complaining except the downtrodden (and who gave a fuck about them).

She'd spoken with Governor Strauss (a Democrat!) about the issue more than a couple times, but his hands were apparently tied. Thinking about it made her blood boil and she forced bile down her throat as Justin continued his story.

"The president himself called me an American hero," Justin said. "Begaye! And look where I am now. You can't trust politicians for shit."

It was just the sort of thing her son would've said. Even the lilt of Justin's voice reminded her of him...

———————•———————

April 10, 2003

The cry of her baby boy was the most beautiful thing Therese Johnson had ever heard. Born six pounds, seven ounces, he had finally arrived. Today would be more important to her than even the day she'd married Jerome.

"We gotta name him after you, baby."

"Jerome Jr.? Shit, this guy's gonna be a killer."

Boston was a great town to raise a boy. They actually lived in Tewksbury, but close enough. And with her husband as the hot-shot lawyer, they'd give their son opportunities the two of them could've never dreamed of. Maybe she wouldn't even go back to work.

Later, after Jerome had left and the lactation consultant had gotten her set up, when it was just her and her baby in the hospital, she closed her eyes and focused on her baby drawing life from her. They said it would hurt, but his mouth against her bosom filled her with warmth. She was his everything, and he was hers.

"Nothing I did before today mattered, and nothing I do tomorrow will matter if you aren't there with me."

For now and forever, her life belonged to him.

———————•———————

July 2, 2009

No wonder Nancy Pelosi was such a great leader, Therese thought. Managing one six-year-old was driving her insane. If you could handle five of them, you should be elected president automatically.

"You're gonna slip and fall down the stairs!"

Bath time had ended, but before she'd been able to drape her boy in a towel, he'd taken off with a toy lightsaber in one hand and his underwear in the other. As he made the crackling energy noises his father had taught him, Therese tried to seize him and at least wipe his feet down so he didn't break his neck. Luckily, the door opened before Jerome Jr. made it to the stairs. The boy stopped to watch his dad stumble inside, dropping his briefcase to the ground unceremoniously, giving Therese a chance to wrap him in a towel.

"Hey honey!"

She saw the pain in his face before he made that sound, that horrible guttural groan that ripped something out from her body.

"Baby!" Holding her boy, she took the stairs two at a time until she was by her husband's side. He was grabbing his heart, telling her he loved them both so much, telling his son to be strong. She grabbed her phone, called 911, but it was too late. He died in the arms of his loved ones, at least.

———————————●———————————

January 7, 2028

And then before her son's eighteenth birthday, before he had a chance to become a man, she'd let the world rip away the last part of Jerome Johnson Sr.'s legacy.

What could I have done?

Something. Surely, something.

"Ma'am?"

Still cuffed to the table, Justin did his best to nudge her from her nightmare, shaking her body. When she woke, Therese found herself sitting on the floor, shoulder slumped against the table.

"Why'd you pass out? Do you need anything?"

His voice made her want to kiss his forehead and rip her eyes out.

Ignoring his question, she picked herself up and forced calmness into her voice. "I'll talk to the DA on your behalf. Maybe we can get you into some classes while you're in jail, get you some skills for when you're released early on good behavior."

"Good behavior?"

"You remind me of someone." She bit the inside of her cheek to keep from crying. "Someone who would've shook the world if he'd gotten a second chance."

Justin smiled and it almost brought her to her knees again. "I'll do my best, ma'am."

She turned and left without another word.

Therese could've heard a pin drop as Luke drove them back to the office.

"Are you all right?" he asked.

Using the mirror on the passenger side to block out the sun, Therese re-applied her lipstick and put on some makeup to mask her crow's feet, a warrior putting her armor back on. "I'm fine."

Chapter Two

January 7, 2028

Kaitlin Lungford found comfort in attending funerals. She'd been to hundreds in her time as Undersecretary of the Army, and then thousands as Defense Secretary. Funerals were humbling affairs, a reminder that we all became worm food eventually, but that you could go out with honor if you were privileged enough to have that opportunity. And the funeral she was attending today was extra comforting. Lucas Brooks hadn't served a day in the military, hadn't understood the meaning of words like *service* and *honor*, but he was dead and at last the world knew what she knew. Well, not *all* that she knew. But enough that they wouldn't begrudge her celebrating publicly. She'd piss on his grave except for the fact that it would end her presidential campaign.

Her phone buzzed. It was her campaign manager, Olivia Stoneburner, reminding her for the twelfth time to make sure no pictures were taken. Her driver knew to "accidentally" break any camera he saw that managed to snap a picture of her here. It had been a risk to come, but the trip would accomplish two goals: smiling at this man's grave and saying goodbye to her uncle. He'd become frail at the ripe age of eighty-two, and when she'd first gotten the call that she'd be attending a funeral, she'd guessed it was his. Uncle Charles missed her, apparently. She knew better. What he missed was having influence over her. But when Brooks's corruption had been exposed, she'd finally been able to break from her uncle once and for all.

She closed her eyes and began tying her curly blonde hair into a ponytail, finding pleasure in establishing order where none previously existed. Breathing in and out as the Suburban drove past Arlington National Cemetery (for Kaitlin had been one of many to ensure Brooks wasn't buried there), she remembered her epic shouting match with her uncle from almost four years ago. Uncle Charles couldn't believe she'd resigned, but what other choice had she had? If her uncle wanted to wed himself to a traitorous moron, that was his business, but she was done. She wasn't putting her neck on the line for Lucas Brooks any longer, and this way she positioned herself as a bipartisan figure poised to run for the presidency herself.

In January 2024, an election year, at a time when he was still seen as the head of the Republican Party, the former president had been revealed to have copied the NOC (Non-Official Cover) list before leaving office and brought that copy to his home in Chicago. And how had the world learned this? Because the moron had left the list where it was stolen by a foreign operative who sold it to FGRN-14.

The NOC list was comprised of only a few dozen individuals around the world. CIA agents posing as mid-level private-sector employees. They had no diplomatic immunity, no protection if their covers were blown. Not to mention the fact that they'd been placed in specific locations because of the incredible intelligence opportunities the U.S. government needed them to seize for the sake of national security. And the former President of the United States had allowed that information to be sold to the largest terrorist organization in the world.

People died.

She and the president had found out from the media. That'd been among the worst of it, to be blindsided by the fucking *New York Times*. One of the few good things that had come out of the crisis was that there hadn't been a debate over whether or not to throw Brooks's ass in jail. Attorney General Leticia Cummings had handled the case herself, and a few weeks after Brooks had reported to prison, Kaitlin had resigned. Begaye had begged her to stay through the election, to help him wind down the war responsibly, but she hadn't needed that burden. End the war "responsibly?" It hadn't been a responsible war from day one, something she'd let the president, her uncle, and the press know repeatedly over the past four years. Whether it was Brooks or Begaye, gone were the days where she'd let some politician who'd never seen combat tell her she "owed it to her country" to do something.

Kaitlin had hit the campaign trail for Republicans after resigning. Begaye's re-election had been secured by Brooks's actions, but her campaign schedule had saved a few downballot, and they'd remembered her when she'd announced her own campaign. Democrats had ended the cycle with a twenty-two-seat majority in the House and flipped five Senate seats, an unmitigated disaster for the GOP, but she'd come away looking as clean as possible under the circumstances. And in just a few weeks, she'd beat Alan Westbrook in Iowa and New Hampshire and then every other state, too. She couldn't believe he had any support, considering he'd been Brooks's VP.

The Party went mad, but I can save it. I can save everyone.

"Ma'am, we're here." Her driver stopped the car at the back entrance to the cemetery. She could see the ceremony had finished, which was just as well. As her driver opened the door and she started to exit the car, she saw the tombstones and found herself unable to go on.

"No."

"Ma'am?"

Returning to her seat, she told the man to close the door lest he let in any cold air, then texted her uncle to come meet her in the car.

She was done going to meet lesser men on their own terms.

Kaitlin wasn't surprised her uncle didn't knock before entering the car and taking a seat by her side. She was taken aback that he looked as if he belonged in a casket rather than above ground. They hadn't met face to face since that shouting match years ago, and she supposed his letters actually were true and not just sordid attempts to gain her sympathy.

"You're dying." She said it as a fact because it was undeniable when she saw the spots on his face, the cane in his hand. He had such a coughing fit when he sat down that she wished he was wearing a mask.

"Life catches up with us all."

His tone confirmed her belief that he was resigned to his fate. At long last, the lion of the Senate had met the greatest predator of them all: time.

"How's Vijay?"

He must've truly been on death's door if he thought mentioning her boyfriend of ten-plus years was appropriate. She'd only brought him to the house in Utah once, right after they'd started dating, and that experience had confirmed for her that she'd never do it again. Few people outside of her inner circle even knew she had a live-in boyfriend.

"Why are you here?" Try as she might to force neutrality into her tone, some hope still pushed its way through.

She hated herself for the longing that showed in her question. What did she care if he asked about Vijay? She knew she shouldn't, that this was another ploy he was using to manipulate her and get his way, but what if it wasn't? What if this time was different? Balling her right hand into a fist, she dug her nails into her skin to calm herself.

After eighty-two years, no one changes. Get a grip.

"The doctors say I don't have long. My urologist is making me wear a diaper these days."

Kaitlin couldn't help but laugh. Her uncle, this titan of terror, soiling himself. She caught her mouth, began apologizing, but he waved her off.

"I deserve that."

He did. That and so much more. But try as she might, she found herself hoping he wasn't in too much pain.

"Looks like the funeral was small and intimate," she said.

Charles laughed, and the effort led to another coughing fit. "Yeah. Brooks would've hated it."

No head of state had attended. His wife, kids, a few members of his Party, like Charles—that was it.

"His wife said a few words, but that was all," Charles said. "At the end of a long life, a life that touched every single person in the world, no one wanted anything to do with him."

Surely those weren't tears in her uncle's eyes. The man hadn't cried when his brother, her father, had died. She balled her left hand into a fist as well and considered knocking him out.

Brooks gets tears but my dad didn't?

The moment passed as quickly as it had come as he leaned toward her, holding his cane for support. His breath was ragged and smelled of rotten tomatoes. "I won't make it through the year, Kaitlin."

Ah. This was it, then. Having had no children of his own, and with Chad long dead, he thought he could have her carry on his legacy. Relief coursed through her whole body now that she understood his end game. It was a simple ask. One she'd never, ever entertain, but simple, nonetheless.

"What do the doctors say?"

"My lungs, my liver, my heart. They're all failing me."

She exhaled, letting him believe it was a sympathetic sigh rather than one of relief. He placed his hand over hers, and to her surprise, she didn't pull away. God help her, she sympathized with the crypt keeper.

They sat like that for what seemed like hours but was probably seconds, his fingers rubbing over her knuckles. "At least I got to see you run for president. I always told you it was your destiny."

She'd indulged him enough; this was one bridge too far. Pulling her hand away from his frail body, she turned to face him, scooting back in her seat and adopting that ramrod-straight posture they'd both learned at West Point. "Running for president has been a notion of my own since long before you mentioned it. And now? I'm running to make sure a piece of shit like Lucas is never elected again. I refuse to give up on the greatest nation on Earth without a fight."

Her uncle looked like he might die right there in her Suburban. Wiping tears from his face, he nodded, and she thought the effort may cause his head to roll off his body.

"Of course," he said. "Your achievements are yours alone. I only wish to be remembered a bit more fondly than Brooks, once I pass."

She'd been harsh with her words, but it was only what she'd learned from him.

"I always wondered what people would say about me at my funeral, but seeing Brooks's, I now wonder if people will even attend."

Turning her perfectly proportioned Greek nose to the side, she smelled the piss filling his diaper. God help her, she had to comfort him.

It's just what family does.

"Every single day you have in the Senate gives you more power than ninety-nine percent of the world."

Charles stared at her blankly.

"Work with Democrats. Get something real passed, something that will leave a good taste in your colleagues' mouths when..." She couldn't say the words: when you die. "The Chief Justice just died. Instead of stonewalling until the elections, try actually working with the Begaye administration for once."

"You think the president would come to my funeral?"

The hope in her uncle's voice was pathetic. She hated herself for wanting to smile and then hated herself for hating that impulse. "He's attended Republican funerals before. But you have to give him something genuinely positive to say about you. Show him you've changed."

Show me you've changed. Kaitlin knew only of death visiting the young, on the battlefield, and of course her father. Her familiarity with it creeping into the old crevices of the decrepit was limited. Still, she dared dream that Uncle Charles was actually authentic in wanting to better himself.

What's one more chance between family?

She wouldn't let him near her campaign, near Vijay or the rest of her life, but she could allow him this one kindness, of how to safeguard some sort of legacy for himself.

"Ma'am?" Lowering the window between the front and back of the car, her driver indicated it was time to leave for another meeting. She opened the door and took her uncle's hand to help him leave.

"Westbrook's got twenty years of experience on you."

Kaitlin refused to look into his eyes as he offered his unsolicited analysis of her campaign.

"That could work in your favor, though. The Party wants to

move on from the last generation."

Move on from the last generation. From you. She refused to let him use that phrase to tug at her heartstrings, locking them away where only Vijay could reach.

"Good luck in Iowa next week. Let me know if I can help."

Getting back in the car, she rolled the window down and offered one last comment before driving off, leaving him alone in a cemetery. "I don't need your help anymore."

Chapter Three

March 9, 2022

The Honorable Bella Ferrari had spent all day fielding calls, but now night had finally come and it was just her, a glass of red wine, and her favorite movie in bed. She'd been a federal judge for less than a year, and already she'd made a ruling that would cement her legacy in the textbooks forever. The Medulla brothers had been blowing up her phone all day, ecstatic at what it meant for their company and its fifteen thousand employees. For tonight, at least, she'd forget the unspoken threat voiced in their most recent conversation.

"It's a good thing we were able to make your past disappear, eh, Bella?" Matteo's thick Italian accent matched her own. A mix of payoffs and threats to the right reporters and political operatives had ensured her smooth confirmation to the 10th Circuit Court of Appeals, but with enough years under her belt, people wouldn't care about her history even if they did learn the truth. Prostitution was legal less than eight hundred miles from here, in Nevada. Besides, it wasn't like she still did it. This generation, with TikTok and OnlyFans and Tinder, embraced messiness. In fact, she thought, they insisted on it as proof of authenticity.

At just forty-two, she'd managed to secure a presidential appointment to a judicial bench. She told herself it was due to the fact that she'd graduated Summa Cum Laude from law school and was a published author making significant advances in her field, but she knew it helped that she was also undeniably attractive in the conventional sense of the word. Green eyes. Wavy, chestnut hair. Freckles that made her look like the innocent girl next door. And, as some of the ruder articles had stated outright, her big tits didn't hurt either. But there was a ferocity behind her looks, a brilliance and tenacity few understood.

She'd just issued a stunning mandate to the federal government, establishing a difference for the first time between refined and unrefined WP. After a series of deaths involving a maritime company using a largely South Indian workforce to handle unrefined WP underwater, Judge Ferrari had determined the cause of those workers later developing delusions of grandeur was due to the existence of two toxic isotopes within WP. In her majority opinion, Bella ruled that Chadium and Karenthium must be removed by the government through a refining process before any mandates could be imposed on private companies concerning WP usage.

It was a grand victory. But there had to be more.

Aditya. She'd only lobbied for the nomination after learning Karthik was dead, that he couldn't threaten her life again. In her dreams, every night she was taken back to that office at One Bryant Park. Karthik was going to kill her until Aditya rescued her. She'd obeyed him, gone into exile, finished law school in Albuquerque and then escaped to her ancestral home in Italy. She watched a similar scene taking place on her TV as Michael Corleone hid in Sicily.

And we both ended up frustrated, ready to seize back our destiny.

Karthik had been dead for years. She'd read Aditya was back as head of his company, Adrsta. There was nothing stopping her from just picking up the phone and calling him, assuming he had the same number.

She picked up her phone and pulled up his contact entry. After staring at it for an eternity, she turned it off for the night and returned to her movie. Apollonia was about to die.

———————————————————

May 16, 2016

Aditya picked up the phone on the first ring.
"Bella, why are you calling?"

His sharp tone was another stabbing of her heart. Leaving NYU, adapting to the dry heat of Albuquerque and the University of New Mexico, it was all too much.

"I'm ready to leave," she said.

"America? You graduated?"

She couldn't believe he hadn't remembered.

"Shit. I'm sorry I forgot. I meant to send you something."

She pushed steel into her voice before speaking again. He wanted to be done with her? Fine. Two could play that game.

"You told me to leave the country after I graduated, so I just thought I'd let you know it's being handled. This is the last you'll hear from me."

"...Bella... I'm sorry..."

"Whatever."

She'd told her parents the whole truth last December; it had been a hell of a Christmas gift. Sleeping with Aditya's boss to try and dig up some dirt on him. Aditya smuggling his gangster friend into the country to kill him. They hadn't been happy about it, but they were immigrants; happiness wasn't their default, safety was. Calls had been made, and Bella had been off to Maranello for the undetermined future to live with her *nonno* and *nonna*.

She hadn't visited since grade school, but it had to be better than Albuquerque.

———————————•————————————•————————————

February 14, 2017

Every day for eight months, Bibiana Ferrari had woken Bella at dawn to go to church.

She had complained at first. "*Nonna*, wouldn't Jesus want me to see him after a good night's sleep?"

"Jesus would like to see you twice a day for what you've been calling 'sleeping.'"

They'd managed to keep the real reason she was here a secret from the town, but her *nonna* knew all about Bella's past and used that famous Italian guilt whenever it suited her, usually around five a.m.

After morning mass, it was off to the supermarket and then back home to cook. Bella learned to make tortellini from scratch and that there were four types of balsamic vinegars in the world. She listened to her *nonna* complain that the vast majority of balsamic vinegars flooding the global market actually had no balsamic in them at all, and instead used red wine vinegar diluted with water.

"Modena is the birthplace of balsamic vinegar!" Bibiana Ferrari announced proudly, referring to their home province. "How you think we get so rich?" Flailing her arms wildly, she pointed at the ornate cabinetry and cookware and Antolini quartz countertops. "All this? Your *nonno* helped a little, not a lot. We sell *my* balsamic vinegar and ham and cheese."

It was true. Bella had seen beyond Maranello that her family owned a farm in nearby Castelvetro with a full staff committed to the business of feeding Italy and keeping her family rich. She hadn't thought much of it when she was nine, the last time she'd visited, but her grandparents had built a genuine empire.

"Amore mio, c'è la colazione?" Oreste Ferrari entered the kitchen and sat at the table as the two women set down three plates of yogurt, fruits, and pastries.

"Use your eyes, you old bear. Breakfast is right there."

"Buongiorno, nonno," Bella said, bending down so he could kiss her cheek. He'd been teaching her Italian for months now and she was finally becoming comfortable with it.

"My two favorite girls," he said, digging into his food. Since he'd retired, his English had gotten rusty, and he was happy to have the practice to stay sharp. No one would believe he was in his eighties. "Do you have a hot date for tonight, *amore mio?*"

Using all her strength to shove Aditya out of her mind, she chuckled and said no. "Who could match the attractiveness of an evening with my *nonno?*"

"Maybe we have a hot date and want you gone tonight," Oreste joked, prompting Bibiana to slap his arm.

"Disgustoso," she said.

"What's disgusting? She knows about the birds and the bees."

Bella stifled a smile, deciding it best to take her grandmother's side in this fight.

"She's here so we can discourage that type of behavior," Bibiana said, using a tone Bella heard often when she was arguing for deals

21

at the supermarket. "Or have you forgotten why she had to leave?"

Oreste waved her off and returned to his yogurt. "Ah, let me eat my meal in peace."

When he was done, Bella cleaned the table and tried loading the dishwasher, only to find her *nonna* unloading the dishes and doing them by hand.

"*Nonna,* I called the guy. He fixed the machine last week."

"*Piantala!* For centuries our family has had the best dishwashers possible: strong women." She flung a finger at the machine. "This? It's the reason you can't hold a man. It made you weak, turned you to… other pursuits."

This time Bella's laugh wasn't a polite chuckle but a hearty guffaw. "Of course, so silly of me to forget what a slippery slope it is from using a dishwasher to becoming a call girl."

Oreste had risen to sit in the parlor with his morning copy of the newspaper, but now returned to the kitchen and offered an out for Bella to avoid another pointless fight with her grandma. "It says here the agreement with the FIA and its partner countries has been approved," he said, referring to the governing body that regulated the F1 racing Maranello was famous for. "Now cars can use WP-enhanced parts. Why don't you go to the track and see if you can entice one of the racers to buy you lunch?"

Silently mouthing her thanks, she left her *nonna* to vent in peace, kissed her *nonno's* forehead, and made herself scarce.

An hour to Bologna. Two hours to Florence. Less than five to Rome. There wasn't much to do in Maranello unless you loved cars, but Bella had access to her family's fleet of vehicles. She'd gotten her driver's license but had only taken the most perfunctory of trips to the track in her eight months here, despite Maranello's global reputation as the home of racing. Instead, she'd spent her days sight-seeing across the country and her nights learning to make zuppa inglese from her *nonna* and discussing the current events of the day with her *nonno.* Riding her Vespa, she decided it was time to give the racetrack the respect it deserved.

She took in the car museum filled with red and yellow cars that looked as though they belonged to Batman. She saw the 350-pound stainless steel statue of the famous Prancing Horse that symbolized one of the most iconic car brands in the world. She even watched as some racers tested their vehicles in advance of the season beginning in March.

It was at the end of watching two cars move through the track that one of the drivers got out and smiled at her. He was nice, with tawny hair and arms molded by a lifetime of racing and shoulders that showed off his great posture. Too bad his short frame reminded her of Aditya. She let him down easy when he asked her out and then found a quiet place to eat lunch alone.

•————————————————————•

January 13, 2018

Bella thought she may murder her grandparents if she had to spend another day with them. She'd perfected her favorite dessert of zuppa inglese, but there were only so many times she could listen to another lecture from her *nonna* on how dishwashers were a tool of Satan or avoid offers from her *nonno* to set her up with "a nice Italian boy." Karthik or not, it was time to go home. She'd sought her parents' advice last night, and now—armed with their approval—she'd go downstairs and tell her grandparents over breakfast. UNM had wanted to hire her to teach when she'd graduated. She'd kept in touch with the Dean of the law school and they were still interested. Albuquerque was two thousand miles from New York, and she was reasonably sure she had nothing to fear from Karthik.

Steeling herself for her grandparents' shouting, she headed downstairs to finally leave the past behind and embrace her future.

•————————————————————•

May 6, 2020

Professor Ferrari.

Those words, emblazoned on her door at the university, filled her parents with enough pride to make the flight from Jersey to visit Bella a couple times a year (they'd only visited twice total when she was a student here, upon admission and for graduation). By all accounts, she was well-loved by both her peers and students alike. She'd been published multiple times, both regionally and nationally, and had just been selected by the Dean to represent UNM at a national conference in NYC on the impact of WP in certain luxury foods. It was on this occasion that she stayed with her parents at their home in Hoboken. The commute to the conference in the city was a pain, but not as much a pain as it would've been to explain to her parents why she couldn't see them when she was traveling so close by.

"Dad? You home?" Bella walked through the door without knocking, knowing her father always left it unlocked despite her repeated warnings. Her *nonno* ignored her, too. She hoped it was mere stubbornness and not Alzheimer's.

"Back already?" Tommaso Ferrari came up from his basement, toolbox in hand. "Spent the day fixing that leak in our crawlspace. Gimme a minute to wash up and I can get some steaks on the grill."

She smiled, following him to the washroom upstairs, putting her briefcase away in her own room as her dad cleaned up.

"I was a big hit at the conference," she said. Her mom always worked late, so she got to treasure this time with her father.

"That's great, Slugger." Walking out, he patted her on the back and then headed down to the kitchen with her. "I'm so proud of you."

"Thanks, Dad." It had taken five years, but things were finally getting back to normal. "Actually... the conference went so well that someone at Parkins and Lee offered me a job."

Tommaso dropped the frozen steaks in his hand onto the floor. They made a loud thump, the same sound Bella's heart was making. "I'm not sure that's such a good idea, Slugger."

"...I'd be in New York again. Right next to you."

"That's what worries me." Tommaso picked up the steaks and set them on the countertop. "Only thing bloody I want to see are my burgers."

"What do you mean?"

Her dad became fascinated with his shoes.

"Dad? Just tell me."

"...I didn't wanna say anything, but we got a few visits from people after you left."

A pit formed in her stomach. "What? Who? When?"

"They came by the day after your flight. Then a few weeks later.

Then less often, but still every once in a while for the next year. Looked like skingrafters."

"Dad!" She'd never liked the phrase.

"Well, what do you want me to call them? Dark-skinned and wearing those dumb muscle shirts and smoking God knows what."

"You think they're still watching you?"

Tommaso sighed. "I don't know, Slugger, but it was a scary time for me and your mom. That Karthik kid is bad news. We knew it from the start. And with this presidential campaign going on? Why poke the beast?"

Bella had read in the news that Aditya was involved with President Lucas's campaign, that somehow Karthik had gotten a gig with the newly created WP Force.

"You got a good thing going in Albuquerque. Leave well enough alone. Besides, your mom and I like coming out for the Balloon Fiesta."

Bella sighed. She'd fill the pit in her stomach with regret and loneliness, but never fear. She couldn't risk her parents' safety just for the chance to come back to New York. "I'll turn down the job."

"Thank you. And do me a favor. Don't tell your mom about any of this."

Bella nodded and watched as her dad turned the grill on and prepared the red meat.

●————————————————————●

March 12, 2021

It'd been four months since President Begaye had won the election, and only weeks since WP legalization had been passed, but Bella had been working on a book since she'd attended that conference in NYC almost a year ago. Her publisher had decided on the title of *Privileged Food*. The book was about 75% oral history of how Caucasian families had come to integrate WP into high-end restaurant cuisine over the past fifty years, 25% blueprint on how this cuisine could be expanded to become more affordable and suit the needs of the broader community now that WP was being legalized. Bella had fought to ensure her voice shined through as one of commanding moral authority, and her argument was greatly bolstered when Begaye won. Sitting in her office, staring at the stack of signed books in front of her and wondering who would ever buy them, she opened her phone for the sixth time and went to Aditya's name.

Does he ever think about me? She'd considered calling him with condolences after Lucas's defeat but wimped out. Squeezing her phone so hard it exposed veins against her cream-colored skin, she dropped it in surprise when it rang. "Hello?"

"Bella Ferrari!"

She hadn't heard that thick male Italian accent in fifteen years, but she remembered him immediately. Gianpaolo Medulla, her on-again, off-again college fling.

"*Come va?*"

"Um, I'm doing fine... What's up?"

"I wanted to congratulate you on your book."

Bella was glad this wasn't a video call. He'd think her blushing proof she still pined for him. "You heard about my book?"

"Everyone I work with knows about your book. You've made quite the splash in the food and beverage industry."

Standing up, she began to pace. The office being as small as it was, that required a lot of turning. "What are you up to these days?"

She could hear the smile on his face as he explained how he and his brother, Matteo, now ran a very successful startup, Famóre. A portmanteau of family and the Italian word for love, the social media app allowed users across the world to share recipes in both written and video form.

"We always wondered what happened to you, eh? A hotshot legal teacher and author to boot!"

"That's very kind—"

"Have you asked her yet?" Matteo's voice drowned out the rest of Bella's words. "Bella, *come va?*"

"I already asked her, Matteo. She's good."

"Um," Bella said, "ask me what?"

"Forgive my brother's enthusiasm, but then again, without enthusiasm, we wouldn't be half as successful as we are today."

Bella chuckled, remembering how boisterous the brothers had always been.

"It's really something to ask in person," Gianpaolo said. "We're in Denver. We can be at your place tomorrow, okay?"

Failing to think of a polite reason to decline, Bella ended up agreeing and giving them her address.

"Tomorrow, then," Gianpaolo said. "And don't worry, your only concern should be loving this idea so much you fall in love with me again!"

Hanging up, Bella thought at least there was no chance of that. Her heart belonged to another.

Before she knew it, Bella was going outside to greet the Medulla brothers as they arrived in a lime-green Lamborghini.

The doors opened vertically rather than horizontally. "You like the wheels?"

Bella used all her effort to not roll her eyes and hoped the rest of the night was more impressive. In her long experience with men, fancy toys existed to overcompensate for less impressive attributes. Leading them into her house, she offered them cheese and red wine. "The wine is retail, but the cheese comes straight from my *nonna's* farm near Maranello."

"No kidding!" Matteo shouted the words. "Our *nonna* and *nonno* are from Maranello as well."

"Cheers to that," she said, making a toast. Their glasses clinked and they took their seats on her couch for what she hoped would be a pleasant opportunity to reminisce and nothing more.

The story of the Medulla brothers' rise to fame required multiple glasses of wine due to both the length of the story and the shocking origin of it.

"You went to Adrsta for funding?" Finishing her second glass, Bella poured herself another.

"The fact that it fell apart was one of the best things to ever happen to us," Gianpaolo said.

"Really gives credence to that saying," Matteo added. "Sometimes, not getting what you want is the best thing in the world."

Bella leaned in as she learned how the two brothers had gotten their big break at a trade show in Denver, where they'd met the mayor's chief of staff, who'd introduced them to the mayor.

Matteo's grin never left his face. Bella wondered how he could talk with it plastered on. "Mayor Denton helped us out with a bank loan and offered us public funding if we moved our headquarters here. And what is he called today? U.S. Senator Denton!"

"Wow." Bella took a long sip from her glass. "You truly are the white knights of Denver."

"And tomorrow, the world!" Matteo laughed. "But enough of that. You must be wondering why we've come."

Gianpaolo smiled. "Now, now, she knows she can make me come."

Bella "accidentally" spilled her drink on the man's pants, blaming it on her tipsiness. It wasn't a total lie.

"Don't worry about it," Gianpaolo said, waving off her napkin and using his own handkerchief. "I was perhaps a bit rude in any case. The universe has a way of delivering karma."

"So," Bella said, "the reason you're here?"

"I don't know how closely you follow judicial vacancies, but there's a seat open on the 10th Circuit Court of Appeals."

She knew of the vacancy. It'd been open since before Lucas had lost. "What of it?"

Matteo grinned once more. "We want you to fill it."

Her first thought wasn't one of fear or doubt. She knew in that moment she was meant to do the job, that it was her destiny.

But Karthik. My parents. She couldn't risk their safety. How lucky it was that women didn't speak before thinking things through. "I can't."

"That's not a no," Gianpaolo said. "You're not interested, that's fine. But there's a story here, eh?"

Finishing her third glass, popping some cheese into her mouth before pouring herself a fourth, she let out a deep sigh. "You should know about my own history with Aditya Shetty."

When she'd finished her story, Matteo was still grinning. Bella wondered if her mother was right and your face did, in fact, freeze in place if you held a pose for too long.

"Karthik is dead," Matteo said.

Bella spit her red wine out all over her white couch. "...what?"

"The full story's classified, but he died overseas in the war."

The boogeyman was gone. WP was legalized. Her mind raced,

but she could think of no reason not to go back to her normal life at long last. This was her key back to respectability, back into Aditya's arms.

"I'm in."

Chapter Four

January 7, 2028

Therese Johnson almost always returned from a full day of work to a home-cooked meal. Jazz played in the background as she sat at a table decked out with a plate of green chile cheeseburgers and a bowl of pozole.

"You really are a native New Mexican," Therese joked to Russell. Thank God he loved cooking and cleaning, because she just didn't have the energy anymore. Or maybe he just loved cooking and cleaning for her. Either way, it filled her stomach and her heart.

Russell handed her a margarita and sat down as well. "How was work?"

She took a long sip of her drink instead of answering. They'd sit outside most Saturday nights, but she was grateful for the privacy of indoors today. Her encounter with Justin had shaken her worse than she'd imagined.

"Babe?"

They didn't have secrets, her and Russell. It was one of the best things about them. Swallowing, she told him what had happened this morning. When she was done, he got up and stood behind her, massaging her neck and shoulders. "Grief never goes away." His fingers released knots she didn't know were tied. "I'm so proud of you. And it's not right Jerome isn't here to witness everything you've accomplished."

Therese let out a sigh.

"In a perfect world, you and I would've never met. I wish more than anything you were still with Jerome and his dad, that you all could enjoy your success together. But life often isn't fair and the best we can do is try to find what good we can."

Tears started streaming down her face as she took a gulp of her margarita.

"Hey, now," he said, kissing her cheek. "Why are we crying?"

"I don't know what I did to deserve you."

Russell smiled, and his face had the power to shape Therese's wildest dreams into reality. "Nothing's deserved, but we work at it every day. Together."

They did the dishes together after dinner, her soaping and him rinsing.

"How was your day off?" she said.

"I finished the Indiana Jones trilogy."

"Didn't they make more than three?"

"Not ones worth watching."

She couldn't help but giggle when he got this way. Their teamwork, his passion for the stupidest of topics, she hadn't thought she'd ever find someone like him.

"Babe," he said. "I also caught up with my buddy at the White House."

Therese dropped a dish, chipping it in the sink.

"No worries," he said. "Damaged ain't broken."

"Every time you bring up Roger Manning, it's something depressing."

"Well, today it wasn't. He just wanted to catch up. Besides," he said, putting away the last of the dishes on the drying rack, "it's always a good thing to have an inside line to the Oval Office. I still can't believe that dude became Begaye's Chief of Staff."

Therese hoped he hadn't invited Roger to the house. She'd yet to meet any of his DC friends, and from the stories he'd shared of his days in the Capitol, that was just fine with her.

"Now," Russell said, sliding behind her and kissing her neck, "that's enough shop talk." His calloused fingers ran down her hips to rest at her waist, playing with her skirt. She was sure he'd feel her quickening pulse. "I believe we have other matters to attend to. From this morning."

Taking his hand in hers, she led him to their bedroom upstairs, sitting on the bed as he took off his shirt and pants, throwing them to the bedside.

"Russell..." The sight of his arousal made her throat dry and her panties damp.

"Relax, Madame Mayor." Pushing her back on the bed, he lifted a leg and kissed it from ankle to hip before parting her thighs.

Therese moaned, a guttural sound. "Make me feel good."

Sliding her panties down, he let his tongue explore her as she bucked against his face.

Chapter Five

March 14, 2028

Kaitlin couldn't believe she was spending her fifty-sixth birthday in fucking Orlando, Florida.

Happiest place on Earth, my ass.

Her campaign manager, Olivia Stoneburner, had told her in no uncertain terms that it was political suicide to skip the Faith and Freedom Conference, even if it was being held in Alan Westbrook's home state. Two months of primaries had effectively drawn them to a tie, with Westbrook winning Iowa and New Hampshire while she took South Carolina and Nevada. Super Tuesday was in just three weeks, and a strong performance here would give her just the boost she needed.

"Should we straighten this hair?" Her beauty consultant, Emily Vanderbilt, applied makeup to her face as she sat as calmly as she could in her changing room before the debate. Although calling it a debate was being overly generous. A bunch of dipshit audience members asking whatever they wanted without a moderator filtering through the riffraff beforehand seemed idiotic to her.

"I like my curls as much as you like yours, thanks." Her tone was more pointed than she'd intended. It wasn't Emily's fault she was here on her birthday.

"And what are we doing about the ponytail?" Olivia asked.

"Emily thinks it'll stretch my old skin and draw attention to my crow's feet." Kaitlin laughed, a genuine spark of joy.

Emily slapped her hand. "Don't be silly. I just think you'll look less bitchy with your hair let loose. You want to project an image where these men can see themselves having a beer with you."

Kaitlin bit her lip, prompting scowls from both Emily and Olivia. "I'd rather give a blowjob to a cactus than get a beer with anyone in the audience."

They'd never admit it, but Kaitlin saw that comment draw grins from her friends. At the end of the day, possibly the best thing to come from this campaign was that the two of them had become genuine friends. She had twenty years on Olivia and thirty on Emily (God help her), but it was an undeniable comfort that they were experiencing this madness together. Just last week they'd made the cover of *Vanity Fair*, Kaitlin and her blonde curls in the middle, flanked by Olivia's straight black hair and Emily's red curls. They looked like a team of superheroes. She'd framed the cover and gifted one to each of them.

"You could've at least worn the red dress I picked out instead of going with white," Olivia whined.

"White is the color of the suffragettes. I'm the first female candidate!"

"Red is the color of Republicans! You know, the Party you want to represent. Besides, red makes your tits pop."

Kaitlin rolled her eyes. "As if Westbrook is choosing what pants to wear based on what'll make his shriveled dick pop."

Emily burst out laughing, dropping the comb she was using for Kaitlin's hair and eliciting a glare from Olivia.

"Just chill," Kaitlin said. "I got this."

The "debate" was as nuanced and educational as Kaitlin expected. She fielded questions ranging from her religion (non-practicing Mormon, an oxymoron) to her role in the war.

"The vice president says he's a Baptist preacher, but during the Brooks administration all I saw him worship was the president." Olivia had blessed her pushing back on the religion issue, and she was determined to go for the jugular tonight. "He says he was so influential during his tenure that he was the last one in the room before President Brooks made any big decisions, so then was it him whispering in the president's ear to take the NOC list?"

She forced herself not to smile as the audience gasped and

Westbrook threw daggers at her. From the way he'd positioned himself at her eye level, she knew he was standing on a stool behind his podium. It must've just killed him that not only was she twenty years younger than him, but she was also about three inches taller.

Maybe he'll die within the month and I won't have to go to another one of these things.

As he spat out some sort of response to her accusation, Kaitlin's mind drifted to more pleasant things, like the memory of getting her wisdom teeth removed.

It took all the discipline of her West Point training for Kaitlin not to leave as soon as she shook Westbrook's hand. Instead, she honored Olivia's wishes and stuck around for selfies with her fans. More than once she felt one of those "fans" rubbing against her ass or breasts as they positioned themselves for photos or leaned in to ask her questions. Her body man, Keith, and Olivia had discussed this issue at length, and the consensus was reporting the assaults would be more headache than they were worth.

I can't believe I go to war for these people.

After a half hour of subjecting herself to the mob, she finally got Keith to take her to the spin room, where Olivia was hobnobbing with reporters.

"And here's Secretary Lungford now," she said.

No sooner was Kaitlin at her side than a microphone was in her face.

"Tell me," the reporter said. "Twitter is blowing up. The consensus is that you dominated tonight. How do you feel?"

Like I'd love to shove that microphone down your throat.

Olivia fielded the question. "The secretary is glad Americans are realizing she's the only candidate who can stand up to the Begaye administration's unfunded mandates and assault on our religious liberties."

As Keith escorted the two of them into a car and back to their hotel, Olivia read Kaitlin all the positive headlines and tweets from her smartphone.

"This was a home run, Madame Secretary."

"Thanks, Olivia. I guess seeing Westbrook flail around in

disbelief that a woman could punch back almost made this worth it."

"You're very welcome."

"Did Emily get home all right?"

"Yeah, her boyfriend picked her up."

Kaitlin sighed. It'd been weeks since she'd seen Vijay.

"Hey," Olivia said, her voice softening. "I know it's been tough. I wish I could tell you the whole country appreciates what you're giving up, but at least know that I do."

Kaitlin patted her friend's hand as they pulled into the hotel.

"Have a good night," Olivia said, exiting the car.

Keith's room was on the same floor as hers, so it was easy for him to escort her. They paused at her door.

"Happy birthday, Madame Secretary."

"It'd be happier if Vijay was here."

He smiled, telling her he hoped she'd enjoy the rest of her night before excusing himself to his own room down the hall. When she opened her own room and stepped through the threshold, she found the lights off. Turning them on, she found Vijay lying on the bed.

"Vijay!" Her heart exploded. If the smile on her face exposed her wrinkles, she was proud to show each and every line. "What the fuck?"

"Keith suggested this would be a great surprise, and Olivia agreed."

"Yeah?"

Vijay laughed, his muscular arms stretching over his head as he interlaced his fingers. He knew the look showed off his abs. "I believe Olivia's exact words were, 'hopefully she'll be in a better mood after she gets laid.'"

Kaitlin let loose a laugh of the purest variety once again. When she'd first met Vijay all those years ago, she'd agreed to a second date because it was one of the few ways she could rebel against her uncle. Little did she know how quickly she'd grow to love his dry wit and taut legs and keen intellect.

He wasted no time, taking her by the shoulders and pushing her against a wall. Squeezing her ass, he bit her neck and ears and lips. He tasted like safety but made her feel dangerous. She gasped at the feeling of his bulge pressing against her thighs, his fingers brushing her curls.

"Let me shower first," she moaned.

"I don't mind."

"I know you don't, but I do." Painful as it was to leave, she excused herself, but not before undressing in his eyeline.

She heard music playing as she turned on the shower, saw the lights turn off as the hot water hit her skin. She touched herself, realizing she was wet in places water couldn't reach. When she returned, she saw candles and massage oils around her, and him naked on the bed.

"I think we can risk the fire hazard." Taking her towel, dropping it to the ground, he kissed her lips before laying her on her front. His strong fingers untied the strains of daily life binding her, letting her actually relax for once. Any man from her life, from the lives of her friends, viewed a massage as a quick thing to get out of the way before sex. But with Vijay Shankar, this was an art form. They could've been there for minutes or days for all she knew. His hands explored every part of her body, applying firm pressure and oils to release every bit of stress from the past several weeks.

Tears wet the pillow her face was buried in, silent until she could hold them in no longer and her chest heaved against the bed.

"Am I that bad at giving massages?"

Flipping over, she revealed herself to him fully. "These are good tears," she laughed. "This is just what I needed. You're so beautiful, and I just, I don't deserve you."

He kissed her again, softly. One hand cupped her head as the other traced its way between her breasts, past her bellybutton, to rest between her legs. "Yes, you do."

His finger found no resistance when he entered her, circling her insides and testing her arousal before introducing a second finger. Bucking her hips against him as he stroked her, she held him tight as he kissed her lips and ears and neck as she finished.

Sated, she took his penis in her fingers and kissed it before taking it in her mouth. He gasped and she remembered the last time they were together, how it was small enough for her to deepthroat without gagging, comforting in her mouth like a Jolly

Rancher she needed to suck all the flavor out of. Licking the underside, she knew he was close.

"Lay on your side," he said. His tone was soft but direct, making her insides squirm. No one told her what to do, ever. She'd always been expected to take charge, to be the leader, and Vijay gave her the safe space she needed to finally not be that person. She loved that feeling more than she wanted to be president.

Removing him from her mouth, she lay on her side, looking at their bodies in a mirror. She didn't see wrinkles or crow's feet or sagging breasts. Instead she saw a woman in her sexual prime and the man who couldn't wait to ravish her. Vijay didn't find the fact that she'd gone through menopause "unsexy." If anything, he found it hot, thrilled he didn't have to wear condoms anymore.

She watched as he kissed her neck and fondled her breasts and smelled her hair. She was glad she'd shampooed.

"I need you inside me," she whispered. And he obliged. Gasping, she rocked her body against his, a piston moving a well-oiled machine. After a few moments, he pushed her on her front again and leaned behind her, grabbing a pillow to place under her hips as he grabbed them and thrust harder. She saw fire in his eyes and innocence in her own. Here, away from everyone else, she could reclaim that feeling for herself.

Kaitlin couldn't sleep. It wasn't Vijay's snoring; she'd been an insomniac since the campaign had started. Reading Apple News on her iPad, she clicked on an article in the *Wall Street Journal* about fatherhood: *The Ties That Bind Us.*

The title didn't pull any punches. Binding was not always good.

She didn't blame her dad for leaving them, for starting a new family when she was twenty-four. He'd stuck around through college, but her mom had been long dead, and he'd deserved happiness. Still, Chad's birth had meant him exiting her life for his final six years. She still remembered the call like it was yesterday: Uncle Charles calling to tell her that her father was dead.

Fucking Chad. He'd stolen her daddy. Charles had wanted to fill that gap, and she had let him. Asking the Devil to enter your house. A tale as old as time.

Turning off her iPad, looking at Vijay's resting face before closing her eyes to try and sleep herself, she asked a question she'd posed to herself at least once a week for the past thirty years: *Why can't I just admit I deserve nice things?*

Chapter Six

March 14, 2028

Bella enjoyed these speaking gigs, and tonight's at American University presented a unique opportunity, with President Begaye's daughter, Anaba, being a recent graduate. Bella had been assured she'd be in the crowd this evening. Walking into a classroom filled with undergraduates and law students alike, she saw Secret Service agents everywhere. Rather than hiding, they wanted to be seen. As the head of the college's legal society introduced her, she spotted Anaba Begaye sitting in the front row. It seemed like she was using all her energy to stop herself from jumping up to give Bella a hug. Anaba's leg shook like a loose tooth as the audience clapped and Bella got up to speak.

"Thank you all for inviting me today."

She spent the next half hour talking about her book and what an honor it was to serve on the 10th Circuit. But when it came time for questions, the first one was the one she'd feared most. It hadn't been an issue when she'd first agreed to speak at AU. The president had named Judge James Francino of the 4th Circuit Court of Appeals to replace Chief Justice Swindell. He was uncontroversial. Boring. Or at least that's what everyone had thought, until *Buzzfeed* had broken the news two week ago that he'd forced himself on one of his clerks at the start of his career. Francino's defense? He'd only asked her for a massage, and she'd given him a happy ending willingly.

"Let's keep the questions focused on Judge Ferrari," a student said, taking the mic from her questioner's hands.

"That's okay," Bella said, waving her off. "This is an important topic and I'm glad to have the opportunity to address it."

Steeling herself, she raised her voice for the whole room to hear. "I am disgusted by Judge Francino's behavior and I'm proud the president accepted not only the withdrawal of his nomination but also the resignation of his judgeship. Less than forty percent of my fellow judges on the federal Court of Appeals are women, despite us being a clear majority of both the country and the electorate. It's not my place to choose who President Begaye nominates, but I do hope he keeps that in mind."

Bella saw Anaba Begaye practically salivating upon hearing her answer, leg still pumping like a locomotive.

Sure enough, Anaba was the first one at Bella's side when the event finished.

"Judge Ferrari, I am *such* a fan!"

"Very kind of you," Bella said. "I do hope you'll tell your father I'm an equally big fan of his."

"Of course."

Bella would've been forgiven for mistaking the man at Anaba's side for the Greek god Adonis. He must've been over six feet tall, with piercing blue eyes and a body fit for a linebacker. "And who are you?" she asked.

"Oh," Anaba squeaked, "so rude of me! This is Luther!"

"Aldrich? The president's body man?"

Anaba looked to her feet. "Um, if you ever see the president, please don't tell him he was here. It's kind of a secret he's my boyfriend."

Bella laughed. "Don't worry. We all have secrets."

Just then, an agent at her side whispered in her ear.

"It's okay, Agent Pierce, I'm almost done." Facing her again, Anaba pulled a copy of Bella's book from her bag and asked for an autograph.

To Anaba, she wrote. *Never stop fighting to shape the America we all deserve.*

"Wow!" Anaba's voice rose to a level only dogs could hear.

"What've you been up to since graduating?"

"I'm at a think tank focused on US-EU maritime trade law."

Bella chuckled. "I bet my book comes in handy there."

Anaba nodded, blushing.

"Have you ever thought of law school?"

Anaba opened her mouth, then closed it again and meekly shook her head.

"Well, you should. AU has a great program."

Before Bella could say anything else, the agent, Pierce, carted Anaba away and Luther followed behind. As they left, Bella caught remnants of their conversation.

"Please, Agent Pierce, promise me you won't tell my father about Luther."

"Ma'am, the president recognizes I can't do my job right if I'm reporting every little thing you do back to him. He explicitly forbade me from telling him about anyone you date unless I think there's trouble."

"And do you?" she asked. "Think there's trouble?"

The agent shook his head. "No. You got a good one."

Bella followed them out onto the quad, watching the agent open a car door for Anaba. Luther thanked the man before heading home himself. Bella made sure to run into his path on the way to the metro.

"Where you headed?" she said.

"I live in Farragut North."

"My hotel's there. Mind if I walk with you?"

Luther nodded his assent and the two walked in silence until they came to the red line.

"Anaba seems wonderful."

"She's the best," Luther agreed, his voice neutral. She supposed he had a job where it was impossible to be warm to a stranger, even one who was a judge.

Still, I have to take a chance. "Any idea who the president's going to nominate next?"

"No one Vice President Harmon suggests." Luther grunted, the bitterness in his tone as sharp as the taste of grapefruit.

"I'd heard the VP fought for Francino..."

"It's not news to anyone who reads POLITICO that his relationship with President Begaye wasn't the best, even before this disaster," Luther said.

Before Bella could say anything else, he took out his headphones and put them on, preparing to board the train. "Luckily, it's not your problem, Judge Ferrari. You got enough to worry about, I'm sure. But it was nice talking to you."

Bella watched silently as he walked away, this perfect specimen with the ear of both the president and her biggest fan.

Surely, that should mean something great for me.

Chapter Seven

March 14, 2028

Therese stayed at the Salamander when she was in DC. It was union-run, and in the southwest part of town, right near the Wharf. She had hopes of doing some pedal boating with Russell tomorrow. Returning to her room after a full day of meetings with the Democratic Mayors Association (DMA), she announced her presence to her husband before beginning to change out of her heels and orange pantsuit.

"What a day," she said. "Had to sit through lunch with Trunkle. You know, the head of the AFL-CIO?"

"Yeah?" Russell emerged from the bathroom, halfway through shaving and looking like Santa Claus.

"I hate how much Piven complains to him behind my back," she said, referring to the state director of the AFL-CIO for New Mexico. "So now they're both on my ass about the yellow tape keeping their workers from getting approved for public works contracts in Albuquerque. And it's like, don't talk to me, talk to your Congressman!"

Russell chuckled before heading back to the bathroom to finish. "But you played nice?"

She let out the sigh she'd been holding all day. "I played nice."

"Good." Re-emerging, he took her by the hand and sat her on the bed. "I had a business lunch, too."

"With who?"

"Roger Manning."

Therese bit her lip. "I'm surprised he could fit you into his busy schedule."

"Therese, baby, Roger's a nice guy. And more importantly, he's a good friend. You need to make more of an effort."

Therese sighed again before standing back up. "You're right. I'm sorry."

"Ain't nothing to be sorry about."

"So, what did you two discuss at lunch? You said it was a business meeting."

Russell took her by the hand again, sitting her on the bed once more. "The president's unimpressed by the current field."

"The presidential race?" Therese laughed. "The president's instincts are as good as ever, because there's absolutely nothing impressive about Vice President Harmon or Governor Ensign."

Russell laughed, a deep sound that filled her heart with warmth whenever she heard it. "Damn, Therese, you savage." He pulled his hands from hers and stood up.

"Just calling it like it is."

"Ensign got elected governor of Texas. That counts for nothing?"

"He's got charisma, no doubt about it. But as Walter Mondale once said, 'where's the beef?'"

"All flash and no pizazz, huh?"

"You know it."

Russell cleared his throat before continuing. "Well, between you, me, and these four walls, Roger shares your analysis of Terry Ensign."

"I guess that leaves Harmon." Therese tapped her foot on the ground. "It sucks, but I guess he won't be too bad. There'd be some sort of continuity in governance, him being the current VP and all."

Now it was Russell's turn to sigh. "You know Harmon lost Iowa and New Hampshire to Ensign, right?"

"Yeah..."

"The money dried up soon after. The president told Roger a few days ago that Harmon's dropping out soon."

Therese's hand closed around her mouth. "Ensign can't beat Kaitlin."

A mirthless laugh filled the air as Russell nodded in agreement.

"Now what?" Therese stood from the bed, grabbing Russell's hands once more. "Tell me Roger has a solution."

"He does, and it's a doozy." Russell smiled. He opened his backpack to get a beer, handing her one, too. "You might want to drink this first." Popping the cap, he took a long swig of his own.

"What is it?"

"At this point, the White House is looking for an amazing write-in candidate to win the nomination. Specifically, a woman."

Therese popped her own tab, taking a gulp and sitting in the room's only chair. Closing her eyes, she let her mind race with possibilities. A woman. Presidential caliber. Hopefully with electoral experience in a swing state. "What about the Senate Majority Leader?"

Kusum Raghavan had served as Lieutenant Governor twenty years ago under then-Governor Harmon in Virginia. Though small and demure, few were better than she was at understanding the political zeitgeist and bringing together different coalitions for shared progress in pursuit of a goal.

"Roger talked about it, but they need Senator Raghavan in Congress. Nobody can do that job like her."

"Okay, great," Therese said, "so he just needs to find a woman willing to wage a suicide campaign."

"Roger's pretty serious about this," Russell said. "He knows Terry can't win and he's willing to get the president involved if the right candidate is identified."

Therese stared blankly at her husband, taking another swig of her beer. "I don't know another woman who might even have a shot at beating Kaitlin."

Russell grinned. "Roger thinks one person can."

"Who?"

"You."

Therese's heart skipped a beat. But not like when she'd first kissed Russell. More like when she'd heard that cop tell her her son was dead. "...what?"

Putting his beer down, Russell walked over and put his hands in hers again. He knelt and told her how he thought she could do it and what it would mean to mothers and Black girls all around the country. "We're not doing anything you're not one hundred percent committed to doing, but this stuff with the DMA was a cover. This is the real reason we're here."

She couldn't breathe. Grabbing at her chest, she grew more panicked when she realized it wasn't just an expression, that she *actually* couldn't breathe.

"Oh, shit!" Russell ran to the sink to pour her some water into one of those Dixie coffee cups. He held her hand and tipped her head back and made sure she swallowed it all. "Better?"

Still unable to speak, she nodded.

"You're a first-rate mayor, and people have noticed."

"I didn't even want to be mayor..."

"But you said yes," Russell said, steel in his voice. "You stepped up, and you made sure Jerome's legacy didn't die with him. And now you have the chance to bring that to the entire country."

"...me?"

Russell kissed her cheek. "It ain't just me saying it either, baby. People at the highest levels of government and the private sector believe in you."

"...the private sector?"

"I'm no fool," Russell said. "I told Roger I wouldn't even think of bringing this up with you unless he assured me at least the first ten million was in place."

Therese needed something stronger than beer. "...and it is?"

"Damn straight." Russell's laugh did things to both her heart and her legs. "Look, I'm on Team Therese forever. Whatever you decide, I'm with you a hundred percent. But I know you can do this, and I know Jerome would be proud to see you in action. Both of them."

She couldn't answer with her voice, so instead just cried. Not the crushing despair of dreams dashed, but the promise of an unrealized one, so beautiful you had no choice but to weep before it.

"Happy tears?" Russell asked.

"Yeah."

"Good. Get them out of your system, because tomorrow you meet the president and begin to wage war in your son's name."

Chapter Eight

March 15, 2028

Therese's smile stretched as wide as the street she was walking down as she made her way to the White House. She left Russell a few steps behind her as she took in what'd been renamed Black Lives Matter Plaza on 16th Street. Emblazoned on the concrete in fifty-foot-tall bright yellow block letters was a truth the whole world knew now: that Black lives were just as valuable as everyone else's. Making her way to 1600 Pennsylvania, she was stopped by a woman not much younger than her.

"Excuse me," the woman said, "are you Mayor Johnson?"

Therese opened her mouth, but found no words came out.

"Yes," Russell said, catching up. "She is."

"Bless you," the woman said, hugging her. "Your strength gives me strength."

Words found Therese only after the woman left. "You think she confused me for someone else?"

Russell's laugh filled her heart once more. "She asked for you by name."

"I wonder why..."

"Because you're a goddamn inspiration, that's why."

She didn't speak again until they'd made their way past security and into the West Wing.

The building's interior wasn't anything like the show she'd loved watching. It was smaller, for one thing, and instead of portraits of dead presidents, photos of President Begaye all over the country lined the hallways.

Making a speech at the Trail of Tears Memorial in Jerome, Missouri.

Paying tribute to the Wounded Knee Massacre in South Dakota.

At the Navajo Code Talkers Museum in Tuba City, Arizona.

Therese was so mesmerized she didn't see the aide who'd come to get them until her husband took her hand.

"Most presidents swap out photos every few weeks," the aide said, "but President Begaye wanted these three up for good."

"This all happened his first year, right?" Therese's voice was a reverent whisper.

"Yeah. I still remember Republicans calling it his apology tour."

"You work for Roger?" Russell asked the aide.

"The name's Walter." He laughed. "It seems like in this White House we *all* work for Roger."

"Drop her off and then gimme a tour?"

Therese finally snapped out of her trance. "Wait, what? You're not coming with me?"

Russell grinned. "You're the big shot. This is your moment to shine, not mine."

Walter chuckled. "Hold on to this one, Madame Mayor." He turned to Russell to let him know he had another meeting, but that he'd send someone else to show him around while Therese took her meetings.

"This way, Mayor Johnson."

Walter showed Therese into a room that wasn't much larger than a broom closet, and by the look of the cleaning supplies within, it might've once served that function.

"Good thing I don't have a big head," Therese panned. "It wouldn't fit in here."

"You'll understand the need for discretion, ma'am." Walter looked at his feet, contrition shining in his eyes.

"Ain't a big deal for me, but I feel sorry for whomever I'm meeting. I take it that isn't the president?"

Walter opened his mouth, but before he could say anything, a white woman entered. She couldn't have been older than thirty-five, with alabaster skin and blonde hair that touched her shoulders. She had some meat on her bones that shaped her hips nicely, and Therese thought that if she'd smiled, she'd look quite cute with that dimple on her chin.

"I've met in worse places," the woman said. "The name's—"

"Rebecca Steinbeck," Therese said. "We still get newspapers out in Albuquerque."

Nodding, Rebecca extended her hand. Therese shook it perfunctorily.

"Good," Rebecca said. "It's a dying media, but we need it to last a bit longer."

"And why aren't I meeting Roger? Or the president?"

Rebecca grinned, not with the cocksure expression of Therese's husband, but with the impulse of a snot-nosed child. "Neither's going to meet with you until we know you're for real."

Therese's nostrils flared. Malibu Barbie wanted to know if *she* was real? "You got a lot of nerve, thinking I may be fake when you've spent seven years as Harmon's Chief of Staff."

Walter tapped his foot. "Yeah... I'mma head out. But y'all have fun. Try not to kill each other."

Rebecca chuckled as he left. "What you said is fair enough. I know it's not my place to tell you anything, but I do think I'm perfect to run your campaign."

"...you want to be my campaign manager?"

"The truth is, I begged Roger to let me pitch myself to you first."

"And why would you want the job?"

For all Rebecca's bravado, the room was small enough that Therese noticed the woman fidgeting with her nails. She turned the question back on Therese. "Why do you?"

Therese scoffed. "I'm not at a hundred percent yet, but I have spent the last eighteen hours giving this a lot of thought and I do think I have something unique to offer the country at this moment."

"No one should make this decision lightly, but you want me to tell you why I think you should run?"

Therese motioned with her hand for Rebecca to continue. "Please."

Holding out four fingers, Rebecca ticked them off as she spoke.

"One: you're a mayor, which means you've got executive experience. Two, your life experience means you can empathize with the working class in a way that no other presidential candidate in the history of our country has been able to. Three, you're a Black woman at a time where our country is begging to take a leap forward on social rights. And four, you're fucking smart."

This time, Therese didn't scoff but instead let out a full-blown chortle. "Being smart has to go last?"

"I'm pretty good at my job," Rebecca said, "but even I won't be able to make the average voter care about your intelligence."

Therese and Rebecca spent the next hour discussing everything from policy to fundraising to the logistics of running a race and the administrative burden that would entail.

"We focus on the states most favorable to write-in candidates. New York. California. Illinois. That's more than enough delegates to make a splash."

"Those are Super Tuesday states," Therese said. "We've only got three weeks..."

"Crazier things have happened," Rebecca said. "Even if Harmon doesn't endorse you, it won't be lost on people that his Chief of Staff is moving to Team Therese."

Team Therese. She couldn't help but smile at hearing it, remembering how Russell had coined the term.

"I'll be real with you: I've got survivor's guilt." Rebecca bit her lip so hard Therese worried it would bleed. "Most nights I'm a nervous wreck. I pop pills to get to sleep."

"You're not making a great sales pitch for being in charge of the most important thing in my life."

Rebecca threw back her head in laughter, her full cheeks turning pink. "I know all about the importance of reclaiming your agency. My sister, Claire? You probably read about her, too."

"I know the Steinbeck name..."

"She certainly lives up to it. She was in the driver's seat for so long and I was the ugly stepchild. But then she lost her job, she lost her influence with Brooks losing to Begaye, and all of a sudden, I was top dog." The room wasn't big enough to pace, so Rebecca just tapped her foot faster and faster. "It should've felt great, but instead it was like survivor's guilt."

"Rebecca..."

"I have a point, I swear. And it's this: don't let your worst moments define you."

Therese sighed.

"It's not like mine, not by a long shot, but you've got survivor's guilt, too. And if you do this, if you run, you can make sure Jerome's life is recognized by everyone in the country in a way that ensures lasting progress, so that maybe it won't ever happen again to anyone else's child."

Therese's lip quivered. A lump started to form in her throat. Balling her hands into fists at her sides, she pushed it down. She would not cry, because the media wouldn't differentiate between the proud tears of a warrior and the shrieking hysterics of another angry Black woman. Instead, she exhaled and nodded.

"I'm in. But why should I hire you? Why *didn't* you go work for your boss's campaign?"

Rebecca sighed, a sound as if she was releasing seven years' worth of tension from her body. "I'm kind of holding my nose working for that Republican-lite fossil. There's no way I'd have taken the job if the president wasn't in charge, but this position gives me a quick line to the Oval Office."

Therese smiled at her honesty. "I respect directness, and I can appreciate your hunger for power; it's the only way to make a career in this city, especially as a woman." She leaned in, her heels allowing her to tower over Rebecca's five-foot frame. The smallness of the room forced Rebecca's back against a wall. "Did you get that from your family? I've heard how they made their billions."

"My father was cleared of any wrongdoing in those experiments," Rebecca said, though Therese saw her shudder, saw the curled lip of disgust when she mentioned Dr. Steinbeck. "At any rate, I haven't spoken to him in years."

"Estranged from your whole family? Must be tough."

"Poor little rich girl," Rebecca said, struggling to choke back tears. "I know my story requires the world's smallest violin."

"That's not what I meant." Therese leaned back, taking the

woman's hands in her own now. "Just because you're privileged doesn't mean you don't have problems. Looks like we both lost our families."

"But you found someone. Russell." Rebecca whispered the name.

"And you'll find your better half, too, one day."

Rebecca shook her head. "No. I fucked that up."

Therese paused, allowing Rebecca to spew her verbal diarrhea.

"Mom and Dad cut me off, said I was as good as a skingrafter. Why? Because I don't believe in the caste system WP created? Because I know now that power is overrated? Power cost me everything. Not just my family, but my one chance at a happy ending."

Therese smiled.

"What?"

"I knew you were good at your job. I just wanted to know you were a real person, too." Therese hugged Rebecca. "Let's build a system where everyone gets a second chance if they need it."

Therese followed Rebecca to a room next to the Oval Office that contained a large rectangular desk. Behind the desk sat a portly woman with thin glasses.

"Is he ready, Mrs. Fish?" Rebecca said.

"You can go in," the woman said. "He's just wrapping up a meeting with the vice president."

Therese protested, saying she could wait, but Rebecca opened the door and let them both in. And then she saw him. Bolo tie and jeans. A frame that told Therese he really did play pickup basketball with his sons, just like Kate Caruso had written in her *Vanity Fair* profile of him when he'd been running in the primaries against Vice President Harmon.

"Like I was saying, Mark, you'll see your decision to drop out was for the best."

Though he might've been a half-foot taller than the president, Vice President Harmon's shock-white hair and old age made him look frail when the two stood side by side. "I'd hardly call what's happening my decision."

"Mr. President…" Rebecca's voice broke the uncomfortable

silence.

"Ah," President Begaye said, "you've arrived."

The vice president's nostrils flared. "Rebecca? This wasn't on your schedule." Turning to the president, he tapped his foot impatiently. "What is the meaning of this?"

Joseph Begaye grinned. "If I know the White House Press Corps, you'll learn soon enough."

"Who is this?" Harmon's tone shifted from obnoxious to rude.

"I'll explain later, Mark."

"Explain it to me now, Joseph!" Pointing a finger at Therese, he demanded to know who she was.

Rebecca begged. "Please, Mr. Vice President..."

Understanding dawned on Mark Harmon's face. "You just couldn't have come work for me, huh? We would've won Iowa and New Hampshire with you on the team, but instead you've chosen to go work for some nobody?" He scoffed so loudly the Secret Service agents keeping watch outside noticed, turning to the windows to ensure the president wasn't in imminent danger.

"Watch it, Mark." Venom dripped from the president's words. "The first Black female mayor in New Mexico is far from a nobody. And if I ever hear you talking like that again, I'll leak it to the press myself." Therese held her breath as he continued. "We're exploring all options to beat Lungford, since it's clear you can't do the job. Now get out of my office and get a hold of yourself."

Chastened, the vice president spun on his heels and left through the side door connecting the Oval Office to Roger's office.

President Begaye chuckled. "Oh, Roger's gonna get it. But it's his own fault for coming up with this plan." Smiling at Therese, he took her hands and sat them on the couch positioned in front of the Resolute desk. "Now, let's get down to brass tacks."

Therese was offered tea, coffee, soda, and even a glass of scotch while President Begaye explained how Roger had come up with this long-shot idea for injecting the Democratic field with some "much-needed energy."

"Can you beat Kaitlin? Can you win the primary? I don't know. But I do know if Terry wins the nomination now by default, if he isn't challenged anymore, we don't have a chance in Hell come

November."

Therese frowned. "It's not much of a pep talk, Mr. President..."

"It's not supposed to be. I'm never gonna be anything but real with you, Madame Mayor. You gotta be your own cheerleader in this race—you and your campaign manager. I can't endorse you, but I do think you'll add the jolt we need to make this race exciting."

Therese rubbed her neck, taking a sip of the water she'd accepted after saying no to everything else. "How do you know who I am?"

"You kidding? My press secretary won't shut up about you."

Therese slapped her knee as she threw her head back laughing. "Alicia? That girl's the daughter I never had." Then, remembering where she was and who she was talking to, she apologized, adopting a somber expression.

"It's okay to laugh once or twice," President Begaye said. "The Secret Service won't shoot you unless it gets out of hand." His comments made even Rebecca crack a grin. "Alicia believes in you, and so do I." Standing up, he clasped Rebecca's shoulders and looked Therese straight in the face. "And so does this one. She's the best there is when it comes to this stuff, and I truly believe the two of you together could do incredible things."

Therese's face grew hot, while Rebecca's alabaster skin didn't hide her pride at all. She stammered out a response. "That's very kind of you, Mr. President."

"I don't say anything I don't mean." Walking to the Resolute desk, he picked up the phone and asked Mrs. Fish when his next meeting was. "I've got the Ag Secretary in five, so I'll leave you with this: don't be afraid to run from my legacy when you genuinely disagree with me."

Therese opened her mouth, thought of closing it, and then ultimately decided against it. "Don't worry, Mr. President. I have no intention of following you blindly."

President Begaye nodded, and Rebecca took Therese's hand to lead her out.

"Okay," Therese said, walking alongside Rebecca as she returned to her husband. "What's next?"

Therese and Russell spent the rest of the day visiting some of her husband's favorite haunts from when he'd lived there. Drinks at Madam's Organ in Adams Morgan ("Try saying that five times fast," Russell joked). Music at the Black Cat in Shaw. A midnight stroll visiting the MLK and FDR Memorials.

"Soak it in," Russell said, taking his coat off and wrapping it around Therese. "After you announce, we ain't gonna be able to do anything like this for a long time."

"Yeah? How long?"

Russell whistled. "I'm thinking eight years."

Stopping at the base of the white granite slab of rock with King's likeness carved into it, Therese rested her hand on it.

"I'm doing this for you, baby." As she read the quote framing the entire memorial, she decided right then and there it would become the mantra of her campaign: "Out of the mountain of despair, a stone of hope."

Chapter Nine

March 16, 2028

Roger Manning's job was ninety percent bullshit. And being White House Chief of Staff was one hundred percent thankless. Contrary to what he'd worshipped on TV during his college days, his job was nothing like Leo McGarry's. The ladies didn't care for his eighty-hour workweeks, reporters found his quips more annoying than funny, and he couldn't think of a single elected Republican leader who'd rather hash out a deal with him than rile up their base on Artie Quiver's nightly talk show on FOX.

Morning staff was at 7:30, but Roger had been in for an hour to read a few dozen digital tip sheets that kept him apprised of the country's zeitgeist. The president would ask him in a few minutes what the world was talking about, and he loved having the answer each day. He read not just domestic politics, but international, too, as well as what Hollywood and Wall Street were thinking that morning. The press called him 'the President's Hawk.' He only pretended to hate it.

"Roger?!"

In eight years of working for the man, Roger could count on two hands the number of times his boss had actually yelled. This was made all the stranger by the fact that his meeting with Mayor Johnson had gone well yesterday. At least, that's what he'd heard from Rebecca and Russell. Downing a cup of coffee on his desk, he steeled himself for the day and entered the Oval Office through the connected door between their offices. "Good morning, Mr.

President."

"It'd be a better morning if Harold Mueller had a dime of sense, and the best morning if we did, too!" The president slammed the *New York Times* onto the wooden table separating the two couches in the room. Roger sat himself on one side as President Begaye unfurled the fists at his sides and took the other. "You know it's the stress talking."

"Of course, Mr. President. We've had some bad days."

Begaye grunted. "We've had some bad months."

"When does the First Lady return from Albuquerque?" Roger definitely spent more time thinking about the president's sex life than Leo McGarry ever did thinking about President Bartlet's. Coordinating her schedule with the president's was an unspoken but essential component of his job: he had to determine how long the president could go without getting laid and make sure it never got that far. As crass as it sounded, the country suffered if they breached that point.

Patriotism took many forms. Roger stifled a grin.

"She's still with Nivol," Begaye said, referring to his youngest son. A recent graduate from the Maryland Institute College of Art (MICA), Nivol spent his days touring the country with his sculptures and paintings. Roger made a mental note to have Luther call Ajei Begaye's chief of staff later that day and suggest the First Lady return home. The president's body man and the First Lady's chief of staff spoke so frequently Roger was sure they had a thing going on.

Biting the inside of his cheek, Roger chided himself. He wasn't a gossip columnist or reality TV producer. He looked at the cover of the paper President Begaye was reading. A photo of an unidentified face with a question mark accompanied the front-page headline: STILL NO JUSTICE FOR THE BEGAYE ADMINISTRATION.

"It's been two weeks since Francino withdrew," Begaye said. "Why don't we have a replacement nominee announced?"

"We need to make sure the next person gets the job," Roger said.

"Were we not sure Francino would get the job when we announced him?"

Roger sighed. "Vetting takes time, too. We don't want to get blindsided again."

"We didn't vet multiple candidates before picking him?"

The president's questions were good, and unlike his press secretary, Roger had no experience when it came to avoiding them. Looking around the room, he spotted Luther in the back, as usual, listening intently in case he was needed. "Luther, what do you think?"

"Sir?" The man waited for the president to nod his approval before joining them in the center of the room.

"Thinking Luther can bail you out, Roger?" Begaye's chuckle eased at least some of the tension from Roger's shoulders.

"You said we're a team here, right, Mr. President?" Roger was actually a bit taller than Luther when they were both standing, as they were now. "You've been in the room for a lot of these meetings. You read the briefing books on most of the potential nominees. Got any ideas?"

Putting his hands in his pocket and smiling, Luther nodded. "Actually, there is one person..."

Roger hadn't realized Luther hung out with Anaba so often. As the three of them sat around the table, Luther filling him and the president in on his encounter with Judge Ferrari at American University, at how much Anaba loved her, Roger wondered if he and Anaba were an item. He'd have to keep a better eye on that; another unspoken rule of this administration was that no one in the White House was allowed to date the president's daughter. President Begaye would've preferred no one in the federal government (or even better, the entire world), but Roger wasn't a miracle worker.

The president was smiling when Luther finished his piece. "What do you think, Roger?"

"I love it."

Luther's voice went up an octave. "Yeah?"

"Politically, it's a dream. Woman. White. From the west. Already been confirmed by the Senate."

"Yes," the president said, "but a SCOTUS nomination is a whole different ball game. I want you working the phones immediately."

When he stood up, the others followed. "Get Denton on the phone. I want him here within a few hours."

"Yes, sir," Roger said.

"He shepherded Ferrari's last appointment, if I'm remembering correctly. Let's figure this out today, please."

Nodding, Roger returned to his office as Luther and the president left through the back door to meet a school group in the Rose Garden.

●————————————————————●

Even though his boss was from New Mexico and Senator Harvey Denton hailed from Colorado, Roger knew the two were old friends from when they'd served in the Senate together. They'd been on a CODEL together to Israel about twelve years ago, and ever since then, Denton had been a loyal ally of the president's. That was the only reason Roger could stand the three-term senator. Denton was too cozy with Silicon Valley for Roger's liking, and the senator made sure his staff knew they could quit if they didn't agree with his rigid views on technology. Denton also didn't believe in such a thing as work-life balance; he had a reputation for having one of the highest staff turnover rates of anyone in the Capitol.

"Joe!"

Roger bit his tongue to keep from reminding the senator that the name was 'President Begaye' and that this was the Oval Office, not the rowhouse they'd shared on Capitol Hill when they'd lived together during congressional sessions.

President Begaye certainly didn't mind the informality, walking over from the Resolute Desk to grasp both of the senator's hands in his own. The pair sported matching bolo ties and jeans. "I believe in Harvey Dent...on!"

Roger refused to laugh at the dad joke. It would only encourage him.

"At least someone believes in me," Harvey chuckled.

Roger was spared having to listen to any more of their banter when Mrs. Fish knocked on the door. Opening it, he helped her bring in lunch.

"I got some lamb biryani, tandoori chicken, rajma with chapati, and mango lassi." The president's grin couldn't have gotten wider if he'd tried. Roger knew how much he loved this Punjabi restaurant, Pi'āra. It was the Punjabi word for love, and that accurately described the president's feelings toward it.

"It's not every day I catch you eating Indian food," Denton said.

President Begaye threw his head back in laughter. Roger mimed throwing up in an empty brown bag after taking out all the food. Mrs. Fish gave him a firm glare and a slap on the arm, the only one to catch him in the act. She hissed under her breath. "Yeah, he sucks, but this isn't about you, Mr. Manning."

"You're right, ma'am."

"Hey," Denton shouted, "leave poor Mrs. Fish alone. If you're so hard up for a date, all you gotta do is ask. My chief of staff's in the market for someone who can show her a nice time."

"Leave it alone," President Begaye said. "This guy's never taken me up on an offer to set him up."

Roger responded by patting the senator on the back and taking his seat as Mrs. Fish excused herself back to her desk. "Well, gentlemen, let's see if we can set America up for success by the end of the day."

"Good lord," Senator Denton said, "I hope he's a better chief of staff than he is a comedian."

"He is," President Begaye said. The pride in his boss's eyes was enough to keep a smile on Roger's face.

They spent the next hour taking in Denton's advice on the political and legal upsides to having Bella Ferrari on the Court.

"Michelle replaced you, of course," Harvey said, referring to Michelle Haaland, the Pueblo Indian who'd replaced Begaye in the Senate once he'd ascended to the presidency. "And she blessed Bella's Appeals Court nomination with a blue slip, that's only right."

Roger rolled his eyes. Everyone here knew it would've been the height of disrespect to appoint a judge who didn't have a "blue slip" of approval from their home state senators. Roger also knew Denton was re-stating the timeline because he enjoyed making snide, implicit jabs about his intelligence.

"But to be honest, Michelle didn't carry Bella's water through that fight. I did."

The president took a sip of his mango lassi before placing his hand on Harvey's shoulder and leaning in. "Well, then, can you shepherd her this time, too?"

Harvey showed all his stupid, perfect teeth when he smiled. "Shucks, Mr. President. You need little ole me to help you out?"

Picking up a fork, taking a bite of lamb biryani, Roger considered stabbing himself in the eye with it.

"Would you help us bring this one home, Senator?" Joseph asked.

"It'd be my pleasure, sir."

Senator Denton left soon after, but not before handing a business card to Roger.

"Call the Medulla brothers tonight. They helped us lobby support last time around, kept the wolves at bay."

Roger had heard of Famóre, the Medulla brothers' company. It was actually one of the few apps on his phone, but he'd never admit that to Senator Denton. Just because something was useful didn't mean it needed to be revered. He asked his boss a pointed question. "You sure we need to throw our lot in so strongly with some tech millionaires from Silicon Valley?"

Harvey spoke before the president could reply. "Try not to sound so jealous when you call them, Roger. Oh, and please don't insult them by calling them millionaires, either. You gotta replace the M with a B."

Roger nodded, leading the senator out and thinking of a word for him that started with a B.

Chapter Ten

March 19, 2028

Tucked away in a strip mall near Montgomery Park was a Lebanese restaurant called Masarab. The word meant 'delicious,' and Bella thought it lived up to its name better than anything else she'd experienced. Doubling as a grocery store, the store stocked olives and chickpeas and tahini and pita bread, but she could also get chicken shawarma to die for and the best baklava in the country. It'd taken some convincing to get the Medulla brothers to dine at a grocery store, and she was pretty sure their lime-green Lamborghini was the only sports car that'd ever entered the parking lot, but now the brothers couldn't stop raving about their honeyed dessert of phyllo dough and chopped pistachios.

"How is it so good?!" Matteo asked with his mouth still full. "*Fratello*, it's as good as we had in Dubai last winter."

"Swallow before you speak, *fratello*," Gianpaolo chided his brother. "Look at Bella. She always swallows."

Bella let the insult roll off her shoulders. Aside from the occasional private jabs at her past profession these past six years, the Medulla brothers hadn't caused her any real trouble. They'd never told her how to rule on a case or done anything else remotely unethical. If the only thing she had to deal with was inappropriate jokes and reminders that once upon a time she and Gianpaolo had slept together in college, that was a fair price to pay for what they'd done for her.

"What brings you to town?" Bella got up to throw away the

Styrofoam boxes their food had come in.

"Not here, eh?" Matteo said. "Let's go back home."

Bella forced herself not to correct him. *My home.* The brothers did this at least once a year, got too comfortable visiting Albuquerque and set up shop for a few days in her spare room. The last time, Matteo had brought a girl back with him after a night of bar hopping. Thankfully, Gianpaolo had spoken to him since then and the pair had decided to stay at a hotel from now on.

Gianpaolo forced Matteo into the virtually nonexistent backseat so Bella could sit up front as they drove home. His grumbling filled her stomach as well as the food had.

When they arrived, she took out a bottle of red wine from her kitchen.

"You'll want something stronger tonight," Gianpaolo said.

Bella's eyes narrowed as she swapped the wine out for some tequila. "*Buona o cattiva notizia?*"

"Only good news for you, *amore mio,*" Gianpaolo replied.

He'd called her his love before on occasion, a sure sign he'd drank too much. Still, it wasn't like he'd listen to her and stop. They'd traveled all this way, and curiosity did get the best of her. Pouring three glasses, she carried them to the couch and sat down. Clinking their glasses together, each took a long sip. Bella's throat burned with memories as she stifled a cough. Coughing in front of these boys would just lead to a dumb joke about her gag reflex.

"So," she said, "what's the news?"

Rather than answer with words, Gianpaolo took out his phone and showed her a series of texts between him and a man named Harvey Denton. Racking her brain, she remembered he was the senior senator from Colorado. Taking the phone to scroll through the full text thread, she dropped her glass as she finished reading.

"Senator Denton wants me?" It was not just the alcohol that made her mouth run dry. Standing up, she began pacing between her kitchen and living room, hand over her chest to try and maintain some semblance of control over herself. Her heart was a jackhammer drilling into concrete. Grabbing the banister to her second floor, she blinked rapidly, trying to focus.

"Bella?" Matteo sounded genuinely concerned, which just made her panic worse. It was as if he was speaking to her underwater.

She hoped he didn't come over to help; she'd probably vomit on his thousand-dollar shoes.

SCOTUS. She could be with Aditya. After six years of being a coward, there'd be a clear reason to call him, to reconnect. Fuck her old life; she could build an even better one.

But what about the risks? A vetting for a judgeship was nothing compared to one for SCOTUS. She had to assume everyone would learn how she'd paid for law school. Her parents would die of shame. Her colleagues would learn the truth. *I can't do it.*

"Bella?" Gianpaolo had come to her side. "I want you to follow my instructions. This is called the 3-3-3 rule; I used it to deal with my panic attacks growing up."

Is that what I'm having? She'd felt this way before, waiting for her LSAT results and before a big exam and after being with certain clients, but she'd just chalked it up to the usual stress of being a woman. Wearing WP-tinged earrings had dulled it in her college years and beyond, but she'd stopped wearing the drug after becoming a judge.

"I want you to look around the room and name three things you see."

Bella complied, and her breathing began to slow. While she processed the next command, to list three sounds she was hearing, her vision returned and her dizziness vanished.

"Now," Gianpaolo finished, "list three parts of your body."

Bella obeyed, accepting a glass of water from him when she was done.

"Buona o cattiva notizia?"

She smiled at Gianpaolo's question. "I want it to be good news, but perhaps it's bad news."

"You don't have to worry," Matteo whispered. It was so much worse when he wasn't his dumb, sexist self. "We'd never reveal the truth about you. And if it comes out? We'd help you navigate that, too."

She wanted this so badly, more than anything in the world. *But it can't be just about me, can it?*

It was her life. The Medulla brothers would never worry about some past indiscretion blocking their path to greatness. And it wasn't just a male thing; women from Meghan Markle to Kusum

Raghavan dealt with sexist bullshit on a daily basis and still managed to push through. Out of the hundred-plus Justices who'd served on the Court, she would only be the sixth woman. Her appointment would mean a great deal to young girls everywhere.

Maybe I can be more than my worst moment.

She didn't have to make a decision tonight, or even tomorrow. Gianpaolo told her Denton wanted her to fly to DC tomorrow with them to meet the president.

"I voted for him," she said.

"Let that slip to Harvey, but the president will probably hold it against you if you mention it," Gianpaolo said.

"Thanks for the tip."

Matteo was already in the car, eager to find a woman to keep his bed warm for the night. "*Fratello,* let's go!"

"I could spend the night," Gianpaolo said. "Be a warm body if you find yourself in the middle of another panic attack."

Bella forced a smile. "It's not a good idea to mix business with pleasure."

Gianpaolo embraced her, pushing his body against her full chest as he grasped the small of her back. "All business should be pleasure." It was thirty degrees outside, and she used that excuse to mask the shiver that ran through her whole body. He didn't notice. "I'll pick you up in the morning for our flight, *amore mio.*"

Brushing her teeth, changing into her nightgown, she opened the desk at her side. Inside was her newest vibrator. She'd worn out three over the last thirteen years. Bella hadn't let any man touch her since Aditya had left. Turning the lights off and her toy on, she let her mind drift to the possibility that she'd be reunited with him soon.

———•————————•———

March 20, 2028

Bella woke to the sound of her phone screeching with an incoming call. Still groggy, she tripped over her covers and rolled off the bed. Her vibrator turned itself on again in the fracas, vibrating alongside her phone. Clenching her jaw, she turned it off and answered her phone.

"Bella?!"

Matteo's panicked voice tore at her sides. Had the president learned the truth? Was she about to be banished to Maranello once again?

"Check the front page of the *New York Times.*"

Turning on her iPad, she saw the headline: DENTON SETS EYES ON 4ᵀᴴ CIRCUIT JUDGE.

Bella let out a sigh. "Denton leaked it?" It wasn't ideal, but at least no one knew about her past... yet.

"Either him or someone on his staff," Matteo said.

"Where's Gianpaolo?"

"Trying to get a hold of the White House to save this thing."

Bella blinked. "What do you mean? This story could sink my chances?" A pit formed in her stomach.

"Duh." She could hear the condescension on his lips. "Politicians don't like being blindsided or forced into decisions."

"Pull yourself together, Matteo. And give me a call as soon as you hear anything."

"Likewise." He hung up without saying bye.

Bella tried focusing on her usual morning routine. Shit. Shower. Shave. It all blew out the window, though, when she opened the door to find a press gaggle snapping photos and shouting questions at her. She thanked her stars she'd already put on a bra and changed from her nightdress to a blue blouse that matched her eyes. Placing her phone on the kitchen counter, pouring herself a glass of water, gulping it down in one go, she wondered if she should call her parents first or try the Medulla brothers again. Her heartbeat raced as violently as it had last night, and she found herself closing her eyes and focusing on the sounds around her. It helped until she heard her phone wailing with another phone call from an unlisted number.

"Hello?"

The voice on the other end sounded like a rose, soft and beautiful yet filled with thorns. "This is Senate Majority Leader Kusum Raghavan."

Bella knew the senator couldn't see her, but she stood up straight all the same.

"I apologize for the enormous violations to your privacy this morning, and for my curt tone. My friends will tell you I'm an incredibly warm person to be around, but we don't have time for that now."

Bella poured herself another glass of water and gulped it down again before responding. "Yes, ma'am."

"Cut it out with the ma'am crap. Senator is fine."

"Yes, Senator."

"I hope we can become friends in the future, but for right now I just need to get down to business."

Bella nodded, then remembered Kusum couldn't see her. "Okay."

"Did you open the door already?"

"Yes, Senator."

"I hope you had a bra on?"

"Yes, Senator."

"At least you're not media stupid. That'll help."

Bella's voice caught in her throat. She took another sip of water. "Senator... am I about to get nominated?"

"Depends."

Bella let the warmth in her heart spread through her entire body. "Depends on what?"

"Are you one hundred percent committed to this? I'm speaking under the president's authority, but we can't have another disaster. We can't survive two failed nominations in an election year."

I won't fail. Nodding her head, she realized again Senator Raghavan couldn't see her. "I'm in."

"Good. Then get ready, go outside, corroborate the official story that you met President Begaye last time he was in Albuquerque and that this DC trip is just a follow up, and then get to the White House. Your official announcement is tomorrow morning."

The senator hung up before Bella could respond. Going back up the stairs to pack, her heart raced at the possibilities that awaited her.

Chapter Eleven

April 4, 2028

Therese had perpetual whiplash. She'd launched her campaign in New York instead of Albuquerque. As much as she hated this city, she couldn't disagree with her campaign manager's logic. Rebecca was thrilled that it was easier to hobnob with donors, and it also centered her roots as a working-class single mom. What she had said no to was the collage of Jerome's photos behind her as she'd announced her candidacy. True to what she'd told Russell those weeks ago at the MLK Memorial, she'd quoted the reverend and stated that it would be the chief goal of her presidency to build a stone of hope out of the mountain of despair that loomed before them. But she'd let them know it would take a communal effort, that in the words of President Barack Obama, "while freedom is a gift from God, it must be secured by His people here on Earth."

In the three weeks since she'd said those words, the vice president had officially dropped out. Harmon hadn't endorsed her, stating he'd needed to stay neutral, just like the president, but he'd given his blessing to a number of his top donors to join Therese's campaign. And it wasn't just his money that flowed to her; Rebecca had been able to bring on most of Harmon's field directors and digital staff. With Super Tuesday just a week away, a staff of two hundred now lay spread out across the entire country. Rebecca managed them all from the headquarters in New York. Therese was glad to be in New York with her tonight, even if they were holed up in a dressing room, minutes away from the last debate before people in New York and ten other states voted.

"Pre-debate poll has us at thirty-two percent in Arkansas and thirty-nine percent in Idaho." Rebecca barked the words as Therese's beauty consultant, Erica Heimstaff, continued applying makeup to her face.

"Are there even thirty-nine people in Idaho?" Therese batted Erica away as the young Latina tried to cover her crow's feet with concealer. "And stop with the makeup, Erica, it's enough. The voters appreciate some wrinkles."

"Can I see some polling on that?" Rebecca muttered.

Therese raised her eyebrows. "You want to say that again?"

"You're right, as always," Rebecca said. "Anyways, what you don't know is how big a deal Idaho and Arkansas are. Our delegate director can break it down if you want to hear more."

Therese rolled her eyes "I don't."

Winning the nomination wasn't about winning certain states, but about amassing more delegates from those states than anyone else. They had a whole team focused on winning these delegates, and each state awarded them differently based on a set of rules Rebecca called "complicated math" and Therese called "bullshit." Ultimately, she'd approved a larger salary for their delegate director than Rebecca earned—at Rebecca's insistence. This guy was the best of the best, apparently, and in a week, she'd know if that was a lie or not.

Standing up, Therese asked Erica to bring over the rack of dresses for her to choose from.

"I really think you should go with the black dress," Erica said. "It makes a point about your son's legacy and your significance on that stage as a Black woman, the backbone of the Democratic Party."

Therese shook her head. "You ever heard about beating a dead horse? You think anyone's forgotten how Jerome died or that Black women represent the most reliable voting faction of the Party?"

Erica's face fell.

Breathe. It ain't her fault I'm stressed. Therese had to remind herself she had thirty years on Erica, that the woman was a force of nature on the campaign trail, but was ultimately just a kid working her first real job and searching for validation. *I'm not just running for president to honor Jerome. I gotta bring a whole generation of women up with me.* The pressure sat on her as if she was Atlas holding up the world, but it was nothing new to a mother.

Taking Erica's hand, she touched the girl's chin and brought her to eye level. "Erica, voters are smarter than we give them credit for."

"Can I see some polling on that?" Rebecca's snide question was met with a glare that silenced her.

"People want to be spoken to like adults. And when we're not? That's when the cynicism sets in. I'm so glad you joined this campaign; I think we women have a lot to teach each other. So I promise I'll keep an open mind on the campaign stuff I don't know about if you keep an ear open for the life stuff you may not know much about. That sound good?"

Erica nodded as she played with her curly black hair and smiled. She'd just turned twenty-four. *Jerome's 25th birthday is in a few days.* They would've been dating in a different life. Therese would've liked that.

"Erica's wrong for another reason," Rebecca said, interrupting Therese's reverie. "You shouldn't wear black because it's a depressing color." Walking to the line of dresses, she pulled out an orange one. "Wear this. I heard Ensign is wearing blue, so it'll make a nice contrast." Therese lifted her arms up as Erica slid the dress over her chest and hips.

Rebecca whistled. "Not bad, Madame Mayor."

"Let's get this thing over with," Therese said, leaving the room with the two of them.

Rebecca offered one last comment that prompted Therese to snort in laughter. "I can't wait to see what trousers Ensign picked out to make his dick pop."

The press insisted on speaking to Rebecca before the debate began. She'd tried getting Therese to take the debate stage immediately, but she'd insisted on joining the press scrum.

"Madame Mayor, Harold Mueller with the *New York Times.*" Therese turned to see a man pushing forty who still couldn't grow a proper beard and mustache.

"Loved the editorial today." She flashed him a big smile that was only partly fake. The *Times* had endorsed her campaign this morning, a much-needed boost ahead of next Tuesday's vote.

"I don't see any other elected officials in your corner tonight, ma'am. Should I read anything into that?"

Therese batted her eyelashes, reminding herself to thank Erica for curling them so well. "If you look at the seats I reserved, you'll see they all belong to Black mothers like me who've lost their sons to gun violence. I value all the voters, but their support is most important to me and I'm so pleased they've agreed to corral this grassroots army for me."

Rebecca stepped between Therese and Harold before he could get another question in. "Mayor Johnson couldn't be prouder of the coalition she's built in less than a month, recruiting thousands of volunteers and inspiring people to give tens of millions of dollars, between the campaign and The American Dream Fund."

Therese thanked her lucky stars every night that Roger had finally left the White House to run the super PAC now tasked with electing her. In truth, she wouldn't have made it to this debate without that support, and the irony wasn't lost on her that her campaign manager had been in charge of the super PAC just eight years ago when its main charge had been to elect President Begaye.

Despite Rebecca's protests, Harold asked a second question. "Wouldn't you agree that it's kind of useless to say that you aren't the president's favored candidate at this point? I mean, the former White House Chief of Staff is running your super PAC, and Harmon's old chief of staff is running your campaign."

Therese chuckled, placing her hand on the man's shoulder. "Harold, come on. You know I don't have any control over what The American Dream Fund does."

Rebecca chimed in. "The president has full confidence that the best way to ensure continued progress is a Democratic victory in November, and we're touched to see he hasn't chosen a favorite." Leaning in, she brought her face right to Harold's microphone. "But let's be clear: President Begaye doesn't have the authority to just declare Mayor Johnson the nominee. That privilege belongs to the voters."

Harold scoffed. "Am I going to get anything out of you that isn't a trite slogan?"

Rebecca's fake smile showed off her chin dimple. "You're welcome to try. We got time for one more question before the debate starts."

Therese bit the inside of her cheek to keep from laughing. Rebecca was good at a lot of things, but one of her best skills was dealing with these bullshit vultures who'd do just about anything to take her off her game to score a bit of news.

"A successful presidential write-in campaign is unprecedented," Harold said. "You're seriously telling me that you aren't being guided by the president's hand?"

"What's unprecedented is the number of cop shootings around the country in the wake of WP legalization, and you'll hear tonight why that's one of the clear reasons why Therese is the only candidate who can deliver the kind of change we need."

Before Harold could open his mouth for a follow-up questions, the lights blinked on and off to indicate it was time for the show to begin.

"So happy you could be here tonight," Rebecca said, carting off her candidate. "Enjoy the debate."

Joy Taylor of MSNBC was picked to moderate the debate between Therese and Governor Ensign. She sat at a rectangular wooden table in the center of the stage to announce Mayor Therese Johnson of Albuquerque and Governor Terry Ensign of Texas. The two shook hands center stage before walking to their podiums on respective sides of the stage, with Therese on the right and Terry on the left.

"On behalf of Barnard College and the American people, I want to thank both candidates for being here tonight. The format of this debate is as follows: for the first hour, I will ask a question of each candidate. A coin toss has determined that Governor Ensign will respond first, and then Mayor Johnson will respond. Each candidate will have two minutes per question, along with one minute for clarifying any other issues that might come up. In the second hour, we will take questions from the audience. These will not be pre-selected, but I will remind our audience once again that any inappropriate questions will lead to your evacuation from the facility and possible further action as deemed appropriate by the staff of Barnard. Now, let's begin."

Right off the bat, Governor Ensign made clear his support for the Begaye administration's approach to WP legalization, stating that everyone across racial lines deserved to use refined WP.

"Mayor Johnson, your response."

"Thank you, Joy." Facing her opponent instead of the audience, Therese straightened her shoulders and followed the president's advice to disagree with him. "With all due respect, President Begaye has not done enough on this issue. Local governments should be given federal dollars to disburse to refinery stations in every single county in America. More than five years after legalization, this remains another unfunded mandate from up high, just like No Child Left Behind."

"You're starting to sound like a Republican, Madame Mayor."

Therese laughed at the governor's statement. He was too dumb to realize it, but that comment had just cost him married white women in the suburbs of Chicago.

"The bipartisan vision of President Begaye and then-Senate Majority Leader Hammond to promote WP access as a way to unlock new commerce remains unfulfilled for most Americans," Therese explained. "There was money allocated to private business, incentivizing companies to encourage WP training for their employees for the sake of developing a twenty-first century work force unparalleled in the world. President Begaye and Leader Hammond created a position of Undersecretary for Drug-Enhanced Commerce under each cabinet agency, but a Republican Congress stripped all funding for those positions in 2023. Democrats didn't fight hard enough, and so the president had to sign off on it. And after we won back Congress? Well, I guess we've decided to not care since no one's pushing to restore that funding. Send me to the White House, and I'll make sure the private-public partnerships WP legalization relies on become a reality. Send me to the White House, and I promise I'll care every single day."

The crowd exploded in applause, prompting the moderator to remind them to hold all applause until the end of the debate.

"Governor Ensign," Joy said, "you do have one minute to speak, if you'd like."

Therese bit her lip to keep from laughing. The governor looked constipated, as if he was trying to do long division in his head. Finally, a light turned on and he snapped out a response. "What about the WNBA? A sport no one cared about, and then the players get some WP and boom, stadiums are being sold out. That's a direct result of President Begaye's policies, and I think they're worth defending, don't you?"

Therese caught Rebecca grinning in the front row, seated next to Russell. In debate prep, they'd so hoped Terry would bring up the WNBA.

"Governor, perhaps *you* didn't care about the WNBA before WP was legalized, but it's a bit insulting to speak on behalf of everyone else."

The crowd gasped.

"The WNBA brought in close to one hundred million dollars last year, and thousands of fans watched the Dallas Wings in your home state. There's been a long tradition of governors working with their local sports teams to encourage increased physical activity in schools and promote leadership lessons. I wonder, Governor, have you hosted the Wings at your mansion yet?"

Terry's lanky frame and cleanshaven face made him look like a baby doe leaping onto the freeway. As he sputtered out a reply that he'd invite them right away, Therese forced down a smile and Joy Taylor moved to the audience segment of the debate.

●————————————●

The second hour of the debate wasn't nearly as exciting as the first. Rebecca had been right; the tone would be set by the end of the first ten minutes. Luckily, it hadn't taken longer than that to establish Terry as a second-tier joke. Or, as Harold Mueller phrased it in his post-debate tweets, "the governor proved he was a one-hit wonder, a boy who stumbled into a man's job and now wants a promotion."

Rebecca read off the tweet as Therese and Russell ordered them and Erica barbecue for dinner. Therese always went to this place in Harlem when she was in town: Locked and Loaded.

Therese made her way to a booth in the back after signing a few autographs for diners up front. She saw a few familiar faces, but mainly her fame was due to Cassie insisting the debate be broadcast on the diner's TVs. In addition to Therese being a good enough patron to have her picture up on the wall, Barnard was just a couple blocks from the restaurant. "No one makes better BBQ than Cassie Washington."

"You should've told Terry that during the debate," Russell said, sliding over a tray of collard greens, mac and cheese, beef tips, and pulled pork.

Therese laughed again, a rich sound she'd been told straightened her sagging cheeks and made her crow's feet disappear better than any makeup. She tried using it during debates for that reason, but her laughs always came out fake; she sucked at pretending to be authentic and spontaneous.

"I love seeing you laugh, Madame Mayor."

"Please, Erica, it's Therese when it's just us."

Erica played with the curls in her hair. "Thanks for taking us out to dinner."

"It's the least we can do," Russell said. "I'm so damn grateful for y'all taking a chance on my bride."

Therese took a sip of her boozy milkshake to keep from choking up. She needed this time with these girls and her husband just as badly as they did, probably more so. Over the last few weeks, she'd come to think of Rebecca and Erica as her daughters. Having this family, weird as it was, was all that was keeping her sane.

"You got a boyfriend, Erica?"

"Russell!"

"What? I'm just taking an interest in the kid."

Erica's voice went up an octave as she squeaked out a laugh, twisting her curls around one of her fingers until they got stuck and she had to ask Rebecca for help getting untangled.

"I didn't mean to make you nervous," Russell said. "Is it a girl?"

Erica coughed. "Um, I like boys. But no one right now."

Therese called out toward a woman cooking in the kitchen. "Cassie, you got a boy about her age, don't you?"

The owner of the diner, one of Therese's newer friends, emerged from the back, caked in grease and wearing a hairnet. "Aaron? Yeah, he's a medical researcher now, in Columbus."

"Ohio?" Therese smiled. "The convention's there in July." Walking to the front of the diner, Therese took Aaron's phone number from Cassie and brought it back to Erica. "You may as well give him a call."

Erica grew fascinated with her feet.

"Come on," Therese said, "what's the worst that can happen?"

Finishing her own boozy milkshake, Rebecca nudged Erica. "Just say yes so we can all move on with our lives."

"I'm still trying to find the right person for this one," Russell said, pointing to Rebecca.

"God, you guys are like our pimps," Rebecca said. Therese noticed her tone shift and made a note to tell Russell not to bring up dating again with her. She didn't want Rebecca feeling uncomfortable.

Erica didn't say anything, but she did take the piece of paper with Aaron's phone number on it.

"Okay," Therese said, "enough of this. We all gotta be up early for flights in the morning."

Closing their tab, she thanked Cassie and got in a cab with her new family.

Chapter Twelve

April 12, 2028

Therese woke up in a Sheraton located in the "Magnificent Mile" neighborhood of Chicago. She'd turned her phone off last night sometime after ten p.m., choosing to spend the night with Russell alone instead of with Rebecca and the rest of her staff in their makeshift war room, eyes glued to the various county board of elections websites as precinct results came in. Arkansas and Idaho were declared wins for Therese early on, but when she'd made her speech last night, they still hadn't called the three biggest prizes: New York, Illinois, and California.

Held in Russell's embrace as 'the little spoon,' she was acutely aware of their nakedness. His mind was asleep, but his body wasn't. She failed in trying not to wake him as she shuffled out, turning her phone on.

"Come back to bed," he said.

"Not that that idea's not appealing, but I've probably avoided Rebecca as long as I can."

"Suit yourself." Russell got up to go to the bathroom, leaving Therese to admire his full form. She bit her lip and considered logging some more 'rest' before heading back to the grind.

A message came through on her phone. "Holy shit!"

"What?" Russell asked from the bathroom, brushing his teeth.

Therese walked in, so flummoxed she didn't even bother throwing clothes on. "...we won California. And New York."

Russell swallowed his toothpaste. "Holy fuck..."

Grabbing her phone, he read the headlines Rebecca had texted over, followed by the desperate pleas to get in touch. Then he turned the phone back off and seized his wife, pushing her back on the bed and spreading her legs.

When they were both sated, Therese finally called Rebecca.

"Where the hell have you been, Madame Mayor?!"

"Good morning, Rebecca." She smiled as she watched Russell jump into the shower.

"I hope you got some rest in," Rebecca said, "because things are fucking nuts here."

"It's not even seven thirty."

"And no one gives a shit. They called California two hours ago and New York just now. Everyone wants a piece of you."

"Illinois?" Therese turned on her mini iPad, pulling up the state board of elections website.

"You're leading, but nothing final yet."

"Where's that leave the delegate count?"

"Fucking competitive!"

Therese pictured Rebecca chewing her lip, pacing back and forth across the war room they'd set up in one of the hotel's conference rooms. "I'll be down in a moment."

Therese entered the room to thundering applause. Not just from her staff, but from hotel workers who'd set up their breakfast.

"Thank you, thank you." Before speaking with Rebecca, she stopped to personally thank each hotel employee, posing for selfies and signing autographs when asked. Fifteen minutes later, she'd finally made her way to her campaign staff. "How'd the Republicans make out?"

"Kaitlin's the nominee," Rebecca said.

Therese took a seat as her digital director handed her a cup of coffee. She took a long sip from it. "Already?"

"She beat Westbrook on his home turf," Rebecca explained. "He was already bleeding support, and losing Florida was the death knell."

Therese sighed. "I guess that makes it official, then. Republicans finally nominated a female presidential candidate.

Maybe with two major female presidential candidates on opposite ends of the aisle, the press will stop harping about this Bella 'scandal' and the president can finally get his nominee confirmed."

Rebecca scoffed. "That's a nice sentiment, but it's a pipe dream. If anything, they'll try to get the two of you to box Bella out even further."

Therese's lip curled. "It's disgusting how the media always wants to pit us against each other. And about something that happened so long ago."

Rebecca opened her mouth to speak, but at that moment Erica ran into the war room so quickly she tripped over a chair and slammed her face into the linoleum floor.

Therese raced to her side, along with Rebecca and a few hotel workers. "Baby, are you okay?"

"I'm great!" Erica smiled, not noticing the small cut that'd appeared on her forehead.

"Erica, sweetie, how many fingers am I holding up?"

"Four!" Erica's voice was as chipper as ever as a staffer placed a Band-Aid on her forehead.

"Are you dizzy?"

"No, ma'am," she said, walking a bit to prove it.

"What was so important?" Rebecca asked.

Therese chided the girl. "How about an 'are you okay?' first, huh?"

"Yes, *Mom*," Rebecca said before asking Erica just that.

"I'm good! Now look!" Reaching into her jeans, pulling out her phone, Erica shoved the headline from the *Chicago Tribune* in Therese and Rebecca's face. "We won Illinois!"

A triple sweep. Therese couldn't breathe. Grabbing Rebecca's shoulder, she had to sit down.

"Can somebody get the mayor a glass of water?!" Rebecca forced it down Therese's throat as soon as a staffer handed her a glass. "Do you need another?"

Therese nodded. "Fuck yes."

A lot of things happened next. Erica ran to Therese's room to retrieve Russell, briefing him on the way down. Rebecca set up a press conference. Therese wasn't anywhere near the delegate threshold to be considered the presumptive nominee, but the first write-in candidate to win three major states? After only a month in the race? It would've been absurd not to take a victory lap.

Russell and Therese ate croissants and sipped coffee as the campaign staff ran around.

"Seven minutes," Russell said.

"What's that?"

"I'd say you have seven minutes or less of down time left in the week," he said. "Good thing we got our fun in last night and this morning because I don't think it's happening again for a long time."

Therese scoffed. "How much more can things change?"

Russell whistled. "You about to find out, Madame Mayor."

Rebecca walked up to them two minutes later. "Ma'am, it's Governor Ensign."

"Should've put money on it," Russell said, standing up to clear their plates. "It was nowhere near seven minutes. Give the governor my regards."

Therese took the phone from Rebecca, walking away to a corner for privacy. "Governor?"

"Madame Mayor, congratulations."

"And to you," Therese said. "You got Missouri, Texas, Ohio. I guess we'll see how Virginia goes next week."

Terry chuckled, a hollow, mirthless sound that echoed in Therese's ears. "Oh, Madame Mayor. I don't think it does either of us or the country any good to deny the inevitable."

"Terry?" Her voice fell enough to draw Rebecca's attention away from staging the press conference due to occur in the next half hour. Therese held a hand up as Rebecca walked closer, motioning for the woman to wait.

"The country needs to see you facing Kaitlin, not me," Ensign said. "I'm withdrawing from the race. Should make that press conference I heard about a bit more interesting."

Therese had prepared herself for this moment, winning the nomination. She thought it'd be suffocating, that the weight of it would send her spiraling. Instead, she found herself cool as a cucumber. In fact, she knew deep within her that this was what her son envisioned for her. "...thank you, governor. You've done your country a great service by running." She was only marginally embarrassed that she said the words with a beaming smile. It'd happened only a handful of times since he'd died, but now she felt her son's hands guiding her, as if they were as real as Terry's hands. Running for president was like a school project she was helping Jerome with. Like all school projects, she'd end up doing most of the work, but it was because of him she was in it at all.

"I hope you want to stay involved with the campaign," Therese said.

"Whatever you need. White male Texans like me got a lot to learn from you and your friends."

Therese threw her head back laughing. Rebecca must've figured out what was going on because she flashed her two thumbs up and attempted what Therese thought was an Irish jig. "Governor, I look forward to becoming friends instead of rivals over the next several months."

"You go talk to the world, and then get Rebecca to call my manager to work out the details. I'll endorse you wherever and whenever you want."

"Thank you, Governor."

Closing the phone, handing it back to Rebecca, she kissed the woman's forehead. "We did it."

Waving Russell over, she gave the two of them a private moment. "Baby..."

"There's nothing to say," Russell said. "I'm so fucking proud of you."

Tears formed on her face before she willed them away. "Wipe my face."

Russell complied, kissing her lips and brushing his nose against hers. "I got you. And you got this."

Nodding her head, she lifted his hand high as they faced the press together.

Chapter Thirteen

July 4, 2028

Bella Ferrari had performed 'rectal exams' before in her capacity as a 'doctor' during her first career. The Senate confirmation hearing process was about as comfortable, except this time she was the one being violated. She'd had about a week of bliss in March after her nomination had been announced before that intrepid reporter at *BuzzFeed* who'd broken the news about Francino had found the big poop on her, too. First, the hearings had been delayed while she'd recounted her entire history as a prostitute in excruciatingly graphic detail to the head lawyer at the White House. Then, she'd had to send her parents on a trip to Maranello to avoid the non-stop press gaggle outside their house. Democrats had started hinting she should withdraw after Therese Johnson had won the nomination, concerned Bella was a distraction the Party didn't need, and she'd even offered her withdrawal to Senator Raghavan.

"That's the dumbest thought you've ever had, and that includes your thought that it was a good idea to become a prostitute."

Angry, Bella had decided it was better to lash out at the senator in her private office instead of in front of millions on TV under questioning. "We can't all be born into privilege!"

Kusum laughed so hard the sound startled Bella. "After coming to America from India to attend a state school for college, I stayed to get a PhD in clinical psychology and then decided to marry a stay-at-home author. Where exactly is my privilege? Can you please locate it for me so I can use it sometime?"

Bella cracked a grin. Even with WP legalized, she'd never seen the senator wearing it around the office or with her two kids. They'd gotten to know a lot about each other these past four months, and Bella was glad to finally know the stories about Senator Raghavan's kind-hearted temperament were true. The woman spoke softly and carried a big stick, and that stick was solely trained on her enemies and the enemies of her friends.

"It's a dumb idea because the only thing that matters is getting you confirmed," Senator Raghavan explained. "Once you're on the Court, no one will care about how you got there or what you did before it. Just look at Kavanaugh. Congratulations, you've found a job where winning is the only thing that matters. Nothing else even comes close."

Bella bit her bottom lip. What she'd told the senator those months ago was true; she was in this one hundred percent. But with the opposition led by Senator Charles Lungford, that decrepit lion of the Senate, her chances were looking as good as the man himself. She couldn't believe his niece was now the Republican nominee for president. Whatever had happened to women sticking together?

The confirmation hearings had finally begun last month. With the Senate on break for the holiday, Bella picked her nose alone in her hotel room as she reflected on the most recent hearing three days ago. She'd bet anything it'd been Lungford who'd leaked her career to *BuzzFeed*. He'd probably used one of the girls from the same agency. WP-laced condoms worked better, and were much safer, than Viagra or any similar drugs. She'd considered calling her old agency, trying to connect one of the girls there with Lungford or Hammond or one of the other Republicans blocking her confirmation, but Senator Raghavan had killed that idea without her even vocalizing it. She'd spoken with every single Democratic senator at this point, and it really was true that Kusum was the savviest of them all, in addition to being the kindest and smartest, too.

And then there was Aditya...

Senator Lungford had ripped her relationship with him to

shreds on national TV. No longer was Aditya a 'job creator,' but instead an ex-con who'd dabbled in unrefined WP and hired prostitutes and suffered from a drug addiction. He'd called her after that hearing, and she was pretty sure he'd shown up at her hotel once or twice, but she'd always been too much of a coward to face him. How could he be anything but angry with her? She'd lose her last nerve if she had to hear him yell at her.

His mom had to see that...

She'd never met Deepika Shetty, but she had enough Indian friends to know the wrath of an Indian aunty.

Aside from Senator Raghavan's confidence, there had been a few positive editorials keeping her somewhat sane. Jessica Newbury at *Vogue* had described her journey as a big step forward for the sex industry. Kate Caruso at *Vanity Fair* had called her a leader for fourth-wave feminism.

She'd also received an offer to be the spokeswoman for Doc Johnson, the largest sex toy company in America. So, she had a backup plan if this SCOTUS thing didn't work out.

Bella rolled her eyes as she stared at the phone, willing it to ring with some good news. Senator Raghavan was meeting with the White House right now, and any minute now, she'd get an update on the status of her life...

———————————————•———————————————

Roger paced back and forth in Senator Raghavan's office as she sat on a couch, tapping her foot on the ground and looking at something on her phone. The office hadn't changed much since Senator Nagaraj had been Majority Leader. He'd truly been blessed. He'd gone from Montgomery, Alabama to the White House, with stops in between as a senate leader's chief of staff and the chief strategist for a presidential campaign. And it was true what they said: the higher you rose, the more room you had to fall.

"My husband had the right idea, being a stay-at-home dad," Kusum grumbled.

"It's lovely to be here with you, too, Senator."

"I should be home with my family. Just look at them!" She showed him a video of her two children with their father in their backyard in Virginia.

"It's like a thirty-minute drive from here," Roger said. "And the faster you see reason, the quicker you can leave. But in any case, it's not like Independence Day means something special to either of us."

Politics was a bunch of bullshit, but one of the chief offenders, in his opinion, was having to pretend to be happy about a holiday that celebrated the liberation of white America while completely ignoring what his own people had endured.

Kusum stood up, putting her phone away. "As corny as it sounds, I still believe in the promise of America. You and me being in this room with our titles is proof that America is still the last, best hope for humanity. And as for seeing reason? You get my support the same way I get yours, both when I agree with you and when I don't care. Neither of those conditions is satisfied here."

Roger cracked his knuckles. "Senator, you know I think the world of you, right?"

Kusum rolled her eyes. "Yes."

"And even if I didn't, I'd still respect the title. At the end of the day, you were elected by 1.7 million voters to lead your state and fifty-three of your Senate colleagues to lead our caucus, and I'm just some guy."

"But—"

"Going back to the Medulla brothers hat in hand isn't going to save this nomination. Senator Denton is wrong; more money isn't working here."

Kusum grinned. "You can speak freely here, Roger. I didn't invite him to this meeting for a reason. Denton's a blowhard, no doubt about it."

Roger exhaled, a weight heavier than those he lifted in his morning gym routine leaving him. "I know he's head of the Judiciary Committee, but you need to circumvent him here. He's too close to Hammond to see it, but getting this Aditya guy involved is our best play at this point."

He could hear the thoughts racing through Senator Raghavan's head.

He's an ex-con.

He was pardoned.

Brooks was the one who issued that pardon.

Did Aditya ever pay Bella for her services, or was it really love? If it was love, why isn't he in her life anymore?

"Senator," Roger said, "the fact of the matter is that we're at fifty-eight votes with the whole caucus behind us, plus four Republicans. Aditya's funded a lot of these guys; he still has some pull in the Republican conference."

"Maybe he gets us to sixty-two, sixty-three," Kusum conceded, "but we need sixty-seven to win the vote, since Republicans increased the voting threshold last session."

"Fair enough," Roger said, "but sixty-two re-opens negotiations. We can't go another week without gaining some ground, no matter how little."

Glancing at the senator's phone again, Roger noticed a picture of her daughter. "I didn't know she was pregnant. When's she due?"

"Any day now." Kusum sighed. "Make the arrangements, but if Aditya fails, it's on your head."

Roger nodded. "This'll work, but even if it doesn't, we got another ace in the hole."

"What's that?"

"We all know Senator Lungford's health is failing. The word is he just got admitted into hospice. If he dies before the vote, it's smooth sailing."

He'd been around the Senate long enough to have heard about Senator Raghavan's temper, and had even witnessed it firsthand a couple times, but this was the first time she'd been angry at him.

"Don't ever say that again." Her lips were pursed, her voice as low as a tiger about to pounce. "I'll call the president, Roger. That's halfway treasonous, what you just put out into the universe."

Not for the first time, Roger feigned contrition with a superior. "I apologize for vocalizing what we've all been thinking. Give your family my best."

Leaving, he called Adrsta to set up a meeting with Aditya.

●————————————————●

July 6, 2028

Bella made sure she wore the honeyed perfume Aditya loved as she waited for him at her house in New Mexico. When Roger had called her with the details of the new plan for salvaging her career, if not her reputation, he'd agreed with her that New Mexico was a better locale than DC. Less press made it easier to make sure this meeting stayed secret until they knew if Aditya could help as much as Roger thought.

For all her brains, for all her growth over the past decade, just thinking about seeing him made her heart skip a beat. She'd worn granny panties and avoided shaving her legs in anticipation of this meeting, hoping it would be enough to keep her from making a bad decision. All her plans went out the window, though, as soon as he knocked on her door and she opened it, seeing his dad bod and wondering if she could ever give him a family in the future. He'd grown out a beard and mustache he obviously kept well-maintained, thin but ever-present around his entire face. She wondered if it would tickle between her thighs. Biting the inside of her cheek, she told herself to get a grip.

"...hi..."

"Hi," he said.

Her wardrobe matched how conflicted she was. The granny panties and hairy legs were below, but on top she wore a floral V-neck that accentuated her breasts and skinny jeans that were a size too small. When they shared an awkward hug, she heard him smelling her wavy, chestnut hair and caught him admiring her freckles. Moving to the couch, sitting opposite from him, she breathed deep as butterflies flitted through her whole body and set up shop in her heart.

"How've you been?" The thick Italian accent she'd worked so hard to control since becoming a judge came out again. She took a sip of the wine she'd set on the table, trying to mask her embarrassment.

Aditya frowned. "That's all you have to say to me?"

And just like that, Bella's anger took on a life of its own. They'd had shouting matches in the past; on more than one occasion, Aditya had ducked to avoid a thrown plate. Examining her wine glass, she considered how much it would hurt him if she cracked it over his skull. Having visited Maranello, she knew now that her hot Italian temper was genetic.

"Why didn't you ever call me?!" Standing up, she raised her

glass above her head so fast the wine in it spilled all over her couch and Aditya's slacks. He leapt up in response, bringing his hands to his chest to try and assuage her.

"I didn't even know you'd come back from Italy until I read about your appointment to the 4th Circuit in the paper."

Bella saw her green eyes blazing with fury in the reflection of the glass as she stepped toward Aditya like a cat, backing him into the kitchen. "You made it pretty clear you didn't want me in your life. You know how many nights I spent crying, wondering what I did wrong?!"

Aditya's voice dropped to a whisper. "You could never do anything wrong... you're perfect..."

In the kitchen beside him now, she dropped her glass to the floor, not caring that it shattered, scattering glass beneath their feet. She was glad she hadn't told him to remove his shoes. "If that's true, why didn't you tell me Karthik died?"

Aditya cleaned the floor as they caught up on over a decade of news. They both cried, good tears and bad.

"Deepika Aunty died?" Bella held him in a tight embrace as he rubbed his nose into her clavicle.

"When I was in prison," he said.

"I'm so sorry..."

"At least my dad isn't sick anymore." Squaring his chest, sniffling, he looked her in the eyes. "The past is the past. Let's talk about the future. From what I understand, it's pretty promising."

Bella hadn't wanted to tempt fate by cooking dinner for him, in case their reunion turned disastrous quickly, but with the yelling out of the way (for now, at least), she began cooking risotto as he laid out which Republican senators he thought he could influence.

"I seem to remember a lot of takeout when we were dating," he joked. "Who taught you to cook?"

"My *nonna*, of course," she said. "And if I remember correctly, the takeout was a mutual decision so we could spend more time doing... other activities." She enjoyed seeing him adjust his slacks as she teased him.

The meal ended too quickly for her, but she forced herself not to suggest a nightcap. After debating with herself all night about whether or not to ask the question at the top of her mind, she finally conceded to her curiosity as they stood by the door, both too happy or afraid to say goodbye. "You've got the big, fancy job again, the influence, the money. Is there a woman?"

He was on her before she had a chance to think, kissing her and brushing her hair and pressing his chest against hers as his bulge grew against her warming thighs. She let him push her back against the front door, welcoming his tongue into her mouth and tucking her hands under his shirt. Their passion might've lasted an hour or a minute, for time had no meaning when they were together.

"There's only ever been you," he said. "I haven't been with anyone else since..."

Heat flushed through her cheeks. "...me neither..."

Aditya smiled. He looked so good she wanted to cry. "Can I come upstairs?"

She got a call before she could answer. It was from an unlisted number. "Hold that thought." She swayed her hips as she walked back to the kitchen for some privacy, knowing his eyes were glued to her.

"You know you can't sleep with him, right?" Senator Raghavan's voice dried her thighs.

Bella hissed her response, a whisper low enough she hoped Aditya couldn't hear. "Are you spying on me?"

"Of course. I hope you didn't shave your legs."

"I didn't," she said. "He won't care."

"Get a grip," the senator said. "Have as much fun as you want after you're confirmed, but the press is on their way to your house as we speak. Someone found out you're meeting Aditya, and you gotta be ready to deny the story when they show up."

"Did anyone ever tell you you're a clam jam?"

Kusum laughed. "What's that? The female version of cock blocking?"

"Yes!"

Kusum hung up without responding, leaving Bella to break the bad news to Aditya.

"It's okay," he said. "I've got a hotel room already. I wasn't sure how this would go. But it went well, right?"

"Yeah," she said, "it's been almost perfect."

Closing the door behind him after he snuck out, she went upstairs to get her vibrator.

Chapter Fourteen

July 8, 2028

Kaitlin Lungford hated being in Albuquerque this late into the summer. Sweat pooled under her skin, which was flabbier now that she couldn't do her usual workout routine every day, due to her campaign schedule. She thought cutting her hair would help with the heat and make her look fiercer, but Olivia and Emily insisted her ponytail illuminated her femininity.

Running for President of the United States and I still have to listen to a bunch of people young enough to be my kids. At least obeying her campaign manager and beauty consultant was better than listening to her uncle. Though one day, her manager was going to grow to be just as ferocious. When she'd tried to give Charles a piece of her mind last month for dragging this Bella woman's name through the mud, Olivia had literally taken her phone away. A Secret Service agent kept all her electronics now.

"Madame Secretary?" Olivia's voice cut through Kaitlin's thoughts.

"They're ready for me?"

"Yes, ma'am."

The woman was only thirty-five, but in campaign years, that made her older than Kaitlin. Before this, she'd managed three senate races and two gubernatorials. Kaitlin wondered if she and Rebecca had their own secret text thread as two long-time female professional operatives at the top of their game.

Despite herself, Kaitlin smiled. Her official reason for being here, to give a speech to some donors at a La Quinta Inn and tell them their nominee was going to beat Governor Strauss in November (she wasn't), was bullshit. But before the plane took them to the next fundraiser in Jackson Hole, she was going to pay Bella a visit.

She'd found out Agent Hanson was the one keeping her phone and bribed him to give it back to her by offering the phone number of one of Vijay's friends. After weeks of holding in her feelings, she'd let her uncle have it. She couldn't believe she'd let herself believe he actually wanted to change before he died. She'd told him flat out that she wouldn't even consider attending his funeral unless he at least met with her. He'd made no promises of supporting her, but had agreed to speak with them in Utah. Now she just had to convince Bella Ferrari to get on a plane with her to visit her arch-enemy as he lay in hospice.

Patting Olivia on the shoulder, Kaitlin walked onto the stage, flashed her pearly whites, whipped her ponytail back in a way that showed off her boobs, and put on a show that would've made P.T. Barnum proud.

⸺●⸺⸺⸺⸺⸺⸺⸺⸺●⸺

Kaitlin wasn't sure if Olivia was more upset that she'd gotten her phone back or that the car was driving them to Bella's house and not the airport.

"This is so dumb," Olivia said, checking her phone every two seconds.

"Would you stop? No one's going to find out where we're headed."

"Yeah," Olivia said, "you're only the first female Republican presidential nominee and you're only headed to the house of a SCOTUS nominee who was secretly a prostitute for years. Why would the press care about that?"

Kaitlin pursed her lips. Enough was enough. "I took my phone back because I'm an adult, and I'm talking to Bella because it's not right, what she's going through. That dry wit and those big breasts might've worked when you were handling the old men who used to run this Party, but you're working for me now, so you better change your tune or find another ride home."

Olivia looked like she'd been slapped, her full cheeks turning beet red. "...I'm sorry, ma'am."

"It's okay to joke about Westbrook's shriveled dick and talk about how stupid reporters are and force me to go to bullshit events when it's actually important, but when you start talking down to me, calling an idea of mine dumb or trying to manage when Vijay can see me or when I can use my phone, that's when we'll have issues. Understood?"

Olivia nodded, her eyes glued to her shoes.

Kaitlin told herself her tone and words had been appropriate and respectful. She could sympathize that it was tough to be a gay, full-figured, single woman in her thirties running in Republican circles, but life was hard for everyone. She let the drive carry on in silence until they arrived.

As much as Kaitlin wanted to see Bella's face when she rang her doorbell, Agent Hanson had insisted he press the actual button.

"I don't think she's going to shoot me, Agent?"

"Well, ma'am," he said, "this way we'll thankfully never know."

Bella was clad in a loose T-shirt and shorts when she answered the door. An Indian man was cooking in her kitchen.

"You gotta be fucking kidding me," Kaitlin said, recognizing Aditya.

"I was about to say the same thing," Bella said. "Wouldn't the sight of you and me together here tank your campaign?"

"Ma'am, may I check your house, please?" Agent Hanson didn't wait for an answer before barreling in to assess the safety of Bella's home. "We're clear. I'll wait in the car." Leaving, he let Kaitlin inside.

"Well," Bella said, "do you want some green chile cheeseburgers?"

The two women had as much in common with each other as Kaitlin thought. Both were whip smart, but habitually underestimated because of their natural beauty. Both had lovers relegated to the sidelines, although Bella maintained that she and Aditya were 'taking things slow.' Kaitlin assured her she wouldn't tell the press; the woman deserved some semblance of privacy.

"Why should I get on that plane with you?" Bella asked.

"Uncle Charles is dying."

"Good," Aditya said, chiming in for the first time. "He's brought us nothing but pain."

Kaitlin balled a hand into a fist at her side, letting the nails dig into her skin until they made a mark. "He's spent his whole life hurting me, hurting others... but I think now, at death's door, he might actually want to make things right."

"I'm not sure that's possible," Bella said.

"Me neither," Kaitlin said, "but right now he's got all the cards. If there's even a chance he could fix this, don't you owe it to yourself to try?"

Leaving Aditya to man the house in her absence, Bella went up to change before meeting Kaitlin in the car, joining their fates together.

●————————————————●

Kaitlin wondered if Bella had ever been on a private plane with any of her former clients before. She thought of asking her if she was a member of the mile-high club before thinking better of it, remembering how she'd just dressed down Olivia for being inappropriate.

"I asked Senator Raghavan if I should withdraw," Bella said. Kaitlin raised her eyebrows in response. "I guess you agree with her that it was a dumb idea."

"I don't think you were making the decision to make your own life easier," Kaitlin said. "You were trying to make things simpler for the country."

Bella nodded. "It kills me to see the president take another hit, and I knew Republicans would drag me through the mud, but poll after poll shows the public doesn't care much for me, either."

"The public doesn't know what it wants until it's right in front of them," Kaitlin said. "And I wouldn't get down on yourself too hard about them. Forty-four percent support means you're pretty popular these days."

Bella sighed. "How sad."

Kaitlin looked out the window as their plane began its descent to a private air hangar in Springville, just an hour south of Salt Lake City. She'd managed to find a facility for her uncle close to the family mansion. "Don't worry about your poll numbers," she said.

"Today we fix all past wrongs."

Uncle Charles had aged considerably in the last six months. The spots on his face that she'd seen in January had now taken over most of his body; one would think the dark brown blotches were his natural skin color. His cane stood in a corner of the room, replaced by a wheelchair he couldn't even operate on his own. Assuring his hospice aide that they'd call her at the briefest indication of an emergency, Kaitlin shooed her off so that she and Bella were the only ones in his room. He lay propped up on a bed, connected to a ventilator and an IV pumping nutrients into his system.

"Bella." Charles's once-regal voice registered as a whisper, forcing Kaitlin to step closer to hear him. "You actually came." His smile showed his yellowed teeth and sunken cheeks. In over fifty years, she'd never seen that desperate, sad, hopeful look on his face. Kaitlin realized at last that facing his mortality had actually changed her uncle. She'd dodged his calls for six months and thought if he had another six months, maybe he'd turn into an actual human with feelings.

"They told me you were in hospice," she said. "You said once you wanted to change before you died. Why don't you prove it today?" Stepping aside, she revealed Bella to her uncle.

"Why'd you bring the whore?" Charles asked, his voice as shaky as his grasp of social norms.

"I knew this was a waste of time," Bella said.

Kaitlin stepped in front of her, preventing her from leaving the room. "Please, stay." Turning to face her uncle, she threatened to pull out his IV herself if he didn't change his tone.

"As you wish," Charles said.

Finding two glasses and a bottle of scotch tucked away inside a cabinet, Kaitlin poured her and Bella a finger each before explaining her plan.

Charles grinned when his niece had finished. "I die with dignity, like I deserve. And you'll attend my funeral?"

"I'll even say nice things about you," Kaitlin said. She'd explained to him how Bella's nomination would help her campaign, would lead to another strong woman owing them a favor. Not to mention the president would definitely attend his funeral if he moved to support Bella's nomination. And the closing argument? Kaitlin assured him that once she was in the White House, she'd have a bust of Charles moved into the Oval Office so he could always remain in the center of the action (a lie, but one he'd never learn).

"You expect that I'd be doing your bidding?" Bella's nostrils flared. "Support me or don't, but I'm not for sale."

Kaitlin's voice was as firm as her posture. "You've been a whore before. At least this way you'll get to remain on top, just how I heard you like it."

Bella gritted her teeth as Charles chuckled, resulting in a prolonged cough. Kaitlin gave him a sip of her scotch. He closed his eyes for what felt like an eternity before opening them again. "I'll do it. Get me a pen and paper."

Charles Lungford dictated his parting words to the world that night, a deathbed confession of past wrongs and future promises. After he begged Kaitlin for a hug, she reluctantly complied and heard his whispered cries that he wished he'd been better. She chose to believe him, though his statue would never sit in her office. She could forgive her family for any past sins without honoring the sins themselves.

"Give the letter to the *Tribune* tomorrow," Charles said.

Nodding, she took the letter and bade him goodbye forever.

Bella scoffed as they made their way back to the plane. "I suppose you want a thank-you. You're not getting it."

Kaitlin laughed, a sound filled with more frustration than mirth. "You'll know. For the rest of your life, you'll know how you got here. That's enough thanks for me."

"Fuck you," Bella said. "I'll sleep just fine. What happened today doesn't change a damn thing."

"Sure, it doesn't," Kaitlin said. "Everyone owes the Lungfords a favor, so what if you do, too?"

As the plane took off, Kaitlin told Bella to shower often. "It helps to wipe away any lingering disgust and self-loathing you may feel. Congratulations on reaching the pinnacle of power."

———————————●———————————

July 9, 2028

Kaitlin got the call bright and early that Charles had passed in his sleep. True to her word, her first call was to the *Tribune* so they could print her uncle's deathbed letter. Her second call was to Roger Manning.

"Madame Secretary?"

She grinned at hearing the confusion in his voice. Life held such few pleasures for her; it was nice to grab on to one when she could. "Tell the president to hold the vote. My uncle died last night; you've got your new Justice."

The letter was reprinted in every major outlet that day, its words re-tweeted by figures as diverse as liberals Joy Taylor and Jessica Newbury to conservative firebrands like Artie Quiver and Tammy Day.

Calling himself "the last flawed warrior of a generation that waged war in Vietnam against not just their corrupt government, but ours, as well," Charles admitted that participating in war crimes like the My Lai Massacre had altered his worldview, broken him so totally that he had no longer been able to tell right from wrong. Repenting for his life, he called for Bella's confirmation to usher in "a new era of politics, led by women who've triumphed despite all odds, women like Bella, who can be supported by Kaitlin." He spoke proudly of how she would restore honor to the Lungford name. Kaitlin wished he hadn't linked her name so closely to a whore's, but it wouldn't have been an authentic letter of repentance if she hadn't found some flaws within it.

"You okay?" Vijay asked as she returned to their condo in Pentagon City. She hadn't felt bad lying to Olivia about how she needed the night off to deal with her grief. It'd been weeks since she'd spent a night with Vijay, let alone one in their own bed. Walking to the kitchen, she kissed his neck as he cut vegetables for their dinner. Pressed up behind him, her hands tucked beneath his pants, she whispered in his ear. "I want dessert first."

———————

Halfway across the city, Whit Pryor's cell phone rang as he entered his hotel room in Capitol South.

"Senator?"

James Hammond's southern drawl was on the other end of the line. "The White House won."

"Sir?"

"They're gonna have the vote next week." His voice sounded like molasses. "I'm gonna lose this battle, but there's still time to win the war."

Whit started pacing back and forth in his small room. "What do you need?"

"Call your girlfriend."

Whit gulped. He'd tried keeping her a secret from his boss, but evidently not hard enough.

"I'm not mad," James teased. "Honestly, after the divorce with Melissa, I was worried about you."

Whit gritted his teeth. "Thank you, Senator. I'm fine."

"Well, you call up your girl. She's gonna be useful to me."

Chapter Fifteen

July 16, 2028

Bella convinced her *nonno* and *nonna* to come to DC to see Bella confirmed as only the sixth female Justice ever to serve on the Supreme Court. Walking past the supporters and detractors who gathered on the steps of the Court each day, flanked by security, Bella passed the Greek colonnades bordering the building's entrance to enter the hallowed ground with her family. She had multiple reasons to explain the wide smile on her face as the morning sun beamed down on her. She'd been confirmed with sixty-eight votes, which was one more than necessary, but far fewer than Charles Lungford would've imagined possible after his impassioned plea to support her. At the end of the day, after Aditya's lobbying as well, Lungford's letter had only moved a half-dozen votes. She almost wished he was still alive to know how few allies he'd had at the end of his life.

While the outside of the building was packed with people cheering and cursing her name, the inside had been virtually emptied of staff. The Court had wrapped up its annual work weeks ago, making today a particularly good time to swear in a new Justice. Bella squeezed her *nonna*'s hand as she guided them into a room where the new Chief Justice was waiting to swear her in.

"I, Bella Bibiana Ferrari, do solemnly swear..."

Bella hadn't told her *nonna* she'd be saying her full name at the ceremony. She could count on one hand the number of times she'd used her middle name, but this occasion certainly called for it. The old woman's tears filled her heart. Now and forever, her *nonna's* name would be part of the historical record.

A small reception followed her swearing in. It was traditionally larger, but Bella had insisted on no fuss.

"My parents have been through enough," she'd explained to Roger Manning. "It'll be my grandparents' first trip here. To be honest, I'd rather take them sight-seeing alone than have to hobnob with members of Congress and my new colleagues on the Court."

The president had respected her wishes, though he did call her and insist on speaking with her whole family. It was extraordinarily gracious of him to joke with her father. She even thought she heard him speaking Italian with her grandparents.

"I didn't know the president spoke Italian," Bella said to Senator Raghavan. It would've been impossible to not invite both her and Senator Denton.

"President Begaye speaks seven languages," she said, "but he won't tell anyone which ones." Kusum laughed, a full sound that spread through the room until everyone was smiling. "He likes to keep an air of mystery around himself."

"Thank you for being here, Senator." Bella meant the words, taking the woman's hands in her own. Finally, after over a decade in the dark, no less than the U.S. Senate Majority Leader had shepherded her home in more ways than one. Aditya hadn't been able to be here tonight, but he was waiting for her in a hotel room near Nationals Park.

"Make us proud, Madame Justice," the senator said. "Sorry I had to bring Senator Dental."

Bella watched the man nicknamed for his fake but flawless teeth trying to speak to her *nonna*. He was pantomiming as he spoke, as if that would make her understand English better.

"I know you wanted it intimate."

Bella grinned. "It's fine. I realize I'm a public figure now, and that comes with responsibilities."

"I'm glad I took a chance on you," the senator said. "Now, you can call me Kusum."

Bella placed Senator Raghavan's hands in her own. "We both

worked hard for our titles, Madame Leader. Let's use them, at least in public."

Excusing herself, Bella left to save her grandmother from Denton's gesticulating arms and increasingly loud voice. "Senator, so good of you to come." Saying a few words to her *nonna*, she watched the woman rush off to join her family.

"I wouldn't have missed this for the world," he said, moving so close that he stepped on her new black robes. "Gianpaolo and Matteo send their regards."

The brothers had spent plenty of money on her nomination fight, but it'd been weeks since she'd actually seen them. Whether they'd wanted to keep their distance in case she lost this fight or were actually busy, she didn't know.

"You must see my house, Bella. Have you ever been to Denver?"

Bella suppressed a shiver. "Only once or twice, and not for years."

Denton smiled, proving why people called him Senator Dental. "No doubt for... work."

She knew just then that she was nothing more than a rabbit in his eyes: cuddly and small and insatiably horny. No doubt his snide remark masked a longing to spend a night in her bed.

But her ancestors claimed Italy as their home, and if she could be compared to an animal, it was a lynx, beautiful and lethal and quick to strike.

"I'm not sure I'll find my way to Denver anytime soon, Senator," she said. "My docket will keep me busy here in DC."

"Of course," he said. "But then again, it's only proper I get to show you around the best state in the union, what with all the fuss of the last several months. You deserve a break, so if I call, I do hope you'll indulge me with a visit."

She didn't have to force a laugh, though he'd never know it was because she thought him an idiot rather than humorous. If this moron thought he could sway a Supreme Court Justice, he had another thing coming. Saying a polite goodbye, she thanked Senator Raghavan again and posed for another picture with her family before taking them sight-seeing for the day.

Bella's parents had offered to take her out for gelato before catching their flight to their new home in Albuquerque, but she'd said no. She was hungry for something a bit sweeter. Entering her hotel room, she saw Aditya opening a box of pizza.

"Perfect timing," he said. "I know it's not much of a celebration, but I figured we can't be seen outside at a fancy restaurant."

She was on him like a lynx before he could say another word. Her hands in his hair, her lips on his neck, the scent of him covering her like a shield against all the shit they'd had to endure, not just over the past year but since their days at Hoboken High. Even now, society told her not to be with him.

Fuck society.

Her hands found his belt, pulling it loose as they tumbled onto the bed together.

"Are you sure?" His voice showed hesitation, but she was glad his body didn't. His erection pressed against her skin as she tugged off her clothes and slid out of her panties.

"It's been thirteen years." Her breath came in ragged huffs as she kissed his lips and felt his heavy balls.

"I'm not sure I'll last thirteen seconds…"

She smiled, biting his lip before kissing her way down from his neck to his groin. Licking his shaft, she opened her mouth and prepared to take him in before he stopped her.

"I wasn't kidding," he said. "I'm gonna end up finishing in your mouth if you don't stop."

She swallowed him whole in response, her head bobbing like she was fishing for apples as she pawed at his ass. Knowing she was the cause of his moans, that she held total control over his manhood, she relished a feeling more powerful than the one wearing her robes gave her. True to his word, his hot warmth found its way down her throat within minutes.

"Your turn," he said, lifting her up to kiss her lips and shove her on the bed. He didn't even bother removing her bra, instead massaging her breasts through them as they made out atop three-hundred-thread-count sheets. She giggled when he licked her freckles, but gasped as he kissed his way down her waist and grabbed at her legs, spreading them to rest his face at her entrance.

His arms gripped her thighs as if they were anchors keeping him safe at home. She heard him smell her scent, lick the folds of her skin before plunging his tongue within her. Her toes curled as she bucked against him, his nails digging into her ass as she grabbed at his hair to shove him deeper inside her. She wondered how he managed to breathe with the ferocity of his mouth on her skin. It seemed like he was down there for thirteen years, equating to a whole lifetime stolen from them by the rest of the world. But for now, for tonight, they were the only two people left in it.

Emerging from between her legs, Aditya let his head come to rest in the valley of her cleavage, rubbing his wet eyes on her bra.

"Are you crying?"

"I just... I always believed this would happen again. I promised myself I'd come for you."

Lying on the bed, she held his head to her chest with one hand while the other traced his sticky member. "I'd say you definitely did."

He laughed, turning to rest on top of her as they shared a passionate kiss while he held her tight and his fingers found their way inside her.

She sighed as an overload of sensations took her from herself: the building climax as his fingers composed a symphony inside of her; his semen painting a picture on the side of her hip as his penis pressed against her, beginning to twitch again with arousal, his lips on her ear.

A surge ran through her body. She shivered as she came, pushing him from her thighs.

The smile they shared was more intimate to her than what they'd just done. With him, she could finally be herself. It had always been him, who saw strength in her vulnerabilities and yearning passion in her anger. "I need you inside me," she said, slipping into her thick Italian accent.

Kissing his lips, she guided his penis to her sex before wrapping her thighs around him as he thrust inside her. If she was his anchor, then he was the boat that would provide for her, keep her safe, guarantee her happiness for the rest of their lives. He moved with such intensity that a breast popped out of her bra; his lips found her nipple as he seized her shoulders and grunted. With another thrust, he emptied himself inside her and rolled to the side, panting in exhaustion.

"That was fun," she said. The sheets were wet with both of them; she got up to wipe them with a towel. As she moved to the bathroom, she saw Aditya's gaze on his seed dripping down her legs.

"I didn't mean to finish inside you," he said. "Are you on the pill?"

"No." Returning to the bed, wiping the wetness away, she kissed his lips once more.

"So... you'd be open to kids?" His smile lit even their dark room.

Bella laughed. "I may be too old, but I always did want at least one. We've had so much taken from us these past thirteen years. What if this is just another thing we can't have?"

Propping himself up on his elbows, Aditya leaned into her, taking the towel from her hands and wiping himself before tossing it to the side. "We won't let the world take this from us," he said. "I've always wanted to be a father, but only with you."

Now it was her turn to cry. Curling into herself as they lay in bed under the sheets, she let him wrap his arms around her. "What if the best part of our lives is over?"

Lifting her chin, Aditya smelled her hair and licked her freckles once more. "Bella, our journey is just beginning."

They held each other through the night, a light still on as they slept, so they could always find each other.

———●———————————●———

Whit Pryor paced through his hotel room in the Southeast as he waited for his guest that night. He'd already cleaned the bathroom and remade the bed. The staff had said they'd done it, but his standards for cleanliness bordered on OCD. Removing some bills from his wallet before locking it in a safe, he opened the door when he heard knocking.

The girl was Indian, but fair enough to pass for white. Dropping a thick jacket to the floor, she exposed an outfit of red mesh lace, with connected tassels at her full hips he could grab on to in order to steer her any way he wanted. The ad had said her name was Kajal Talwar. Four foot ten and 144 pounds. He licked his lips in anticipation.

"You got the money?" she said.

His nostrils flared as she undid her own bra. He wanted to do that himself, to treat her like a rag doll. He'd certainly paid enough for that right. "All $500. Want to count it?"

She nodded, taking the bills and tucking them into her purse. He growled as she bent over, stepping closer to rub himself against her satin panties. Pressing her against the wall, he undid his belt and moved to bind her arms. Before he could, she turned and shoved him onto the bed. "Don't do that again, or I'm out the door."

His ego bruised, he considered calling the cops right then and there before realizing he was thinking with his balls instead of his brain. Hammond needed this, but more than that, he did, too. It'd been weeks since he'd found relief in a woman.

"LISA said you were the best," he said, referring to her agency: Ladies Into Sexy Adventures. There wasn't much online about Kajal's employer, but he'd finally found what he needed by calling up Claire Steinbeck. Turns out Claire's ex-husband had used a whore from the same firm years ago, Bella Ferrari.

"It's nice when your boss thinks so highly of you," Kajal said. Kneeling at the foot of the bed, she tugged his pants and boxers down. "So, what's your story?"

He wasn't about to tell her about his divorce, how he couldn't see his kid unless Melissa agreed. "What's yours?" He grabbed her ample breasts, standing so that his erection pressed against her closed lips. "You must be a real attention slut, huh?"

She giggled. "This? It's only temporary. It pays the bills for law school."

Whit wondered if LISA was a front for getting prostitutes JDs.

"You never heard of an educated courtesan?" Kajal smiled, grabbing her purse again to take out a condom.

He stopped her before she rolled it on. "I heard LISA uses WP-laced condoms now. Unrefined."

Kajal frowned. "...it's dangerous."

If Whit was going to do this for Hammond, he was going to enjoy himself. "I don't care."

Nodding, she went back to her purse and dug around until she found another condom, this one sparkling with white residue at the base as she tore open the package. She used her mouth to put it on, and Whit gasped as he grew inside her. The drug warmed his package, enhanced every sensation. The heated wetness of her lips didn't just thrum around his cock, but around his whole torso, a warm bath heightening every element of his being.

She stopped too soon, standing back up and facing the wall. Looking back over her shoulder, she yanked her panties down to her ankles, spread her legs, and rested her hands against the wall in one swift motion. "Grab my hips and thrust."

Whit took a moment to collect himself. "What? Romance is dead?" He'd hoped five hundred bucks would entitle him to a bit more.

"You don't want romance," Kajal said. "You just want to get your rocks off."

Chuckling, Whit stared at their reflection in the hotel mirror. "Fair enough." Her body smelled of cumin, earthy and pungent, as if they'd been rolling together between bedsheets for hours already. Digging his skin into her bottom, he thrust himself inside her and was amazed the drug allowed him to hear her heartbeat; the physical bond between them transcended their bodies touching. His toes tingled and his mind raced as he listened to both their hearts pounding and watched himself in the hotel mirror as they fucked.

She'd told him it'd be extra if they cleaned up in the shower together, so he wiped himself down alone. She had her jacket back on when he emerged from the bathroom, clad in just a towel.

"Call me if you get lonely again," she said.

He grabbed her arm when she reached for the door. "You ever heard of a woman at your firm, Bella?"

She slapped him as understanding dawned on her face. "That's not how this works, and if you ask me that again, I'll go the press about you."

Whit smirked, grabbing her wrist when she tried slapping him again. "No, you won't. They teach you about mutually assured destruction at law school?"

There was fire in her eyes, from anger, yes, but also a yearning he knew she wouldn't voice. She'd probably never fucked with an unrefined condom before; he'd wager his passion had injected her with more than just dopamine. Taking a chance, he kissed her before shoving her back onto the bed and spreading her legs. Ripping off her panties, he buried himself inside her, clawing at her ass as she bucked against him. She came violently in minutes, kicking him aside immediately after. She shuddered as he wiped WP and her juices off his face with her jacket.

"You've never had hate sex?" It'd been like this with Melissa, with Claire, with so many others. Women hated him, but it didn't stop them from returning to his side. He had no patience for lectures on morality from people willing to get in bed with monsters. Fuming, Kajal stormed off to the bathroom to clean herself, emerging fully clothed.

"Here's another $1,000 for your time."

"That's too much," she said.

Whit grinned, knowing the movement highlighted his flawless jawline. "Not for what you're going to do for me these next few months. Keep your phone on."

He knew she wanted to slap him again, to break his beautiful face. But like all the women he'd ever fucked, she left in silence, no doubt trying to deny the satisfaction so evident on her face.

Chapter Sixteen

July 16, 2028

The private plane had left an hour ago from Sunport in Albuquerque. There weren't any direct flights to Columbus, and Therese had to be there a few days before the Democratic National Convention started on the 20th. After weeks of protesting, she'd finally let Rebecca convince her it was worth it to spend the extra funds on a plane that allowed them to avoid everyday passengers and make better use of everyone's time.

"Feels wrong," Therese said, seated next to her husband. "Don't private planes send the wrong message about where I stand on climate change, on government waste?"

"If it'll help you de-stress, we can go in the back and join the mile-high club," Russell joked.

Therese slapped his hand, looking across the plane to make sure Erica and Rebecca hadn't heard him. The two were seated near the back of the plane with her vice-presidential nominee, working on a third draft of his speech.

"That's enough scotch," Therese said, getting up. "We land in an hour. Get some water and some sense in you."

"You're leaving?"

"I should check on Tiffany. I heard her husband accepted my offer without even checking with her first."

Russell laughed. "Well, rest assured I'd never do anything like that to you."

"I know," Therese said. "You enjoy being alive and married at the same time."

Making her way to the back of the plane, she sat across from Tiffany and Terry Ensign. "Doing OK?"

"Oh," Tiffany said, smoothing her dress as she took another sip of her champagne. "First flight jitters, you know?"

The governor kissed his wife's hand.

"You'll get used to it," Erica said. She had a copy of the latest issue of *Vanity Fair* in her hand, page opened to reveal a photoshopped picture of Therese, Kaitlin, and Bella together.

"What's that?" Therese asked.

"Kate Caruso's latest," Erica said. "Talking about how the nominations of you three mark a turning point in female rights for America."

Therese scoffed. "Kaitlin wouldn't think twice about reversing eighty percent of the rights Bella and I are fighting for. And I'm sure she doesn't think the upward mobility of a Black woman and a sex worker says much about America's progress."

Russell joined her at that moment, massaging her shoulders. "Pilot says we gotta sit. Turbulence is coming."

Before Therese could return, Rebecca looked up from making notes on Governor Ensign's speech, raising her voice to ensure everyone could hear her. "The mayor's right. The press will devote themselves these next few months to trying to get the three strongest women ever in national politics to rip each other apart."

"Well, then," Therese said. "We just gotta find a way to win this election and keep our dignity intact at the same time. Let's get to it."

PINNACLE

There was once a queen named Amani Renas from what has become modern-day Sudan.

Little is known about her, since the native language remains untranslated, but we do know she halted the Roman Empire's southward expansion into Africa.

Legend has it that during her three-year war with the Romans, she had an ambassador deliver Augustus, heir to Julius Caesar, a quiver of golden arrows with a note:

"This gift is from the Queen. If you want peace, this is a token of warmth and friendship. If you want war, keep them, because you will need them."

We do not know much, but at the end of it all, Augustus agreed to a peace that highly favored Queen Amani Renas and her people.

The final humiliation for the Romans was that the queen sent her envoys to negotiate the deal, deciding not to meet with Augustus herself.

Chapter One

July 18, 2028

Kaitlin Lungford didn't bother keeping her voice down as Agent Hanson drove her from Salt Lake City to Springville in a standard-issue black Suburban. He'd been her personal agent when she'd been Defense Secretary, and when she'd become a presidential candidate, it had never been a question that he'd return to her side. He could always be counted on for discretion, and if forced to admit it, she'd agree he was probably her only male friend.

Her lover, Vijay, wanted to know how Hanson's date had gone with the man they'd set him up with. Maybe she'd ask him after her phone call. Nearing the end of the drive, she found herself hitting it off with a vice presidential prospect. With the convention in just two weeks, the entire Party was shocked she hadn't chosen a running mate yet. But it was her decision, not theirs. Today she buried not just her uncle, but any expectation that she'd allow herself to be bullied by lesser men. Especially into making decisions she wasn't fully invested in.

She put her phone on speaker, reaching for her steel water bottle. It was overly ambitious of her to think she could get a hike in after the funeral, but looking at the mountain through her window, she wished she could; it had been too long.

"Forgive me, Governor, I'm a bit distracted with my uncle's funeral. What were you saying?"

"My condolences, once again. I was just saying, a blending of old and new is just what this country needs right now." A pause followed, long enough to fill the car. "...not that I'm saying you're old. I only meant your family is old money, while I'm a second-generation immigrant."

"Of course," Kaitlin said. Flipping her phone's camera on, she noted her crow's feet and frowned. She would never admit it to her beauty consultant, Emily, but she did buy into the bullshit about makeup playing a pivotal role in her public appearances, about the ageism that worked against her just as much as the sexism.

"And I know a thing or two about winning tough races," the governor continued. "I'm not only the first Asian governor of Georgia, but the first female, too."

"What's something about you I can't learn from a briefing book?" Kaitlin asked. "You can speak freely here, Mirai."

The woman chuckled. "We do all have to put on acts, don't we? The truth of the matter is that I couldn't be prouder of where I came from and where I am today. I'm the living embodiment of the American dream. Raised by a janitor and a convenience store clerk. Not only the first in my family to graduate college, but I also went on to law school and met a man who's now general counsel for Delta. Got a kid in elementary school, learning at the best private school in the Atlanta suburbs, a hotbed of economic, cultural, and political growth. Beat out a room full of old, white men to capture a congressional seat, and then did it again to become the Republican gubernatorial nominee just four years ago. And now? I'm talking to our presidential nominee about the vice presidency."

"Hell of a story." Kaitlin was sure her grin could be heard over the phone. "Although I must say, you're laying it on pretty thick."

"Madame Secretary, I've had to scrap and fight for every inch of progress in my life," Mirai said. "No offense, but you haven't. And that's another thing I'll bring to the ticket: a sheer carnal thirst for victory. You fought for this country, and I couldn't be more grateful, but I've fought, too."

Kaitlin pursed her lips. She could count on one hand the number of people who'd spoken to her like that. She was sleeping with one of them; it was probably worth keeping the other one close to her as well.

Mirai took her silence as permission to continue. "It's not a bad thing to want something so badly you're willing to do anything for it. And as women, we're preconditioned to not go after those things with the same gusto as men because we're scared we'll be called bitches. Well, Madame Secretary, bitches get stuff done. I'm proud to be a bitch."

Kaitlin's brow furrowed as she took another sip of water. She knew Governor Shimizu spoke the truth. She'd let Uncle Charles bully her. She'd taken orders from President Brooks. And for what? She'd known she was superior to these men in every way, and yet something had held her back. But Mirai? She seized her destiny by the balls, refused to let it go. Her confidence was inspiring, and— Kaitlin hoped—contagious. Beyond the country benefitting, Kaitlin knew she would learn from the woman's tenacity, too.

"Why now?" Kaitlin's question echoed as the Suburban pulled into a parking lot. Others were here already, but the ceremony wouldn't start without her. She was the only family Charles had left. For all his machinations, he'd died alone, with no heir or wife to mourn him. "Why do you believe your moment is now, with me?"

The governor responded without hesitation. "Have you heard of the concept of kintsugi?"

"No," Kaitlin said.

"It's a method of repairing broken pottery, a philosophy for life. The Japanese take the broken pieces and apply lacquer and powdered gold to highlight the imperfections that make the piece whole again."

Kaitlin smiled. "Are you saying that President Brooks broke the country?"

"You said it, not me." Conviction rang through Mirai's voice, her tone as strong as steel. "I'm saying that together, two women at the pinnacle of their careers, we can build something even better than what was broken."

Just feet from Kaitlin lay the man who had broken her. But by burying him, by dismissing the legacy of her uncle and the former president, by embracing what the future could be if she had the courage to seize it, could she make something better from the broken pieces of the past?

"And is it what will make me great?" Kaitlin muttered under her breath.

115

"Madame Secretary?" Mirai broke her from her reverie.

"You've given me a lot to think about, Governor," she said. "Thank you for your time. I'll be in touch."

"Of course. Thank you for the opportunity."

Hanging up her phone, Kaitlin climbed out when Agent Hanson opened the door for her. She welcomed the sunny, oppressive heat.

Kaitlin knew her uncle would've wanted to witness his funeral. She had to admit, it was quite impressive. The junior senator of Utah was present, as were the governor and Senate Minority Leader Hammond. President Brooks's wife had come as a courtesy, perhaps also hoping the Lungford Estate would make a gift toward the Brooks presidential library. Kaitlin chuckled again, knowing that was a pipe dream, almost hoping the woman would ask so Kaitlin could turn her down.

Uncle Charles was draped in temple garb, complete with the white underwear, long-sleeved shirt, and his best tie. The priest made a good speech, reminding everyone that her uncle had kept with the Mormon tradition until his dying day, tithing ten percent of his income to the Church. It was her turn next, and she was able to string together some kind words about his hospitality after her father had died and her uncle's pivotal role in getting Justice Ferrari confirmed—with his dying breath, no less. Despite knowing better, she found herself disappointed Bella hadn't attended today, or at least sent flowers. She supposed the woman was naïve enough to think that just because Kaitlin had blackmailed her, that meant they weren't allies.

As guests shook her hand after the ceremony, conveying their condolences with one side of their mouth while using the other side to not-so-subtly indicate what favors they'd prefer once she won the White House, Kaitlin noticed Harold Mueller speaking with Senator Hammond. She'd asked for no press, but no doubt the Minority Leader had overruled her. At least his presence guaranteed a mention of her speech in the *New York Times* tomorrow. Olivia, her campaign manager, would be pleased.

She made her way to him as the last of her guests drove off. "Senator." A curt nod between them revealed to anyone watching the true nature of their relationship: an alliance of convenience that couldn't be broken no matter how much both would prefer that option.

"It was a great speech," Hammond said. "Your uncle would be proud. I'm glad you two ended things on a positive note. And it was particularly savvy of you to give that speech in front of a reporter, to make the world believe in the sanctity of your relationship."

"Thank you for coming." She took his hand as they spoke, squeezing it as her eyes darted across the room, confirming that even the cleanup staff had left them alone. "But there are no cameras here. You can go now."

Senator Hammond glared at her, rubbing his hands before shoving them in the pockets of his suit. "You'll want to watch how you speak to me, Madame Secretary. You haven't won the race yet, and you won't, if you make an enemy of me."

"I'll take that under advisement, Senator." She drew out that last word, his title, making it clear she had no intention of doing anything of the kind.

"You need to seriously consider what I said about naming Westbrook VP again. He's raised the money and he's got the political influence."

"You'll be among the very first to hear when I've made a decision, James." She used his first name since she couldn't actually slap his face, then walked out on him before he could respond. She wondered if she was leaning toward picking Mirai as just another way to stick it to her uncle and the men arrogant enough to think they could control her. If so, was she just allowing them to control her in another way?

Back at the Suburban, Agent Hanson was talking on the phone, and Kaitlin wondered if he was speaking to Vijay's friend. She was just about to ask him when the priest intercepted her.

"I was hoping to speak with you, my child."

Kaitlin hoped he couldn't hear her sigh. "What can I do for you?"

"Your uncle did indeed tithe to his dying day, just as I said."

"It must've given you quite a bit of funding. I'm sorry for your loss, but I don't intend to continue his generosity."

The priest stared blankly at her. "My dear, the Mormon church will survive without your uncle's generosity. A great tragedy has occurred, but it has nothing to do with losing something as corporeal as money."

"Of course," she said. "Father, I'm in a hurry—"

"Kaitlin, I'll be blunt, as you appreciate forthrightness. Charles set aside some money for us, yes, but there is funding in our ledger for a monument dedicated to you."

Now it was Kaitlin's turn to stare. Soon, though, she composed herself, running her hands down her slacks to smooth the fabric out. "That won't be necessary. Feel free to use those funds however you see fit."

"Kaitlin..."

"Save yourself some time, Father. Since you've recognized I appreciate blunt talk, I'll take it one step further. It wasn't exactly a surprise to anyone that I attended services as a child only because he made me, and my mind hasn't changed in the last forty years. I'm simply not a believer."

"Oh, my child." The priest looked at her as if she'd been sliced to ribbons. "It doesn't matter if you believe in God or not. He believes in you."

She turned to storm off, but as Agent Hanson opened the door to the black Suburban, she saw her uncle's ghost hovering over his grave. The man's WP-laced cufflinks gave him an almost corporeal form. When she blinked, though, his body disappeared, assuring her she'd imagined the whole thing. As they drove away, she wondered if she would ever be free of him.

Before leaving Utah, Kaitlin directed Agent Hanson to stop at a modest rowhouse. She was going to leave her past behind forever, but not before seeing her dad. The mansion in Springville had existed since before her father had died; Matt Lungford had been notably jealous of his brother's success when he'd been alive. But Kaitlin had never quite felt as at home there as she had at her dad's place. It was here that she'd believed in Santa Claus and learned to ride a bike. Chad Lungford had never crossed the threshold of this humble home. Nor had President Brooks. Even Charles had avoided it.

It was unsullied by lesser men. And, unbeknownst to all but a few, the property had been purchased years ago, by an LLC in Vijay's name.

Unlocking the door while Agent Hanson kept the Suburban running outside, she let herself in and noted the paintings and TV. She'd paid well to restore the place, and it looked as if her father had never left. The one good part of her past, kept pristine.

Her uncle: gone. Her half-brother: gone. Her president: gone. The men in her life were obsolete, save for one: Vijay. His generosity had made this whole endeavor possible.

It was time, then. A photo of her father embracing her five-year-old self sat atop the fireplace mantelpiece, and she touched it before pressing her fingers to her lips.

"I'm done being afraid, done running from my future. I'm going to marry that man."

Chapter Two

July 22, 2028

Kaitlin had learned three things in the four days since she'd returned from Utah: Agent Hanson hadn't hit it off with Vijay's friend, Olivia had hit it off with some woman she'd met at a bar in Wisconsin, and it was impossible to schedule time to ask her boyfriend to marry her between now and the convention. She figured it was just as well she asked him then; she needed this time to perfect her speech and finalize her vice-presidential decision.

When she'd told Olivia her marital plans, the woman hadn't been able to contain her enthusiasm.

"It's a manager's wet dream," she said. "You get a poll bump from the convention, and then we announce the engagement a couple days later and get a second boost. Not to mention the fundraising bump: Indian-Americans are loaded."

"So glad my choice of fiancé could be a political asset," Kaitlin said, her voice as dry as the martini in her hand.

That'd been last night. Right now, she was sitting in Atlanta at the Governor's Mansion with Mirai Shimizu. A long-scheduled fundraiser downtown tonight had given Kaitlin sufficient excuse to visit her without setting off too many alarm bells.

Sitting in an ornate dining room, handed porcelain dishes from China, Kaitlin sat in mild surprise that the governor hadn't changed anything from the past residents. Italian marble and Persian rugs still adorned the rooms, along with paintings that were at least two hundred years old.

"Thank you for hosting me, Governor."

"Of course." Waving a maid over, Governor Shimizu had the woman pour them both tea, then dismissed her. "Take a sip."

Kaitlin did, then winced.

Mirai grinned. "Raspberry tea goes very well with saké."

"It's four thirty," Kaitlin said.

"Which means it's still party time in Japan."

"Fair enough." Kaitlin laughed, a rare sound that filled her with confidence that she was making the right decision. She just needed to learn a few more things she wouldn't discover from the team vetting the governor. She needed to make sure Mirai had never done anything that could embarrass Kaitlin politically. "Your grandparents brought your dad over, right? Why did they choose America?"

Mirai took a long sip before answering. "For the same bullshit reason we teach our children."

"Bullshit reason?" The woman was as audacious as James Hammond at his most arrogant.

"Opportunity. A rags-to-riches story. Ingenuity that can only be found here. That pioneer spirit unique to us."

"Why is that bullshit?"

"Don't get me wrong, Madame Secretary. I believe in the promise of America. I would've gone back to Minato City if I didn't believe it with all my heart. But the promise has been spat on by men like Brooks and Begaye. It isn't all their fault, not really. The American Dream has been degrading since the days of FDR."

Kaitlin smiled with her eyes. Now they came to it. She knew she liked the governor personally, and the woman would be a political asset, as an Asian female governor from a state that both Brooks and Begaye had won previously. But she wanted to know her personal politics, why she opposed Begaye and—it turned out—FDR. "FDR?"

"Saying his name was more forbidden than repeating the name of the Devil in my house." The governor's voice shook. "My grandparents were proud people, but by the time my father was born in the fifties, that pride had been beaten out of them. Dad never learned it."

"They were interned?" Despite an entire career in public

service, Kaitlin had never met someone with such a personal connection to FDR's racist policy of throwing Japanese-Americans into camps during World War II. Why hadn't she ever asked one of the many Japanese-American soldiers who'd served under her? The failure to do so burned her cheeks.

"Yes," Mirai said. "They never wanted to talk about it, so I didn't even know until they died and dad mentioned it in his eulogy. They knew a man, Gordon Hirabayashi. His case was actually decided before the Supreme Court."

Kaitlin knew about Korematsu, the case that had upheld the constitutionality of the internment camps, but not this other one.

Bowing her head, Mirai continued. "Hirabayashi's case held it was legal to have curfews against members of a minority group when the U.S. was at war with said group."

"...I don't know what to say..." Kaitlin gulped down the rest of her sake before setting it aside. Leaning forward, she took the governor's hands in her own. "I'm sorry."

Mirai gritted her teeth. Lifting her head to look Kaitlin in the eyes, she squeezed the woman's hands in solidarity. "It isn't your fault, but it is your responsibility to make sure we never forget our history. Learning about all this growing up, and then learning about my grandparents later on, it shaped every part of my political upbringing. It's why I believe in limited government and it's why I despise Roosevelt, a man so weak he was too afraid to show the country his true self."

Kaitlin rested her back against the upholstered mahogany chair she sat in. "Isn't that a bit extreme?"

Mirai laughed, a mirthless sound, as she finished her drink. "His weakness had nothing to do with his polio. No, it stemmed from his being a philandering racist who ultimately didn't trust the American public any more than Brooks did."

Kaitlin bit her lip to keep from smiling. This was it: Mirai was the real deal. Together, they'd move mountains. And yet, she had to keep playing Devil's advocate. "And what do you think about Begaye? Electing a Native American didn't restore the promise of America?"

Governor Shimizu rolled her eyes. "Don't worry, I've got a convincing answer ready for when the press inevitably tries to pit the Asian woman against the Native American man."

Kaitlin appreciated her bluntness. "And that is?"

"What exactly is revolutionary about another male president accelerating a war we should've never been in? President Begaye's surge of troops did nothing to protect the homeland. His recklessness over a drug we don't even fully understand endangered countless lives. And besides that, he's embraced the same type of corporate politics he campaigned against. In all honesty, what's the difference between Vice President Harmon and Vice President Westbrook, as far as their economic views are concerned"

Kaitlin's grin was so wide someone could have driven a school bus through it. "You've been practicing that one for Fox News, haven't you?"

The governor took a bow. "I'll be ready for Artie Quiver, don't worry."

"And us? Do you really think we'll be such a change to the status quo?"

Mirai's eyes burned with passion. "Two women? A female defense secretary and a minority whose grandparents were interned? We're gonna be such a shock to the system it'll burn itself down."

Kaitlin was well-practiced at masking her emotions, but even she had trouble hiding her enthusiasm at this response. She just had one final question. "I gotta ask, since you mentioned the drug: do you wear WP?"

Mirai shook her head. "My husband does sometimes, and our son is half white, so he likes to wear it on occasion, but I meant what I said. We don't fully understand its effects on people like me yet. It gives me headaches even being around it for too long, so Ralph doesn't even wear it unless he's at work."

"Well," Kaitlin said, "you lucked out. I'm the one Republican woman who doesn't like wearing it constantly."

The tea was going right through Kaitlin after over an hour of talking. "Do you have a bathroom I can use?"

"Of course," the governor said, pointing her in the right direction.

When Kaitlin was finished, she found the governor's soap was jasmine scented. Returning to Mirai's side, she was preparing to ask Mirai if she'd be her vice president when she noticed a TV had been turned on. Artie Quiver was spouting his usual nonsense about Therese Johnson.

"...thank God her thug son isn't around anymore, but the fact remains, if you raise a kid like that, what makes you think you can be trusted? I did ask her manager, Rebecca, to come on the show, but of course she turned me down. Probably because she's on a date; we all know why she left her husband. That whole clan's been avoiding coming on this show so much that at this point that I'd settle for her husband, a man so effeminate it's no wonder he gets along with Rebecca."

Kaitlin's nostrils flared as he kept speaking. Seeing her return, Governor Shimizu turned off the TV. "I don't know how the Party became so enthralled with him," Mirai said. "To be honest, the only negative about being your VP would be having to do his show."

Kaitlin smiled. "Why don't we give it a shot?"

Mirai's eyes bulged. "Is that an offer?"

"Yes." Kaitlin's voice was firm, tempered with steel. "Will you be my vice president?"

Mirai poured herself two shots of sake, handing one to Kaitlin. "It would be my honor." Clinking their cups, they both gulped the drinks down. "But don't announce it at the fundraiser tonight. Let's make the world wait one more day."

Kaitlin took the bottle from her new VP, pouring another round. "I agree."

Clinking their cups once more, they toasted to the future and downed more sake. As the liquid ran down her throat, Kaitlin noticed for the first time that their cups were actual examples of kintsugi—broken porcelain pieced back together with gold.

Mirai had been right: it was more beautiful this way.

Chapter Three

July 22, 2028

Therese and her husband, Russell, had invited their staff up to their hotel room in Columbus, Ohio for a little powwow on the final night of the Democratic National Convention. Rebecca and Erica, Therese's beauty consultant, sat on the bed as Russell assisted with Therese's makeup and wardrobe. Despite Rebecca's protests, Artie Quiver's show played in the background because, as Therese put it, "We gotta know what the other side is saying about us. He's got over three million regular viewers. We're supposed to just write off those voters?" She hadn't been amused when Rebecca had said "yes" without hesitation.

"...I did ask her manager, Rebecca, to come on the show, but of course she turned me down. Probably because she's on a date; we all know why she left her husband. That whole clan's been avoiding coming on this show so much that at this point that I'd settle for her husband, a man so effeminate it's no wonder he gets along with Rebecca."

Therese stopped Erica when she reached for the remote to turn off the TV. "Oh please," she said. "It's nothing I haven't heard before."

Rebecca rolled her eyes. "Another dig at me for being a lesbian. How original."

Therese sighed. "I'm fair game, but you'd think Artie would have enough class to lay off you and Russell."

Her husband laughed. "How'd he put it last week? I'm

'whipped' and you 'wear the pants?'"

"You know it's not true," Therese said.

"Hell yeah, I know it's not true. But even if it was, what of it? Money, influence, even WP, these aren't the things that give life meaning. Life is about forging a partnership, about recognizing that we really are stronger together, and about crafting a way to maximize happiness through that understanding. That's knowledge that escapes even the smartest guys in Washington. And don't forget, I'm a King. I serve my queen proudly."

Therese kissed him, tracing her hands down his waist and forgetting for a moment that other people were in the room.

Rebecca coughed loudly. "Okay, lovebirds. Let's save that energy for later."

"You hosting the post-convention party?" Russell asked Erica as they all made their way to the elevator that would deliver them to the black Suburban driving them to the convention center.

"She can't," Rebecca interrupted. "She's got a hot date."

Erica shot daggers at Rebecca's smirking face.

Therese squealed. "With Cassie's son?!"

Erica smiled despite her best efforts. "Yes, *Mom*." She drew out that title into multiple syllables. "We've met up a few times over the last couple months. He's flying in to see the speech."

"He's flying in to see a bit more than that," Rebecca muttered. Erica shot her another glare.

"Maybe we'll have more than just an election to celebrate by November," Therese said as they all crammed into the car.

Now it was Erica's turn to roll her eyes. "Ma'am, you need to focus on your speech, not my love life."

Therese laughed, a sound richer than ice cream. "I can do both."

Rebecca handed Mayor Johnson a mint as their car took off. "It's a bold move to give your speech with Governor Ensign on stage," she said. "I still can't believe you picked him for the VP nod."

"We need more boldness in America," Therese said. "Ensign's the kind of guy who'll shake up Washington for good."

Russell nodded as the car pulled into the parking garage. "It's time to make history, Madame Mayor."

Giving Russell another kiss, she stepped out of the Suburban when a Secret Service agent opened the door for her. She waited for the rest of her group to gather before heading to the elevator.

"Give 'em hell, baby," Russell said. "I'm so proud of you."

Stepping inside with her agent, she blew him a kiss as the doors closed and she was taken to new heights.

⸺●⸺

Therese heard the crowd roaring from backstage as Governor Ensign finished his speech. He'd announce her in a moment and then stay on stage, behind her, as she delivered her remarks. They'd decided the visual of a white guy letting a Black woman take center stage, listening to her intently, made a stronger statement than giving her the stage herself.

She'd practiced a million times at this point. If she was being honest with herself, she'd had a form of this speech rattling around in her head ever since she'd confronted Officer Jackson the day he'd announced his resignation from the NYPD. She'd told him he wasn't worth her time, that joy was resistance. She believed that with all her heart, that embracing hate and resentment was like swallowing poison and expecting the other person to die.

Ensign's voice grew louder. "And now, the moment you've all been waiting for. She is a woman who needs no introduction, the woman named top mayor in America, my dear friend and the next President of the United States: Therese Johnson!"

There were so many campaign signs flapping in her direction as she stepped onto the stage that it was as if she was an Egyptian princess being fanned by her enraptured public. The signs in red and black and white stuck out amidst the bright LED lights towering over the stadium. Fifty thousand attendees chanted "Mayor J, Justice Today!" as she waved and pointed at the enthusiastic crowd, flashing a smile that showed all her teeth. The chant was catchy, and definitely preferable to the phrase embodied in some homemade signs made during the primary by her most passionate supporters: #JusticeforJerome. They meant well, but she didn't need to hear them shouting it every time she made a speech. After a debate coach had informed her about the value of using anaphora, she'd resolved to give them a new catch phrase today.

"My name is Therese Johnson. I am a child of Boston and Brooklyn. Of Albuquerque and the AME church. And I am here to tell you that you are Enough!"

The word was emblazoned on the signs in every supporter's hands, but she hadn't told anyone what it meant to her, choosing instead to keep it a surprise until now. Even Rebecca didn't know the extent of what that word meant.

"We have had enough, God knows that's true. Enough of dads working triple shifts and not being able to spend enough time with their kids. Enough of moms coming up to me across the country, scared they can't send their children to school because of their very real fears of gun violence. Enough of women being told by old, white men that they can't control their own bodies. But I'm not here to just tell you the world is tough and we're all tired. We all know how tired we are. We feel it in our bones. We come home to it at the end of every shift at work, when we only have the energy to warm up a microwave dinner and watch a rerun of *The Office* for the millionth time. Yes, we've had enough, but I am also here to tell you that *you* are enough."

She jabbed her finger at the crowd on that final word, prompting applause that didn't fade for several moments.

"I see your imposter syndrome rearing its ugly head. I've heard from the men and women of Illinois and Iowa, how you're afraid to ask for that raise you know you deserve. I am telling you today: you are enough!"

Another roar from the crowd gave her the moment she needed to calm herself. She hadn't practiced her next words, not wanting them to sound rehearsed or trite. She'd insisted on having a pitcher of water on stage, and as the audience continued to applaud and wave their signs, she took a sip and steadied herself.

"You all know why I'm on this stage. It isn't because I'm the best mayor in America. Although, at the risk of sounding arrogant, I'll say I'm pretty damn good." That remark drew laughs and applause that steeled her will further. "It's because my son was murdered and I'd had *enough* of staying silent and accepting it as just the cost of being Black in America."

You could have heard a pin drop in the convention center.

"Forgiving Jerome's killer really did give me peace. I draw comfort from the fact that his murderer is still in jail, from the fact that Curtis Levitt is the Mayor of Manhattan instead of Pete

128

Jackson." At this, she saw the cameras steer toward Curtis's face. He sat somber in his seat among the New York delegation. "Curtis wouldn't have been elected without the #JusticeforJerome movement, without the great work of Black Lives Matter. That's an uncomfortable fact, but it's a fact all the same. And while the country remains imperfect and cruel at times, I draw more comfort from knowing in my bones that Jerome would've wanted me to move on and build the next chapter of my life. He would've loved to meet my husband Russell, and I know beyond a shadow of a doubt that he would've been proud of this campaign."

The crowd roared back to life, waving her campaign signs and chanting a new word: Enough!

"Our oppressors do not deserve forgiveness, but we do! We are *enough*!"

Governor Ensign stood at this point, leading the crowd in chanting her name, lifting her arm as if she was a prizefighter. She couldn't remember the rest of her speech; it was as if she was having an out-of-body experience. She spoke of why she'd picked Ensign and why she was a Democrat, but those first several minutes would be what the newspapers and pundits led with tomorrow. Finally, it was time to end the speech.

"Before I leave you today..." she began.

At those words, an audience member interrupted her. "Don't leave us!"

She smiled as the crowd laughed. "Don't worry, I'm not going anywhere for four years."

"Let's make it eight," another audience member shouted, to rapturous applause.

"Before I leave you today," she said, a wide grin on her face, "I'd be remiss if I didn't mention the president. He's got quite a lot on his plate, but he's done a pretty good job, hasn't he?"

More applause from the crowd. She saw her campaign team smiling from a balcony and knew Rebecca was thrilled she'd finally learned to manipulate an audience's emotions.

"You all know President Begaye wants to get paid family leave passed before he leaves office. He and I agree: we have had *enough* of being told you can't be both a loving, doting parent and a productive employee at the same time. If that law had existed when Jerome was still alive, it would've made all the difference."

More tempered applause from the crowd, reverent and hopeful. "I have such respect for Senate Majority Leader Kusum Raghavan," she said, drawing more cheers. "She just became a grandma. She gets it. She knows this bill will make all the difference in becoming a better parent, employee, and member of society. If it can't be passed by November, send me to Washington and it'll be the first bill I sign as president!"

As the crowd started chanting "Enough!" again, Therese took Ensign's arm and lifted both their hands up as if they'd just scored a knockout blow. Soaking up the enthusiasm before her, she knew they had.

———————————————•———————————————

Rebecca Steinbeck certainly didn't feel like she was enough. Alone in her hotel room, she popped open her suitcase and found her vibrator and a package of Twinkies waiting for her. She'd been self-medicating with food and sex for the last three months. The number of strangers she'd let into her hotel rooms across the country astounded her. It'd never been this way when she'd lived in DC; she'd had two long-term girlfriends over the last seven years and zero one-night stands. But campaigns were all about indulging in self-destructive behaviors, right?

Regrettably, no woman would enter her room tonight. Too many familiar faces, too much press. Jamming a Twinkie in her mouth, she pulled a nightshirt on as someone knocked at her door. Hip fat jiggled out at the edges, not quite covered by her shirt, but all that did was make her ass look better. At the door, she handed the pizza delivery girl a twenty.

"Keep the change." Watching the woman walk away, her thighs burned at the thought of inviting her inside. Instead, she closed the door and started eating the pizza on her bed, straight out of the box.

One hand held her pizza while the other held her phone so she could scroll through Twitter and chomp down on hot cheese and sauce at the same time. Therese's speech was trending; #Enough was the number one topic in America. And yet, she had no one to share tonight with. Staring at the vibrator again, she replaced her pizza with the toy and thought back to the last time she'd used it with someone she loved: Maadhini Kedilaya. It'd seen other women since then, but Maadhini was the last one who'd made her believe she was enough.

Tears ran down her face, silent at first, and then she allowed herself to ugly cry, her chest heaving. Without realizing it, her fingers found a life of their own and she found herself on Maadhini's Instagram. The most recent pictures revealed her lying on a beach with her wife, Sadiya Murthy. She looked as stylish as ever, with a two-piece hugging that lithe body. And there was someone else, a baby girl.

Rebecca should've been happy for her. That was what a good person would've felt. Instead, she wondered how, with all her family money and WP, she'd ended up less content than some Indian immigrants. She wanted to banish the thought as soon as she had it, yet it lingered like a sore at the top of her mouth.

Taking another bite of her pizza, she considered messaging Maadhini. And what would she say? "Congratulations on the baby! I see you're still rocking those killer thighs. I've grown a pair of my own since last we met, so if you ever want them around you give me a ring!"

She'd failed with Maadhini, just like she was failing with the campaign. She hadn't told Therese yet that they were broke, but she'd have to do so soon. Governor Ensign had injected some funds to keep them afloat for another month, but the September and October travel schedule and media buys (not to mention expanded payroll, once they filled out the post-primary team) made things significantly tougher for them. The easiest solution would be to call her sister, Claire. Claire had lost most of her political power when Begaye had won, but her beauty and brains kept her powerful enough to hold down a job on Wall Street, even after Aditya had fired her from Adrsta. Going back to Claire would be humiliating, though, especially after all these years. They'd been estranged for so long, and Rebecca knew it hurt Claire more than it hurt her. She'd been Claire's only real friend, and perhaps Claire was the only person who understood her...

These were all "tomorrow" problems. Finishing the pizza, she opened the mini-fridge and took out the pint of Ben & Jerry's she'd picked up in the hotel lobby. Piling ice cream onto her spoon, she realized the closest she'd get to Maadhini now was gorging on the Karamel Sutra ice cream in front of her.

●————————————————————————————●

Erica Heimstaff had never felt more alive. The energy of fifty thousand people cheering on an effort she was an integral part of, the sense of pride warming her heart as DNC executive director Jamie Braun congratulated her on picking a killer outfit for Therese tonight, and the makeup job she'd done all filled her with pride. DNC chairwoman Patricia Williams had even snapped a photo with her without Erica having to ask like some fangirl. Finally, finally, she was one of the cool kids. And now, to top it all off, a boy was in her room. No, not a boy: a man. Dr. Aaron Washington. Almost thirty years old and built like a boxer.

She let him kiss her, press her against the wall, run his fingers from her curly black hair down her waist and grab her full butt, squeezing it as their bodies pressed against each other. The warmth in her heart moved southward as he pulled her shirt over her head and tossed it to the side. His own shirt was already off, and when he placed her hands against his abs she didn't protest. She let him grab her legs and wrap them around him, let him kiss her neck and bury his face within her ample bosom as he licked her in spots she'd never been touched before. Moans turned into giggles as he threw her on the bed and crawled atop her.

"Have you done this before?"

"Not since college," she whispered.

He unbuttoned her jeans and pulled them off, kissing the inside of her thighs as he did. She wriggled in anticipation, a wet spot already forming on her panties. Pulling them down, he buried his tongue inside her and she trapped his head between her thighs until her squeals of excitement turned to moans once more.

Sated, she pushed him on his back and pulled his own pants and boxers down. Kissing his chest, she made her way upward until her lips were on his, her hand finding his penis and stroking it as she wrapped her other hand against the back of his head and pulled him closer.

Turning so he had full view of her ass, she moved her head to his thighs and took him inside her mouth. She gasped in pleasure as his fingers entered her while she brought him to completion, swallowing his seed and bucking her hips against him as she came once more.

There was nothing like the high of a campaign.

They slept naked that night, his strong arms wrapped around her. But she slipped from bed before he woke the next morning. She was already up and dressed when he stirred.

"You were fantastic," she said as he blinked the sleep out of his eyes.

"You weren't too bad yourself," he replied.

"But I can't do this right now."

Getting up, he threw his shirt back on and stepped into his pants. "What do you mean?"

"If I let you into my life, I know I won't be able to help myself," Erica said. "I'll want you to be the most important aspect of it, but that has to be the campaign right now. I can't risk focusing on you and ignoring Therese."

Aaron smiled, and Erica noticed in the daylight how he ran his tongue over his lips when he was excited. "No worries," he said. "Casual works for me right now. Besides, it's not like you won't be back to Columbus before November. Ohio's a pretty important state."

He told Erica she didn't have to wait up for him, that if she had to go, she could. Making her way to the elevator to join the campaign team for their flight out of Ohio, she couldn't stop smiling. The pay was shit and the hours were long, but the warmth filling her heart and thighs made the campaign lifestyle worth it.

Chapter Four

July 30, 2028

Kaitlin paced around the podium of the conference room of her hotel in Denver, having dismissed her campaign manager, Olivia, an hour ago. She'd run the speech she would give tomorrow at the Republican National Convention a few times with her, but the last hour had just been with Vijay. He was the only one with the guts to confront her and give her notes that were actually helpful when she got like this, a caged lion sick of performing for the spectators.

"Your tone is still too brusque," he said, seated in the front row. "You're accepting your Party's nomination and outlining a vision for America, not insulting a board room full of corporate sellouts."

"Have you seen the guest list?" Kaitlin deadpanned. "Considering who's going to be in the convention hall, I'd say slamming a bunch of corporate sellouts is exactly what I'm doing."

"Well," Vijay chided, "those suits are going to fund the final months of this campaign. At least pretend to be excited."

Kaitlin tapped her foot as she reviewed her notes again. She'd built her whole speech around the concept of kintsugi. Mirai had been a big hit since she'd been introduced as the VP pick last week. She'd give her own speech, and then introduce Kaitlin and stay on stage. It hadn't been the original plan, but seeing Ensign on stage as Therese spoke made it clear Kaitlin had to follow. Two women contrasted against a woman and a man gave the advantage to the Republicans.

"Hey," Vijay said, "there's such a thing as overthinking things.

Let's just go to dinner."

Katlin sighed in relief. "I knew there was a reason I loved you."

Taking her by the hand, he walked them to the elevator and up to their room. They'd gotten the penthouse suite, courtesy of the owner of the hotel chain, who hadn't believed Olivia when she'd told him in explicit terms that the penthouse suite didn't guarantee him a White House job. That would be a rude awakening in November. But for now, Kaitlin would enjoy the full-length bedroom mirror and stocked mini-fridge and rainforest shower, Roman style for her and Vijay's comfort. Undressing to get ready for dinner, she noticed Vijay staring at the backfat that'd resulted from months of campaign eating. Frowning, she turned to face him. "They've got me doing four events a day. I miss the gym some weeks."

He laughed, and for a moment she was insulted, until he grabbed her waist and pulled her into his arms for a deep kiss. "You think I care about any of that? I was just thinking, 'fuck, this woman is so beautiful. I can't believe she's mine.'"

Pushing her breasts into his chest, she kissed him again and announced her intentions. "Make me yours—forever. Marry me."

He smiled, biting his bottom lip and sighing, the most wonderful sound she'd ever heard. "You're serious?"

"Yes." The confidence in her voice had been a lethal weapon on the battlefield, but she'd never used it in personal affairs. Only now was she ready.

Rather than answering her immediately, Vijay turned to his suitcase, bending over to open it. The view of his taut legs (and other parts of his body) did things to her heart and legs. Returning to her, he revealed a box with an engagement ring inside.

"I've had it with me for about a decade now."

Silent tears ran down her face, probably ruining her makeup. Getting on one knee, he slipped the ring onto her finger before standing back up and pushing her against the bathroom wall. "I can't wait to become Mr. Lungford."

Throwing her head back in laughter, she agreed with him that they should skip dinner and move straight to dessert. Pushing her on the bed, he pulled her pants down. He crawled atop her, his breath growing ragged as she tugged his slacks down and he shoved his hard member against her chest. His muscular arms pinned her arms above her head. He kissed her neck and guided his lips all the way down her body to rest at her thighs, parting them with fingers that soon found their way inside her. And when she began bucking her hips against his hand, when she begged for more, he spread her legs and sucked her wetness off his fingers before opening his mouth and licking her mound. Grabbing at his hair, she locked his head between her legs and refused to let him breathe until she screamed in pleasure.

And then it was his turn. Flipping over, wiggling her ass at him, she invited him to squeeze it, slap it, bite it. Here, alone in the bedroom, she was all his and he knew it, putty for him to shape however he wanted. She loved watching him seize her by the hips in the mirror, the sound of his pelvis slapping against her butt more beautiful than any music. Moaning in pleasure, she gasped at seeing his soft fingers glide up her neck, grasping at her blonde ponytail, tugging her head back and kissing her neck as he slid inside her. It wasn't long before he erupted, pulling her back into a warm embrace. Back under the covers, they slept in each other's arms.

Kaitlin awoke that night in a cold sweat, though she was fairly certain she hadn't had a nightmare. Vijay's snoring confirmed dawn hadn't broken yet; he was always an early riser. His arms around her brought her heart rate back down, and she was about to try sleeping again when she noticed a third form sitting on the bed. The sight of WP-laced cufflinks filled her with dread. "Uncle Charles?"

He stood, revealing a translucent form that ruffled her blankets.

"I'm dreaming." She blinked, but he didn't disappear.

"I would've advised you to pick a woman, but did it have to be that Asian governor?"

His voice was gravelly, as if he'd swallowed sandpaper and was trying to throw it up. Reaching out to punch him, she found her fist went right through. Her arm locked up with an intense coldness that ran through the rest of her body.

"Georgia's on your mind." He sang the words in that same tone, spitting out sand with each syllable. A smile revealed he'd lost half his teeth in the underworld or wherever he now resided.

"Mirai told me about kintsugi," Kaitlin said. "Out of something broken, something even better can be made."

He threw his head back and laughed, a haunting sound that pierced the soul. "And you think that applies to you?"

Kaitlin bit her lip in thought, but after a moment, the ghost disappeared, leaving her with no one to answer but herself.

Chapter Five

July 31, 2028

Kaitlin and Mirai peeked past the curtain to see what awaited them. The convention center was packed with what Olivia had said was close to one hundred thousand people. They'd doubled the Democrats' audience, thanks to their proximity to a larger city and the fact that they were two women (not to mention one was Asian). Kaitlin had let her beauty consultant, Emily Vanderbilt, dress her in gold and black to match her campaign logo. Her dress had lines of gold running across a black background, as if she were laced with royal history. And at her side was Mirai, clad in red and gold to showcase the Japanese colors of strength. A white scarf was draped around her to make her long black hair stick out even more.

The two women were smiling, joking as Alan Westbrook prepared to introduce Mirai.

"It must kill him to have to introduce you," Kaitlin said.

"Yeah," Mirai agreed. "He's still quite salty about not being picked to return as VP."

Kaitlin laughed. "He's salty about a lot of things, not the least of which are some marital issues, if my sources are correct."

Mirai smiled, her eyes saying far more than her mouth. "How sad. We must all mourn the demise of the privileged old white man."

With another laugh, Kaitlin joined the applause as Westbrook welcomed Mirai on stage.

"Thank you, Denver!" Mirai appeared demure, but she had a quick wit that made her instantly appealing. Hugging Westbrook as he left the stage, she walked the whole length of the stage and waved to the crowd. "My name is Mirai Shimizu, and I am here to tell you that the American Dream has never been stronger, no matter what Joseph Begaye and Therese Johnson tell you!"

The crowd roared with applause as Mirai launched into her family story. "My grandparents didn't grow to hate America after being locked up; they grew to love limited government." Speaking about how she'd met her husband, how they now had a loving son who could grow up to do anything he wanted because of his God-given right as an American, she revealed the quality that'd allowed them to raise $30 million from small donors in the week since her announcement. Mirai made everyone in a room feel as if they knew her intimately, despite the fact that she never said much. Kaitlin had no doubt she'd be a presidential candidate one day, and she was equally certain the governor wouldn't outshine the top of the ticket.

As Governor Shimizu's speech came to an end, Kaitlin steadied herself to go on stage. Olivia'd told her she had resting bitch face, so now five minutes before each public appearance, she had to close her eyes and think about Vijay.

"Are you all ready to meet the next President of the United States?!" Mirai shouted to the crowd; Kaitlin heard her unassuming giggle as she took in their applause. "Well, shucks, let's give her a big welcome, then!"

Bathed in the public's adoration, Kaitlin walked from behind the curtain and waved at the attendees before hugging Mirai, taking her hand and raising their arms above their heads as the audience gave them a standing ovation and began chanting. "Kaitlin and Mirai! Never gonna die!" For once, Kaitlin didn't have to fake a smile. With this team, with this crowd, with this energy, she could remake America. Brooks's bullshit. Begaye's theater. Her uncle's casual cruelty. It'd all been worth it to get to this moment.

The crowd didn't stop applauding for several minutes, but eventually they quieted and Mirai took a seat behind Kaitlin. Diving into her speech, Kaitlin gave them red meat from the beginning. Begaye had waged an illegal war and that was why she'd had to resign in protest. Because, as someone who'd actually served in combat, she'd never stand by and allow America to fail in its unending and vital quest to preserve and protect democracy. Instead of conducting an "apology tour," as Begaye had done when he'd visited places like the Trail of Tears Memorial in Missouri, she would present a strong united front for other world leaders to know "we will never apologize for our way of life. It's time to stop being ashamed about the past and to start letting people know how bright the future is under strong American leadership!"

Only when Kaitlin had the crowd riled up so much they would've run into fire for her did she unveil the meaning behind her campaign slogan. "I know you're all wondering what kintsugi means," she said, pointing to some audience members waving gold and black campaign signs emblazoned with the word. "It's a concept I learned from America's best governor," she said, pointing to Mirai and getting another cheer from the crowd.

"Kintsugi's a Japanese word that literally means 'joining with gold.' More than that, it's an idea that what is broken can be rebuilt, better than ever. You see, when pottery breaks in Japan, they don't throw it away. No, they join the broken pieces with lacquer and gold to make a more refined product. They take what has been shattered and make it better than before, and that is the story of America!"

The audience rushed to their feet, stamping their approval until Kaitlin raised her hand for silence. "I can't think of a better slogan for this campaign, because that concept, kintsugi, celebrates the richness of our culture, the promise that we will always grow and become better, in large part because we do not fear being broken. No! We understand that you have to break in order to heal."

Kaitlin saw Mirai's husband, Ralph, weeping in the audience. She hoped the governor was shedding a few tears, too. That kind of emotion would guarantee them another point or two in the polls.

"Breaking is not losing," she continued. "America never loses! We either win, or we learn to become better, stronger, and more resilient than ever! So, my fellow Americans, I ask you today: will you join me in becoming better, or will you accept—as the Democrats do—that we are trapped by our worst moments?"

The crowd chanted now: kintsugi. The word was a reverent whisper on their tongues, a promise they'd all make to support her the best they could. Once again, she didn't have to fake a smile. "Join me, join us, and let us restore the promise of America together!" When she took Mirai's hand and brought her to center stage, only then did the audience's chants grow louder. Holding the woman's hand above her head, letting herself bathe in the crowd's love, she allowed herself this happiness. It'd taken decades and broken her more than once, but finally she'd become who she was meant to be.

•————————————————•

Kaitlin told Emily to enjoy at least one night with her boyfriend and recommended Olivia drink alone in her room (and put it on Vijay's tab) rather than risk a night of drinking too much next to the top brass of the Republican Party. This made her look like a great boss, but practically, it also meant Kaitlin could enjoy one last night of peace with Vijay. They'd agreed not to announce the engagement publicly; she hadn't even told Olivia, though she had told Vijay that Olivia expected him to help arrange some Indian-American fundraisers.

"Don't worry," Vijay said. "I'll talk to Olivia in the morning."

The rest of the night had been bliss, with room service and service of other kinds, as well. Lying naked in bed, Vijay's arms around her, she wondered if this was what happiness felt like. Did she just not recognize it, or was she missing something? When she pictured her wedding day, try as she might, she did picture her family beside her. Who would walk her down the aisle if not Uncle Charles? As awful as he'd been, at least he'd been there.

Closing her eyes, sighing deeply, she wondered if she was just marrying Vijay to avoid being alone, to forge a connection God would recognize and protect forever. She knew that couldn't be the foundation of a successful marriage. Wrapping Vijay's arm tighter around her, kissing his fingers, she closed her eyes and told herself she was, indeed, happy.

Chapter Six

July 31, 2028

Bella thought of how much she loved Aditya. He must've been her whole world for her to have agreed to host a convention viewing party in their Union Square apartment. Bartenders stood at the ready to prepare bellinis, negronis, and mango lassis with rum. A private chef accommodated made-to-order dosas, bhel puri kati rolls, and other Indian street food, taking orders from a who's who of the Democratic Party. None other than Senate Majority Leader Kusum Raghavan and House Speaker Kent Munroe headlined the event. Bella actually liked Senator Raghavan, but Speaker Munroe was about as interesting as traffic. Besides that, Senator Denton of Colorado was also there with Gianpaolo and Matteo Medulla. The two tech billionaire brothers still thought her their lapdog just because they'd helped her secure a seat on the Supreme Court. With Kaitlin's speech done now, she hoped the guests could take a hint and exit stage right.

She realized she'd have no such luck when Senator Denton cornered her at the dosa bar.

"Justice Ferrari. Thanks for hosting."

"My pleasure, Senator." She hoped her Italian accent was thick enough to mask how she really felt.

"And congratulations on your wedding!" Kusum cut in. "Though my husband instructed me to voice our displeasure that we weren't invited." She grinned to let Bella know her outrage was feigned.

"We've been in each other's lives for so long; we didn't want a big fuss," Bella said. "Having it with just some family as witnesses, at the Court no less, made it special enough."

Kusum raised her eyebrows. "Speaking of that, which Justice performed the ceremony?"

"Justice Lyman," Bella said. Kusum's nose crinkled at the mention of him.

Bella laughed. "He's not as bad as you think."

"Does he still hate gay people?"

Bella rolled her eyes. "You know, Ginsberg and Scalia had one of the best friendships the Court has ever seen. We can still get along with those who disagree with us."

"Anyways, speaking of work, you've got a big case coming up in just over a month."

Bella nodded. *Hokkam v. Famóre* was one of many cases that'd been brought up in the wake of WP legalization, asking a central question about whether or not a public company could be held liable for its users abusing the new freedom found with using refined WP versus unrefined WP. Simply put, could the Medulla brothers be held liable for the recipes people posted on their platform that involved using refined WP? Some had substituted unrefined WP and ended up dead or severely injured.

"Thank you, Senator," Bella said. "I know the Court docket."

Denton flashed his pearly whites and dipped into that fake folksy voice he liked to whip out on the campaign trail. "Of course you do. And I trust you'll come to the right judgment. After all, it'd be political suicide to invite your benefactors to a party and then turn around and vote against them."

Bella thought about decking him right then and there, but luckily Senator Raghavan and Speaker Munroe approached the center of the room to say some words to close out the evening.

"Thank you all for being here," Kusum said. "And a special thanks to our generous hosts. The concept of dosas and mimosas is delicious!"

Kent patted Aditya on the back as Kusum beamed at Bella.

"That was a hell of a speech," Kusum continued. "Kaitlin and Mirai are going to be tough to beat, that's for sure. And I gotta be honest: seeing them speak, seeing Therese last week, while in the home of one of the few women to ever sit on the Supreme Court, this makes me so proud. You all know that I just became a grandmother." At this, Bella led the rest of the party in applause. "Because of the work of everyone in this room, Asha is going to grow up knowing nothing but the power of strong women. That's going to be the norm for her. So, I won't say much else, but thank you all for being here and now I'll let the congressman from Denver, our very own Speaker Munroe, say some words before we all wear out our welcome."

Lighter applause followed as Kent gave his remarks. Bella noticed Matteo wasn't even paying attention, focused instead on his third serving of bhel puri. Gianpaolo, though, stood right at Kent's side.

"Thank you, Madame Leader," Kent said. "From my earliest days in Denver, giving Gianpaolo some seed capital for Famóre and hosting Harvey's earliest events when he first ran for Senate, I knew we had something special here."

Bella rolled her eyes. The speaker couldn't miss an opportunity to remind everyone he was not just a multimillionaire but also political royalty out west.

"When Democrats vote, Democrats win. And thanks to the people in this room and the tens of millions of voters like us, I was honored to become the 56th Speaker of these United States less than four years ago."

He stopped, and once again received a polite smattering of clapping. The way Senator Raghavan told it over brunch, the stories about Kent were true. He'd somehow failed up to the speakership because of his failure to have attached his name to any substantial legislation, not in spite of that fact. It was just as well, because Kusum said he had other interests. His wife leaving him about a decade ago had given him more time to chase tail and trade stock tips for favors. Despite Bella's best efforts, she had to admit he was handsome even at the age of sixty-one. Admiring his compact frame and cropped black hair, she rubbed a finger over the wrinkles forming on her hand and cursed the world for making men silver foxes while women became decrepit the moment they passed fifty. She only had seven years to go, come September.

Bella tuned back in to Kent's speech as he wrapped up, hearing him mention how he'd tried to get the DNC hosted in Denver this year and hoped it didn't cost Therese Colorado in November. When he was finished, Senator Raghavan walked to the door, clearly encouraging people to leave. Instead, Gianpaolo approached Bella as she also moved toward the door in an attempt to shuffle people out.

"*Ciao bella*," Gianpaolo said. "*La cena andava bene, ma voglio il dessert.*"

Bella wondered if he was arrogant enough to think she wouldn't mind him flirting with her as long as it was in Italian, if he actually thought Aditya couldn't understand him telling her he was done with dinner and now wanted dessert. Looking to her man, she saw him step toward Gianpaolo and waved him off, trying her best to avoid a scene.

"Thank you for coming, but it's now time to go." She opened the door, making it clear the night was over.

Matteo left, grabbing one last kati roll before the servers cleared the kitchen, but Gianpaolo stayed put. "The concept of kintsugi: do you feel like it applies to you and your past life? That this is your second chance?"

Aditya's hands became fists and Bella had to physically restrain him. "*Metti giù il tuo drink. Ti stai abbracciando.*" She would let Gianpaolo's impudence slide, out of respect for Senator Raghavan and the responsibilities of hosting. Guiding Matteo's hand, she recruited him in leading his brother out the door, along with Senator Denton and Speaker Munroe. No doubt the four of them would find their way to another bar.

As they left, Matteo asked his brother why he'd say such a thing to Bella. She heard Gianpaolo's response before closing the door. "I'm surprised you noticed while you were so busy stuffing your face with that Indian rubbish."

Aditya tipped the event staff as Bella and Kusum shared a hug goodbye, and when everyone had left, she collapsed on their couch. "We're not doing that again."

Aditya sighed, taking a seat next to her. "You're right; the party was a mistake. I'm sorry."

He paused. "You don't believe that, right? That you're broken?"

Rather than answer, Bella wrapped her legs around him. Sitting on Aditya, she ran her fingers through his short, black hair, down over his dad bod, letting her hands stop over his heart. "Let's not waste any time on what some *stronzo* thinks of me."

Pulling his shirt off, tossing it off along with her bra, she wrapped her arms around his neck and pulled him into a deep kiss. His hands cupped her ass under her dress and she pulled it over her head; it crumpled onto the couch next to them. She gasped as he thumbed her nipples and kissed down the valley between her breasts. Throwing her head back, she shoved her breasts in front of his mouth for him to suck on. As his tongue traced over her most erogenous zones, she saw all of New York through their full-length windows.

She'd reached it at last: the pinnacle of personal and professional bliss.

Feeling his trapped cock bumping against her body, she granted him time off for good behavior, standing to remove her panties before sinking to her knees to take it in her mouth. He lay back on the couch as she took in his full length, his hands stroking her chestnut hair. She knew he loved this show: her wavy hair and big tits and bobbing head. Certain he was close as his body tightened, she stood again and sat on him, sliding his penis inside her. Placing his hands on her breasts, kissing his neck as she stared out the windows at the unlimited possibility of the greatest city in the world, she rocked her hips against his as they both grunted. His nails dug into her ass as her lips found his and her arms wrapped around his entire body. Riding him, controlling the speed and touch of their bodies, she reveled in the depth of her control. And other things. She'd served at the pleasure of the johns who'd hired her and now the politicians who thought they owned her—for weren't they one and the same? Here, though, moaning with unrestrained pleasure, she was free from having to put on a show.

He was dangerously close to finishing before her, so she pinched his nipples and bit his clavicle. He yelled in pain, but she knew he liked it: they'd talked about ways of slowing him down. His head found its way between her breasts, and he kissed her all over as he continued thrusting inside her until his face was red and they were both sweating. Only then, on her terms, did she let him finish as they both screamed in ecstasy. Finally, she allowed herself to collapse in his arms.

They lay in bed at midnight, the sun long set and the sounds and spirit of New York City thrumming through Bella's whole body. Her arm was wrapped around Aditya since she insisted on being the big spoon.

"You don't believe what Gianpaolo said, right?" Aditya's question poked at her insides, at the itch in her eyes that just wouldn't disappear. "You know you're not broken." His fingers brushed her hair as if trying to banish the thought.

She sighed and turned his body to face hers. "Broken or not, I'm ready to make something beautiful even better. Let's adopt."

He buried his face in her neck and cried, then. "You're sure?"

"Positive." Whether childbirth was possible for them or not, she didn't want to wait any longer to start their family. And the nobleness of adoption called to her, as loudly as the cabs driving up and down Fifth Avenue outside.

"I'll start researching agencies tomorrow," he said.

Kissing his lips, she rested her head against his flabby chest and took comfort in the audacity of her future.

Chapter Seven

August 18, 2028

Bella smiled as her father-in-law drove her and Aditya to LaGuardia Airport in a 2025 Subaru Forrester. Finally, after years of being pestered, Puli Shetty had allowed his son to replace the 1985 Justy. After dropping Bella off to fly to DC for work, he and Aditya were going to do some father-son bonding. Despite Aditya's best efforts to move his father to NYC, Puli rarely left his Hoboken home. She knew the two men would see Swapnika and her husband for dinner after this. Puli hadn't seen his wife's best friend since Deepika had died while Aditya had sat in a prison cell upstate. It didn't seem like it, but today was a huge step forward for her father-in-law's mental health. She and Aditya had also decided he would talk to his dad about the adoption process one-on-one while she was gone. They'd been unsuccessful so far in their research, but she knew some of Puli's friends in Hoboken had adopted, so maybe he could help.

"Have a nice trip, *sose*," Puli said. "Study well."

She laughed. It was the same thing her grandparents told her, the words of an elderly generation more at home outside of America than in it. *Study well.* As if she was still in school and didn't have job security for life. Short of committing murder, she'd never be fired. Stopping the car, Puli encouraged her to leave quickly before the police got on their case about parking for too long.

"I'll call you when I land," she told Aditya. She tried kissing him goodbye, but he merely patted her on the head.

"I know what happens behind closed doors," Puli laughed. "You can kiss your wife."

Blushing, Aditya did just that.

After pulling her luggage from the trunk, Puli waved goodbye. She walked away, baggage in tow.

The plane ride to DCA was just an hour, but there was still enough turbulence that Bella threw up in one of those paper bags. Waving off a flight attendant's words of comfort, she drank a ginger ale to settle her stomach. Kusum had offered to let her stay in her guest room since her lease in DC wouldn't begin until September, but Bella had opted for a hotel room; she'd inconvenienced the senator enough these past months. Once alone in the hotel room, she could pore over her briefing books in peace. Grateful the trip was ending, she closed her eyes and squeezed the armrests as the plane landed.

Though Bella had refused Senator Raghavan's hospitality, a car detail did pick her up at the airport. Apparently, it was a legal necessity that Justice Ferrari be outfitted with a Secret Service detail. Bella couldn't imagine taxpayers agreed with the expense, but President Begaye himself had spoken to her when she'd tried turning it down. She tried to protest as an agent opened the door to a black Suburban for her, but ultimately got in and opened her briefing book. They drove to her hotel in Foggy Bottom. She flipped through the pages, reading the stories of people who'd brought suit against Famóre after relying on their platform for safe recipes and instead finding permanent disability or death when using WP in their food. As she read, she grew more convinced that the plaintiff, Hokkam, had a solid class-action lawsuit against the Medulla brothers. Oral arguments started in two weeks, and it didn't look good for the tech bros. Though they'd won in district court and at appeals, she suspected money had changed hands in those situations. She knew the judges involved in both circumstances, knew the reach of Senator Denton's influence and the depths of the Medulla brothers' pockets.

Sighing as her car stopped in front of the Watergate hotel, she hoped her "benefactors" understood she couldn't be anything but impartial.

Chapter Eight

August 18, 2028

Therese wasn't much for ballgowns and glamour, but she knew it was past time to play the game. Even before Rebecca had confessed they were running out of money, she'd known enough about the finances to realize they needed to lay off some staff and spend more time fundraising and less time talking to voters. She'd ordered a fifty percent salary cut for senior staff across the board, and Erica was on unpaid leave until the first debate on October 11. *Not that she minds*, Therese thought. It gave her ample time to spend with Aaron in Ohio.

Therese finished putting on a gold and black ball gown (Kaitlin's campaign colors, in order to prove, as Rebecca had said, that Therese looked good even in "the enemy's wear") just before her manager knocked on the changing room door at the Marriott.

"Your adoring crowd waits, Madame Mayor." Rebecca wore a blue and yellow gown, the skirt cut just high enough to show some leg. It was clear to Therese from the way Rebecca fidgeted with the ruffles at the bottom and tried smoothing out the top that she'd have rather been in her standard pantsuit.

"Did Patricia and Jamie come?"

"Of course," Rebecca said.

The Democratic National Committee's chairwoman and executive director stuck to Therese like white on rice. While the campaign was aggravated about the money situation, the DNC was downright panicked.

"Is Jamie wearing a hat?" Therese joked. The woman hated formal wear as much as Rebecca, opting for jeans and backward caps with slogans like "F*ck the Patriarchy" and "Women belong in the House... the White House."

"I bet she asked Patricia if she could," Rebecca said. Adopting a somber expression, she touched Therese's arm and sat them both down. "I have to tell you something."

"Don't tell me we're broke." Therese smiled, but a pit formed in her stomach. "I thought we had enough to at least make payroll on the thirty-first."

"We can get past the end of the month, but this event's only going to bring in half a million and we're about to start burning twenty million a month between travel, ad buys, and field events nationwide."

Therese bit her lip.

"Don't do that," Rebecca said. "We don't have Erica here to fix your face."

"But we do have you here to cheer me up," Therese said.

"I do have a solution, but you're not going to like it."

"I'm not sure I've liked much since giving my speech," Therese said.

"That's the spirit," Rebecca said. "Nowhere to go but up."

Therese rolled her eyes. "Feel free to take your time. I prefer this to hobnobbing with donors."

"Roger will kill me if I don't get you out there in the next few minutes."

Therese raised an eyebrow. "Roger's here?" As the executive director of The American Dream Fund—the super PAC supporting her—Roger legally couldn't speak to her directly, but if they happened to be mutual attendees of a fundraiser hosted by the DNC, well, it was a free country, right? Beyond that, though, his presence told her the White House was taking a personal interest in the weekly press hits saying the Johnson campaign was running out of money and energy.

"Don't freak out," Rebecca begged. "I always thought the White House would get a bit closer as we head into Labor Day. Roger's probably here to suggest some optimal timing and location ideas for when the president can schedule a joint appearance with you."

Therese sighed. "Yeah, right. You said you had a solution to the money problem?"

"I can call my sister..."

Therese didn't yell or stamp her feet. Instead, true to form as the stand-in mother to every staffer she met, she brought Rebecca into a deep hug. "I'm sorry it's come to this," she said, her voice barely above a whisper as she brushed the woman's blonde hair and touched her alabaster cheeks. "I know there's a reason you two haven't spoken in years."

"It's my fault," Rebecca said, her voice threatening to crack as she dug her head into Therese's shoulder. It was good Therese's shoulders were bare, or Rebecca's tears would've stained her dress. "I had the gall to tell her happiness was more important than power. I made the choice to cut her off from the White House."

"And after all that, she'd still help?" Therese offered her manager a tissue from the sink next to them.

"Claire will answer my call in a second. One good thing about her, the reason she's always excelled in finance and politics, is she has no ego when it comes to power. She'll find her way into the most advantageous situations, no matter what."

Therese looked Rebecca straight in the eyes. "I wish you didn't have to, but I understand we gotta kick things up a notch. I'm sure as hell not about to admit defeat."

Blowing her nose, Rebecca threw her Kleenex in the trash and said she was ready to face the music if Therese was.

"How bad is it going to be?"

Rebecca shrugged. "It's no secret the DNC didn't want you as the nominee."

"You'd think Patricia and Jamie would like seeing another strong Black woman take center stage."

"Patricia's had a hard time raising money as chairwoman," Rebecca explained. "They liked that Ensign had a lock on raising grassroots money in twenty-five-dollar chunks."

"I'm not dumb," Therese said. "I put him on the ticket for a number of reasons, including his rapport with small-dollar donors."

"And it's helped keep us afloat, but it's not the same as him being on the top of the ticket."

"So what can I expect to hear from those women tonight?"

"Well, Patricia would never use the language Jamie did when I saw her in Columbus."

Therese scoffed. "What'd Ms. Executive Director say?"

Rebeca laughed "You and I are 'pussies who don't have the balls to understand power or money.'"

Therese threw her head back in laughter. "Oh lord, I needed a good laugh."

"You aren't insulted?"

"I'm only insulted they don't know better. Isn't Jamie a lesbian?"

"Yes..."

"Then maybe she doesn't realize how laughably weak balls are. One good kick and a man is down for the count."

Rebecca bit her bottom lip, a grin forming on her face.

"A vagina, though? Strongest part of the body. I shoved a whole person out of mine and it still works. The human race would be extinct if men had to give birth."

Rebecca couldn't control herself any longer, laughing openly and with such fervor that cracks formed in her makeup. She used another Kleenex to wipe some off her face. "No one out there would take me seriously with this stuff on, anyways. They know it's not my style."

Therese squeezed Rebecca's hand before opening the door. "We just gotta make our own style an asset."

"Game on?"

Therese smiled. "For now. But come November? You and I are gonna win this race on our own terms and change the game forever."

When she entered the ballroom, Therese refrained from stopping one of the waiters passing out hors d'oeuvres. Rebecca, on the other hand, exercised no such control. The woman scooped up a bacon-wrapped fig, some kind of potsticker, and the most elaborate mini grilled cheese Therese had ever seen, then excused herself to a table near the open bar. Counting down the days until their next event in Texas, which would no doubt be filled with barbecue, Therese made a mental note to scold Rebecca the next time they had a moment alone.

She forced herself to bat her eyelashes at two of the DNC's largest donors, a power couple from Los Angeles that just happened to also fund The American Dream Fund.

"No wonder Roger's here," Therese muttered.

"What was that?" The wife gulped down her champagne, not interested in the answer to her own question.

"I was just wondering if you needed another drink." Therese smiled and the donor laughed—despite no one telling a joke—while the husband mentioned how they'd just returned from Switzerland. It was a fairly obvious attempt to convince Therese he deserved an ambassadorship posting there if she won.

Looking past them toward Rebecca, Therese noticed her manager's table now featured Roger and Jamie as well.

———————————•———————————

If Rebecca had been straight, she would've wanted to be with Roger. It wasn't just that he was tall, dark, and handsome (though that helped). He was just so brilliant. A stint at the DSCC had turned into a posting as Chief of Staff for Manish Nagaraj when he'd been Senate Majority Leader. Then a personal recommendation from Senator Nagaraj had resulted in Roger being chosen to become President Begaye's chief strategist during the campaign before he'd entered the White House as Chief of Staff. And now? Executive Director for the best-funded Democratic super PAC in the country? She was gay, but that kind of power still wet her thighs.

"You sitting here puts us on legally thin ice, doesn't it?" she cooed.

"I'm just another volunteer working on behalf of the Democratic Party tonight," Roger said, batting his eyes. Some people looked terrible bald, but all hairlessness did for him was bring out his best attributes. Even his voice made her feel secure.

With Roger on her left, Jamie Braun sat on her right.

"And what's Patricia got you snooping around for tonight?" Rebecca said.

"It's Chairwoman Williams to you, Rebecca." Jamie's shoulder-length black hair couldn't mask her resting bitch face.

"If I send these kinds of loving chats to Whit Pryor, he'll just lie down and let us destroy ourselves," Rebecca said.

Jamie's eyes scanned Rebecca from head to toe, as if she actually believed the woman would record their conversations and mail them to Whit.

Rebecca rolled her eyes. "Have a beer, Jamie."

"Moscato, if I must," she said. "But I don't drink while I'm working."

"Aren't you a saint?" Rebecca made a point of taking a long swig of her bourbon and Coke.

Roger grunted. "Ladies, let's be civil for one night."

"You're right," Rebecca said. "Besides, Jamie, you should be thrilled at how tonight's going."

"And why's that?"

Rebecca finished her drink before answering. "I talked to the mayor, and she's down with the idea you suggested."

Jamie stood up so fast she spilled Roger's beer. Darting to his side, she used a napkin to clean up her mess.

"What's this idea?" he asked.

"I told Jamie about the campaign's money issues one night in Columbus, after too much drinking."

"And?"

"And I had the perfect solution for her," Jamie said.

Rebecca scoffed. "Yeah, I just had to swallow all my pride."

Jamie laughed. "You're running a presidential write-in campaign for a Black mayor and she's got a realistic chance of actually winning. Take pride in that and swallow whatever else you have to."

"What's going on?" Roger asked.

"Jamie said I should run back to my rich, powerful sister. And after some soul-searching, I recommended the idea to Mayor Johnson, and she agreed."

Now it was Roger's turn to stand. His tall frame leaned over the table as he gritted his teeth. "Have you all developed amnesia?"

Jamie sighed. "We all know you slept with her, but put your feelings aside."

"I slept with her, sure, but so did Whit," he said. "This isn't personal; she can't be trusted. She played both sides and she lost last time, so who's to say she doesn't cost us this race?"

Rebecca pretended to listen while Roger and Jamie argued, but her attention was drifting to the president's daughter, who'd just walked in. Waving Anaba and Luther to their table, she hoped their presence would make her "allies" shut up.

Luther Aldrich stood over six feet tall and was easily over two hundred pounds of muscle. A former linebacker for Stanford and current bodyman to President Begaye, he was ostensibly there to protect the president's daughter, but Rebecca was fairly certain he was fucking Anaba, too.

"Anaba, come join us," Rebecca said. "Save me from Roger and Jamie's bickering."

Roger feigned offense as Luther and Anaba sat on opposite sides of Rebecca.

"You two can sit next to each other," Roger said. "We all assumed you were an item."

Luther began to protest, but Anaba cut him off. "I'm so tired of hiding it," she said. "I should've guessed you'd be the first one to discover the ruse." She used her lithe fingers to brush her bangs out of her eyes. "Just… please don't tell anyone. We're not ready for dad to know yet."

Jamie patted Anaba's back. "I can only imagine what it's like to date as the president's daughter. Don't worry; your secret's safe with us." She glared at Rebecca, perhaps thinking she'd be the one to spill the beans, either innocently or even on purpose.

"I'm not quite the evil bitch you imagine," Rebecca said, rolling her eyes.

"I don't think you're evil." Jamie excused herself to the bathroom. Rebecca thought she heard her mutter under her breath that rather than think her evil, she merely thought she was dumb.

Realizing she'd left her candidate alone for far too long, Rebecca scanned the room and spotted Therese speaking with Senator Raghavan and Speaker Munroe.

She jumped up from the table and went to join them.

●————————————————————●

Therese hugged Rebecca as she came to her side, squeezing her shoulder tightly enough to let her know she was in trouble.

"I was just about to give my remarks," she said. "Senator, Mr. Speaker, how are you?"

"I'm sure you heard how Senator Hammond has halted any progress on paid family leave," Senator Raghavan said. As Rebecca nodded, Speaker Munroe halted a waiter to grab a couple wontons.

"These are delicious," he said, and Therese nodded politely. "We want ten weeks for new moms and six weeks for new dads. Hammond thinks four weeks for moms is enough and laughed at the idea of leave for new dads."

"One of the many good things that's resulted from WP legalization," Therese said. "The drug's many benefits have expanded the productivity frontier, making the five-day, forty-hour workweek a bit of a fossil."

Rebecca smiled. "Okay, Madame Mayor, save it for the speech."

The crowd was as boisterous as ever after an hour of drinking, but Speaker Munroe took special pride in quieting them down. His introductory remarks focused on how the gridlock of Congress made his job unbearable (Therese wagered the lack of actual work and the promise of insider trading made it, in fact, quite appealing), but the prospect of a Black woman as president and an expanded majority was all the hope he needed to keep him working as hard as ever through November. Then it was Senator Raghavan's turn. She spoke about how she's found a great friend in Mayor Johnson and joked about how, as great as President Begaye was, it'd be nice to have a fellow woman in the White House.

By the time Therese spoke, the audience was high on the campaign and stuffed with enough liquor to sign checks big enough to get the campaign through mid-September.

"It means so much to me that you all came out," Therese said.

She launched into her talking points, covering how she had cut crime in Albuquerque by getting smart, not tough, and how she'd worked with the community to empower the people instead of just forcing cops down everyone's throat (although married white women *loved* how she mentioned that she'd increased police salaries by fourteen percent). Next was her weekly mention that "politicians have no business getting all up in *our* business. If they want to legislate our bodies, they're free to find a way for men to have babies." That line always got a laugh. The standard daily talk about being "enough" followed, and she sprinkled in some feel-good talk about the Begaye administration and a couple political jokes Rebecca had written for her. But to mix things up for this crowd, she ended with a passionate defense of paid family leave.

"I wish it would become law before I'm sworn in, but my good friend, Senator Raghavan, has just informed me Senator Hammond's the key legislator holding it up." The audience booed on cue until Therese waved them down. "No, no, we appreciate the passion of the other side," she said. "We need a vibrant opposition party, and God knows we don't get it right all the time, but on this particular issue, he's wrong. And so I have some news to make. I know there's at least one of you here who's gonna leak my remarks to the press." Her smile told the crowd it was okay to laugh. "I'm calling on Kaitlin Lungford tonight to call Senator Hammond and request that he step aside in the name of *all* American women."

As the audience cheered, Therese caught Anaba's twinkling eyes before the girl left with Luther. Therese hoped she'd go back and tell her father about this moment. They needed the money.

———————————●———————————

Late as the fundraiser was, Anaba wasn't expected to check in with her dad until after leaving the hotel tomorrow. And good thing, because Luther had made reservations weeks ago, and now planned to take her for drinks at a fancy new restaurant/bar in Dupont Circle. The burnt-orange walls of The Maharani's Voice were adorned with large paintings smeared with vivid colors. Directional lights were spread over the large tables and upholstered chairs and booths. And the bar section itself was pressed against a semi-tall glass window that revealed the chef's staff hard at work. Scents of saffron and onions and cumin filled the entire restaurant, encouraging, Anaba suspected, those who'd merely entered for a drink to order the entire menu.

"I heard about this place from a friend," Luther said.

"Good thing you made a reservation." A hostess seated them both at a booth near the bar, giving her a view, and more importantly a smell, of the cooks' work. Without asking, Luther ordered her something called "Bath of the Temptress" and himself a Kingfisher, along with an appetizer of paneer pinwheels.

"More food?"

"Trust me," he said, "you'll thank me."

Anaba scanned the entire restaurant, taking in the paintings portraying women in various states of power: someone nursing a child, someone leading an army into battle, a queen holding court. "I've turned you into quite the feminist, haven't I?"

Luther chuckled. "No offense, but I was a feminist long before I met you."

Anaba beamed. "I only tease." She took a sip of her drink when it arrived; a concoction of honey and lemon and date-infused gin with foam, poured into a martini glass. She squealed in delight at the complex array of flavors, letting her feet brush his under the table.

"I'm glad you like it," he said. "Actually, I brought you here because I love this." He wiped foam off her upper lip as she put her drink down, and she giggled. "I love you; I never want to spend a day without you." The strength and directness in his voice disappeared, replaced with a low, urgent tone that lunged at her heart, refusing to let go.

"Luther, what do you—"

When he bent on one knee, she became acutely aware of the fact that the restaurant's patrons had hushed.

"Marry me."

Someone in the crowd recognized her, no doubt, and snapped a picture with his camera phone as she stared blankly at her man. "Oh, Luther..."

"You're not happy?"

She heard the pain in his voice and kissed his cheek to reassure him.

"This is the happiest day of my life," she said. "But I don't want to say yes until you've spoken to my dad."

Luther smiled, and her heart melted. "I did speak to him, and not for the first time. We've been chatting it up a few times over the last couple weeks." He stood, waving a waiter off who was about to deliver their paneer pinwheels.

"When?! He's okay with this?!" Her voice was always a bit shrill, but now she was truly in danger of breaking the glass champagne flutes in the hands of the patrons around her.

Luther chuckled. "He wasn't thrilled at first, but I told him my intentions, how I've never worn WP around you and I'm fine being known as 'the president's son-in-law' for the rest of my life."

Anaba's bangs masked the tears that'd begun to form.

"Crying's good?" Luther asked. "Is that a yes?"

Nodding, she kissed him in response. "Yes!"

The crowd exploded, and she saw several people now taking photos, no doubt about to post them to Twitter. At least her father knew this was happening already. She'd be disowned if one of his staffers informed him after learning about it online.

The waiter from before returned, paneer and dessert menu in hand. "Congratulations, Ms. Begaye. I'll return to take your order. On the house, of course."

Savoring Luther putting on the ring—which must've been over a carat of diamond in a princess cut—she turned to her food options, trying to ignore the press who'd started to arrive. She could hear waitstaff telling the reporters they had to order if they insisted on being here, and she made a note to always recommend this place.

"What about the Italian's Dream?" Luther asked, pointing to a menu. The dish was described as a mixture of ras malai and tiramisu, pistachios and mascarpone, lady fingers and cardamom. Licking her lips, Anaba decided it wouldn't be as good as the dessert she'd have when they returned to her apartment, but it sounded delicious, all the same.

Ignoring the press and the patrons snapping her photo, she stared at the blue-eyed all-American in front of her. Rubbing her leg up his thigh, brushing his manhood, she batted her eyelashes and imagined their future together. "Let's take it to go."

Chapter Nine

August 18, 2028

Whit Pryor's son would be ten before he knew it, and yet he was missing all the big moments in the kid's life. He was supposed to have him for the weekend, yet his ex-wife, Melissa, had just called to say the kid wanted to stay at her place instead. It was bullshit; what the kid wanted was to spend time with Melissa's new boytoy, who was quickly eclipsing Whit as a father. The man had showed the boy Indiana Jones, had taught him how to build Legos. It was an outrage.

For that reason, Whit found himself dropping $850 for a night at the Ritz. It'd been three weeks since he'd used Kajal's "services." Her visits hadn't given him any good intel on Justice Ferrari, but that didn't mean they weren't fruitful; Kajal had many gifts. Waiting for the hooker to knock on his door, he applied some gel to his blond hair and combed it into a style reminiscent of Joseph Gordon-Levitt. Winking at himself in the bathroom mirror, he heard a knock on the door and moved to open it.

"You wore what I sent you," he said, commenting on the black sequined dress he'd bought for her. It had an open back that ran all the way down to her sizeable hips.

She answered him with a kiss, running her hands over his abs and pushing him inside before closing the door behind them.

Her lips tasted of mangoes, and when he ran his fingers over her thighs, he was pleased to discover she'd forgone wearing panties. It was raining, thundering outside, and as he touched her, he found her dress wasn't the only part of her that was wet. Pinning her to the wall, digging his nails into her arms, he ripped the dress enough to expose her large breasts.

Her hands found his belt, throwing it to the floor as he sat on the bed and she tugged his boxers down.

"Use the unrefined stuff," he growled. Kneeling so that her full cheeks brushed against his member, she used one hand to stroke him while the other found a WP-laced condom in her purse.

"Put it on like before, with your mouth."

She hesitated, but only until he handed her a fifty-dollar bill from the wallet in the slacks she'd dropped to the ground. He threw his head back in bliss as she deepthroated him and pushed the condom all the way down his shaft. The drug coursed through his body as well as hers. If she'd really wanted to say no, he would've let her, but he knew she wanted the drug as badly as him.

The WP gave him energy to cum twice. After he'd shot his load, Kajal pulled the condom off and was about to throw it in the trash when he stopped her.

"WP's in there," he said, taking it from her and downing the contents in one gulp.

She turned her nose up, yet still asked the question. "...was it nice?"

He cackled, the sound of a super villain. "Fuck yeah. I bet I could jump out that window and fly."

He considered doing just that for a moment before grabbing her ass and shoving her onto the bed, pushing her head into the pillow. Whit spanked her, the sound in sync with the crash of lightning.

Kajal tried slipping the dress over her head, but he swatted her hands away; he wanted her to keep it on for this next part, loved how her body stretched the fabric. He bit his bottom lip and focused on the sound of his pelvis slapping against her ass.

When he was in heat like a lion like this, he could almost get the thought of Melissa and her new man out of his head...

He left Kajal's money on the table as he washed up. To his surprise, she was still there when he returned.

"I'm not paying you extra to just hang out," he said. "Even WP has its limits. I can't go more than twice in a row."

Kajal rolled her eyes. "Do you feel... different?"

"What do you mean?"

"Using the drug... You're the only client I've used it with. You're the only person, period."

Whit grinned. "I'm flattered. Why do you ask?"

"I think it's affecting me," she said. "My memory, my sexual preferences..."

Whit pulled her toward him, licking her lips before kissing them.

"Like that," she said. "I'd have banned you a year ago for doing that, but now I think it's hot."

Whit licked his lips, her taste clinging to him like a blanket keeping him warm. "The difference is that I've grown up using it daily, and at the end of the day you're nothing but a skingrafter. No offense."

He feared he'd pushed her too far, but she merely closed her eyes and counted to ten. The money he was shelling out was way too good for her to ignore. He knew you could treat people like shit as long as you gave them some crumbs once in a while.

"You know," she said, "it won't always be like this. You better get your kicks while you can, because in a few months, I'll have enough to leave LISA for good."

"Oh?" He started packing as she talked. Staying the night would make him feel dirty.

"I've got dreams, you know. Graduate with my JD, get married, have kids."

Whit grunted. "Marriage isn't a silver bullet. Alimony is a bitch."

She packed as well, applying some makeup over the spots where he'd grabbed her too roughly.

"You ever been in love?" Whit's question surprised even himself. She may not have let him grab her a year ago, but even a week ago, he wouldn't have cared to ask her that.

"Once," she said. "Actually, the woman was a bit famous." Whit worried she'd start crying when he looked at her face.

"Anyone I know?" He wanted to slap himself for asking these inane questions. What did he care if a hooker was once in love?

"Claire Steinbeck."

Whit bit his tongue to keep himself in check. He hadn't heard that name in years. "Never heard of her."

After escorting Kajal out, he took out his phone to confirm he still had Claire's number. She'd been the best kisser he'd ever had until he'd met Kajal. Maybe that was where Kajal had learned it from.

●————————————————————————————●

August 20, 2028

Claire was the happiest she'd been in seven years. After dissing her at the Begaye election party and turning her back on their family legacy, her sister had come crawling back, calling her yesterday to beg for help. Gracious as she was, Claire had agreed. Rebecca was her only female friend, but she'd once crushed Claire's spirit like it was nothing. As if the bond of sisterhood was insignificant compared to the greater good of "saving democracy" and "the moral arc of the universe." What a bunch of bullshit.

But now, Whit Pryor was on the line and Claire had two hands in the cookie jar once more. No matter if Kaitlin or Therese won, she'd be on the fast track to wielding real power once more. She'd made out okay for herself in the past few years, but an in with the White House would change everything. Truthfully, she'd prefer if Kaitlin won; Rebecca needed to lose her "holier-than-thou" attitude.

"Did you hear what I said?" Whit asked. "Are you interested in helping Kaitlin win?"

"Yes," Claire said, pacing in her New York penthouse, rubbing the pendant around her neck, which was encrusted with stones made of WP. "How can I help?"

Claire couldn't believe her past with a prostitute was catching up with her. Closing her eyes, she remembered Kajal's smell and touch as Whit filled her in on his own rendezvous with her. She'd found the woman in New York, shortly after Rebecca had abandoned her. Her sister had made such a show of being a lesbian that Claire had wanted to try it out, but of course she hadn't been about to actually date a woman. Calling LISA had been ideal; the firm had sent over someone entirely opposite of her usual type. They'd had fun for a few weeks, but it'd gotten way too intense when the woman had told Claire she loved her.

"Are you listening?"

Claire opened her eyes, licking her lips at the memory of her last encounter with the girl. "It would be fun, but how does Kajal get Kaitlin elected?"

She heard Whit tapping his foot impatiently. This was why they'd have never worked as a real couple; he insisted on treating anyone he deemed "less than him" as an idiot. And he thought everyone was less than him.

Waiting him out, content to hear his frustrated sighs through the phone, she grinned when he finally revealed his plan.

"String Kajal along," he said. "Reach out to her, tell her you were scared of the depth of the relationship before, or some shit like that, but get in with her and then poke around about Bella. She's hiding something."

"And your pencil dick can't poke it out of her?" Claire grinned.

"Watch it," Whit said, ice in his voice.

"It's not a bad idea," she admitted. "The agency gives out a personal number if you've got a regular with them. What's hers?"

She hadn't told Whit she was raising money for Therese. The thrill of working both sides almost matched the high of WP. After all, if you weren't at the table, you were on the menu.

Playing with her pendant, rubbing her nails over the drug, she smiled. Kajal's taste was a fond memory she was eager to explore once more. And Rebecca? Even if Therese won, with Claire at her side, her sister would still learn a valuable lesson: that it wasn't a crime to be beautiful and white and rich and smart all at the same time.

Chapter Ten

August 26, 2028

Therese's feet had perpetual corns. At first, Russell had soaked them in warm water each night, but after four days of nonstop rallies, she'd told him not to bother. They hadn't slept in their own bed for weeks, but at least they were together. St. Louis to Wichita to Oklahoma City and now El Paso. Officially, Rebecca called it their "Midwest is Enough" tour. Unofficially, she called it the "Midwest is more than Enough" tour. She didn't see the point of traveling to "states we aren't going to win," but Therese wanted to bring her message to every region of the country.

Therese, Russell, and Rebecca sat in a black Suburban outside an Indian-BBQ fusion restaurant called NaanStop BBQ. They'd brought a sizeable party with them to Texas, and three people had ridden in a second car. Erica was back at Therese's side, along with her digital director, Gael Rodriguez. She didn't understand TikTok and Instagram and whatever else Gael recorded footage for daily, but she was glad he did. The strangest part of the campaign was the reality that it'd be won by single people in their twenties posting memes.

Rounding out her retinue was the former District Attorney of Manhattan, the man who'd defeated Pete Jackson: Curtis Levitt. He was now the mayor, a real leader in the Black Lives Matter movement and a big hit among single and married women above forty, if her polls could be believed. She was sure that had nothing to do with the fact that he looked like a Black Adonis.

"I gotta speak to Rebecca for a moment," Therese said to Russell as an agent opened the door for them. "I'll join the team in a moment."

"Sure," Russell said, stepping out. "I'll tell them to go ahead and start eating."

When the agent closed the door, Therese turned to her manager. "Where are we on money?"

"Claire's already scheduled fundraisers in Dallas and Austin over the next couple days."

Therese sighed. "Dallas and Austin? We gotta go there after this speech?"

Rebecca grinned. "That's the best part: you don't even need to be there. Claire can handle all the spotlight herself."

"My favorite type of fundraising," Therese said.

Running through worst-case cash scenarios based on what Claire and their grassroots fundraising operation might bring in over the next two weeks, Therese decided they'd make it to October 1, at least.

"One day at a time, right?"

"Absolutely, Madame Mayor. It won't do you much good to think about much else."

Stepping out, Therese thanked Rebecca for the long nights and constant travel. "Don't think I don't recognize your sacrifice."

"Thank you, Madame Mayor, but this is nothing compared to what the people at this rally go through daily." Her words were as earnest as her hair was blonde.

Hugging her, Therese told her she'd left something in the car and to go ahead and get situated with the others. Waiting until she was out of sight, she walked to the second car, where the agent opened the door. Telling him it was of vital importance that no one come around for the next ten minutes, she entered and found Russell waiting. He already had his pants off.

"I thought we'd never get this opportunity," he said.

She bit her lip, kissed him, and got on top.

●————————————————————————————●

Therese joined her team with Russell fifteen minutes later, hoping their flushed cheeks and ruffled clothes didn't give them away. They'd ordered a fusion dish of saag paneer made with collard greens, tandoori chicken served with biscuits, and cardamom bread pudding.

"Hey, Russell," Curtis shouted as the married couple sat down, "you want some of this pudding?"

"No, thanks," he said, squeezing his wife's hand under the table. "I already had something sweet today."

Therese changed the subject before anyone could pry further. "Anyone order some mango lassi for the table?"

"Erica's got it," Rebecca said, pointing to the woman approaching with a carafe.

Turning in her chair, Therese saw not just Erica, but about a dozen people snapping photos. No doubt the pictures would be on Twitter in minutes.

"We don't have long before the press gets here," Curtis warned.

"We want them here," Gael said.

Rebecca raised her voice. "Have you been the one telling the press where we're eating?"

Gael suddenly became fascinated with his shoes. "How else am I supposed to generate viral moments?"

Rebecca rolled her eyes as Erica poured them all drinks.

"So," Therese said, grinning at Erica, "how was your time off?"

"Yes, I saw Aaron, and no, I don't want to talk about it."

"Is it time you and I had 'the talk?'" Therese joked.

Erica's brown skin turned crimson. "Um, that's okay, my mom already gave me that..."

Therese laughed, a rich sound that warmed her belly more than the paneer. With Russell and the staff all around her, she could actually have fun on the campaign trail.

It didn't take Therese and her team long to eat (they'd mastered the art of stuffing food down their gullets before jumping onto a conference call or speaking to a donor), but it'd taken her another half hour to get through posing for selfies and signing autographs. When they loaded back up into the Suburbans, Rebecca steered Therese into a separate car, lumping her, Curtis, and Gael together while she rode with Russell. Therese heard her husband scold Rebecca before they left.

"Spoilsport," Russell said.

"You've got her lipstick on your chest," Rebecca replied, prompting a smile from Therese.

Curtis asked her what she was happy about as they drove away.

"I'm just so thrilled you're with us, Mr. Mayor."

Curtis grew somber. "I never wanted to be here," he said. "In an ideal world, no one would've ever have heard of me."

"Mr. Mayor," Gael said, "you've done so much good for the campaign. Our stuff featuring you always goes viral."

Curtis sighed, elbows on his knees and face in his hands. "I'd've never become DA if it weren't for the fact that Jerome died. And I'm only mayor because the country's finally reckoning with its epidemic of dead Black boys."

"And I'd still be a nanny if my son was alive," Therese said. "We can play this game all day, but what matters now is how we move forward. We know their lives mattered; no one's gotta tell us they did. But did their deaths matter or not? That's on us."

Gael offered a hand on Curtis's shoulder. "You've helped a lot of people with your Instagram Live discussions. It's because of you that #JusticeforJerome is still trending nationwide."

Curtis grunted. "You're right, Madame Mayor."

"I'm not riding with you again if you're always this dour," Therese said.

Curtis cracked a grin. "I heard you've got a month on the road, Gael. Staffing celebrities and all kinds of bigshots."

Gael's eyes lit up. "I'm not sure anything beats hanging out with the two best mayors in America, but I do hope I get to meet T-Swift and JJ."

Therese chuckled. "Nice sucking up, but Rebecca sets your salary, not me."

"I'm gonna assume you mean JJ Abrams," Curtis said. "If you do see him, let him know how much I hated *Rise of Skywalker*."

"Yeah," Gael said, fascinated again with his shoes. "I'll probably avoid that topic..."

It was well past two p.m. by the time they all reached the rally site.

"We're late," Rebecca said.

"Looks like they waited," Russell replied, stepping out of the car and pointing to a crowd of about ten thousand. As Therese walked behind stage, she ran into one of her older advance staffers, Molly Higgins.

"Excuse me, ma'am, I hate to be this person, but can you sign this toy for my son?"

"Of course." Therese looked at it as Molly handed her a pen. It was a WP Force solider; she thought this one was Abhinav Iyengar. The way she'd heard it in the press, the original WP Force soldiers were all dead or distraught these days, haunted by memories of what they'd had to do. Handing the toy back to Molly, she barely heard the woman's appreciation. Whether she won or lost this race, whether WP legalization was expanded or rescinded, the impact of the Brooks-Begaye war was part of this country's legacy now.

Rebecca went on stage first. Therese beamed as the woman introduced herself to the crowd in flawless Spanish. At each rally she attended, Therese gave a shout out to the local field organizers who busted their asses in these communities for maybe thirty-five hundred dollars a month and no benefits. When she was president, she'd replace Patricia with a DNC chair who believed in unionization for political campaigns. It was the biggest joke of the Democratic Party that unions were untouchable until you needed cheap labor to get re-elected. Biting her bottom lip, she tuned in to Rebecca's remarks. A translator stood at her side, signing the words as a big screen played them in English.

"Que privilegio estar de vuelta en el paso," Rebecca said. *"Pronto, muy pronto, Texas se volverá azul gracias a ti."*

Therese made a note to remind Rebecca that they weren't here just to turn Texas blue, but because these families were in pain and needed to know their president would defend them against ICE and anyone else who tried to deport them.

"Tengo el honor de presentar a continuación es un alcalde para todos."

Therese saw Curtis jumping up and down near her, getting himself psyched up as Rebecca prepared to bring him on stage next.

"¡Dé la bienvenida a mi querido amigo, un luchador contra la

injusticia en todas partes, el alcalde Curtis Levitt!"

Curtis gave Rebecca a big hug before she left the stage, and waved and pointed in response to the crowd's rapturous applause. Therese smiled at her manager as Rebecca returned backstage.

"You didn't think the Spanish was too much?"

"Girl, please," Therese said. "They ate it up. You just got us another dozen volunteer shifts."

Their attention turned to Mayor Levitt as he began his own spiel, bringing his hands above his head to lead them in further applause. "November or Bust! Justice is a Must!" Dressed casually in a shirt and shorts, his V-neck rode up his waist with each clap, exposing the start of a six-pack.

"Curtis might've made a better VP pick than Terry," Rebecca joked.

Therese rolled her eyes. "He can put on a show; that's for sure. But the country won't accept two mayors suddenly joining the national stage in the biggest way possible, never mind the fact that they're both Black. Besides, Terry's a governor of one of the largest states in America; no question he can do the job if anything happens to me."

Rebecca's eyes wandered to the two agents nearby. "You stopped reading the threats, right?"

Therese sighed, thinking back to the start of the campaign, when she'd still insisted on reading a few pieces of hate mail weekly. She'd thought it'd bring her closer to understanding that part of the country; she realized now there was no understanding that kind of attitude. "Yeah, the agents shred them and track them down if needed."

Rebecca reached for Therese's hand. "My old bosses never faced death threats, but it's just proof that what we're doing matters."

Curtis's speech was winding down. Therese had her hand on a railing leading from backstage past the curtain to front and center. Her head was bowed as she repeated the mantra she always did before embracing the crowd:

"Jerome and Jerome, you are my home. One day I'll join you, 'til then I'll roam.

What's right is right and what's wrong is wrong, I'll fight in your name for justice; with you at my side it won't take long."

Curtis's voice grew louder, taking her out of her reverie. "Please, join me in welcoming the next President of the United States: Mayor. Therese. Johnson!" The crowd rose to their feet, stamping in thunderous approval as she came from behind the curtain, waving and smiling at those who'd chosen to endure the hundred-degree heat to see her.

"Good afternoon, El Paso!" Her Spanish was a joke compared to Rebecca's, and they'd decided that rather than do some blatant pandering, it was more authentic of her to just speak English. She hated those politicians who ran TV ads that'd obviously been dubbed.

"It's great to be back in Texas!" She'd done a trip to Dallas during the primaries—Rebecca's idea of psychological warfare against Ensign in his home state. It hadn't worked; she'd finished in a distant second and wasted time and money she could've spent elsewhere. But the experience had given her the much-needed confidence that just because she was a small-town mayor who'd never run statewide before, let alone nationally, she shouldn't trust her staff's opinions over her own judgment.

"You all know about NaanStop BBQ?" Therese hadn't given a speech to a crowd larger than a few hundred prior to running for president, but even her worst critics admitted she could now work a crowd even better than President Begaye could. "That place is bussin'!"

It was the kind of thing that made Gael groan, but she actually enjoyed using Gen Z slang. Hanging around a bunch of kids in their twenties meant she'd picked it up naturally over the last few months. Still, she knew it'd end up being a TikTok meme from some Lungford supporter and Gael would give her shit about it. Cheers from one kid in the crowd reassured her at least someone thought she was hip.

"We love you," the child shouted.

"I love you back!" Her beaming smile wasn't a front. She was baking in the sunny weather, but Therese never felt more alive than she did here among the people. "And before we get this party started, I wanted to give a special shout out to the awesome team of field organizers here today." Scanning the crowd, she found them all bunched together at the exit, clipboards ready so they could jot down the names of attendees and ask them to volunteer for canvassing shifts.

"Bruce, Tiffany, Shivani, Vivian, and Sean! You're the heart of the campaign and the reason we're going to win Texas in November!" The crowd went wild. "Please, all of you, remember to give them your deets before you leave. They need you to sign up for one, five, ten volunteer shifts." Scanning the crowd, she noticed Gael groaning in the corner when she said "deets."

"Speaking of Texas," she continued, "I'm sorry your governor isn't with me today, but he was needed in New Hampshire." Terry had won the state during the primaries, and they'd need his charm to win it in the general election. She couldn't believe it'd elected a Republican governor and senator two years ago. "My apologies for taking him from you for so long."

"Take him for another eight years!" someone shouted, prompting a sea of foot stomping that shook the stage.

Therese grinned as she launched into her stump speech. She was running because she'd learned some things in Albuquerque that Washington needed to adopt, like how to work across the aisle to reduce crime by embracing policies that didn't just sound good but actually did good. She was going to make sure senators like James Hammond understood that paid family leave led to stronger businesses and a stronger stock market. And finally, at the end, she brought out a cross she wore around her neck some days, kissing it.

"I'm here because of Jerome Johnson Jr." The cheering crowd fell silent. "There's nothing I'd like more than to be back home in New York with my boy, except winding the clock even farther back so that we were still with his dad and never left Boston." She saw audience members wiping tears from their faces. "But we can't go back, we can only move forward." She didn't believe in delivering paint-by-numbers remarks, choosing instead to tell these people what she'd told Curtis.

"I've had *enough* of being sad. *Enough* of being told how brave I am and how much Jerome's life mattered. I know his life mattered, but did his death matter? Texas! In just ten weeks, you get to decide if my son's death mattered!"

Therese saw Gael record footage on his phone as the crowd came alive, chanting "Justice for Jerome!" She noticed more than a few on their phones as well, no doubt because they were donating through the campaign website.

"Our oppressors don't deserve grace, but we do! You must always remember: you are *enough*!" Watching FOX News's and the other media outlets' cameras rolling from the rafters sectioned off for the press, she hoped Artie Quiver wasn't missing this. On November 7, he and everyone else who watched that propaganda would know Jerome's life had mattered.

Chapter Eleven

September 1, 2028

Bella loved Aditya's entire body and soul, but sometimes she wished that body's familiarity with a six-pack extended beyond Yuengling. Today was move-in day for her new apartment at the Watergate in Foggy Bottom, and they'd already spent a couple hours shifting heavy boxes of law textbooks, shoes, and clothes up to her place on the tenth floor. He'd eagerly agreed to the task when she'd offered him pizza and sweeter treats, but he was already panting and they hadn't even had sex yet.

"Is this the last box?" he said.

It wasn't, but she nodded, because his face was the color of a tomato.

Wheezing, he opened his last box: the pizza. DC wasn't known for their pies, but the buffalo chicken from Wiseguy N.Y. Pizza had to rank among the best she'd experienced outside of Italy.

"Lunch time," he said, stuffing a piece into his mouth so quickly she worried his tongue would burn.

Throwing the crust in the metal trashcan next to her kitchen, he poured himself a glass of water and gulped it down. "Really something when the best pizza your city has to offer has the name of another city in it," he grumbled.

"Be nice," she said, her thick accent coming out as she surveyed the view. The Watergate made up six buildings, and her ceiling-to-floor windows exposed the residents of all of them. Curtains gave everyone the illusion of privacy, but to her, the view served as a reminder that the higher up you went, the more your life was laid bare for all to see and judge.

"You sure you'll be fine here alone?" He'd offered to stay with her, but he had meetings of his own in New York and she wanted some freedom to get acclimated to this new world of hers before opening arguments for *Hokkam v. Famóre* began in four days. Besides, someone may as well use their place in New York if they were going to keep it.

"I'm fine, *amore mio*," she said.

Joining her at the window, Aditya took in the view. "My first thought every time I think about you living at the Watergate is about the Nixon scandal."

"I'm pretty sure that's the first thought everyone has," she said. Today's scandals made Watergate seem like child's play, but at the time, the break-in and ensuing cover-up had been big enough to bring down a president. "But Kusum said this location can't be beat. It can house my security detail, not to mention they're so familiar with the layout because so many other politicians stay here."

"You're a politician now?" Aditya smirked.

"In everything but title," she said.

She'd had the good sense to pay for white-glove service with her bed and couch, but they wouldn't be delivered until tomorrow, so for now, Aditya sat against her bedroom wall. "I talked to my dad," he said.

"Yeah?"

He talked to his dad daily, so his mentioning it meant something special was happening.

"His friend recommended this adoption agency, New Beginnings."

Bella sighed and sat next to Aditya, taking his hand and leaning in to rest her head against his chest. "Do you think we're young enough for a new beginning?"

Aditya brushed her chestnut hair, sniffing at it. She'd worn that honeyed perfume he loved. He kissed her lips softly. "No one deserves a new beginning more than us."

It wasn't the first time he'd told her that. They might've been in their forties, but their relationship was young, torn apart by death and racism. Now shielded from reality by money and power, they could finally say it was their time. Looking at where she now lived, remembering the pride on her *nonno* and *nonna*'s faces when she'd been sworn in, she was starting to believe it. "Can we call them now?" She didn't want to lose her nerve.

"I thought you'd never ask," he said. He opened his phone, and she saw he had the number saved already.

He hit a button to put it on speakerphone.

"New Beginnings, where we're dedicated to helping you find yours. My name is Heather; how can I help you?"

They'd been compiling a list of questions for weeks on Aditya's phone, and over the course of an hour, asked every single one.

"Do you have any references?" Bella asked.

Asking for Aditya's email address, Heather said she'd send them the name of "a lovely woman who adopted a child with her wife a few years back."

"It's happening so fast," Bella said.

"Well, some things are," he said. "Getting scheduled and checking references and making sure we're CPR-certified, that's the easy part. Then we have to actually be selected."

"But one day not too far away, we'll get our happily ever after," Bella said. "We'll fly in *nonno* and *nonna*, and my family from Jersey, and your dad, of course. It's all coming together."

Sweat stains darkened Aditya's shirt from the hours of lifting, and he had dried sauce on his shorts, but she'd never wanted him more. Grabbing him by his flabby arms, she kissed him as if his lips were oxygen. Shoving him to the bare, hardwood floor, she crawled atop him and ran her hands over his chest, throwing his shirt off and tossing it to the side. They rolled together on the floor until he was on top, kissing her freckles and her neck. Grunting, he tugged his shorts off and she followed. Gasping at the feel of linoleum on her bare ass, she watched him pull at one of the boxes of clothing, sending it toppling down as they laughed at the ridiculousness of the situation. He pulled out a green pea coat, laying it under her as he kissed her from pelvis to neck. Kissing her lips again, he began to move to her groin before she stopped him.

"Take me now," she said. Moving her hand down, finding his

hardness, she guided it to her entrance. "I can't wait."

Her breath caught as he thrust inside her; she closed her eyes, hearing his grunts and remembering the first time they'd made love inside an apartment. She'd been a lowly law student fucking strangers in order to make ends meet; he'd endured racism with a smile to work his way up the corporate ladder. They'd sacrificed so much, but look where it had gotten them, to the pinnacle of success. She held him close, kissing his neck, biting his ear as he grunted. The pain and pleasure rushing through her had been a constant her whole life. She didn't notice how her hips and shoulder blades dug into the floor each time Aditya moved, but instead focused on the fact that she'd be just one of nine votes soon on a case that impacted law for the most powerful country in the world. She would finally become a mother. All her newfound wealth and privilege? She deserved it. Therese Johnson was right: she was enough. She was done apologizing for her past and would do whatever it took to secure her future.

Aditya yelled as he finished, panting as he rolled off her. Lifting her head as she hugged him close, she caught sight of her judicial robes in the box that'd fallen down.

She smiled.

Claire answered the hotel door wearing a jade dress that showed off her clavicles. She didn't have Kajal's curves, but what she did wield was dark red lipstick that complemented her dress and a thigh slit that revealed her red thong whenever she bent over.

"Why'd you call?" Kajal's voice dripped with curiosity and eagerness.

This would be the hardest part of her show to sell. If Claire could convince Kajal she'd actually missed her, the rest of this charade would be easy.

"I was scared... before." She tightened her throat as if a frog lived in it. She'd used some drops before opening the door to make it look like she'd been crying. She wiped her eyes as Kajal stepped toward her. They were feet apart; she inhaled the woman's scent, the smell of cumin and saffron.

"And you're not anymore?" Kajal's question brimmed with

possibility.

For the slightest moment, Claire thought of telling Whit to fuck off. Leaving him and Rebecca behind. Finding happiness in Kajal, of giving her the money to leave prostitution behind so they could live out their days on some island far from here. The moment passed like bad gas. It was childish, idiotic. Her purpose was here; she'd never stop. Why give others the satisfaction of seeing her down when she knew her place was on top? "I'll never doubt where I belong."

"And am I there?"

Claire batted her eyelashes, biting her bottom lip as she held Kajal for the first time in years. Her fingers ran down Kajal's waist, resting at her hips. "I need you with me more than ever." She kissed the woman softly before biting her lip. Kajal gasped at the pain. She tried kissing back, but Claire retreated while also pushing the woman against a wall.

"Claire... don't make me wait."

"Just a little longer," Claire said. One hand found its way up Kajal's dress, rubbing over her panties and finding her wetness.

"I was so scared," Claire said, pouting. "I didn't know I was gay... but I do now. I'm almost forty. I don't want to run from who I am anymore, but I need help. Will you help me?"

People were suckers. Pretend you needed their help, show one act of vulnerability, and they became putty in your hands.

"Claire..."

"I didn't know I was worthy of love. Coddled my whole life, told I had to act a certain way, trapped in a gilded cage..."

"Let me show you."

Claire let Kajal control her hand, the one resting on Kajal's panties. Kajal took two fingers, used one to brush her panties aside while the other entered her. A sharp exhale and the tightening of Kajal's body told Claire her work was done. Claire's wet fingers and the smile on Kajal's face showed her the woman was all hers.

After, as they both lay naked under the sheets, Claire rested her head against Kajal's breasts. Her fingers traced figure-eights on Kajal's thighs as her mind drifted to the memory of having her head between them. They'd both been generous lovers; the thought of leaving Whit and DC behind crossed her mind again before she snapped to her senses and remembered why she'd called Kajal at all.

"I never slept with another woman after you," Kajal whispered.

Claire got up, resting her back against the headboard. "Really? Women don't call you?"

"That's different," Kajal said. "I meant... personally. I dreamed of it. You coming back."

Claire smiled, leaning in for another kiss as her hand slid over Kajal's thigh and came to rest on her knee. "I'm sorry I kept you waiting. I think it's because I knew if I did return, I'd be admitting to myself that I love you."

A pause filled the room, large enough to give birth. "...what?"

"It's you, Kajal. It's like those women running for president say: I finally realized I'm enough, and that what was broken can be rebuilt even better."

Kajal sniffled, and Claire bit her lip to keep from smirking, knowing the gesture would be misinterpreted as lust and not laughter. The whore was as easy to manipulate as ever. Flashing Kajal some Bambi eyes, she moved her hand from Kajal's knee to brush against her mound as she kissed her again.

Kajal gasped, leaning back to take in Claire's full body. To her credit, Kajal wasn't bawling, thanking Claire for her love like she'd done the first time Claire had shown her any interest. Perhaps she was waiting for Claire to leave, eager not to embarrass herself.

Kajal spoke as if nothing special happened, as if the sniffling was due to a cold. "I always thought you'd go into politics. You don't know Mayor Johnson and Secretary Lungford?"

"Who?" Claire thought she may be overselling it, but Kajal didn't question her ignorance.

"Never mind," Kajal said. "You know, I'm sleeping with a guy on the Lungford campaign."

"Yeah?"

"He's a lousy lay," she said.

Claire choked down a smirk; she couldn't wait to mention that to Whit one day. "Are any of your clients good?"

Kajal smiled. "Some of them are great, but nothing like this. Nothing... real."

She'd ruin this woman beyond recognition. Standing up, walking to her purse, Claire put her pendant on, rubbed the WP-encrusted stones. Instantly, her guilt disappeared.

"DC's clientele is a lot better than New York's," Kajal said.

"Oh?"

"You'd be amazed what all you learn from these political types."

"I imagine it makes blackmail a real concern," Claire said.

"We take pictures of them," Kajal said. "No one's gonna spill the beans about anyone else if they know we've got photos of their dicks, proof of their fetishes."

Claire wasn't sure what she was looking for, but she sensed she was getting close. "You ever let them take photos of you? If they pay extra?"

"No way," Kajal said. Her voice wasn't convincing.

"You're lying," Claire said, stepping back into bed.

"I shouldn't tell you this…"

Claire found Kajal's neck with her mouth; her hands ventured under the sheets, between her thighs.

"You can't tell anyone…"

It was too easy. "Of course not," Claire purred, her fingers exploring Kajal.

"There was one woman, she's actually a huge deal now."

Claire bit her tongue. Surely it wasn't who she was thinking of.

"Bella Ferrari," Kajal said, gasping as she bucked her hips against Claire's fingers.

As Kajal finished, Claire decided she wasn't the only one getting lucky.

Claire had all she needed by the end of the night. She didn't know what was so irresistible about Bella Ferrari, but it seemed as if half the men in Claire's life had fucked the woman. Aditya Shetty, but also her ex-husband, Oliver. She'd left things in a bad place with Oliver; he wouldn't take her call. But he would take Whit's, especially if there was money involved. Kajal couldn't confirm whether the photos of Bella still existed, but Claire knew Oliver's kinks. He would've loved to snap some candids; she'd used photos just like those in her divorce case. After telling Kajal she'd call her soon, she pulled out her phone and called Whit.

"Claire!"

His voice was different, higher pitched. She heard him pacing.

She hesitated. "You okay?"

"Never better! Why are you calling?"

He kept sniffling as she told him about Oliver and Bella.

"You've got shitty judgment, letting your husband fuck a professional. So what?"

She thought about telling him what Kajal had said about their sexual trysts, but decided she wanted to share that in person. "She let people take photos sometimes. If anyone has evidence of her whorey self, it's Oliver."

Nothing came over the line but Whit's sniffling.

"This is a nuclear bomb," he finally said.

She nodded before realizing Whit couldn't see her reaction. "We gotta track him down. This wins us the election."

"And then some," he said. "We flip Congress if we can track down your ex."

Claire returned to bed, enjoying the way the soft sheets hugged her naked skin. Tracing her fingers between her thighs, she realized power turned her on more than anyone's touch. "Let's get to work."

———————————•———————————

September 5, 2028

Bella thought the moment she got used to walking up the stairs of the Supreme Court—the day her heart didn't sing at the sight of the stone columns—would be the day she should retire. Today, with the new term starting and the work of *Hokkam v. Famóre* leaning so heavily on legal arguments derived from her book, *Privileged Food,* Bella found herself hovering at the foot of the building. Security hated it, but what did she have to lose by saying hi to a few tourists? She could make their day with just a hello.

Bella ignored Supreme Court Officer Brandy Knowles's warnings and approached the audience gathered around the entrance, getting ready to shake hands.

"Good morning, I'm Bella!" She beamed, shaking hands with a girl sitting on her father's shoulders.

"Can I touch your hair?" The girl's voice shone like the weather.

"Of course!"

Officer Knowles cringed as she leaned in to let the kid touch her wavy, chestnut hair.

"Can I get a photo with you and my daughter?" the father asked.

Bella held the girl close as she posed. The starstruck dad fumbled with his phone as Bella talked to the girl about Doc McStuffins.

"What an inquisitive young woman," Bella said, after learning her father had planned a DC trip from South Carolina for a long weekend. Handing the girl back, she spotted a mother and son at the other end of the building and waved before heading over.

Officer Knowles rolled her eyes. "You know you work here, right?"

"Come on," Bella said. "They love it!"

It happened while Bella was walking over, in the blink of an eye. A sound like a firecracker, a noise that threatened to pierce her eardrums. And then she was on the floor, Officer Knowles shoving her to the ground with one hand while firing her pistol with the other. The concrete scraped her knees, cut through her robes, but nothing could erase the visual in her head. She'd seen a body fall to the ground in front of her, seen blood leaking from the attacker's head. Screams consumed her as the surrounding groups dispersed and other cops joined the fray. Knowles patted her down, asked if anything hurt. She could've been shouting or whispering; Bella couldn't tell, but Knowles must've been satisfied because she handed her off to two other cops and ran off to do something else. Those two shielded her body as they hauled her up the stairs of the Court and shoved her into a room. One stayed guard over here while the other left, probably to do some crowd control.

"Ma'am, are you okay?"

Bella nodded as he poured a glass of water from a faucet and handed it to her. "Drink."

She obeyed. When she was done, he exchanged her glass for a bit of chocolate from one of his pockets. "Eat."

She resisted at first, but he insisted. To her surprise, the candy pushed warmth down her throat and into her entire body.

Patting her robes, she found her phone and took it out. She

dropped it on the floor, leaning down to pick it up with clammy hands. "May... may I?" She was struggling to form words, but the man understood, telling her he'd wait outside to give her some privacy. Her heart was going to leap out of her body; she felt more helpless now than she had when bullets were flying around her.

Her cellphone rang before she could dial Aditya's number. The shock of the call made her drop her phone again. Bending down to get it, she answered without understanding what her fingers were doing.

"Are you okay?! I got a CNN alert!"

"I'm..." What was she? A word didn't exist to describe her state now versus her state mere minutes ago. She wanted to laugh about how a person could even ask that question after something like this had happened.

Aditya swore as she tried finding words for her emotions.

"It can't be..." she mumbled. Someone had shot at her? Or was it at the Court in general?

"What happened?"

Her mind began to relax as she looked around. She was in what looked like a staff meeting room. A fridge stood next to the sink where the cop had gotten water. Opening it, she found a chicken salad labeled for "Brett" and a box of cookies. She ate a cookie as Aditya spoke and her heart rate stabilized.

"Twitter's got the man's suicide note."

Warmth trickled down her cheeks. Finding a chair, she sat and put her face in her hands. Still, she had to know. "Read it to me."

"My name is Abhinav Iyenger, and for years I was part of the WP Force, forced to participate in the illegal war waged by Presidents Brooks and Begaye."

A political manifesto, then, she thought. A way of settling old debts and explaining himself before taking his own life through "death by cop."

"The war was always a tragedy; you can't steal something you've had since birth, like WP. We were told men like DeLeón were terrorists, then sent to far-off places like Guatemala and Rwanda and Croatia to kill them. But the truth is, DeLeón was just a man trying to get his and maybe do a little good at the same time. Our presidents aren't any different."

Bella poured herself a second glass of water, forcing it down as Aditya continued.

"I was happy the Court ruled my career illegal, happy to come home. But what I returned to was PTSD and little support from my government. This government, which refuses to tell the truth about what really happened to my best friend, Rakshan Baliga. Rakshan deserved better, and so do I. I'm homeless today, left on the streets of DC with bums and vagrants, even though I fought for the politicians working mere miles from where I sleep each night."

Bella's crying had ended; she was pacing now.

"It's fitting that this end at the Court. They took my career, my livelihood. But even beyond that, I have not mentioned Aditya Shetty until now. The man took the most important person in my life from me, and so now I will take the most cherished woman in his life from him, a whore the world won't miss. *Amma, Appa:* I love you. Don't believe the lies they'll tell about me."

Heavy breathing filled both sides of the phone.

"Why does he hate you so much?" she finally managed.

"They'll come for me because of this." There was hesitation in Aditya's voice, and fear. "My enemies will seize on this news, say that making deals with Adrsta isn't worth the hassle."

She'd been in a haze since the attack, but his comments focused her like a laser. "You're honestly worried about money right now? About your fucking job?!" She stopped walking.

"My fucking job is how we afford two places and the stipends we send back to our parents," he said. "First thing I did was call you, ask how you were doing. But now we need to do some damage control. You think the adoption agency is going to love that we were personal targets of a madman?"

He was right. He was an asshole, but he was right.

"What happened to this Rakshan guy? You knew both of them?" Her pacing continued as Aditya explained how Abhinav and Rakshan had robbed him, how he'd gone to jail, only to leave in President Brooks's good graces, how they'd been sent off to war with Karthik Thakur as their boss.

"That motherfucker?" She dropped her phone in disgust. Picking it up, she heard him apologizing.

"I'm sorry for the way I put it. I know I'm an asshole

sometimes, but everything I do is because your happiness is at the forefront of my mind. Always."

She smirked. "*Ti perdono, amore mio.*" Aditya would know her accepting his apology in Italian meant all was well, that she was comfortable.

"Nevertheless, I'll be with you tonight."

"You don't have to do that," she said. "You have that client meeting tomorrow."

"I wasn't asking you," Aditya said. "My flight gets into DCA at 6:45."

She smiled, and emotion spilled over into her words. "I'll make pasta and zuppa inglese. I'll have time, since Court has to be cancelled today."

The conversation was over, but she hoped they wouldn't end on such a sad note. "You mentioned the adoption agency... Did they email you a reference?"

Aditya sighed and her heart froze. What more could be wrong?

"The woman they mentioned, half of a happy couple? It's Sadiya Murthy."

Bella rolled her eyes. "Do you know every Indian in this country?"

Aditya laughed, and she had to join him, releasing all the tightness in her chest.

"No, but I do know this one." He explained Sadiya's connection to Rakshan, then shared that he couldn't call her but trusted that if the agency was able to do right by her, they'd be the right choice for them, as well.

"Rakshan," he said. "Abhinav. Karthik. Do you think death is destined to follow me everywhere because I tried to be more than just another skingrafter? Is that my curse for past sins?"

"*Come può una persona così intelligente essere così stupida?*"

"You think I'm smart?"

She just knew Aditya was smirking through the phone. "I also called you stupid. Just because bad things happen around you, even if you've done a few bad things in your life, doesn't mean you're a bad person."

Aditya sighed, loud enough to make her think he was expelling demons through his nose. "...I've done more than a couple bad things."

Bella ran her fingers through her wavy hair and sat again. "I'm no innocent flower, either. I suppose it was naïve to think only my past would come back to haunt us."

Aditya laughed again. "We're a mess."

"Yes," she agreed. "But we do our best, and our best is pretty good if you look at where we are today."

The clock in the room showed Bella it was half past nine. She needed to shop before cooking, though she supposed her security detail would insist on doing that for her. "I need to go, *amore mio.*"

"Hey," Aditya said. "Despite everything, I did care about Abhinav in my own way."

"...and?"

"They say he had unrefined WP on him... Is that true?"

Bella closed her eyes. "I didn't get a good enough look at him, but I wouldn't be surprised. The world has become harder since I left Maranello. That feels like a lifetime ago."

"We've seen the pinnacle of excess since WP was legalized. Maybe it wasn't a good idea. Maybe the Court should've gone further than banning the WP Force."

Bella hung up instead of answering.

———————●———————●———————

September 19, 2028

Kaitlin Lungford preferred war to campaigning (and *hated* how Olivia and the other staff had a Sun Tzu saying for every incident over the last seven weeks). Debating tactics over TV ad content. Caring about her personnel more than poll numbers (she'd signed off on laying off a tenth of her staff due to money problems). And, most importantly, developing a familiarity with guns over ghosts.

Uncle Charles's specter appeared to her the night before each rally, whispering campaign strategies and offering his bigotry free of charge: that dress didn't compliment Kaitlin's ass; Mirai looked like she was dozing off during interviews with those eyes. At first, rubbing her eyes and biting her arm had been enough to make him disappear. Now, though, his form lay next to her on the bed until she faded to sleep alone in some hotel room.

Kaitlin wished Mirai was here; their joint rallies always injected her with energy. But with less than fifty days left in the campaign, they'd agreed Mirai was needed elsewhere. Besides, the fine folk of Raleigh didn't care about kintsugi as much as they wanted to hear about Kaitlin's military record and how Therese couldn't be trusted. Kaitlin wasn't about to refer to her opposition's "thug son," as Artie Quiver put it, but she'd promised Olivia she would draw a stronger contrast between herself and Therese. She had some ideas she'd try out today.

Standing backstage outside the local VFW chapter, she smiled as Preacher Barry Whitlow announced her. Behind him were rafters filled with people.

"The woman you're about to meet is extraordinary!" His voice echoed through the hall even without a microphone. Whitlow was a local legend among Raleigh's Catholic community. He'd convinced his followers that Kaitlin wasn't a lost cause since she hadn't been seen in a Mormon church. Olivia hadn't found it funny when Kaitlin had remarked that her agnosticism was finally coming in handy.

"It is my privilege to introduce to you the next President of the United States: Secretary Kaitlin Lungford!"

Pastor Whitlow, clad in robes, bent down to shake hands with several audience members before moving to embrace Kaitlin as she walked through the curtains. He whispered in her ear before retreating, a line from the Book of Proverbs—*trust in the Lord with all your heart and lean not on your own understanding.*

Kaitlin smiled, not at her audience but because she was impressed with her ability to keep from groaning. "Good afternoon, Raleigh!"

The crowd gave her a standing ovation, stomping their feet with enthusiasm. Glancing at the audience in the rafters behind her, she saw all but one were women. She wondered how one lone man had made it up there, but figured her Advance Director had his reasons.

"First Corinthians tells us to be on our guard and to stand firm in our faith." She had a whole staff dedicated to writing scripture into her speeches. Mainly Christianity, but on occasion she would appeal to Vijay or Mirai for help and reference the Baghavad Gita or Shintoism. "We know now more than ever to be on our guard."

She locked eyes with a mother standing at the front of the crowd, hand firmly grasping her daughter's.

"I'm speaking of the attack on the Supreme Court a couple weeks ago. My thoughts are with Justice Ferrari and the other Justices, but also with that soldier."

The audience murmured.

"We must show grace. Luke tells us to love our enemies, and Ephesians reminds us to be tender-hearted."

By sprinkling phrases she'd Googled into these speeches, she hoped to avoid extended conversations about her faith until she was elected.

"That soldier did his duty, but did we do ours?" She saw men shaking their heads. "Too often, our brave men and women are denied mental healthcare after returning home. The man had WP on him—are we to blame for giving him access?"

Veterans shouted now, letting her know what they thought of the president and legalization. She waited until they quieted down to continue.

"America has become a harder place in the last few years because of what the Democratic Party is doing."

The sole white man behind her made his opinion known. "And because of what you've let them do!" Leaping over the women in front of him, he moved to tackle her with his fist outstretched.

Her body reacted instinctively, readying to swipe his legs and break his arm, but Agent Hanson was upon him within seconds.

The chaos that ensued was more like a zoo disaster than war. The audience stampeded to their cars, tripping over each other as a rafter at the back filled with press tried getting closer. CNN and FOX and NBC captured footage she knew would lead the nightly news. Passing the attacker off to another agent, Hanson took her hand, leading her to a black Suburban.

"No!" she shouted. "This man does not get to control my campaign!"

Hanson sighed. "Ma'am, please. We can't secure you here, and the people are already fleeing."

Kaitlin pointed at the cameras. "Not them. I have something to say."

A woman who couldn't be older than twenty was at the foot of the stage now, notepad in one hand and phone in the other.

Kaitlin approached to find she was scrolling through Twitter. "It's Tammy, right?"

The woman dropped her phone in shock. She was blonde and leggy and exactly the sort of person who'd be leading a show on FOX one day. "You know who I am?"

"I keep tabs on all the up and comers in the conservative movement. You're with Shapiro News."

Tammy nodded in reverent silence.

"Anyone saying anything about this guy?"

To her credit, Tammy's blank expression cleared as soon as Kaitlin asked the question. "Twitter thinks his name was Rob Engleman. If so, the *News & Observer* had an article last week about a Rob Engleman who was drunk and disorderly around two a.m. outside his ex-wife's apartment. It was bad enough that police took the gun he had on him."

Kaitlin's lip curled. She'd had plenty of suitors in her thirties and forties; the reason she hadn't married any of them was because she'd known they would turn into someone like Rob with enough time. Turning to Agent Hanson again, she asked him if the man had WP on him.

"Yes, ma'am. Judging by the way he acted, and knowing he had such exposure to WP during the war, we suspect it was unrefined."

Walking back to Tammy, she thanked her for the news and asked her to tell the rest of the press to gather round, because she had something to say. When the cameras surrounded her, she invited them onto the stage before calling Tammy over. "Want to interview the next President of the United States?"

Snapping her fingers, Kaitlin had her staff bring out two chairs, sat down, and invited Tammy to proceed. Gone was the fangirling bimbo she'd seen just moments ago; Tammy crossed her legs and got right to it.

"Madame Secretary, you talk about how America is becoming a harder place, and we saw proof of it just now. How would you be able to guide us out of this position?"

Kaitlin took a breath, letting the cameras capture her "thinking" face. "I've thought a lot about this, and I agree with the Court's decision that the WP Force was illegal." Olivia would wring her neck when this was all over. For agreeing to this interview and for changing her position on the WP Force and SCOTUS. "People like Abhinav Iyenger shouldn't have access to WP."

"Because of their skin color?" Tammy couldn't hide her smile. The thought of being the one to expose Kaitlin as a racist trumped any personal political affiliation of hers.

"This has nothing to do with race," Kaitlin said. "It's science. You heard it during the congressional hearings from none other than Dr. Jocelyne Clark. We just don't know enough about the effects of the drug on certain members of our community."

She hoped that was enough dog whistling to win her North Carolina.

Tammy continued. "Pardon my bluntness, but your running mate isn't white. Do your comments include her?"

Kaitlin smirked; she'd had this answer ready for weeks. "Let the cameras zoom in real close," she said. "You'll notice I'm not wearing any WP. Neither is my staff. I don't wear it out of consideration for others. I know it is our birthright, but I urge my supporters to think about how the drug impacts their surroundings and change their behavior accordingly."

Poll numbers raced through her mind. That remark might've cost her ten percent in Alabama or even twenty percent in Idaho, but that wasn't enough to make those states competitive. She was going to say what she wanted to, or else what was even the point of running? "America needs compassion and grace now more than ever."

She saw agents waving off press trying to get on stage, saw Olivia mouthing out talking points she ignored. Everyone wanted a piece of the action now that they'd learned she was making big news today. With the crowd gone and the world watching, she was going to draw that big contrast with Therese her staff so desperately wanted.

"Whether it's that veteran at the Supreme Court or this Rob person today, I want people to think about kintsugi. And I want to take this opportunity to explain the difference between me and Mayor Johnson, because while traveling the country, I've heard too many people say we're the same."

She tried not to smile as Olivia tried and failed to get on stage, no doubt thinking of the best way to get Kaitlin to stop talking.

"Kintsugi asks us to hold on to our pain so we can make something better, while this mantra Therese Johnson has, this belief that you are *enough*, requires forgiveness, asks us to let go of that pain."

She saw more than a few members of the crowd returning from the parking lot. She knew reporters were tweeting her speech, knew her words would lead the nightly news instead of some abusive ex-husband's tirade. She'd turned a story about domestic violence into one of hope, one focused on issues. It was kintsugi in action, and it reassured her that she deserved to be president.

"Letting go of the pain, that devalues Abhinav's experience, devalues the experience of all who are hurting because of real, legitimate trauma."

Tammy had more questions, but Kaitlin could only spend so much time per day using other people's pain as a political prop. Deciding the interview was over, she stood up and left, letting Agent Hanson take her to the car.

Doing the interview had been worth it for the sole reason that Olivia told Kaitlin she'd never question her political instincts again.

Kaitlin chuckled. "Agent Hanson, did you get that?"

"Yes, ma'am," he said, as he steered the Suburban out of the parking lot.

Smiling, joking with her manager, Kaitlin turned to see a pale figure racing behind the car. And then the ghost of Charles Lungford was sitting in the backseat. Leaning in, he whispered in her ear—congratulations for embracing racism in her attack on WP legalization.

"Shut up!" she hissed.

"Boss?"

Olivia couldn't see him, of course. She must've looked like she was losing her mind. "Sorry," she said. "It's been a long day."

Her uncle's smiling body swam through her own; she shivered as goosebumps broke out over her skin. Teeth chattering, she swung a fist that went right through the ghost. The punch almost connected with Olivia's face.

"Fuck! Are you okay?"

Kaitlin apologized again. When she touched Olivia's knee, the woman pulled away.

"Jesus, you're freezing. It's like eighty degrees outside." Olivia turned to Hanson, telling him Kaitlin must be sick and to swing by a pharmacy. "Vijay's flying in tonight, since we're here for another two days. I'll clear your morning and afternoon."

"I'm not sick," Kaitlin said, resting back in her chair. "I just saw something that should be long gone."

Olivia bit her bottom lip. "Do you mean a ghost? Because this is Raleigh, not Roswell. These people believe in Jesus, not aliens."

Her uncle's specter gave a gravelly laugh, as if the rocks the car was speeding over were in his throat.

Kaitlin hoped Jesus and aliens were the worst of it.

Chapter Twelve

September 21, 2028

Even two weeks after the attack on the Court, Bella's heart still pounded like a jackhammer each time she heard a loud noise. Squeezing the hands into fists before releasing them, taking deep breaths, she calmed herself before answering the doorbell to her and Aditya's place in New York.

"*C'è la mia bellezza!*"

Bella's nose twitched as Gianpaolo and his aftershave walked through the door, Matteo behind him, holding a cup of frozen yogurt doused with toppings.

She wanted to slap Gianpaolo for calling her his beauty, but restrained herself, remembering Senator Raghavan's lessons on decorum. The majority leader had told her if she responded to every sexist comment, every biting flirtation, she'd never have time to actually accomplish anything.

Instead, Bella batted her eyelids and closed the door behind her. "You know I've got just one love, *fratello*, but I appreciate the compliment. Come, sit."

It was laying it on a bit thick to call Gianpaolo her brother, especially given what had happened the last time he'd been in this apartment, but she'd been tasked by Kusum to make nice with the Medulla brothers. The senator needed to show Denton some love before Election Day, and no one had his ear like these two. Bella knew she had to learn to do favors if she was to thrive in this city; if she couldn't perform for her best friend in DC, what hope did she have of acquiring goodwill from anyone else?

"Where is Aditya?" Gianpaolo grabbed a glass from her kitchen and poured himself a finger of bourbon before taking a seat on her couch.

She forced a smile, offering a glass to Matteo, too. When he declined, Bella drank it in one go. "He's meeting some investors in New York."

"I would never leave such a delicate flower alone," Gianpaolo said.

Bella raised her eyebrows, sitting on the arm of the couch so she loomed over him. "Delicate?"

Gianpaolo chuckled. "Aren't all beautiful things delicate?"

"What about a rose?" she asked. "You must risk being pricked to touch something so alluring. Not everyone can handle it."

Matteo laughed, throwing his finished cup of froyo away in the kitchen before returning to sit next to his brother. "She's got you there, *fratello*."

Gianpaolo smirked. Bella bit her tongue and remembered what Kusum had said; she needed to charm and disarm. Taking a seat at his side, she placed a hand at his knee. "Forgive my innocent remarks; I get carried away. It's a defense mechanism."

Running his own hand down his leg, he interlaced his fingers with hers. "And why must you defend against me?"

"Against everyone," she said. "What happened at the Court hardened me."

"How so?"

Biting her tongue harder, she was able to draw some tears to help sell the story. Gianpaolo leaned in further; she let him put his arms around her and brought her head to his chest as she pretended to cry. "My first thoughts were of Aditya, and of my family. But then I imagined a life where I never got to tell you I'm sorry, and I didn't want that."

She fought the urge to choke in response to Gianpaolo's overwhelming cologne.

He shushed her and stroked her hair. "*Non piangere*," he whispered. "What happened in August? It's nothing; all is forgiven."

Pulling back, composing herself, she flashed him a genuine smile. Was it so easy to manipulate the rich and powerful? She wasn't entirely surprised; years of dealing with johns in NYC had unveiled plenty of secrets. Perhaps it would be even simpler in DC.

Standing up, Gianpaolo poured two more drinks for them. When she tried to say no, he shoved it in her hand. "Drink. It will make you feel better."

She took a sip before putting it down on the table. "Shall we go out to dinner? I can make reservations at this Indian place we like."

Gianpaolo laughed. "That's not real food," he said. "And besides, we have a flight to catch in a couple hours."

"A flight? You came all this way just to make sure I was okay? I'm so touched."

Matteo stood and went to the windows to take in the view while Gianpaolo placed his hand on her knee. "We came to deliver a message." His voice dropped an octave as he scratched the underside of his neck with his free hand. He looked like a character out of *The Godfather*. "That incident with the soldier pushed back the plan, but perhaps it's even better this way."

A shiver ran down Bella's spine.

He noticed her freezing up. "Don't take it like that. We're so thankful you're safe, but the attack showed the country that a madman can do anything on his own. How is a third party supposed to stop it?"

It dawned on Bella: these *stronzos* thought they owned her and were eager to cash in on their favor. If the Hokkam case didn't go their way, it'd cost Famóre hundreds of millions in reduced market value and a blow to their reputation.

Standing up, looking Gianpaolo straight in the eye, she delivered a message she knew Senator Raghavan would approve of. "I am no longer a prostitute, *fratello.*" The words were laced with venom this time, her intention unmistakable. "I'm not for sale; I am a member of the Supreme Court of the United States and my votes are more powerful than your little company."

Chuckling, Gianpaolo stood, finishing his drink and pouring himself a third. "Do not shut the door on this just yet, *sorella.* You will regret it."

"I'm not your sister," Bella said, "and I think you should leave. You should also know that I'll have to report this conversation to my security team."

Gianpaolo shrugged as he snapped his fingers, drawing Matteo to his side.

"You seem nonplussed," she said. "Is that because Senator Denton's on your payroll?"

Gianpaolo snarled. "Have it your way," he said. "You're nothing but a dumb whore; soon, the whole world will know that and so much more."

He stormed out the door, and Matteo followed behind him, but not before giving Bella one last look, like a hurt bunny. "I still like you."

She touched his hand before pushing it away, hoping she was closing the door on more than just her past.

Chapter Thirteen

September 21, 2028

Rebecca's team found themselves exploring Boston's Faneuil Hall neighborhood hours before Mayor Johnson's fundraiser. Erica and Gael and the rest of her staff were walking the Freedom Trail and catching dinner before work tonight; she herself had a more embarrassing task ahead of her. Getting off the T at South Station, she walked from the bus to the corporate headquarters of Thunderbird Bank. President Begaye's eldest son, Sani, had become one of the richest Native Americans under the age of thirty when he'd founded the institution seven years ago, shortly after his dad had become president. The Harvard graduate had put his entrepreneurial spirit (and his connections) to good use when he'd founded the bank during his junior year. Call it nepotism or cronyism or whatever you wanted, but the man had a knack not just for business, but for mentorship. Trading alongside stocks like JP Morgan and Citigroup, Thunderbird had seen success *and* led to an explosion of Native American-owned companies on the NYSE; Sana was more popular than his father in several financial and cultural circles.

Walking through the bank's lobby, Rebecca introduced herself to the security guard and told him she was here to see Mr. Begaye. After confirming she had an appointment, the guard walked her to the elevator and used a keycard to let her up to the 49th floor. The clear glass elevator revealed a gorgeous view of the Waterfront's still waters, but the butterflies in Rebecca's stomach made her insides churn with a ferocity that would've transformed those waters into lethal waves. Begging Claire to join the campaign had given Rebecca enough funding to make it a few more weeks, but payroll was October first, and once again, she wasn't sure they could honor their media buys after meeting their staff obligations. Unless something drastic happened in the next week, she'd have to either cut back their advertising or lay off field staff just a few weeks before Election Day; the press would slam the Johnson campaign regardless of her decision.

There was another way, though: Sani. He'd said himself he wanted to help with the campaign. He was a multi-millionaire determined to join the three-comma club before turning forty, and presidential relationships certainly helped on that front. Native Americans hadn't raised big money for the president until his second campaign, but now Sani and his partners understood the power of their dollars, and had gotten accustomed to the influence they wielded. Sani was Rebecca's answer to not just saving the campaign, but also saving her dignity. Admitting her failure to Claire once had been humiliating enough. She wasn't sure she had it in her to do it again.

Sani was there to greet her when the elevator opened.

"No assistant?" Rebecca raised her eyebrows.

Sani laughed. "I send her home after five. I'm more than capable of greeting honored guests and taking any messages."

Rebecca grinned. "I'm an 'honored guest?'"

"Of course," he said. "Come, sit." Leading her into his office, he waved her toward a leather couch across from his desk before getting two bottles of water out of his mini fridge and joining her. "You look great."

She'd dressed for the fundraiser since there wouldn't be time to change after speaking with him, and wore a navy-blue dress with full sleeves and floral lace near the neckline.

"Not as good as you," Rebecca replied. She'd seen him in the occasional issue of *Entertainment Weekly*, usually with an actress on her arm. Now he wore a yellow shirt and black slacks, with a black tie to match. The cleanshaven look and well-fitted shirt, which barely concealed his muscular arms, made him appear far more desirable than any of the twenty-eight-year-olds she'd dated in her youth. "I can see why the ladies can't stay away."

The sun had set, but his earnest smile made the room light up. "The red-carpet premieres? I tell Mom it's all part of the job. I'll settle down eventually, but for now I keep up appearances for the business. If you look successful in this country, people treat you differently. And getting photos snapped by the press at the Golden Globes? My funders read those magazines and watch those awards shows."

Sani was savvier than the president, for that was the key to building generational wealth and an enduring legacy; the first generation raised you from nothing to something, and the second generation started at the level of 'something' so they could bring the family even higher.

"Your parents must be proud," she said.

Sani chuckled, swatting her compliment away as if it was a fly. "Ah, you didn't take time out of your busy schedule to talk about my dating life. What's up?"

Rebecca sighed, standing up to pace before stopping at his desk and looking out the window. "This view..."

Sani walked to her side. "You're not the introspective type, nor do you ever stop and smell the roses. What's wrong?"

"I fucked up."

"I'm sure it's not that bad."

"The campaign needs money."

Sani smiled. "Good thing you're headed to a fundraiser."

Rebecca stared at her shoes—Manolo Blahniks that matched her dress, glamorous and expensive and utterly useless. "It isn't enough."

"What about your parents?"

Rebecca laughed, a genuine cackle devoid of mirth. "They wrote me off around the time your dad became president."

Sani's eyes twinkled like the stars above. "The way I've heard the story, you had something to do with that."

"It was for the best."

"Okay, but your sister helps, yes?"

"I've been keeping her at a distance. She's not full-time or anything, just a couple simple favors tapping her low-hanging fruit."

"Sounds like there's more there."

Rebecca's eyes met his. Balling the hand at her side into a fist, digging her manicured nails into her palm, she steeled herself to make the ask she'd wanted to make the second she'd walked into this office. "I think there're better ways to raise the money. I think it's time you and your partners showed how serious you are about the campaign."

Sani whistled, staring at the T.C. Cannon painting on his wall before shaking his head. "It's not a good look."

Rebecca chuckled. "It could look as good as that painting, if you wanted."

"Being rich and powerful isn't the same as being happy and fulfilled," he said.

"Meaning?"

"You miss your family, Rebecca." Sani placed a hand on her arm, stroking the fabric, crooking his neck in sympathy. "You think one more win will erase the pain, but nothing is stronger than family."

Rebecca shuddered, shaking his arm away. "I can do this without Claire."

"Can you? I know she's hosted for you in the past; just ask for more help."

"It's not that simple."

"It can be."

Rebecca finished her water bottle and tossed it in his trashcan. "My family's played games their whole lives. Mindfucking. Going to her once was embarrassing enough. I'd have to give her an official title in the campaign if I want more, promise her an ambassadorship or something."

Sani scoffed. "Doling out power is nothing new to you. What's really holding you back is the humiliation of it all."

He was right. Rebecca bit her bottom lip; Erica would need to redo her makeup at the hotel.

"I get it," he said. "Niyol's life is so different from mine; I barely get to see my brother. But you can see on my desk: T.C. Cannon may be on the wall, but Niyol's art is framed at my side."

Rebecca didn't speak.

"There's also a practical reason to go see Claire."

"What?"

"It's a bad look to lean on the president's son and his banker friends to save a Democratic campaign," Sani said. "The press would have a field day."

Rebecca crinkled her nose, but he was right. "I'll call her in the morning."

Sani nodded before walking her to the door. "I'll see you at the victory party. And if you need to vent or something before then, just call."

Rebecca smiled. "I'll see you at the wedding, too."

"Ah, yes," he said. "Luther is coming in next week for some brotherly bonding and suit shopping."

"Have they set a date?"

"December," he said, hitting the elevator button for her. "They couldn't wait, but wanted to avoid any disruption to the campaign."

Rebecca hugged Sani as the door opened. "Thank you."

"Any time," he said.

"You're not coming down with me."

He flashed a grin. "No rest for the wicked."

The door closed behind her, sending Rebecca plummeting down forty-nine floors in a speeding metal can with no seatbelts.

⬤────────────────⬤

September 22, 2028

Rebecca woke with a two-million-dollar hangover. Two hundred people at ten grand a pop would equate to life-changing money for anyone else, but it'd pay for less than a week of ads in the swing states they needed to win. Wisconsin, Pennsylvania, Colorado, North Carolina. Media buyers loved this time of year.

She'd taken a bottle of Grey Goose from the event to her room. Checking her phone, she saw she'd drunk-dialed Maadhini. It must've been the liquor talking, because she knew from past experience the woman had changed her number years ago. She should've deleted it back then, and yet she needed to hold on to something she knew didn't exist.

Therese hadn't called in yet, and for both their sakes, Rebecca hoped it was due to a 'good morning' with Russell. One of them should be getting laid, and it'd put a smile on Therese's face when facing the press and meeting voters. Pulling up her calendar,

Rebecca saw they had nine events across three states in all four time zones this weekend.

Going to her contact list, she stopped at the number she'd dialed more in the past month than she had in the last several years: Claire Steinbeck. Biting her cheek, she paced around the small hotel room, then forced herself to just get it over with.

Claire answered on the first ring. "My darling sister."

"Hey, sis!" Rebecca used one foot to stomp on her other. What a fucking stupid thing to say. Even when they'd been best friends, she'd never called Claire 'sis.'

"How's Boston?" Something in Claire's tone sent chills up Rebecca's spine, as if she should look in her bathroom for a ghost.

"Red Sox are gonna make post-season!" Rebecca hit her head against the wall, telling herself to get a grip. The only balls Claire cared about were attached to men.

"What can I do for you this fine Friday?"

Those words cut like a knife. "Um, I wanted to invite you... officially... to join the campaign."

Claire laughed, a sound that knocked Rebecca off her feet. She back down on the bed.

"Raising millions doesn't make me part of the campaign?" Claire said. "Sister, how much have you given to the cause?"

Rebecca wanted to answer truthfully, to say she'd been living off fast food for six months and had the body to prove it, but Claire would take that as weakness. Sacrificing your health, your time, that was irrelevant. Instead, she played to Claire's ego. "Of course you're one of us," she said. "What I meant was that you see the same polls we do."

"Actually, I see more," Claire said. "I've still got a few Republican friends, and they like to try and impress me."

"I'm sure," Rebecca said. Muting the phone, she took a big breath before speaking again, trying to calm herself. "We're going to win this race, and when we do, we want to offer you a nice prize." She couldn't say it over the phone, but she knew Claire understood her. An ambassadorship to the country of her choice, a position on some executive business roundtable, an endowed chair at some federally funded college—the world would be her oyster.

"Oh... Becky."

Claire hadn't called her that since they were children. Back then, her sister had locked her in the cage of their pet rabbit until she'd started bawling her eyes out. Claire had told her she'd done it to build her character, but in truth, Rebecca had always known Claire had done it to prove she could, to show her capacity for unbridled cruelty. Because after that, Claire had always been top dog. Being older wasn't enough for her. She had to bring everyone she called a friend to heel, especially someone she called her 'best friend.'

"I want to congratulate you for learning to swallow your pride," Claire said. "I know what it's like to swallow things you'd rather not."

Rebecca got up again to pace.

"Dear sister: fuck off."

Banging her knee against the hotel bed, Rebecca stopped and bit her bottom lip to keep from cursing. "What?"

"We could've been a great team, but you ruined that when you left us."

"Who is this 'us?'" Rebecca asked, her voice rising to just short of a scream. "You see Mom and Dad like twice a year, if your Instagram can be believed. I can't imagine they call. Why do you have a stick up your ass?"

Claire's voice grew hot as flames, each word burning Rebecca. "They gave you everything and you walked out because you thought it was dirty money, but that money granted you the time and education to think there was another way to live! And then you left me in the lurch! We weren't just sisters!"

Rebecca knew she should apologize if she wanted a chance at gaining Claire's help, that she should at least pretend Claire had a point, but they shared not just blood, but a quick temper. "This isn't like you."

"No?"

"The Claire I know isn't so petty as to throw away one last chance to become relevant again."

"Oh... little sister." The words were ice against Rebecca's heart. "I'm not throwing my chance away; I'm seizing it."

The line went dead before Rebecca could ask her what she meant.

205

Chapter Fourteen

September 22, 2028

Saying no to Rebecca was better than sex. Afterward, Claire had caught the 5:25 from LGA to IAD to meet Whit. After three weeks of searching, they'd finally tracked down her ex-husband, Oliver. She wasn't sure if appearing with Whit would piss Oliver off or work to their advantage, but they'd both decided she should be nearby.

She waved down Whit's car in the arrivals section, and he popped the trunk without getting out.

"Are you going to kidnap me?" she asked.

"You don't have any luggage?"

She smiled. "I find it best to live your life without any baggage. Whatever I need, I'll buy."

Gritting his teeth, Whit got out of the car and closed the trunk as other cars honked in protest. When he returned, Claire was in the driver's seat. "Seriously?"

"I know where you live. Get in."

Scratching his left arm, he scoffed as he complied.

Claire darted through traffic like she was an F1 racer.

"This isn't a video game," Whit hissed. "You don't get multiple lives."

"Maybe you don't," she said. "But I'm a pussycat, and I'm only on my third life."

She'd worn a white sweater that was one size too small on purpose, to tempt him. She'd been a lamb for him to feast on when they'd fucked around all those years ago, but things were going to be different this time around. She saw his wandering eyes focused on her breasts, saw his hand move to grope her. Claire seized him by the wrist. "Uh-uh."

She tossed his hand aside, catching him agape. He scratched his arm again when she released him.

"You're the one who broke things off between us," she said. "It's all business, now."

"That's not quite what happened," he said.

Pulling onto I-66, she clucked her tongue. "Doesn't matter what happened, only what people remember."

She smiled as he dug his nails into his left arm. She drove to her room at the Watergate while his eyes lingered on the pendant around her neck, which was encrusted with WP stones.

Claire checked in as Whit parked the car and came in through the back door. She'd thought of booking a dump to reduce the chances of them being photographed together, but she couldn't stomach staying in a place like that. Besides, it was almost October —reporters had better places to be than DC.

She had two flutes of champagne waiting when he knocked on the door.

"We should go over the plan first," he said, refusing the drink.

"Take a sip; we'll talk business later."

He shook his head, but it was clearly a half-hearted denial of what he desired, and she watched as he ended up downing the drink all in one gulp.

Claire had sensed it in the tone of Whit's voice over the phone, and saw it now confirmed during their drive—he was nothing more than a skingrafter. Worse, he didn't even realize it. She bit her tongue to keep from laughing in his face. Boy wonder, blessed with the physique of Adonis and the intellect of Machiavelli, was going to lose it all because he just didn't know when to say no. Men were so weak. She wondered if his divorce had broken him or if he'd always been this pathetic and she just hadn't seen it.

Pouring him a second glass, she sat in a chair and motioned for him to sit, too. "You're meeting Oliver for dinner at RFD?"

He nodded.

"I'll come to Chinatown, too, but I won't be with you. It's best not to shock him."

Whit's eyes were everywhere but on her face. Standing to get a third glass, she wondered if she'd opened the bottle too soon; this wouldn't work if he passed out. When he was done, she took the bottle and stashed it in the mini fridge. "We want some for celebrating with later." He nodded before pacing around the room.

Excusing herself to the bathroom, she saw him taking out a pouch of white powder as she closed the door behind her.

───────────●────────────────●───────────

There was no reason for Whit to see Kajal after learning about Oliver. She'd been a means to an end, an avenue for incriminating evidence. So why, as he waited at RFD, nursing a beer, could he not get their last encounter out of his head? They'd met twice in the past couple weeks; theirs were the only trysts he'd had where he was the one demanding to wear a condom.

"Whit?"

A burly man tapped his shoulder, pulling him from his thoughts. Oliver's fingers looked like Polish sausages, and Whit's eyes were drawn immediately to the WP-encrusted ring on one of them. His game plan for getting the photos flew out of his head as he licked his lips and scratched his left arm.

"Take a seat," Whit said. He'd gotten a booth in the back. Oliver took up one whole side as he sat across from him.

Oliver waved a waitress over and ordered a double of whiskey, neat. "Couldn't believe my luck that you called."

"Yeah?" Whit cleared his throat. His eyes followed Oliver's ring as the man cracked his fingers.

"The great Whit Pryor." The bitterness in Oliver's voice matched the beer in Whit's hand. "I was a big man like you, once."

"You can be that man again," Whit said. "You give me those photos, let me use them to ensure our victory, and there'll be a place for you in this city."

Oliver sighed. "She was the best lay I ever had."

Whit waited until the waitress delivered Oliver his drink before responding in a whisper. "Bella?"

Oliver sipped his whiskey as if it were a holy thing. "Claire. Did you really fuck my wife?"

"She isn't yours anymore," Whit said.

Oliver laughed. "Don't kid yourself that she's yours."

Whit smiled. "I don't care about Claire anymore." His eyes lingered on Oliver's ring, and the condensation of Oliver's glass as it dripped down over the stone.

"We're Eskimo brothers," Oliver said. "I suppose that means you can ask me for a favor."

Whit licked his lips. "Do you have the photo of Bella on you?"

Oliver laughed. "You got money?"

Whit's foot moved like a piston under the table. "I thought I get a favor?"

"You get a big one," Oliver said. "It's actually three photos, and you get them for the reduced price of fifty grand."

Whit whistled. It'd cost that much to pay for both of Senator Hammond's abortions and the required hush money. Thinking about how he'd pay Oliver, if it was even worth it, he scratched his left arm again.

"You okay, buddy?"

Whit's nose crinkled as he answered, his voice rising. "I'm fucking fantastic."

Oliver leaned in to hold Whit's hands still. Being so close to that ring warmed Whit's insides. "I knew a guy like you once, but he was a skingrafter. You don't use that unrefined shit, do you?"

Ignoring his question, Whit forced some fingers free and stroked the ring, trying and failing to pull it off Oliver's hand.

Oliver shoved Whit back. "You're fucking nuts, brother." Standing up, he took his wallet out and threw a few bucks on the table to cover his drink. "Keep your money, and your dignity, too. If you still can."

Whit watched the man leave, holding back tears as the ring got farther and farther away.

●————————————————————————————●

Whit ordered food as he sat at the Capitol Hill Club, not caring to wait until Senator Hammond arrived. When his ex-boss finally did enter, Whit was deep into some scrambled eggs and toast. Crumbs dotted his chin as he stood and offered his hand. Hammond looked at it as if it was decaying.

"Jesus Christ," he said.

Whit tried speaking, realized his mouth was full, and gulped a glass of water down. "What?"

Hammond sneered. "Have you been crying?"

Whit paused, wondering if his eyes were red. "...no." Taking another swig of his water, a hand went to scratch his left arm.

"Pull yourself together, man." Hammond's nose twitched; he stood, apparently refusing to sit next to his old employee. "You're acting like a fucking skingrafter."

Whit's mind cleared for a moment as he considered not the repercussions of punching out the senator, but just how it would make him feel. Like Muhammed Ali. He smiled, wishing he lived in that simple world, devoid of consequences, where his actions were all he needed and the future could be postponed whenever he'd liked. Alas, he was trapped, trapped in his gilded cage: power and privilege had demands even money couldn't free him from.

"What are you smiling about?" His boss's voice cut through him.

"I've got news."

James finally sat, then leaned back, ordering a bourbon on the rocks from their waitress before cupping her ass as she walked away. "Tell me."

They ordered two more rounds of drinks as Whit told Hammond about how Bella had been a client of Claire's ex-husband, about how Oliver had pictures of Bella in compromising positions. "Claire's working on getting them."

Hammond sighed. "Remember what I told you last time, Pryor. Don't stick your dick in crazy."

Whit stared at Hammond's cufflinks, which were embedded with WP. They didn't call to him like Oliver's ring, like Kajal's condoms. But of course, he thought: a U.S. Senator wouldn't wear unrefined WP, at least not in public. "I'm not sleeping with her," he replied, his eyes never leaving Hammond's sleeves.

Hammond scoffed. "I don't want to know."

The senator stood and left without saying goodbye, throwing some cash on the table to settle the bill.

●————————————————————●

September 23, 2028

Claire wore a cashmere sweater and yellow heels that erased the six-inch advantage Whit had on her. No matter what he said, the other six-inch advantage he had was closer to four. Walking into Central Michel Richard, she spotted him sitting at a table and joined him for lunch. He was already two drinks in, by the looks of it.

A gentleman would've stood to pull her chair out, but all he did was snap his fingers to call a waiter over. "We'll take two grilled cheeses."

Claire scrunched her nose. "Grilled cheese?"

"Trust me," he said.

She sighed. "But I don't. You don't have the photos, do you?"

"That fucking guy. How did you ever stand him?"

"There were benefits."

"Don't be gross."

Claire smirked. "I don't mean the sex—that was mediocre, at best. But the power? The parties at Ben Blackstone's house in the Hamptons? That was divine."

Whit scratched his left arm. "Well, he's out, at any rate."

Claire gritted her teeth. "What did you do?" They sat in silence until the waiter returned with their food. Whit took a bite out of his grilled cheese.

Claire raked her eyes over him. "He figured out you're a skingrafter, huh?"

Dropping his sandwich, Whit lifted his hand and moved to slap her. She grabbed his wrist and kicked his shin under the table, digging her heel in. "Do that again, and I'll force the heel into your balls." Her tone was colder than the ice in her drink.

He gritted his teeth. She knew he was struggling not to shout and upend their table. He was so obvious and so boring, the strait-laced Republican pretty boy with a kink for rough sex and clean suits. Only now he'd lost his way because he'd actually gotten what he wanted, and too much of a good thing—in his case, WP.

"Don't call me that," he hissed.

"It's all over you," she said. "The scratching, the red eyes. Oliver would've noticed as soon as you walked through the door."

Once upon a time, she'd let men like Oliver and Whit shove her against walls, smack her ass so hard it left marks, bite her neck and tell her they'd only left 'love marks.' Never again.

"I'm not... I'm not that."

She rolled her eyes. "Fine. I'm sorry for saying it. Happy?"

He nodded, yanking his arm away and taking another bite out of his sandwich. He dipped the bread in the accompanying gravy boat filled with cheese sauce. He looked as happy as if he'd just done a line of WP.

"I've got a way to get to Oliver."

"How?"

"Remember those tech bros who got Bella on the Tenth Circuit?"

"Those Italian pricks? They helped kill Senator Hammond's immigration initiative. What do you want with them?"

Claire smirked. Men couldn't see beyond their dicks and wallets. "The way I hear it, Justice Ferrari told Gianpaolo the reliable vote he thought he had on the Famóre case isn't sewn up. He's got as much reason to ruin her as we do."

Whit smiled. "You're thinking he'll give us fifty thousand ways to humiliate her?"

"Fifty grand is a rounding error for him. He gives us the cash, you get the photos, I send them out into the world with no way to trace it to your super PAC, and on Election Day, we all win."

Chapter Fifteen

October 2, 2028

It'd taken Claire longer than expected, but she'd finally scheduled a meeting with Gianpaolo. He'd wanted neutral territory, and so she found herself at The Great Dane in Madison, Wisconsin, munching on cheese curds and nursing an IPA when he entered. Ostensibly, he was there to get the lay of the land before the first presidential debate next week.

"This cloak and dagger shit turns me on," he said.

"The way I've heard it, not much doesn't turn you on."

"What's wrong with that?" He grinned, showing all his teeth. "We all just want some *fighetta* at the end of the day, no?"

Claire crossed her legs. "I'm not offering you anything more than a chance to get back at Bella."

"That *stronza?* I would've answered your call sooner if I'd known you had something on her."

Claire sipped her beer. It was one thing for Whit and Gianpaolo to be rich and powerful. They had penises, good breeding, and luck; such was the way of the world. But Bella? Rebecca? She was better than both of them combined, so what right did some whore and a social justice warrior have to be sitting pretty while she had to wait nine days to schedule a meeting with a billionaire? "Let's talk."

Claire took her guest to Essen Haus after dinner, a German place known for serving large glass boots filled with the beer of your choice. Though the boot was usually shared between several friends, Claire convinced Gianpaolo to split it with her. As the night grew longer, she let him slide his hand further and further up her dress.

"You think you can spare fifty grand?"

He grinned, looking her up and down. "I've spent more."

She slapped him, not as hard as Whit had once to hit her, but enough to leave an impression. "Not for that. I've got a business proposition."

Handing her the last sip of beer in the glass boot, he laughed. "It's been ages since someone's had the balls to slap me."

She rolled her eyes, grateful he couldn't see her in the dark room; this idea that balls were strong had to end. "For fifty grand, I can make all your troubles disappear." She snapped her fingers, pulling him from a sleep that was imminent after all the beer he'd had. Claire doubted she had more than a few more minutes.

"What you got, Barbie?" Gianpaolo slurred his words, leaning to rest his head against her breasts. She let him.

"My ex-husband used to sleep around with her, Bella."

Gianpaolo's head snapped up. "No shit?"

"Straight up."

"And he's got, what?"

"Pictures."

Gianpaolo licked his lips. A feral gleam lit his eyes. "She shouldn't have said no to me."

Claire knew he wasn't talking about any court case, that instead, he'd tried to sleep with her. That was just what men like him did, and if he couldn't fuck Bella, he'd fuck her over. "The cash?"

"No problem," he said. "I'll go straight from your place to the bank tomorrow morning." His head found a resting place against her chest again, his hand now cupping the side of her ass.

She traced her hand over his silk pants, rested her hand right on his member. Then she squeezed. "Listen here, you *cazzo*." Claire had made Rebecca teach her all the dirty words in Italian the moment she'd become fluent in it. "You're valuable to me because you have money and a grudge against a person I want to destroy. Our interests align, that's all."

She released her grip, then smiled as Gianpaolo tried to get up. He winced in pain before sliding back into their booth.

Taking out a piece of paper, she wrote her account number down and slid it to him. "Deposit the funds there. And don't make me wait. The opportunity I'm offering you is one of a kind, but rich pricks like you are a dime a dozen. Don't forget that."

She walked out the door, but not before catching him taking some ice out of his drink to cool his balls.

Claire called Whit from the road as she drove back to her hotel room. "Fifty grand secured."

She heard him pacing. "In one night, from one person? You should've worked for my Super PAC."

She gritted her teeth. "That wasn't an option at the time." To remember their affair seven years ago was to remember how he'd cast her out of DC, painted her as Hester Prynne during his own divorce proceedings, made her into a woman to be exiled because she'd dared be more than what society could handle.

Whit paused before answering. "I was wrong."

More than anything else, those words worried Claire. The old Whit Pryor never, ever apologized. These weren't just trips; WP had transformed him. "Whit... Do you need help? I know a doctor; he helped out our family more than once. He's very discreet."

She felt the heat of Whit's rage through the phone. "I'm fine."

Parking at her hotel, she cut the engine but stayed in the car to avoid anyone overhearing. "Okay, you're fine." Him. Rebecca. People lashed out if you tried to help them, so why bother? "I'll have the cash tomorrow. You need to set another meet."

The sound of his pacing increased. She pictured Whit's heartbeat leaping out of his chest. "You don't tell me what I need! Besides, are you stupid? I already told you Oliver won't talk to me."

She was losing him. Adopting the tone she'd reserved for seducing Kajal, she tried a new tack. "He'll take a meeting as long as he knows you're good for the money."

He paused again; she wasn't sure if he was snorting another line of WP or actually reflecting on what she'd said.

"I'll call you when it's done."

Whit Pryor poured himself a finger of bourbon in his hotel room. Who the fuck was Claire to tell him who to call?

Melissa had their son this weekend, and Hammond was barnstorming the country with just around a month to Election Day. He was all alone.

Taking a long sip of his drink, he tore off his shirt and admired his abs in the bathroom mirror before shoving his bottoms down, too, and stepping out of them. He'd had Kajal leave some condoms from last time; he took one out of his suitcase now, laying it on the bed and stroking himself as he called her.

"Come over. Yeah, same address, same room number. Just come right up, they'll have a keycard for you when you enter." He smiled at seeing his member grow. "Hurry, or the fun'll be over before you arrive."

The inside of an unrefined condom wasn't just lubricated—it had WP, as well. As one hand pumped his erect cock, Whit lay back on the bed, totally naked, using the other hand to pinch his nipples. He'd shaved every hair on his body, sighing at the feeling of his bare skin against his manicured hands, his toned ass on the sheets. Moaning in pleasure, bucking his hips as he finished inside the condom, he removed it and swallowed its contents. Lost in bliss, his seed melting on his tongue, he closed his eyes and didn't hear Kajal opening the door.

"Aw," she pouted, "you finished without me."

Opening his eyes, he growled. "I'm just getting started."

He was on here like a lion. He gripped her waist, kissing her neck and pulling her shirt off. His cock pushed against her hip. She'd worn jeans tonight; he enjoyed ripping them off so the buttons bounced on the floor and scattered everywhere. Flipping her around, shoving her against the wall, he pushed his hardness between her cheeks. She'd worn that green thong he loved. Licking her back, inhaling her scents of cumin and saffron, he pawed at her breasts before dropping to his knees and peeling off her panties, his hands sliding down her body as he explored every inch of her. And when his eyes were level with her most forbidden hole, he spread her cheeks and plunged his tongue inside.

She resisted at first, but his strong hands held those thick, heavenly thighs in place and within seconds, the WP on his tongue did its job. Now she was rubbing her ass against his mouth, in danger of suffocating him. What a way to go. Everyone wanted to be filthy; they just needed an excuse.

Gripping her with one hand, he used the other to reach around, entering her wetness. She gasped, and after only a few moments, her knees finally failed her, causing her to fall backward, toppling them both over as she came. His neck ached and she'd bruised her elbows, but they looked at each other, then laughed until their guts ached.

"That was different," he said.

She kissed him, not caring about (or perhaps wanting) the taste of her ass on his lips. "I'll have to share that with my other clients."

He seized her hand. "No."

That word meant nothing to Melissa and Claire anymore, but he'd not have it become useless when dealing with someone like Kajal. "This is ours."

She tried pushing him off, reclaiming her hand, but his grip was too strong. When she brought her other hand up to slap him, he seized that one, too.

She emitted palpable fear as they lay on the ground, his body on top of hers. He smiled, a cruel gesture. "I'm not gonna rape you or anything; you just need to know that I can." Letting her go, he dressed himself, leaving her on the floor, as useless to him now as the used condom. Taking his wallet out from a side dresser, he tossed it to her as she still lay naked on the ground. "Take whatever you think is fair."

Leaving to brush his teeth, he heard her ruffling around. When he finished, she was gone, along with his black AMEX card. He'd known she would take it, just as surely as he knew she'd return it to him next time he called.

Chapter Sixteen

October 8, 2028

Bella's life had changed permanently on the day of the shooting. She'd been dumb to think it could stay the same. Aditya had hired someone to train her in basic self-defense and ways to handle herself during a public shooting or private encounter. It was excessive, given her security detail, but whenever she protested, he reminded her that "those guys" hadn't been able to protect her on "9/5," a date he considered more dangerous than 9/11 itself. Now he didn't let her leave their places in NYC or DC without her (very) noisy hand-held alarm and pepper spray in her purse. On the plus side, he'd blown off more than a couple meetings to be at her side. And the adoption process was moving forward with a home study, with people looking into their financials, their medical histories, every aspect of their lives. It was every bit as intrusive as the FBI background check the White House had conducted before nominating her, but it would be even more fulfilling.

Unbeknownst to Aditya, she was pushing forward in her own way on the adoption front, stalking Sadiya and Maadhini's Instagram profiles for any tips on navigating the process. She hadn't mustered up the courage to message them yet, but there had to be some clues there to help them. People thought being in a powerful position meant you were guaranteed things like a baby, but if anything, it made the process tougher, as she and Aditya had to avoid any perception they'd used their influence to make their lives easier.

She'd spent the morning making crepes and espresso, a lazy Saturday in DC. Hearing the shower stop, she raised her head as Aditya emerged from their bedroom.

"Want to walk around Georgetown?" he said.

"Too touristy. Let's walk around the memorials and museums. It's been too long."

Aditya rolled his eyes. "Because that's *not* touristy?"

She laughed, coming close to give him a kiss and run her hands over his body. "I like watching the kids."

He sighed. "I know you do. And I know this is tough, that our lives have changed so much, but give it a year, and our lives will be transformed again in the best way."

She thought about who she'd call first if and when the agency delivered the best news of her life. Her parents were everything to her, but *nonno* and *nonna* had taken her in when there'd been no one else. They'd let her find her way back to her roots, renewed her faith in herself. She'd call them first.

"I love it when you smile." Aditya's voice was as soft as their blanket and just as warm. "Do you have your noisemaker and pepper spray?"

Bella showed him the items from her purse.

"Good."

Bella and Aditya held hands as they entered the largest memorial in DC, the one honoring President Roosevelt. This celebration of FDR's life spanned over seven acres and twelve years. Over one hundred thousand gallons of water flowed through four rooms that depicted each of his terms in office. And at the very beginning was a fifth room with a statue of him in a wheelchair, though the chair itself was masked by a cloak.

Aditya smiled as a family pushed their wheelchair-bound son past. Bella's security detail asked them to move along.

"You know, FDR didn't want to be seen like this," Aditya said. "He thought his disability made him less than and worked hard to conceal it from the public."

Bella scoffed. "Men are often quite dumb." They walked from the statue of the man to one showing a breadline, revealing the poverty that had accompanied the Great Depression. "It would've been nice for people to know that while they were suffering, so was their president, in his own way."

Squeezing her hand, Aditya led her to yet another room, where waterfalls crashed over boulders. "Fighting Nazis, solving the Depression... Maybe showing his weakness would've been a mistake, for how could a mere man be enough to tackle the challenges of the day?"

Bella kissed his cheek before responding, looping a piece of her wavy, chestnut hair around her ear. "*Amore mio*, what some see as weakness is really a way of humanizing people, and when we humanize our icons, we let others know that their greatness is possible for anyone to achieve."

Aditya sighed, reading one of the many quotes adorning the walls: *The only limit to our realization of tomorrow will be our doubts of today.*

"Humans are drawn to the mysterious over the mundane because it lets us off the hook," Bella said. "We want to believe that WP is what makes athletes gifted and the wealthy powerful, because if that's true, then we don't have to feel bad about all we haven't accomplished. But even before legalization, Jackie Robinson and Denzel Washington and Beyoncé all existed. All greatness can be learned."

Aditya turned to face her, his mouth agape. "Madame Justice, are you saying WP doesn't matter?"

She shushed him as her security detail warded off a group of nearby teenagers. "Of course it matters, but its real gift is taking away obstacles from people's lives, not injecting them with anything extra."

Spotting a vendor selling Greek food, Aditya kissed her on the cheek and motioned toward it. "That's enough philosophy for one day. Let's get out of here and let other families enjoy the memorial."

"Just one last thing," Bella said, walking to a mother and daughter she'd caught looking at her.

"My apologies, Madame Justice," the mother said. "We didn't mean to stare."

"It's my privilege to meet you," Bella said. Bending down, she asked the girl if she wanted a photo. The girl bounced with enthusiasm, so Bella hoisted the girl onto her shoulders as the mom snapped a picture with her cell phone.

Aditya and Bella's agents sighed audibly as Bella returned to them.

"I'm not going to live in fear," Bella said before Aditya could speak. "I made that family's day. That's what life's about."

Holding her hand as they walked to the food truck, Aditya changed the subject. "Speaking of families, I noticed an interesting name in your Instagram search history."

Bella bit her lip. "I gotta stop logging in on your phone."

"I told you Sadiya was off limits."

"Technically, you said you can't call her."

Aditya rolled his eyes. "Leave it to a lawyer to find a loophole. Tell me you haven't called her."

"No," Bella said. "I'll end my stalking here, for now. Although they do have the cutest girl."

"So will we, *amore mio*. One day."

Bella laughed. "Your accent is so bad."

She ordered for them and her agents, ignoring Aditya's feigned outrage as he motioned with a hand as if he were a button man for Don Corleone.

She let her security walk them back to the car they'd arrived in; they wouldn't eat, otherwise, unwilling to take their eyes off her for a moment as long as she was in public.

In the car, Aditya turned to her with a somber expression. "Nothing from the Medulla brothers?"

"It's been three weeks," she said. "Looks like Gianpaolo's threats were just talk."

"Still, keep an eye out."

As the car revved into gear, Bella licked some tzatziki sauce that'd dripped onto Aditya's lip. "Between you, the training you made me learn, and my agents, I'm bulletproof."

⸻

The Capitol Hill Club had a tunnel leading to a basement for only the most secretive meetings. Rumor had it that Teddy Roosevelt had murdered a man there that the then-owner had then helped him bury, and on windy nights, you could hear the dead man's whines.

Whit didn't believe in that bullshit, but did need an exclusive space in which to meet Oliver. Scratching his left arm, he laughed as the burly man squeezed his way out of the tunnel into the sparse room. Whit wondered if this place had been a prison at some point.

"You said you had the money?"

Tracing his fingers over the back of his shirt, confirming his gun was tucked into his waistband, White took out a piece of paper and handed it to Oliver. "Write your account and routing numbers down, and I'll make the transfer right in front of you."

Oliver's nostrils flared as he found a pen on a small table by their side. "I need to log in to my account to confirm."

Whit grinned. "You don't trust me?"

"I'd say I trust you as far as I can throw you, but I bet I could launch your ass into the sun."

Whit spat on the ground. "You crawl out first. Keep me captive in this hole until you check your account."

Oliver chewed his lip. It seemed like hours passed, but he finally nodded. "Okay."

Whit was so close. Do this right, and no one would ever call him a skingrafter again; they'd call him a queen maker. And queen slayer. Maybe Melissa would even realize she was lost without him. "First debate's in three days," he said. "Show me the photos."

They were beautiful in more ways than one. Bella Ferrari was stark naked in each one, vulnerable not just physically, but politically, too. Begaye's judgment would be ruined after these got out, and with it, Therese's chances. The first page of Whit Pryor's obituary would recount how he'd been essential in electing the first female president, and how only he could've ensured that barrier was broken by a Republican.

He bared his teeth as he admired the photos on the table. Bella's legs spread, a pout on her face as she lay on her back. On all fours, facing away, her head turned so the camera could capture her freckles and ass at the same time. A close-up of her standing, smiling as she squeezed those big tits together.

"Well done," Whit said, stashing the evidence in his jacket.

"These are just copies," Oliver said. "I'm keeping the originals."

"I'd expect no less."

After crawling out of the hole together, Oliver cornered Whit, watching like a hawk as he transferred the funds. "Looks like you kept your word."

"I'm a man of integrity," Whit said.

Grinning, Oliver took out his wallet. "You know, we don't have to leave things like this. I've got the funds and you've got the access."

Pretending to rummage through his back pocket, Whit made sure his gun was still there. "What'd you have in mind?"

"I've had the refined stuff my whole life, but how about I give you some company tonight and we hunt down some unrefined WP?"

Whit licked his lips. "I was so hoping you'd ask me for some."

Oliver had an oafish smile as Whit drew his gun. Shifting his weight so the tunnel was behind Oliver, he shoved the pistol into the man's gut and fired two rounds. The body slumped backwards, and Whit used his considerable strength to force it into the tunnel they'd just emerged from. He'd planned ahead, leaving a shovel in the basement to hide the body. But first, he had to push it back through the hole. It took several hours and left both him and the tunnel stained with blood, but he was able to finish the job.

He'd been right to take his jacket, slacks, and shoes off before starting. Shedding the rest of his clothes, he crawled back outside. It was past midnight, and he had enough clean clothes to walk a bit without arousing suspicion. He couldn't risk hailing a taxi, but his Super PAC's offices weren't far from here. He'd fitted the space with a shower and bed since he'd be working long nights, and now he was so glad he had. He'd wake up tomorrow morning in a bed with fresh clothes and tell Claire the good news. No one needed to know the specifics. Besides, Oliver had just gotten fifty thousand reasons to leave DC. It wouldn't be hard to convince people he'd skipped town for the Bahamas or Italy or wherever else.

President Roosevelt himself had buried a man here. Whit was merely following in the steps of greatness.

Chapter Seventeen

October 10, 2028

Kaitlin hadn't dreamed about her wedding day growing up, but Vijay had. To please him, she donned a red and gold sari while her beauty consultant, Emily, worked on her makeup.

"You look stunning!" Olivia said as she entered.

One of the rooms in Kaitlin's Utah mansion had been turned into a bridal suite. She would've preferred getting married somewhere else, but Vijay had wanted the ceremony to take place at one of their homes and she hadn't thought it'd be possible to fly them to India right now.

"Always the tone of surprise," Kaitlin said.

Olivia's sari was gold and black, mirroring her campaign colors. "We're up two in Wisconsin and Arizona. One in North Carolina and Georgia."

Emily stopped her work to meet Olivia's eyes. "Pennsylvania?"

"Stop it," Kaitlin said, cutting her staff off. "I wouldn't have invited you both if I'd known you'd just talk about the campaign."

Emily returned to curling Kaitlin's eyelashes. "Not *just* the campaign."

"Right," Olivia said. "We're also obsessed with how fire you look."

Kaitlin rolled her eyes. "I know you've got more on your mind when you start complimenting me. Say your piece."

Olivia spoke so fast her words would have tripped over themselves if they'd had legs. "I know you've said no to this four times already, but I really think you should reconsider not having the press here. Just one shot of you and Vijay together would get us two points in the swing states, and also, that sari is fierce and it's a crime not to show it off on Twitter, and okay, now I'm done."

Kaitlin grinned. "Nice try, but I told you we'll announce the wedding on our own terms later. Vijay and I value our privacy more than polls."

"I'm going to pretend I didn't hear that," Olivia said. Saluting her boss, she left the room to check on the Hindu priest they'd flown in from DC.

"Thanks for inviting us," Emily said, grabbing a mirror so Kaitlin could comment on her finished work. "But it is a little strange having just the two of us and Agent Hanson here, right? Didn't you picture a big fairytale wedding as a kid?"

Kaitlin shook her head. "There are practical reasons for keeping it small, too."

"Yeah?"

"The first debate is tomorrow. The press learns that I got married? That'll be what all the questions are about. Just another woman finding love, and how can a newlywed be focused on the country?"

"So... why today? Why not just wait a few more weeks?"

Kaitlin twirled her blonde hair; Emily had done a great job shifting her usual ponytail into a mermaid braid for the wedding. "I wanted to remind myself about what really mattered. Win or lose, I can't wait to start building the future I deserve."

Emily laughed. "Are you saying you're enough? Therese would be proud."

Kaitlin nodded. "Yes. And I'm also declaring to the world that what was broken becomes stronger today."

Emily opened her mouth to say more, but at that moment, Agent Hanson entered. "Madame Secretary, your groom's ready for you."

When Kaitlin stood up, her smile could've powered the entire state. "And I'm finally ready for us."

•———————————•

Vijay was stunning in his golden sherwani and salmon-colored dupatta. Kaitlin didn't understand the Sanskrit the priest had her repeat or why anyone would design clothing you couldn't wear without multiple safety pins, but she knew now what love was and it was nothing like she'd expected. She admitted to herself, though no one else would ever know, that victory on Election Day was merely a bonus at this point; she had what she needed.

"Congratulations, ma'am." Agent Hanson opened the door to the dressing room after the ceremony. She'd change before joining the others for a small reception.

"Thank you." She started unwrapping her sari the moment he closed the door. She'd just as soon wear a T-shirt and jeans tonight, but the purple dress Vijay had picked out was almost as comfortable. She'd just finished putting it on when Olivia burst through the door.

"Jesus Christ, Olivia, I could've been naked!"

"That would still be less shocking than what just hit Twitter!" She shoved her phone in Kaitlin's face.

A hashtag took over the entire screen: #ScotusSlutScandal.

Taking the phone from her manager, Kaitlin scrolled through the accounts. It was the same three photos, posted over and over and over again with the cruelest comments.

"I hope you enjoyed the ceremony, because you're missing the reception. The press is going to be on our ass immediately for a response, and if you want to keep this wedding a secret, we gotta catch the campaign plane *now*."

Kaitlin nodded, calling Vijay to tell him just how sorry she was as she, Olivia, and Agent Hanson drove to the jet waiting for them. She hadn't eaten a bite but was ready to hurl. This was not how her campaign was supposed to go. She was supposed to win clean. But perhaps that'd never been an option—only angels got to win clean, and angels had to die first.

Boarding the plane, sitting up front, she spotted an unexpected guest—a dead one.

Uncle Charles wore a grin wider than the Grand Canyon. "Victory is yours. Do you have what it takes to claim it?"

POSTERITY

"I am brave, I am bruised, I am who I'm meant to be, this is me."
– *The Greatest Showman*

Chapter One

October 10, 2028

Bella slept in nothing but her robe most nights. Tonight, she woke to Aditya's hardness pressed against her, his hand brushing her inner thigh, his hot breath on her neck as he kissed it. She gasped, rocking her ass against him. He pulled her robe up as she parted her legs and let him slide between them. Their moans grew louder the deeper he thrust inside her until they were like lions in heat, him pawing at her breasts and biting her neck and clawing at her sides.

After, she cleaned herself in the bathroom before returning to bed and grabbing her phone from her nightstand. Deep in the throes of passion, Bella had ignored the telltale chime of a text. When it rang in her hand with her customized ringtone for Senator Raghavan, though, a pit opened up in her stomach.

She answered, knowing trouble awaited. The woman was her best friend in DC, but that wasn't saying much, certainly not enough that she'd call after 10 p.m. unless it was an emergency.

"Kusum?"

The senator's voice was flatter than the Great Plains. "For the purposes of this conversation, you might find it easier to call me Senator Raghavan."

The pit in Bella's stomach grew into a chasm. "What's wrong?"

"Get on Twitter. Go to the trending topics section."

Sandwiching her phone between her neck and ear, Bella grabbed Aditya's phone from his hands and opened his Twitter account, ignoring his protests. Usually, his profile name (Gangsta4Life, some dumb inside joke he'd never explained) made her chuckle, but this time she went straight to the list of U.S.-wide trending topics.

The chasm widened until craters formed all along her insides, disrupting her ability to stand, to swallow, to breathe. Bella dropped both phones and made it three steps into the bathroom before vomiting into the toilet. She heard Aditya's shouts, felt his arms around her as he pulled her hair back. He always loved saying she smelled of honey, but the stench of her past returned once more to consume her.

This is the end.

One of Aditya's hands guarded her hair as she hurled again, and she heard him reaching to grab his phone with the other. He'd find the number one topic: #SCOTUSSlutScandal.

She hoped Twitter's policies forbade people to post the photos themselves, but who knew? It was so fucking dumb to have let anyone ever photograph her, but they'd paid three times her rate, sometimes four or even five. As far as they'd been concerned, if they could rent her body, they could also buy her privacy.

She flushed when she was finally done, throwing water on her face and hoping to wake herself from a nightmare. When it didn't work, she went back into her room to take her phone.

"What can you tell me?" Kusum was good enough to not mention the hurling or ask if she was okay. It would be several weeks, if ever, before Bella felt some semblance of okay.

Aditya scanned the search results on his own phone as Bella talked. "It's true; there's no point denying it."

"How large is the list of suspects?"

"Small. I only let a handful of guys take photos like that, and I've got all their names and social security numbers written down in my files."

"Give me that list. We'll make life hell for all of them."

Walking to the kitchen, Bella took a Parle-G biscuit from their cabinets and ate it to settle her stomach. "No."

"No?!" Kusum's tone was like a punch, but Bella's insides had evaporated and there was nothing left for the fist to connect with.

"This guy wants to become famous; I'm not going to let him."

Kusum let out a deep sigh. "There's a high chance this scandal will break both your marriage and you personally. Your life is about to become hell."

She knew. Her past had caused her to flee from Aditya once already. Maybe happiness was an illusion, but if that was the case, she'd face reality on her own terms. "My house has always been on the corner of Hell and Heaven." Her voice held resolve, but Kusum couldn't see her trembling lip or reddened face or flared nostrils. Aditya joined her in the kitchen, his hand resting on her shoulder as he continued scrolling through the comments.

"What news outlets have picked this up?" Bella said.

Kusum's tone lifted. "Luckily, none. No one seems to have the actual photos, and no reputable outlet is going to run a hit piece against a sitting Justice without seeing the evidence themselves. That being said, there's a whole ecosystem of far-right media that's made finding enough to run an article priority number one. I'd say you've got maybe twelve more hours to get ahead of this."

Bella began to pace, Aditya following, his hand attached to his shoulder in a poor attempt to massage her. "What does that mean?"

Kusum's explanation fell like bullets, fast and sharp. "An outrageous claim is made, one the *New York Times* couldn't possibly report on. But a few hours pass and some far-right blog on the fringes of society comments. Then FOX News books some whackjob the next day who happens to mention he read that blog post. So now FOX News can report on this second-hand madness they heard from one of their guests. Another day passes and more mainstream blogs comment on the madness. The insane claim is now bringing in ad revenue for all those outlets and gaining enough attention that some editor at the *Times* thinks the claim is newsworthy. Now, the *Times* still thinks it's a bullshit claim, but it's bringing in those sweet, sweet clicks at other outlets and so, while they refuse to comment on the actual claim, they are willing to report on the fact that all these people are talking about the claim, bringing it to an infinitely wider audience."

Bella sat on their couch, rubbing her temple as her elbows rested on her knees. Aditya sat at her side. "...that's the dumbest thing I've ever heard."

Kusum whistled. "Bella, things are about to get so dumb your hair will go gray. This is going to be a thousand times worse than the confirmation hearings."

She heard optimism in the senator's tone for the first time, and that alone gave her the first injection of strength she'd had since receiving the call, enough that her heart finally began to slow. "But?"

"But I'm aching for this fight. I'll be damned if a revenge porn scandal is going to allow Republicans to steal yet another election from us."

After heaving out her insides, there was nothing but steel left in her gut. "You have a plan?"

"I've been thinking as we've been talking," Kusum said.

Acutely aware now that she was still naked, Bella returned to her room to grab clothes from her closet, putting the phone on speaker so she could dress and allow Aditya to hear.

"Is there any video out there?"

"Absolutely not." She wouldn't even let Aditya film her.

"Are there other photos?"

"...maybe."

Kusum paused before speaking. "Well, how much worse could the photos get, right? The descriptions on Twitter seem graphic enough." She kept going when Bella didn't respond. "I'm sure we'll have plenty more awkward conversations, but for now I think I've got enough to stave off any calls for impeachment that may come from my caucus."

Bella's heart dropped. She hadn't even considered yet that Congress could impeach her. The fact of the matter was that Congress had a long leash when considering what was and wasn't worthy of impeachment.

"I won't lie," Kusum said. "Impeachment is a real possibility. But so far I've only heard it mentioned by one of my members."

Bella stood, her grief shifting from hopelessness to anger. "Senator Denton."

"Yes."

They were both whores, Bella realized, only she'd retired. He'd do whatever Famóre asked, as long as they continued to fill his coffers.

"Get some rest if you can," Kusum said. "And then wake up tomorrow and put on your sunblock, because the heat on you is going to be incredible."

Walking back to her bedroom, Bella sat down again on her bed, Aditya still at her side, one eye on her and the other on Twitter.

"Thanks for calling." She meant it. It would've been so much worse if she'd heard about it from the president, or the press, or, God forbid, her parents.

"We'll be in touch."

Bella wished her phone call could last forever, because when Kusum hung up she finally had to take in Aditya's entire face. The half-smile, the tilted head, the offer to make zuppa inglese (she did laugh at that suggestion; his baking was atrocious). She would've preferred his sadness or even anger to his pity.

Finally, he convinced her to eat something, putting together some yogurt rice from the evening's leftovers to calm her stomach.

"I can try and find the photos, if you want."

She lifted her plate to throw at him before forcing herself to stop. "Why would you say that?" Bella took grim satisfaction from seeing Aditya cringe. Knowing she could still wield an emotion like fear reassured her that she hadn't lost all her agency yet.

"It may help to know what we're up against."

But it wasn't him who was up against anything. It wasn't even Kusum. Bella was the one who'd become a punchline for late-night talk show hosts.

Aditya's voice wavered when he spoke again. "Some girl on Twitter said she saw the pictures. She says you're showing everything, but you're not having sex."

She thought a moment before responding. "That narrows it down a bit."

"I can make a couple calls and find the guy, rough him up."

Bella sighed. "What's the point? Besides, I don't want to give the public the satisfaction of suspecting I had someone whacked."

Turning off the light in their bedroom, Aditya laughed. The sound injected rage into Bella's veins.

"What is remotely funny about this?"

"You're clearly Italian," he said. "Most people would think the 'whacking' occurred while he looked at the photos."

Chapter Two

October 11, 2028

The University of Wisconsin's campus sat along the southern shore of Lake Mendota. What had been quite beautiful in the summer, just a few months ago, had frozen over for an unnaturally chilly October night. Therese and her team had bundled themselves into scarves and sweaters and now walked by a statue of the school's mascot, Bucky the Badger, before entering the theater which would serve as the venue for tonight's presidential debate.

"What do we know?" Therese had asked that question several times over the past hour. She'd dialed Bella's number this morning to check in on her friend, but Rebecca had torn the phone from her hand, saying, 'Bella can't feel pressured by a presidential candidate right now.' Therese had wanted to scream, to tell Rebecca to piss off, but the woman had been right. In this situation, Therese wasn't a friend. Bella had enough going on without political pressure adding to her shame; she shouldn't have to think about how her scandal weighed down Therese's chances this November.

"Miles is going to start the debate by asking both candidates about the scandal for sure," Rebecca said. She, Therese, Erica, and Gael were in a dressing room behind the stage. Therese heard students and adults alike begin to fill the auditorium as Erica put the finishing touches on her hair.

If the dictionary included phrases, Miles Parker's face would be under 'generic white guy.' In his sixties, he hosted the last political talk show in America that was actually watched by more than a few million people, *Poly Ticks*—a worn-out joke that politics came from the root words meaning 'many blood sucking insects.' Miles was seen as the last actual bipartisan arbiter in America; when he'd reported with righteous anger on President Brooks's betrayal of the country, Therese had known the former president would go down as persona non grata, even among Republicans.

A woman knocked at their door, then opened it without waiting for an answer. "Two-minute warning," she said. "Is the temperature okay? Need anything?" She held a clipboard and a headset.

Therese smiled. "Got a time machine connected to that headset? I'd like to talk to a young law student."

The woman made a sound that might've been a giggle, but it came out like nails on a chalkboard.

"Don't worry," Rebecca told Therese. "You'll do great!"

"How do you know?" Gael asked, before Therese could.

"Because there's no other option," Rebecca said. Handing Therese a bottle of water, she pushed her out the door, toward the big white lights on stage.

Miles made it seven minutes before mentioning Bella, allowing both Therese and Kaitlin to give opening statements first. Therese rattled off statistics about how the few private companies that'd been able to take advantage of WP legalization without access to federal or state funds were thriving, how as president, she'd offer federally backed loans of WP to companies at all levels in order to keep America at the forefront of global prosperity. Kaitlin spoke of a new birth of progress for America and the opportunity to turn the page on 'moral crises of old.'

Miles cleared his throat before asking the first question. "Thank you for those remarks, ladies, but we all came here tonight expecting one topic in particular to be addressed. This question is for both of you, but I'll ask Secretary Lungford first. Madame Secretary, I speak for the entire country when I say we were quite taken aback with the reporting on photos of Justice Ferrari. As president, would you ask Congress to pursue impeachment charges against her?"

Kaitlin answered immediately. "That's a question for Congress to pursue, and believe me, I'm doing everything in my power to make sure we have a Republican Congress again in November, so we can start turning the page."

The response drew some applause, seeming to rattle Miles, who was no doubt disappointed at her answer. "Madame Mayor, same question."

Therese sighed, her fingers squeezing the podium. "I agree with Kaitlin—that's a question for Speaker Munroe and Senator Raghavan."

Polite applause came from here and there, but the silence of the auditorium was far louder.

"Moving on from Congress, Kaitlin, what do you think failing to call out the Justice's behavior says to the young girls of America?"

Therese imagined hurling her podium at the man.

Again, Kaitlin's response was immediate, yet authentic. "I hope we can turn the page on the misogynistic tendencies of our past and highlight this scandal as what it is—revenge porn weaponized on a national level. I'd welcome a conversation about that."

The audience boomed to such a level that Miles reminded them to please hold any applause for the end of the debate. Therese saw a brief scowl on his face as he adjusted his bowtie. "Your thoughts, Madame Mayor?"

She didn't hesitate this time. "I think the young girls of America should grow up in a world where a man's cruelty is punished more aggressively than any mistakes of youth."

Therese's applause was as genuine as Kaitlin's this time. Rebecca and her husband, Russell, flashed her a thumbs-up from the front row. Still, her heart pounded and her face felt hot as rage clouded her eyes. The debate was only scheduled to last ninety minutes, and they'd already spent fifteen on Bella.

Families across America faced daily challenges regarding education and immigration, but Miles only saw a chance to slut-shame Bella on a national stage. The confidence of a mediocre white man would not be denied. "The whole world is watching," he said, "including, I hope, Justice Ferrari. Mayor Johnson, is there anything you'd like to say to her?"

Therese's vision tunneled. The thousand-plus-person audience disappeared, and the haze of anger turned into a tidal wave, drowning her in hopelessness. Bella's scandal. The scorn far-right bloggers and anonymous Twitter accounts had heaped on Jerome. The constant travel and loss of agency over her schedule. For months, she'd been the frog in the pot of water, getting just a little hotter each day. And now the heat was too much, and she was ready to burst.

"Miles, it isn't anyone's business but Bella's!"

Reporters from Tammy Day to Artie Quiver had searched relentlessly for a story about Therese losing her temper in Albuquerque, to no avail. She'd refused to be seen as the 'angry black woman.' Now, though, she'd picked a national stage to confirm everyone's worst thoughts about putting someone like her in power. And she didn't care. The relief of being able to shout her truth from the rooftop overwhelmed any other instinct, a cool salve over a body that'd endured the flames of righteous rage in silence for decades. "Are we here to talk about some woman's sex life, or are we here to debate the issues facing us each day? And we all know the truth about you, Miles. I don't need a morality lecture from anyone who voted for Lucas Brooks!"

Miles stuttered.

"While you're searching for your questions, let me ask a few of my own! Why does a Black graduate of an Ivy League school make as much money as a white graduate of a state school? Why do banks get away with undervaluing Black homes? Why did a zip code determine my son's educational potential?"

She'd scratched up her podium; her nails were chipped. She'd kept most mentions of Jerome to a private group chat with moms who'd gone through similar tragedies, but Miles had burst something within her. She'd liked it for a moment, but now, staring out into the audience, her tunnel vision faded. She did her best to hold back tears, suddenly feeling as if she were the naked one instead of Bella.

She bowed her head, said a prayer, and bit her lip so hard it bled, then licked her lips to keep it from showing on TV.

"Madame Mayor?"

She emerged with a smile the entire world must know was fake, and yet they accepted it at face value, because it allowed them to avoid the hard conversations. "I'm sorry. Let's move on."

Everyone pretended like nothing happened. It wouldn't be until the morning shows tomorrow and the battleground-state polls later in the week that the true extent of self-inflicted damage would be revealed. Miles went on to ask questions about furthering WP legalization, as if their answers would lead the conversation, and both Therese and Kaitlin played along. Kaitlin offered up the brown soldier attacking her as a reason for limiting WP use to sanctioned military officials (read: white officials), and evidence that Congress should continue to refrain from funding an Undersecretary for Drug-Enhanced Commerce for each department under the U.S. government. Therese spoke again of the need to have those positions so that the Department of Housing and Urban Affairs or Commerce or any other department could form the public-private partnerships necessary to extend loans at the federal and state level to companies working to keep America leading in innovation, that failing to do so gave up economic superiority to countries like China.

Therese felt ninety minutes stretch into ninety hours, but thankfully the night did eventually end. She couldn't remember what she'd said in her closing statement, but recalled shaking Kaitlin's hand before they both left the stage. Kaitlin squeezed her hand twice—a gesture borne either of pity or solidarity.

Gael and Erica weren't present when Therese returned to her dressing room. Russell waited next to Rebecca, kissing Therese on the lips before excusing himself to their hotel. "I'll stay up for you," he said.

Rebecca was on her as soon as the door closed. "I've done a lot of debate spin in my career, but that shit made me dizzy."

"Can you just... not?"

The weight of the world was already suffocating her. And as if that wasn't enough, she hated herself for being this weak here, in the final month of the campaign, when people were counting on her most.

"I can't just not, Therese." Rebecca was half a foot shorter than her, but her tone made up those missing six inches. Her chin dimple followed Therese like the evil eye as she shook her head.

"All America will remember tonight is the angry Black lady screaming at them. How could you be so stupid?"

Therese's nails dug into her palms as she formed fists at her side. For the second time tonight, she took pleasure in her rage. "Who the fuck do you think you're talking to?"

Rebecca's bravado evaporated like water exposed to a hot pan.

"It's Mayor Johnson or Madame Mayor or the next President of the United States, as far as you're concerned. You think I don't know what I did tonight? You think I got this far in life by accident?"

Rebecca stepped back, finding a chair and sitting as Therese loomed closer. "You ever talk to me that way again, and I'll make sure you can't find a job managing a dog catcher's campaign."

Silent tears rolled down Rebecca's cherubic face, and Therese enjoyed seeing them fall.

"You just can't help yourself. For all the work you've put in, your privilege bleeds out of you at times like pus, a scab you just can't help but pick at when times get tough."

"...I'm sorry."

"...I know." And just like that, just like on stage, Therese's anger left her and she felt naked again. After a flame exhausted itself, there was nothing left but emptiness.

"Emotions are high, to say the least." Therese wiped her makeup off. "Get some rest, and we'll talk tomorrow."

She walked out before giving Rebecca time to respond.

In the car, she finally took out her phone and checked her group chat. The moms she'd brought into her confidence were from all over the country. Their messages of support ranged from righteous anger to uninhibited joy, lauding her hair and outfit as well as her talking points. Not one of them mentioned her outburst. Reading through them, she actually laughed. This was her North Star, these women and Russell. And Jerome. If she did right by them, nothing else mattered.

Alone at last, she let herself cry until her security brought her back to the hotel.

Chapter Three

October 12, 2028

Kaitlin's honeymoon had consisted of joining the mile-high club on her campaign plane as she'd flown from Utah to Wisconsin for last night's debate. Olivia had shielded her from facing any press in the immediate aftermath of Bella's problems (she refused to latch on to calling it the #SCOTUSSlutScandal), but unless she wanted to cede all media attention to the Democrats, she needed to start talking to someone with a microphone. And so she found herself this morning at a rented office space, sitting in a chair in front of Tammy Day. As she'd predicted, the woman had found (fucked?) her way into leading a show on FOX. Kaitlin hoped the fact that Tammy was a college dropout—who'd risen to prominence thanks to Kaitlin granting her an interview after the attack during her rally—meant she'd be able to control Tammy's narrative. She wanted her to focus on actual issues of importance instead of Bella.

Not that she didn't have an opinion about Bella. Sexting wasn't dumb; God knew what'd happen if someone ever hacked Vijay's phone. But allowing a client to do that? That was breathtakingly stupid. Still, she had a unique appreciation for the inclination to want to outrun one's past; the memory of her uncle's ghost from the plane still lingered in her mind.

"Don't worry," Tammy said, perhaps interpreting Kaitlin's frown as nervousness about the interview. "This'll be nothing compared to the wars you've been in."

She hated when people compared politics to war, but

understood the impulse. Everyone liked to think of themselves as brave soldiers, willing to bleed for right and wrong. But words were cheap.

Tammy smiled as the cameras flashed on, and Kaitlin didn't miss a beat before flashing her own TV smile.

"Good morning, Wisconsin! Last night's debate was eventful, to say the least. I had to wash down all that tension with a beer and some cheese curds. Here to join me today is none other than Secretary Lungford. Madame Secretary, thanks so much for joining us, especially with less than four weeks to go until Election Day."

"Thanks for having me." Luckily, her lack of enthusiasm for these interviews was eclipsed by her height. Kaitlin was six-foot-one, and people assumed her reserved nature was part of a "strong and silent type" personality. It annoyed interviewers, but her team's polls revealed it resonated with single women, a constituency usually abandoned to Democrats. She wouldn't win them, but making inroads could be enough to win states like North Carolina and Georgia.

"The question at the top of my mind doesn't actually have anything to do with the debate. Viewers, I just found out this morning that we have reason to celebrate! Can someone bring out the cake?"

Someone rolled out a cake from offstage. It had a photo embossed on top, of Kaitlin and Vijay, with lettering that said, 'Congratulations on your marriage!'

Kaitlin's nostrils flared. Pinching her thigh, she forced herself to stay calm and regained control of her body after a moment.

"Now who told you that?" Kaitlin asked, with a sing-songy voice she'd never used before but hoped people would attribute to newfound wedded bliss. When she got her answer, she'd throw that person out a window.

"Oh, I've got my sources." Tammy clearly hadn't noticed Kaitlin's rage. "I would've done something grander than the local grocery store, but I really did just find out an hour ago."

"This is perfect," Kaitlin said, taking the knife Tammy handed her and reminding herself it was for the cake and not Tammy.

The cake was rolled away after a ceremonial cutting. "Our

viewers don't want to see us having our cake and eating it, too," Tammy joked. "Now, to the topic at hand. How about that debate?"

"I'm looking forward to the others," Kaitlin said. "Unfortunately, we weren't able to focus on substantive issues last night."

"I'd have to respectfully disagree, Madame Secretary," Tammy said. "You came out looking like such a bad ass."

Kaitlin knew from focus groups that it was a word used frequently to describe her: bad ass. She knew it was true, but like all things political, it wasn't seen as true until a majority of voters agreed.

Tammy continued. "I mean, I hope Vijay takes your last name. Vijay Lungford sounds better than Vijay Shankar anyways."

Kaitlin bit her tongue before responding. "We haven't had that conversation yet."

"Well, it is so nice to see one presidential candidate leaning into that female bad ass image that's gained such popularity these days. Especially with Democrats so obsessed with being angry."

Kaitlin kicked herself in the shin to keep from scolding Tammy. It was enough to hear men like Artie Quiver attack Therese for being an angry Black woman, but to hear it from a young woman just beginning to shape her career filled Kaitlin's heart with rage.

"I just think anyone who votes against you at this point must be nuts. You are such an inspiration, and so respectable, unlike other women in positions of power. You took it way too easy on Justice Ferrari last night."

Kaitlin flashed her fake smile once more. "Oh, Tammy, you're not gonna rope me into that conversation."

Tammy laughed. "Well, I had to try."

The rest of the interview was harmless enough. Kaitlin regurgitated her standard talking points on what kintsugi meant to her and why she'd run for president. Her mind drifted to Vijay and what they'd order for dinner that night, until Tammy ended the interview with one last barb. "I want to thank Secretary Lungford for joining us today." She turned to face Kaitlin. "I've said it before and I'll say it again: you have elevated the reputation of all women by running, and I think we'll fall far behind if Therese wins and excuses the kind of behavior we've seen from Democrats like

Bella."

Kaitlin smiled once more before taking off her mic and leaving for her dressing room.

Olivia handed Kaitlin a slice of cake as she walked through the door.

Kaitlin refused to take it. "How can you eat?"

Olivia spoke with her mouth full. "It wasn't me that just had to pretend to be nice to that sanctimonious bimbo."

Kaitlin laughed. "I can't believe I helped her get FOX."

Olivia threw her empty plate in the trash. "Don't feel too bad. You may have accelerated the process, but she was always going to end up at FOX. She's a conservative woman whose legs are long, hair is blonde, and head is empty."

Kaitlin chuckled. "I don't know what I'd do without you, Olivia Stoneburner."

Olivia's eyes found her shoes. "Well, at any rate, you just kept Wisconsin alive for us. Latest poll has us up two."

"Cracked fifty percent?"

"Not yet, but forty-seven isn't bad."

Kaitlin sighed. "We've been at forty-seven for months."

"So has Therese," Olivia said. "How many years did you date Vijay before deciding to marry him? People always come home at the home stretch."

"Does that mean I'm at the end of the line? The home stretch?"

"It's not a perfect metaphor," Olivia said.

Kaitlin rolled her eyes. "How did Tammy learn about Vijay?"

Olivia's back went as straight as her raven hair. "I do have an answer to that. One of his buddies is dating a producer on Tammy's show."

Kaitlin cricked her neck. "I hope it wasn't Tim. I actually like him."

"It was someone named Chad."

Kaitlin smiled. "I'm gonna enjoy telling Vijay. Chad's the worst." She cut herself a slice of cake. "Fuck it. I deserve carbs and sugar for enduring this mess."

"Want me to wrap up the rest?"

"Leave it for the crew, but take a slice for Emily." She'd given her beauty consultant an indefinite leave of absence upon learning her dad was sick. Olivia would cross paths with her on the flight back to headquarters.

Sitting, Kaitlin swallowed a bite before continuing. "Obviously, Bella's a mess. And Therese was out of line. But my wedding shouldn't be an opportunity for others to use my happiness to frame against other women's problems. Life isn't a zero-sum game."

Olivia nodded, letting her candidate vent.

"Can't my happiness belong only to me? Just because I'm a public figure, does that mean literally my entire life is up for public scrutiny? Every second of ever day?"

Kaitlin shoved a second bite of cake in her mouth, knowing it was as close to a satisfying answer as she would get.

Chapter Four

October 12, 2028

Bella's father hadn't been able to resist smiling the first time she'd told him about a fight she'd had with Aditya after getting married. When she'd asked why he looked so smug, he'd reminded her how he'd disapproved of Aditya as a child.

"I thought that was because he was brown," she'd said.

"It was because he was breathing and I knew he'd hurt you one day. Because everything worth doing will hurt you. You just have to decide if the pain is worth it."

He'd said if she was hurt enough to tell him and still stay married, he knew the pain was worth it. He knew their love would last.

Aditya was testing that theory now.

That afternoon, Bella and Aditya watched Kaitlin's interview from the couch in their apartment in New York, where they could control the press frenzy a little more. The bellman was making a whole second salary from tips paid to ensure no one got inside the building unless they were a resident.

Turning off the TV, Bella huffed. "Kaitlin gains a half point in some swing state every time she defends me."

Aditya rolled his eyes. "That bitch."

They'd been fighting nonstop ever since Bella'd told him she didn't want to track down whoever had taken the photos. Aditya's apoplexy about the situation remained, and, unable to turn his rage on the culprit, he'd settled for the victim.

Bella closed her eyes and took a breath as she prepared herself for yet another brawl, but before they got into it, her phone rang. "Yes?

The scowl on her face dissipated as quickly as she shifted from English to Italian. It was her *nonna.* Setting the phone on speaker, she walked around the room as Aditya followed behind. It wasn't the frenetic pacing of a woman on a mission, but the soft gait of someone talking to their best friend. She was overjoyed to speak of cooking and her career instead of the #SCOTUSlutScandal.

Her *nonno's* voice broke in after a few minutes. "She's a smart girl. She knows why we're calling."

"Hai problemi lì?" The press had already badgered her parents so much that they'd taken their phone off the hook. They'd lost friends over the photo incident, but Bella hadn't thought to ask her grandparents if they were having trouble, too.

"Faremo un viaggio in America," he said.

"I don't need a babysitter," Bella said. "There's no reason for you to come on my account."

"We're telling you," *Nonna* said. "We're not asking."

"Besides," *Nonno* interjected, "it's no good for your parents in Jersey right now. They said they'd come over to watch the house while this whole thing plays out."

Bella bit her lip, forcing herself not to cry, since she knew her tears of gratitude would be interpreted differently. She nodded before realizing her grandparents couldn't see her, and merely told them thank you.

"Family doesn't need to say thanks," *Nonno* said. "It's self-evident. *Ti amiamo e vogliamo stare con te."*

She stayed on a bit longer to get their flight details; they'd be here in three days. Hanging up, she turned to Aditya. "I don't want to fight anymore."

Aditya's shoulders relaxed. "Me neither. I'm just so angry all the time."

Bella smiled. "Such a strong man. So used to control. But this, the adoption process, living in DC part time? There's no control, and it's scary for both of us."

Her words were soft, but looking at the bedsheets on the side of the couch where he'd slept, the anger she'd unleashed last night resurfaced. He'd called her a whore. Blamed her for taking the photos because "some asshole offered to up her rate." How easily he forgot how he'd suggested using her particular skillset to steal his company so many years ago.

She'd yelled back just as fiercely, unleashing fire on him since she could never turn it on its rightful subjects. "You don't seem to mind when I send *you* photos of my tits."

"I'm your husband!"

He'd said it as if being a wife meant you were your husband's property. She'd thrown him a sheet and a pillow at that point, telling him to sleep on the couch, then locked their bedroom door. But she missed his scent, his touch, even his smug smile. If he was ready to apologize, she'd hear him out.

"I'm sorry," he said. "I know it's not your fault. I chose this life and I'd choose it again."

"Go on," she prompted. "I know you can do better."

"I was childish. It's your body, and it's our life. We both did what we had to, and thank God we did because it brought us here, together."

She drew near enough for him to take her hand; he took the opportunity and squeezed, rubbing his fingers over her knuckles. "And every time you feel the impulse to show off that body, I want you to take it. Society does enough to condemn women for feeling good about themselves."

Bella laughed, able to joke and let happiness inside her, knowing her grandparents would be here soon. "You just want more photos."

"Can you blame me?"

They kissed, her fingers running down his frame as she pressed herself against him.

"Does this mean I can stop sleeping on the couch?"

She smirked. "Yes, but you're on probation until you can prove you're not an idiot."

"Good thing I have my whole life to do that."

●————————————●

Whit Pryor's insomnia proved useful during election season;

tonight was spent eating cheesesteaks while editing ads in his office. Cutting the latest TV spot to exactly sixty seconds, he didn't even notice as cheese dripped onto his shirt. Rather, his attention was on the video testimonials of single female minorities talking about how great Kaitlin Lungford was for standing up for "traditional families and the American way of life." It was a tale as old as time—"traditional families" and the "American" way of life were code for "not Black." With any luck, the average voter would see it as a dig against not just Therese, but Bella, as well. Not many traditional families used whores.

Speaking of whores, he thought of Kajal and picked up his phone, his slacks tightening. It'd been almost two weeks since he'd last enjoyed her company. But when he rang her number, it went straight to voicemail. Staring at his empty cheesesteak wrapper, staring at the breadcrumbs, he ran a hand over the WP-encrusted buttons on his shirt sleeves and listened to his heart race.

Was Kajal avoiding his calls?

Did she know Claire didn't love her?

Did she know she was to blame for Bella's public shaming?

Did she know Oliver was dead?

Whit bit his lip so hard it bled, forcing himself to focus on that and nothing else. There was no way for her to know any of that, especially about Oliver. It'd been days since he'd murdered the guy, and the incident hadn't even shown up in the *Washington Post*'s daily police blotter. Still, his hands shook as he gripped his phone so hard it creaked. When it rang, he swore at the empty room and dropped it. Swearing again, he picked it up. "Hello?"

"You don't have my number saved?" It seemed as if Senator Hammond's southern drawl was a physical entity, wrapping around Whit's body, prepared to squeeze him like a boa constrictor.

"Forgive me, Senator," Whit said. "It didn't show up. Damn phones from China."

The senator's laugh stretched on for ages and reminded Whit of Emperor Palpatine's. "You know what an American-made phone would cost? Let the Chinese build us our toys; we'll focus on the real stuff: missiles and cars and food."

Whit stayed quiet; his old boss loved the sound of his own

voice. What politician didn't?

"You still at work?"

"Yes, Senator."

"Good," Hammond said. "We need some new ads. This Bella stuff isn't moving polls as much as it should."

"I'm editing a sixty-second spot about it right now," Whit said, explaining the subtlety of having non-white women passing judgment on her.

"Subtlety would work if Kaitlin was actually talking about the scandal," Senator Hammond said. "We need ads from a Super PAC to be as subtle as a baseball bat to the head."

Whit muted the phone, taking in a deep breath and releasing it before unmuting. He didn't feel guilty about killing Oliver, but the fear of being caught, mixed with his insomnia, had wrecked his heart over the past couple days; his blood pressure this morning had been 160/92.

"What do you want me to do?" He'd never deny his boss, the man who'd given him a seat at the table and was positioned to be Majority Leader of the U.S. Senate once again.

"You think I can't guess you played some role in the photos getting out?"

Whit muted the phone again, taking an audible gulp before unmuting it again.

"You underestimate my intelligence at your own peril, son."

Son. Senator Hammond was more than a friend, more than a boss: the man was basically his father. He'd never disappoint him.

"Get those pictures on the Internet. I will not fold a straight flush because of some bitch's ethics."

He hung up before Whit could respond.

He was so close to having it all. He'd told Claire that Oliver was in Europe, spending his newfound cash and waiting out the election. He'd given up the month of October to Melissa and gotten a two-week trip to Africa with his son in return. And now he was on the precipice of having his old job back: Chief of Staff to the U.S. Senate Majority Leader.

Scratching at his nose, Whit licked his lips in anticipation.

Chapter Five

October 13, 2028

From backstage at her latest rally, Kaitlin heard the roar of tens of thousands of people awaiting her at Topiary Park in Columbus, Ohio. Still, the one person she cared about wasn't here: Vijay. Once she was president, they'd honeymoon properly in Greece. The birthplace of democracy would be an excellent spot for the first female president to make her first trip. And he deserved the world; just this morning, he'd called to tell her that, despite spilling the beans about their wedding to Tammy Day, Chad had still had the balls to call Vijay up and ask him for an intro with Bella. Vijay's righteous indignation, his ability to stay pure despite being by Kaitlin's side for over a decade, it gave her hope that she really was more than her worst moments. If someone as good as him loved her...

Kaitlin's thoughts were pierced by a phone call; she rolled her eyes when she saw who it was. "I can't talk long, Senator. Governor Shimizu is about to bring me onstage."

"Then I'll keep it quick," Hammond said. "Quick question: why the fuck are you ceding the moral high ground to a whore?"

"Be careful, James," she hissed. "You're talking to the next President of the United States."

He sighed before responding, desperation in his voice. "You think anyone's gonna elect you after you blow this thing?"

Refusing to dignify his comment with an answer, she waited until he continued.

"Look, I'm just giving it to you straight. My staff is on the phone weekly with the newly energized youth leaders who loved President Brooks's 'Team USA' propaganda."

"You mean neo-Nazis?" Kaitlin said. She'd just as soon expel those new people from the Party.

"I mean voters," Hammond snapped. Sighing again, he continued. "They're giving me shit over you picking an Asian woman for VP, but I can manage that. It's not just them, though. The megachurches were on my ass over you picking a lesbian to manage your campaign, and now you not wanting to hit Bella over this photos thing is grinding them down to their last nerve."

"Then tell them to find someone else to vote for." Kaitlin smiled, almost wishing she was with Hammond in person to see him pulling out his hair in frustration.

"You think you're funny? You're gonna lose Nevada, Arizona, maybe even Wisconsin if you keep alienating racist white men."

Kaitlin couldn't contain her laughter at that remark. "Ever think we need a new base, if that's the case?"

Hammond's answer came out through gritted teeth. "It is what it is."

She'd done this while her uncle was alive, complicitly supporting the racist and misogynistic candidates he backed. Showing up at fundraisers for them if she was in town. Offering the occasional quote slamming Democrats on military funding, as if that was a reason to vote for an outright xenophobe. But no more. The presidency deserved better. Vijay deserved better. She deserved better.

Gritting her own teeth, she was about to tell the senator just that when she heard Mirai announce, "My friend, and the next President of the United States!"

"Well, James, as fun as this talk has been, I gotta go." She hung up without waiting for his response, flashing a smile for the cameras as she got onstage.

⎯⎯⎯⎯⎯⎯●⎯⎯⎯⎯⎯⎯

Governor Shimizu's chief of staff was from Columbus and knew the owner of the Indian fusion restaurant Kaitlin found herself at with Mirai that night. The restaurant was cleared of all other guests so they could have a bit of privacy and still enjoy a nice dinner before going their separate ways. With just a few weeks to go until Election Day, a grueling campaign schedule for both of them meant time for sharing meals together was sparse, and Kaitlin wanted to form a genuine friendship with the woman before assuming office. She sipped on a cocktail consisting of paan-infused vodka, lime, and bitters. The heat of the betel leaves complemented the tartness of the lime.

"Are we going to talk about it?" Mirai adopted a tone hotter than Kaitlin's drink.

"I thought the rally went well," Kaitlin said.

The governor's nostrils flared. "That's not what I meant."

"I know." Kaitlin sighed. She'd been avoiding her vice-presidential nominee for as long as possible, eager to postpone this conversation, but wishing something away didn't make it disappear.

"You're fucking up the campaign." Mirai spoke as plainly as she had that day in the governor's mansion, when she'd convinced Kaitlin she was worth elevating to the vice presidency.

"You sound like Hammond."

"The Republican leader in the Senate?" Sarcasm dripped from the governor's lips. "Why would I ever want to listen to the most powerful Republican in Washington?"

Kaitlin had given herself a pep talk in the car on the way to this dinner in case her nerves got the better of her. She suspected she was failing Mirai, denying a woman of color an honest-to-God shot at unbridled power, but to run this race any other way than how she wanted would be to fail herself. And those days were over. "I always said you could be straight with me, so let's hear it."

Mirai stabbed her fork into a piece of paneer, perhaps wishing it was Kaitlin. "Where do I begin? Let's start with the debate and your refusal to talk about Bella."

"How is it relevant to what we're trying to do?"

"How is it not?!" Mirai pointed the fork accusingly. "Don't give me some bullshit about morality; it's about poor decision making."

"Therese didn't appoint her."

"But Democrats did!"

Kaitlin rolled her eyes. "And my uncle gave his blessing."

Mirai looked like the steam from their dishes would exit

through her ears. "Don't get me started on him."

"You know there's no love lost between us. Say your piece."

Mirai chewed before setting her fork down. "Developing a conscience on your deathbed doesn't cleanse you of all your sins. He's not Anakin Skywalker."

Kaitlin scanned the empty room, halfway expecting her uncle's ghost to appear. Relieved, she turned back to the governor. "Believe me, I don't forgive him his past sins."

"But you've allowed that perception to last. When the press was enthralled and reprinting his regrets over past sins, I don't remember you giving any context as to what the real-world implications of committing those sins were."

Kaitlin frowned. "Mirai, I had a race to run..."

"And you chose the most convenient time to dissociate yourself from your uncle, after his death." Mirai's laugh was cold enough to chill their food. "White royalty like you will never understand what my family gave up to be here, to give me this seat at the table."

Kaitlin gripped the table, leaning back as if she'd been slapped. "You want the truth?" Her voice began to climb. "When my team put names of vice-presidential candidates in front of me, I didn't even consider your race. It didn't matter to me at all that you're Asian."

"I bet it didn't."

"What's that supposed to mean?"

Mirai stood, leaning toward Kaitlin so that their noses almost touched. "It means my race matters! Being Asian matters. For fuck's sake, it's been less than a hundred years since a U.S. President declared my entire race traitors and locked us up! My son's classmates can't decipher whether he's Japanese or Chinese or Korean to this day; I have to hear about how some of them make funny accents around him or joke about his food to his face."

Kaitlin opened her mouth, but Mirai didn't give her an opportunity to speak.

"Are we going to establish a national tax credit to fund movies and TV shows lifting up non-whites? Are we going to lean on the state parties to start recruiting more diverse candidates no matter what? Of course not! But what we can do is hit Democrats on being complicit in elevating a woman like Bella. What we can do is use every advantage we have to elect me and maybe move the ball five feet forward toward progress."

Mirai was shaking. Eyeing a waiter approaching with dessert (jaggery ice cream), Kaitlin motioned to him to bring it over, using his presence as an excuse to motion to Mirai to sit back down.

A rush of emotions hit Kaitlin like a tidal wave. But she forced herself not to speak until the impact passed, trusting that Mirai wouldn't care for her tears and knowing that her sadness was nothing compared to what Mirai and her family had suffered. "You're right," she said. "But don't you think you deserve more than five feet of progress? We won't lose; Americans will appreciate us showing grace to another woman. And even if I do lose, it'll be my loss, not yours. You'll be the nominee four years from now."

Mirai scoffed. "Republicans won't elect an Asian woman to go up against the first Black president. They'll retreat back to racism." She took a large scoop of the ice cream, finishing it and chewing as if in combat. "This was our chance to sneak progress into the Party, and you blew it. You'll have to live with that the rest of your life."

Kaitlin frowned. "There are worse things to live with." Like the ghosts of the past. Because she knew now: her silence over Bella was what would make Charles's ghost leave her. She'd been served the presidency on a platter, but it was a Faustian bargain and she would not take it like he would. "If the Party needs to be tricked to accept progress, then maybe it doesn't deserve to exist."

Mirai dabbed her lips with her napkin before responding. She was demure in public, but behind closed doors even an act like wiping her face made her look like a pit viper ready to strike. "You can't possibly be that naïve."

Kaitlin didn't want to end their dinner on such a sour note, but she owed it to herself and her nominee to understand America better. Because that was who they were: the old and new faces of America having an honest conversation together. And understanding each other was the only way to progress beyond those five feet. "Do you actually think Bella is in the wrong?"

Mirai's lip curled. "Why shouldn't Bella suffer for her mistake?"

Kaitlin blinked. She'd thought Mirai an opportunist this whole time, but did the woman also genuinely hold Bella in disdain? "That's bullshit to call it a mistake," she said. "She's just owning her sexuality. Aren't we beyond slut-shaming as a country? Photos like that exist for almost every woman."

Mirai remained unmoved. "Not me. How about you?"

Kaitlin didn't answer. "I just don't want to win dirty."

Mirai stood, clearly ready to leave. She paid the bill, leaving a generous tip before walking out the door, leaving Kaitlin to follow. It was raining, big sheets falling on them as they huddled together under one umbrella. As they waited outside for their cars (Mirai had a rally in Phoenix tomorrow while Kaitlin would stay in the Midwest), Mirai responded. "There's no such thing as winning clean or winning dirty—only winning."

Agent Hanson wasn't driving just Kaitlin back to her hotel. Her uncle's ghost was seated beside her in the backseat of the Black suburban.

"Ironic," he said, still sounding like he'd swallowed sandpaper and was trying to throw it up. "Even though the Asian woman is willing to take down the Black woman, she can't get racism to work for her without the white woman's cooperation."

Kaitlin closed her eyes, taking deep breaths and trying to expel him from her mind, but when she opened them, her uncle was still there. She shivered as he placed his hand on her knee. A chill ran through her whole body.

"Relax," he said. "I'm just along for the ride."

She sat in silence the rest of the journey, doing nothing, just hoping the situation would resolve itself.

Chapter Six

October 14, 2028

Luther Aldrich played pick-up football twice a month with three of his old buddies at Stanford. Of course, "old" was only a word used in your thirties if you'd spent your twenties being battered around on a football field or in the political trenches. Luther had suffered both.

Nothing in the DMV (DC, Maryland, and Virginia) beat the greenery and views of Great Falls National Park. It'd rained last night, so the grass was slippery enough that a strong kicker like Jeff might throw away a few points. And the mud meant Dwight would play conservatively, keeping the game tight without attempting his aggressive plays.

The game of two-on-two set Luther and Jaime against Jeff and Dwight. It'd been three-on-one in the past, but since legalization, they could all wear WP now while playing.

Of course, that meant the game had to become harder. It had taken the NFL two years to agree to revised rules that accommodated everyone, but now games were played with three main differences that made the game seem like a blend of football and Quidditch: large physical objects (e.g., a stone wall so you couldn't just throw the ball one hundred yards straight through the goal post), a goalie, and strict limits on the amount of WP a player could bring onto the field.

For Luther's amateur games, the four friends settled on carrying one small object with WP each, and a larger playing field.

They'd gotten lucky today; no one else was in their area of the park, so the game was played over three hundred yards.

Jaime snapped the ball to Luther before taking off. Jaime wasn't strong, but his WP-covered shoelaces propelled him forward to catch the ball Luther threw ninety yards. Luther smirked until Dwight slammed into Jaime like a truck, launching him fifteen feet.

Luther ran to Jaime's side, relieved he hadn't hit a tree. "How many fingers am I holding up?"

"Fuck you, I'm fine." Standing up, Jaime cricked his neck as Dwight and Jeff joined them.

"Sorry," Dwight said. "I lose myself to the game."

"First and ninety, right?" Jaime shoved Dwight, smiling at the same time so Luther knew he was okay.

"We're a bit too close to the ravine," Luther said, indicating the nearby gorge. He heard the rapids, the splash of paddles as people kayaked below. "Frisbee instead?"

"You forfeiting?" Jeff asked.

Luther laughed. "Sure, man. You win."

When the four of them returned to Luther's backpack, he took out the Frisbee and told Jaime to go long.

"I could go long with Bella," Jeff joked. "All night long, that is."

"Knock it off," Luther said, nostrils flared. "We don't talk business, remember?"

Jeff smirked, his hands in his shorts. "This isn't business," he said. "It's pleasure. I'm just saying, if the White House is gonna cut her loose, send her to me."

"What are you even talking about?" Dwight asked. "She's married."

"Didn't look married in those photos," Jeff said.

Luther gripped his Frisbee so tight it broke. "You saw them?"

"All of them," Jeff said. "And she didn't look married; she looked open for business. It's true Anaba's friends with her, right? Just ask her to do an intro."

Luther lost it and threw a left jab. Jeff wouldn't have been able to dodge if he hadn't been wearing WP. As it was, the fist cuffed his shoulder, sending him to the ground. Luther moved to connect his right foot with the man's head, but Jeff rolled out of the way before launching himself back up to land on his feet and throwing his right fist toward Luther. Jeff was bigger than him, but Luther had more experience with WP. Stepping back, he grabbed Jeff's shoulder and flipped him back on to the ground.

"Have you lost your mind?!" Jeff got up, ready to throw another punch before Dwight got involved, holding him back as Jaime did the same with Luther.

"Shut up about my wife!"

"You aren't married yet, remember?"

"And don't bother coming to the wedding." Luther could've pushed Jaime aside, taken another swing at Jeff. But sense was returning to him.

"What a shame," Jeff said, sarcasm and rage in his tone. "I so wanted to be there." Shrugging Dwight off, he stormed away.

"He's been different since he upped his WP dosage," Dwight said. "He's like Icarus, getting so close to the sun he can't see the danger in front of him."

Luther let out a mirthless laugh. "He's gonna get fired if he doesn't see it soon. NASA doesn't have tolerance for drug addicts."

Dwight sighed. "I know you went out on a limb to get him that job, and I appreciate it. I'll try talking to him."

Luther sighed. "You've been with him since before Stanford, but he's not your brother. You don't have to stick with him through the bad times."

"Family's more than blood," Dwight said. "He needs me, especially through the bad times."

They were supposed to have lunch at Taco Bamba after, but Luther preferred being with Anaba. "I'll catch you guys later."

He headed toward the parking lot, but Jaime threw out a question before he got far. "If an intervention is needed for Jeff, are you going to be there?"

Luther rubbed his face. "Call me if it happens. Game day decision."

●————————————————————————————●

Even after seven years, President Joseph Begaye never tired of flying on Air Force One. It could be refueled in midair, giving the president close to twelve hours of uninterrupted time as he returned from Finland, but he rarely slept in-flight. How could he sleep while charged with the safety of hundreds of millions of people?

The stress of being president and the fact he was almost sixty had turned his hair gray, but he'd never complain. Reading his notes from his meetings over the last couple days, he reflected on his last meeting with Finland's Minister of Defense. It benefitted both countries for the U.S. to increase their military presence on the Russian border, so that should be an easy sell. President Begaye's team had considered having him making a formal speech to Parliament since it was currently in session, but he'd shot it down. It was uncouth to make a grand speech to another country's legislative body instead of just taking private meetings. Besides, his economic goals required a bit more sophistication.

WP hadn't plagued Finland like it'd poisoned America, and even during the military engagements with Rwanda, Croatia, Guatemala, and others, Finland had remained neutral. Asking them to lower their rates for exporting kaolin required finesse only possible in one-on-one conversations with their key leaders.

It was a miracle mineral where WP was concerned. Used in everything from skincare to the paper the president read his notes on, kaolin had represented a $4.4 billion industry before WP legalization and had tripled in the past five years after the discovery of what the drug did when fused with the mineral. American ingenuity had revealed what kaolin and WP could do together, and the implications were staggering. As one of the largest exporters of the mineral, Finland's assistance in bringing down the price of kaolin was crucial to continuing American hegemony.

Lawyers reading legal briefs on paper coated with not just kaolin but also WP read through their reports faster and remembered more of the information, allowing them to increase their billable hours and win the most expensive cases. Houses covered with paint derived from a kaolin/WP blend stood up to natural disasters better, erasing billions of dollars in property damage annually. The mineral/WP mix could even be used in manufacturing plastic, creating more sturdy water bottles, furniture, and more.

Joseph loved being president, nerding out over things like

kaolin, understanding its real-world applications, and then actually having the power and influence to do something about it to improve people's lives. But in addition to those duties, he also had to worry about the presidential race. Roger briefed him on it every Monday and Saturday. Polls were too close for comfort in Wisconsin and Pennsylvania, among other states, and his political team would prefer he spend more time campaigning in Philadelphia and Madison to shore up not just Therese but senators running for re-election as well. President Begaye had his reasons for avoiding the campaign trail, though. At a base level, he didn't want to be asked about the Bella scandal. But there was also a more strategic reason for spending so much of his time abroad these days.

Securing international deals like this one with Finland would establish infrastructure Therese could lean into to convince Congress to finally give her the resources she needed to establish Undersecretaries for Drug-Enhanced Commerce under each agency. Until those positions were created, the federal government couldn't assist the private sector to fund the types of public-private partnerships President Begaye knew would keep America at the forefront of global innovation.

Looking out a window, the president saw the country appear on the horizon. He'd be home soon and should sleep. Instead, he called his daughter. It wasn't going to be a pleasant conversation, but as a friend of Bella's, she deserved to hear what was about to happen from him first.

Anaba answered on the first ring. "Daddy?"

"Anaba, is Luther sleeping over?"

"Would you want me to tell you if he was?"

Begaye paused. "Good point. Have you talked to your brothers?"

"They're good."

"And how's your mother?"

He heard her rolling her eyes. "You live with her."

"You settled on a wedding dress?"

"Dad, I've got swim practice in a few hours. What's up?"

He sighed. "Roger told me about Luther's football game."

"...and?"

"There was a fight, right?"

"Yeah... he didn't want to talk about it."

Anaba's voice exuded warmth as the president finished explaining what happened. "Men are so dumb, never wanting to share good news. Luther acted so honorably!"

The president slumped in a chair. "Luther's friends aren't political."

"And?"

"And it means this scandal is filtering out to ensnare even the most non-political people."

"So?"

"It means the risks of not commenting about the scandal are starting to outweigh the risks of commenting this close to Election Day."

"You're gonna say something? Like what?!"

The president closed his eyes and kicked his feet up on a table. He was overly familiar with what his wife and daughter would like him to say to the whole country, but he'd been committed to starving this story of all oxygen for as long as possible. "I won't say anything, but the Speaker's been badgering me about holding a vote to impeach her."

There was venom in Anaba's response. "He'd lose his seat."

"He wants to hold the vote to embarrass Republicans. He guarantees the vote will fail."

"What do you think?"

"I think it's too risky, but we're at a boiling point here. Therese has shed six points in Virginia and Colorado. Probably antsy Democrats, but she's also given up three points in Pennsylvania. That's the ball game."

"And you think this vote failing will shift support back to us?"

"I think this whole thing is stupid." The president stood up and started pacing, his irritation bleeding through the phone. "But with Kaitlin not commenting on this, the press is looking more toward Congress to pass some sort of judgment on the matter."

"Politics is so dumb."

He pictured his daughter blowing air out of her mouth in frustration, saw her bangs getting in her eyes. "I agree."

"This whole thing is an abomination," Anaba said. "I can't

believe this is happening in America."

Begaye laughed. "America is the one place this sort of thing is most likely to happen. I just came back from Finland and I'm pretty sure no one would care if the Prime Minister had a video out there."

"Gross."

"Anyways, baby, I love you."

She kept him waiting before saying it back. Hanging up, cricking his neck, he got ready to make another tough call.

"Mr. Speaker?"

"Mr. President? What can I do for you?"

The man could've been in his bed or could've been in Vegas for all President Begaye knew. Kent had been Speaker for almost four years, and half that time he'd spent partying. But because half a million voters in Denver and over a hundred of his colleagues had voted for him, he was now second in line for the presidency and a man Begaye had to speak with daily.

"I hope you're as good as you say you are, Kent." He pictured Speaker Munroe playing with his bolo tie, pacing as he forced humility into his voice before responding.

"Mr. President, thank you for trusting me with this. I know it was a tough decision, but Bella and Therese are going to thank us. It's nice when we can do something for women, isn't it?"

The president suppressed a gag. "Hold on. I gotta conference Kusum in. You two need to be in lockstep on this." He was relieved she answered at this hour. "Senator, you're on with me and Kent."

"You've made your decision."

He heard the heartbreak in her voice. She'd stewarded Bella's confirmation at his request, and now she must think he was betraying her.

"This is for the best, Kusum," Kent said.

"It's Senator Raghavan," she said.

"Senator," Begaye pleaded, "if the plan works, we're all going to come out of this bulletproof."

"And obviously it's going to work because it's being led by such a master." The acid in her voice stung him.

"If I didn't know better, I'd say you were insulting me," Kent said.

"It's only been a few days," Kusum begged. "Give it another week; voters will move on."

"People are voting as we speak," Begaye said. "The early voting numbers aren't as good as they should be, and we need that cushion going into Election Day."

"I've spoken to Bella daily since the photos came out. It's not like there's a video out there or anything."

"I'm sorry," Begaye said. "This vote will buy us a little time, and luckily, that's all we need."

Kusum spoke, clearly resigned to being overruled by men once again. "You've made up your minds."

Begaye sat down. Closing his eyes, he said a prayer for Bella and for the country. "I know I can count on your ability to whip votes against this, Senator Raghavan."

She hung up without responding.

"You can count on me, too, Mr. President."

Begaye hung up, too.

Chapter Seven

October 15, 2028

Aditya was ebullient when he arrived at JFK to pick up Bella's grandparents and found the arrivals section half empty. He'd taken his Ferrari, hoping they'd appreciate both the connection to their homeland of Maranello and the fact that he obviously had the means to take care of their little girl. But for all this, in ten minutes of waiting, airport security made him take two loops around JFK rather than just letting him stay at the entrance.

"Literally no one else is here," Aditya argued, indicating a wide empty swath.

"Yeah," the woman said, "because it's against the rules and they can read."

He was about to pull around again when he spotted Oreste and Bibiana Ferrari.

"Look!" Pointing them out to the security guard, he stepped out of the car to get their bags. She threw up her hands and walked away.

"Oreste! Bibiana!" Aditya smiled, popping his trunk and squeezing a bag inside. The second would have to sit on someone's lap in the back.

Oreste's forehead scrunched. "Why you bring *piccolo* car for so much luggage?"

"It's not that small, Oreste," Aditya said.

"What are we, strangers?" Bibiana hugged Aditya, kissing his cheek before shuffling into the passenger seat up front. "You call us

Nonno and *Nonna.*"

Aditya changed the subject. "Bella wanted to be here, but, well, you know..." She couldn't leave their building these days without some intrepid reporter hounding her or some creep asking for a selfie.

Oreste slid a hand over Aditya's car before getting seated. "*Buona macchina. Grande spendaccione.* You think that makes you a big man?"

Aditya's Italian was rusty, but the disdain in Oreste's voice couldn't be misinterpreted. He gripped the steering wheel but bit his tongue and merely smiled in response. Fighting before even reaching Bella wouldn't do any good.

The ride back was like saying bye to someone and then realizing you're both walking in the same direction to your next location. Bella's grandparents spoke Italian the whole way, leaving Aditya lost in his thoughts. One positive outcome of Bella's forced retreat from society was that they'd had ample time to fill out all the adoption paperwork their agency needed. They'd both gone through FBI background checks yesterday and met with their accountant and doctor to gather the financial and medical paperwork required.

"How long are you staying?"

"Family stays as long as needed," Bibiana said.

Aditya wondered if Bella had told them about their last fight. It'd explain why they were pissed, but that stuff should've stayed between them. Besides, they'd made up. Frowning, he parked outside his apartment building and tossed the keys to a bellman as another one got the luggage.

"Park it in the usual spot," he said.

"Yes, sir."

"I can carry the bag," Oreste said, tearing his suitcase from the man's hands. "*Non sono la regina.*"

Bibiana smirked. "No one would ever call you a queen. Let the man do his job."

Chastised, Oreste let the bellman take his luggage to the elevator.

I guess all Ferrari men take their orders from their women, Aditya thought. *But am I Ferrari man or is Bella a Shetty woman?*

The smells of biscotti and chai assaulted Aditya as soon as they entered the apartment. Forgotten as Bella threw her arms around her grandparents and kissed them, he directed the bellman to their room and went to throw some water on his face. His mind had raced like a Ferrari in the car, and even now, it refused to stop until met with the splash of cold. Gritting his teeth, he opened the medicine cabinet and tucked a bottle of powdered, unrefined WP in his pocket. But not before dipping his finger inside and swallowing the contents.

The photos. The adoption. His grandparents. He was smart enough to know he needed help dealing with it all.

He rejoined the others to find them seated around one of his most prized possessions, the glass-encased fireplace with a crystalline ember bed. Aditya went to the kitchen to pour himself a cup of chai before returning.

"Aditya loves this piece," Bella said, rubbing her hand over the glass with pride. "It'd broken years ago, but it got fixed and it looks even better now, right?"

His head throbbed as he remembered how it had broken. His mind brought him back to that fateful night when Rakshan and those other idiots had succeeded in stealing his WP. He winced, physically reliving how Abhinav had thrown him through the glass box. Aditya dropped his drink on the floor, sending broken shards flying. "Fuck!"

"Aditya!"

"It's nothing we haven't heard before," Bibiana said, standing up. "Where's your broom?"

As Bella pointed her grandma in the right direction, Oreste finished his chai and joined Aditya. "The wives need some alone time, anyways," he said. "Join me for a walk."

"Oh," Aditya said. "Shouldn't I stay to clean up?" He wanted an excuse more than a broom.

"They've got it," Oreste said. "Show me around one of those parks I've heard so much about." He tapped Aditya's gut. "Besides, we can both use the exercise."

●———————————●

Though Union Square Park was at their fingertips upon leaving the building, Oreste wanted to walk to Washington Square. "You could use the extra steps," he said.

They did two rounds, walking at first, then jogging until Aditya had to stop to catch his breath. Each time he bent over to grab his knees, Oreste found some kid to joke with or bird to admire.

"You trying to kill me?" Aditya joked.

"I'm trying to show you how Bella feels," Oreste said. He'd been smiling with the kids and animals, but no trace of lightness lingered in his face now.

"What did you say?" Forcing air into his lungs, Aditya faced the man eye-to-eye.

"She's been running for over a decade, and it all leads back to you."

"Oreste..."

"It's *Nonno*, God damn it! You're adopting a kid and you still won't admit we're fucking family."

Aditya had never seen the man angry. His eyes could've been flamethrowers and his voice was sharp as a knife. "She told you about the adoption..."

"Of course," Oreste said, each word a nick to Aditya's body. "You need to do better for her, but more importantly, you need to do better for the child."

Aditya sat on the grass; Oreste loomed over him like a giant. "What do you mean?"

"You've got WP buried under your fingertips. What you wear isn't enough?"

Aditya chewed his lip. "This morning's the first time I took more. It's only because I was nervous meeting you. Otherwise, I'd never..."

Oreste waved a hand before offering it to pull Aditya up. The two found a bench to sit. "I don't ask you to call us *Nonno* and *Nonna* out of ego. Seeing us as family, knowing you can count on us, that'll help with the nerves more than any drug."

Aditya shuddered as he remembered how WP had landed him in jail, how he'd missed his mom's funeral. How it'd led to Bella fleeing the country. He dug his fingernails into his hands. "I'm going to stop."

Oreste shook his head. "Ninety percent of the people who say it was a one-time thing are lying to themselves."

Aditya looked at him. "It isn't my first time, though. Just my last time. Trust me... *Nonno.*"

Oreste smiled. "It's good you want to do better for yourself and this kid, but remember to do better for my Bella as well. Leave everything in the past behind."

"What do you mean?"

"Bella told me about your fight."

Aditya sighed. "Can you blame me? I spoke harshly, but what she did was careless."

"Hey, *coglione,* you won."

Aditya's face blanked.

"Honestly, you need to learn at least a little of our language," Oreste said. "I called you a fool. She married you, so what else matters? Stop shaming her for her past."

Aditya found the ground fascinating.

"You think I didn't look into you? Your family came from nothing, so I'm sure you had to do God-knows-what to come so far, but I won't ever judge you. You understand how tough it is to be an immigrant and successful at the same time. Offer Bella the same courtesy and let's move on with our lives."

Raising his face, Aditya finally cracked a smile. "Can we stop running?"

Oreste laughed. "God yes. Let's go home, but don't tell your *nonna* I took the Lord's name in vain so much."

Aditya laughed as they walked home together. "Where do you want to go for dinner?"

"Anywhere but Italian," he said. "Nothing can beat what I get in Maranello. And since you're such a bigshot, you can pay."

Chapter Eight

October 17, 2028

Tammy Day knew politics moved fast, but the speed at which her world had shifted in just the last week bowled her over. Most girls new to FOX spent years trying to get a spot on Artie Quiver's show, yet here she was in the greenroom, about to go on. Artie was fifty-six, thirty-five years her senior, but those forearms and that scathing wit could get it. For her, his salt-and-pepper hair was a mark of honor. She'd been watching him take down sanctimonious liberals her whole life. He had the battle scars to prove it, and all good girls knew scars were hot.

"On in ten! Let's make some news tonight!"

Tammy caught Artie as he walked to his desk on set. "Mr. Quiver, thanks so much for having me on." She flipped her hair, brushing her fingers against his and smiling. "I've watched you since I was a little girl."

"You were the popular kid on the playground, huh?"

She giggled. "Whoever said to never meet your heroes clearly didn't know you."

Tammy knew why she was on the show instead of a more established anchor like Jen Crew. Jen and most of the other women at FOX thought the network was "above" issues like "revenge porn," but they failed to understand the post-Brooks conservative movement. The voters deserved to know their thoughts had a national voice like Artie's, and it wasn't about revenge porn but about judgment.

"Listen, we gotta knock you off the show tonight."

Tammy's voice quivered. "What? Is it something I did...?"

Artie brushed his fingers through her hair. "Nah, nothing like that. We just think your voice will be so much stronger after those photos leak, so we want to have you on after that happens."

"Mr. Quiver..."

"Yeah?"

She grabbed his arm, forcing him to look her in the eyes. "Have you heard of the Silk Road?"

"That website that got taken down? People could buy drugs and weapons and stuff from it?"

"Yeah. There's a copycat site up, and it has more than that..." Tammy followed him as he sat at his desk.

"Listen, we're about to start. I promise we'll have you on later."

"The site has the photos."

It was Artie's turn to look as if he'd been slapped.

"I have them on my laptop. I just wasn't sure where we stood ethically on releasing them... I don't want to lose my job."

Artie chuckled. "The networks all agreed not to post them, but if the photos wound up on Reddit or something and made their way through all the far-right blogs? That's news we can report on, and of course we'd link back to all the original news sources carrying the photos."

Artie took her hand, pulling her close before handing her a key. "This'll get you into my office upstairs. Let's talk after the show."

The lower half of his body was blocked from the set where he sat, and she blushed as he rubbed her hand over his crotch before letting her go. "Now scoot," he said. "I got Kaitlin on tonight."

"Thank God she finally agreed to an interview."

Artie laughed again. "Hammond probably called her to set her straight. There's only so long you can go without taking a swing at a sure thing."

Tammy thought the same thing as she made her way to Artie's office.

———•————————————•———

Being willing and able to do stupid shit without complaining was one of the top attributes one could have when working on political campaigns. Unfortunately, that trait was ranked pretty far down Kaitlin's list of skills. Still, she'd agreed to do Artie's show after only rejecting Olivia's pleas twenty-six times.

She'd crossed paths with Tammy Day walking to set; the woman hadn't even said hi.

When the cameras rolled, Kaitlin flashed her trademark fake smile as Artie began.

"Good evening, patriots! Tonight, a very special guest, Republican nominee Secretary Kaitlin Lungford! I know you all can't wait to hear from a woman with integrity and grace, so let's get right to it."

Grace. It was not earned but given. There was no monetary value to it, so a man like Artie Quiver would never understand it. She knew she was no paragon of virtue, either, but she was trying to do better. And now, because of this scandal, she could show it.

"Madame Secretary?"

She'd missed his first question. "Sorry?"

Artie smiled thinly. "I asked you if you were as disgusted as our viewers by this Bella Ferrari thing? Your answers during the debate were as classy as you are, but you can tell us how you really feel, now that you're amongst friends."

Kaitlin's heart pulsed within her like a car hitting 7,000 RPM. God knew she wasn't religious, but she prayed for mercy for her staff and Mirai for what she was about to do. She wasn't Jesus on the cross, but she hoped the next words from her mouth would save not just her, but the whole Party. "I'm disgusted that people like you are attacking a woman whose only crime was feeling good enough about her body to share it with others."

For a brief moment, Artie's face resembled a lost duck's. It was there, captured by the cameras for all eternity. She had no doubt liberals would meme it in years to come. But he tried his best to ignore it, gritting his teeth the next second.

"I beg your pardon?"

"I agreed to do this interview because you have the largest audience of Republican voters in the country. You use that platform to poison their minds on a daily basis, and I wanted to do my part to stop it."

She thought Artie might launch himself across the stage to take a swing at her, and wished he would so she'd have an excuse to clock him.

"Republicans used to stand for something," she continued. "Lowering taxes because Democrats think they know how to spend our money better than we do. Securing our borders because we can't all just hug each other if we want to maintain our status as the best country the world has ever seen. People want to blame President Brooks for the shift in Republican politics, the obsession with 'owning libs' over all else, but Brooks just tapped into a sickness that people like you injected into our body politic years ago."

Artie Quiver's anger was the stuff of legends in profiles written by people like Kate Caruso of *Vanity Fair*. There were anonymous quotes about how he'd thrown a bottle of scotch through his window after Obama had won. Cussed out interns if they messed up his dry cleaning. And now, on national television, he was revealing that rage to the entire world.

His face turned red, spittle settling on his chin. Searching for words, he found none.

Kaitlin was the mirror opposite, her shoulders relaxed and voice calm. "I wanted your viewers, especially the female ones, to know I'm going to fight for them. Because misogyny and sexual shaming know no Party. And if elected, I'm going to work with Congress to get things like fair pay passed so corporations run by the same fat cats as ever can't prey on the innocence of the hard-working men and women I've fought for my whole life."

She took off her mic and walked off stage before Artie could find his voice.

Kaitlin held her breath the whole walk back to the green room, only exhaling upon seeing Olivia inside.

"You just lost the race."

Kaitlin chewed her lip. "Maybe I lost Nevada. The women of Wisconsin and North Carolina will reward me." That'd been the most thrilling thing she'd done in fifty-seven years of living. The applause in her head replaced anything she'd heard from colleagues and presidents upon winning a battle. Win or lose, she was confident she'd rewritten the rules of revenge porn and banished Uncle Charles from her head at last.

Olivia smiled. "I'm proud of you."

"...thank you." She wanted to say more, but just then her phone rang.

"Why are you obsessed with ruining my life?!" Whit's voice was so loud it probably could have reached her even without the phone.

Kaitlin smirked. "How'd I look?"

"Like a failure!"

She put the call on speaker, indicating to Olivia to stay silent. "I don't know how, but it was you who got the photos, didn't you? You can't be caught with them because of your closeness to Hammond, but the outlets talking about them, the people discussing them, they're all just a bit too perfectly placed."

A silence fell over the line.

"Fuck you, Whit."

"You stupid bitch. I'll be here long after you've lost in disgrace, so you better—"

"Watch your mouth, Pryor. The anonymous quotes questioning my campaign's judgment. The 'scheduling conflicts' preventing senators and congressmen from attending my rallies and fundraisers. It's all going to stop, or else I won't go to the press with what you've done to Bella, I'll go to Melissa. You'll never see your son again."

Kaitlin thought she heard Whit's heartbeat through the phone.

"I... I... I..."

"Do better, Pryor. For the country, for your son, but most importantly for yourself."

She hung up as Olivia punched a fist through the air. "*That* was bad ass."

Kaitlin offered her a reluctant smile as they left the green room. "Get the car ready," she said. "I'm going to the bathroom."

Inside, she threw some water on her face and gripped the counter. As much as she hated Whit, she knew she needed help. But he'd never listen to her. Her half-brother Chad had stuttered years ago, during the worst of his WP addiction. She considered calling Melissa, arranging an intervention; the man had a son who needed his father.

Thinking about Chad, she glanced in the bathroom mirror and

saw Uncle Charles leaning against a stall.

"I don't need you anymore," she said, refusing to face him except through the mirror's reflection.

"If that's true, then why am I still here?" He smiled, and she shuddered at seeing half his teeth missing. She threw more water on her face, but when she opened her eyes, he was still there.

October 20, 2028

Tammy's daytime show was okay, but ten minutes into her segment on Artie's nightly broadcast, she knew she could never go back to airing at the same time as *Days of our Lives.* It'd taken three days, but she'd found the photos and gotten them onto Silk Road, where they'd stayed for a full half hour before making their way to Reddit and 4chan. Kaitlin's lawyers had them erased from those sites soon after, but plenty of users had downloaded them by that point.

Despite her best efforts to sabotage herself, Kaitlin was going to win the presidency and it was all thanks to Tammy. A thrill warmed her body as Artie continued interviewing her.

"FOX has a strict policy against showing these photos," he said, "but we do thank you for sharing your expertise on the blogs and social media networks obsessed with them. How do you think this affects the race?"

Tammy beamed. "Well, like you said, as FOX hosts, we strongly condemn this invasion of privacy. But as you well know by now, no one can control the Internet. And you're right, these pictures are all the rage among my generation."

"And what are the kids saying?" Artie winked at her. His smiles were condescending, but his wallet was big, along with other parts of him.

"Most women I talk to admit to taking photos like these, but they aren't on the Supreme Court. People expect more from our leaders."

Artie chuckled. "Well, one can hope they'll rise to the occasion. Thanks for being here, Tammy. We'll be back with Whit Pryor. Stay tuned."

Artie handed her his keycard as soon as the cameras stopped

rolling.

"Hey," Tammy said, pocketing it, "can you put in a good word with Whit about me? Make sure he knows I got the photos out?"

Artie flashed that same condescending smile. "No problem. Let's have another nightcap when I'm done."

"Can't wait," she said. She blushed as Whit exited the green room and came their way.

Artie got up to steer her toward the elevator. "I never use my whole closet, so feel free to leave some of your clothes inside, if you want. I don't mind sharing the extra space."

Tammy nodded, turning back to see Artie shake Whit's hand.

●————————————————————●

Whit wished his son was impressed by politics. He also wished Senator Hammond appreciated the sacrifices he'd made for him. And, as long as he was wishing, he'd prefer it if Melissa had never left him, either. But if no one could value his contributions to bettering their lives, at least he knew they'd understand power. His super PAC had pulled in more than $100 million over the past two months, and though he'd never be credited with releasing the photos, he'd finally found a taker to share them on the Silk Road. He didn't know their real name (and it was better that way), but whoever it was had done a great job. Kate Caruso at *Vanity Fair* was condemning their release, Breitbart and other far-right blogs were slut-shaming Bella over them, but everyone was talking about the issue.

Straightening his tie, he flashed his pearly whites as his interview started.

"Whit," Artie said, "it's no secret you have the ear of Senator Hammond, maybe the next Senate Majority Leader."

Whit laughed. "I'm honored to be one of many he trusts."

"Has the senator seen these photos? Have you?"

Whit shrugged. "The senator's got bigger issues to deal with, like trying to stop President Begaye's job-killing quest to enact paid family leave. As for me personally, I've got no interest in photos taken over a decade ago. But voters do look toward the Supreme Court for strong moral leadership. More than the executive and legislative branches, voters have always held the Court in extremely high regard. The fact that photos like these could come out and be used to shame a Justice, to blackmail them? I think that matters, and you also have to ask yourself what to make of a president who, no doubt, learned about this during the vetting process and still chose to appoint Bella."

Artie nodded his assent so furiously that Whit thought his head would fall off. "It's a shame Mayor Johnson rejected any other debates."

"Well," Whit said, "voters are wondering what's she got to hide. We see it in our focus groups all the time. Unlike the secretary, Mayor Johnson's only ever governed a small city. Some might say she's the least qualified major presidential candidate in our history."

"These final days will certainly be interesting," Artie said. "Whit, thank you so much for being here. That's our show; until tomorrow, good night, patriots."

As soon as the cameras cut, Whit asked Artie if he wanted to go upstairs for a beer.

Artie winked. "Can't. I got a girl up there, waiting."

Whit made an X shape with his fingers. "I don't want to know."

Artie patted Whit on the back as he walked him to the exit. "Who are you fucking these days?"

Whit licked his lips. It'd been three weeks since he'd used Kajal. She'd ignored his texts, his calls. He'd even called her agency, LISA, but they'd changed their number after the #SCOTUSSlutScandal. The association with Bella was bad for business; he'd heard they called you directly now if you were a current client. And if you weren't a current client, they didn't want you.

"Whit?" Artie waved a hand in front of his face. "You're thinking of her right now, aren't you?"

"Yeah," he said. "She smells like saffron and sin."

Artie snickered, leaving him to catch a cab back to his empty apartment.

Chapter Nine

October 20, 2028

Therese hated watching cable news, especially FOX, but Rebecca had insisted tonight's interview with Whit was important for her to see. She rolled her eyes as Whit droned on about the "moral leadership" she apparently lacked, eating some Cheetos as she paced around a hotel room in Omaha, Nebraska. Since the state split their electoral votes by congressional district, Rebecca had insisted Therese could pick up a vote here. And every vote mattered: Therese knew from her team's electoral modeling that she'd win or lose with anywhere from 261 to 277 votes. With 270 needed to win the presidential election, any thought of a landslide mandate was gone from her thoughts.

She'd finished her rallies for the day and was now on hold as Russell and Rebecca dined on a nineteen-dollar grilled cheese from room service while listening to the TV. Therese was just fine with her vending machine food; FEC reports were public, and she didn't need the press calling her to task for excess spending.

"I can't believe my sister used to sleep with Whit," Rebecca groaned.

Russell laughed. "I can."

"At least his wife knew to leave him." Rebecca watched her candidate pace, neck crooked to hold her cell phone. "Why are you on hold?"

Since the Wisconsin debate, Therese had been texting and talking with Kaitlin. No one knew except the two of them. But now, it was time to fill Rebecca in. "I'm getting connected to someone."

"Who?"

"Kaitlin Lungford."

Rebecca muted the TV. "What the fuck?!"

Russell raised an eyebrow. Therese had told him the first time Kaitlin had called, right after the debate in Wisconsin, so his surprise now must've been at her finally clueing Rebecca into her plans.

To Kaitlin's credit, she'd called Therese first. Therese had thought it'd been to twist the knife, to pile on with Artie Quiver and everyone else about her "anger issues." But it wasn't like that at all. Kaitlin hated how Miles Parker had goaded her, wanted to work with Therese to issue a joint release condemning revenge porn and the media that'd poured gasoline on this story for profit. They'd texted back and forth about the details after that first call, wanting to wait until closer to the election to maximize the impact of the statement. They'd even come up with nicknames for each other in case Rebecca or Olivia saw their phones. Therese had chosen the name of one of the moms she talked to regularly in her group chat: Isabella. Kaitlin had chosen the Greek goddess of war: Athena.

They hadn't spoken by phone again until yesterday, when Kaitlin had proved to Therese yet again that she was every bit as ferocious as her moniker.

Kaitlin came on the line, sounding apoplectic. "That motherfucker is going to kill himself and take us all down in the process!"

Therese excused herself to the bathroom before responding. "... Kaitlin?"

"I told Whit to do better, and he's done the exact opposite."

Therese held the phone away from her ear. "What are you talking about?"

"Bella's photos are online."

Therese thought about using the toilet in front of her to hurl. "Where?"

"Twitter and Reddit have them uncensored. *Breitbart* and *The Daily Caller* posted the photos with her privates blurred out."

Therese started her breathing exercises, the ones she'd

practiced with her moms group weekly for the last several months.

"I give it another few minutes before Rebecca gets called with a request for comment," Kaitlin said. "Olivia already got one."

"And?"

"I told her to ignore the guy, but if he calls back, to tell him I said fuck off."

"Yeah," Therese said, "it's none of our business. That poor woman…"

"No," Kaitlin said, "that's my quote. 'Fuck off.'"

Therese's laugh held no mirth. "Does Olivia know about our calls?"

"Olivia doesn't need to know everything… but Vijay supports what we're doing."

"So does Russell," Therese said. "Thank God we married great men who understand that humility and compassion aren't weaknesses to be exploited."

"God's never been there for me, but Vijay has."

"I'm sorry you didn't get a proper honeymoon."

"Well, he'll forgive me once we're in the White House."

Therese smiled. "At times, I forget we're opponents."

"Some advice? Don't."

"Noted."

Kaitlin sighed. "But this isn't combat. There's room to work together, and we should, on issues like this. We've waited long enough; I want to speak."

They spent the following hours texting each other fragments of a joint release they wanted to issue tonight. Timing the joint statement to post on Twitter right after Whit's interview would maximize coverage.

"I'm putting the phone on speaker, Kaitlin," Therese said. "Rebecca's here, so I'm filling her in." Therese chuckled at seeing her manager's head steaming. "She's upset about us talking."

"Olivia's here, too," Kaitlin said. "I wonder who's more furious."

"Me!" Rebecca and Olivia shouted at the same time.

"It's now or never," Therese said. "Rebecca, can you get Gael?"

Her digital director was going to post the statement, and Kaitlin would retweet it soon after. Therese had asked Kaitlin if she wanted to post it and Therese would retweet, to which Kaitlin had replied, "I want to not know what Twitter is."

"Madame Mayor?" The young man wore his hair like Goku or one of those other anime characters. Sitting him down, she filled him in as Rebecca and Olivia made snide remarks at each other in the background.

"Can I see it?" Therese handed Gael a piece of paper to type out on his laptop. He gasped upon reading through it.

Therese was always sleep deprived these days, but last night's texts back and forth with Kaitlin had gone past three a.m. Therese had inserted phrases like "Grace doesn't need to be asked for, and as the leaders of the two major political parties in America, we offer it to Bella unequivocally, from both sides." Kaitlin went a step further, stating that "America is the greatest country in the world because of our freedoms. And if freedom doesn't include a person's bodily autonomy, what does it stand for? As president, I will instruct the Justice Department to prosecute as many cases of revenge porn as possible so that sexual predators know there is nowhere they can hide from our legal system."

Gael finished typing out the statement. "Madame Secretary, did you become pro-choice?"

Kaitlin sighed. "Who are you? Kate Caruso? The State has a compelling interest in the case of abortion. There's no such issue here."

"It's ready," he said. Stepping right up to Therese's phone, he spoke into it. "Madame Secretary, thank you so much for serving your country."

Therese tightened her grip on her phone. She knew he was being honest, but his youth and earnestness was cringeworthy.

"...kid, I've been serving the country since you were in diapers. Shut up and just post the thing."

Slack-jawed, Gael did so before excusing himself.

"Can I have the room?" Therese shooed the rest of her team out before returning to Kaitlin. "Seriously, thank you."

"I believe what we said," Kaitlin said. "Showing grace is important, because I have to believe that everyone is more than their worst moment."

Therese touched her chin, pondering a response. Kaitlin hung up before she could give one.

Chapter Ten

October 21, 2028

Gianpaolo Medulla hated the never-ending noises of NYC, but whenever he had to stay overnight, he avoided hotels, preferring instead the apartment his grandparents had moved into in 1940 on Arthur Avenue in the Bronx. He'd bought the complex years ago, offering to pay rent through his private foundation to first-generation immigrant families as tribute to his own family. And if some of those families had daughters sent to thank him for his generosity? Well, he was only human.

He pulled himself close to the naked woman in his bed, embracing her fully and smelling her red hair before getting up to shower. "Last night was fun, but you should go. I've got a meeting to prepare for."

If she was offended by his curtness, she didn't show it. He heard the door open and close as he turned on the water. Tenants in the building usually turned over after a year, but she'd just bought her parents another three months.

Washing his hair, he thought of his upcoming breakfast with Senator Denton. Harvey wasn't just his hometown senator; as head of the Senate Judiciary Committee, the success of any impeachment vote would begin and end with him. Giving Whit Pryor $50,000 to buy Bella's nudes was the second-best money he'd event spent after his initial investment into Famóre. With the pictures out in the world, he'd worked with the senator and his CTO to set up a dummy account on Congress's servers and email the photos to every individual member and staffer on the Hill.

Buttoning his shirt, lacing his shoes, Gianpaolo paused before leaving to shrug on his suit jacket. WP was woven right into the threads.

●————————————————————————●

Gianpaolo viewed Harvey as a brother. He wasn't Italian by blood, but Gianpaolo thought him savvier than Matteo at times. Matteo had never liked the man, wanted nothing to do with politics, but he didn't understand that politics was everywhere. Denton was key to their continued success. With Bella out of the way, this *Hokkam v. Famóre* nonsense would disappear.

Entering a diner, he spotted Harvey and Matteo already seated at a booth near the back. The two regarded each other in the manner of lions from different prides forced to play nice.

Walking to his brother, Gianpaolo kissed his cheeks twice before seating himself at his side and pouring himself a cup of coffee.

"You gotta pay extra for that at the Venetian," Harvey drawled.

"Have you ever been to Venice?" Matteo's question was as bitter as Gianpaolo's coffee.

Chuckling, Harvey didn't answer.

"Did you guys order?" Gianpaolo asked.

"Why is he here?" Matteo replied. "You said we had business to discuss."

"This is business," Gianpaolo said. "Trust me, you're gonna want some eggs first."

"But don't drink," Harvey said. "Not all of us have stomachs strong enough to do what's necessary."

Matteo looked as if he'd vomit when they'd finished telling him everything. How Gianpaolo had used Famóre funds to buy the photos. How Denton had helped him hack into Congress's servers and had manipulated the president into supporting an impeachment vote.

"Why?"

Gianpaolo hadn't lied to his brother once in forty-two years and he wasn't going to start now. The court case mattered, but that was just business, at the end of the day. He could've found an easier way to win the case: bribing another Justice on the Court, or having Hokkam himself killed. But Bella had embarrassed him, and that offense he would not let pass. Leaving him in college, and then marrying that *stronzo*, Aditya. Everything had worked out for the best, though. If Aditya had invested in Famóre it never would've taken off like it had. And he had more ambition than marrying a whore. He wouldn't lie to Matteo: this was personal.

Matteo actually choked upon hearing the truth. *"Cosí meschino?"*

"I'm not being petty!" Gianpaolo's voice rose, such that patrons from other booths looked his way.

Harvey hissed. "Keep your voice down."

"Paolo..." Matteo used his brother's pet name; he hadn't called him that since grade school. "This cannot stand..."

"You like your four-thousand-dollar suits? You like having a table at every Michelin-star restaurant in the country? This is what it takes!"

Matteo's voice cracked, falling to barely a whisper. "Thank God our parents can't see you like this."

Harvey got up, trying to leave. "This seems like a family thing..."

"And yet you are always here!" Rising to his feet, Matteo threw his coffee at the man's tailored suit, not caring that they now definitely had an audience. "You and your politics stole my brother from me!"

Harvey's drawl was as pronounced as ever. Taking out a pocket square, he dabbed coffee off him. "Politics isn't about stealing; it's about convincing everyone things belonged to you in the first place."

Matteo leaned over the table and slapped the senator across the face. Turning to his brother, he said one last thing before leaving. "I did not change, *fratello*, you did. The money is nice, but it wasn't about that. We were creating something for posterity. Somewhere along the journey, you decided there were more important things than leaving something behind. But I will bring you back from the madness, even if you're kicking and screaming while I do. Because that's what family does."

Gianpaolo watched as his brother left and his and the senator's eggs arrived. They ate in silence.

Kusum scrolled through the most recent photos of Asha, her granddaughter, on her phone as she waited in the lobby of the Democratic National Committee. Her meeting with Chairwoman Williams was ostensibly to discuss strategy around deploying senators to swing states where they were needed most to boost Democratic turnout ahead of the elections. Kusum secretly thought three colleagues were hopeless cases in Wisconsin, Pennsylvania, and New Hampshire, but to show them anything less than her full support with both a significant financial commitment and by sending high-value surrogates to campaign on their behalf would lead to stories in the press about how Democrats were giving up on their own. And so Kusum pretended to be happy about wasting upwards of ten million dollars.

Her phone dinged with a notification from *Vanity Fair*. Kate Caruso had just published a piece: "Lungford v. Ferrari: Feminism's Next Battle." Kusum rolled her eyes. Kaitlin couldn't have been more direct in her joint statement with Therese about her feelings regarding Bella's troubles, but the media had to create conflict if none existed. And people like Kate loved pitting women against each other.

"Secretary Lungford has a problem. Though she's never run for office before, she won't be able to assert her own legacy if elected, because the White House has reeked of the Lungford name for decades. As governor of Utah and then senator, Charles Lungford dined with Democrats and Republicans alike inside. Who can forget his infamous dinner with President Brooks, where he offered Brooks's executive assistant a private tour of his Utah home? Republicans tolerated him because of his friendship with the president, but there's a reason his funeral was sparsely attended. How, then, would a President Lungford distinguish herself?"

Kusum sighed, scrolling past photos of Kaitlin back in Utah with her uncle or in uniform at the White House. The article claimed the joint statement was a brilliant move by Kaitlin to win over Democratic-leaning women and those women who didn't traditionally vote in elections. From the private polling she'd seen, Kusum knew it was working.

Kate's piece went on to quote Nanda Taylor, a recent graduate of Howard University who now ran one of the top liberal podcasts in the country: *Let Freedom Ring.*

"It's a fact that Secretary Lungford wouldn't hesitate to work with a Republican Congress to sign anti-choice and pro-gun legislation," Taylor said. "But it's also an inconvenient truth that Republicans have more women and minorities in major offices right now. Whether that's governors or U.S. Senators, voters see one party elevating marginalized people to real positions of power, and it isn't Democrats."

Kusum's shoulders sagged, the weight of the world upon them. As great a fund raiser as she was, she'd spent even more hours speaking with the national and state committees to recruit more women and people of color to run. She'd even considered refusing to fund any non-marginalized candidates this cycle before her chief of staff had begged her to "be reasonable."

Kusum kept reading, stopping at an anonymous quote from "a person in regular contact with senior leaders of the Party."

She gritted her teeth when reading that "our voters are starting to outrun us, and the fact that our VP nominee is some white guy from the South isn't helping. Everyone I've talked to on this issue wonders why Senator Raghavan isn't sharing the ticket." She'd heard this type of talk ever since Therese had picked Ensign. Funny, though, how the chatter always manifested from anonymous sources.

"Madame Leader?" Patricia's receptionist approached her. "The chairwoman can see you now."

Standing up, angry at the quote and confident she knew where it had come from, she walked through the double doors of Patricia's office.

In a world run by men, where people thought the only successful women were single, Kusum knew she and Patricia stood as symbols that women *could* have it all. Kusum didn't care about the corner office or the view of the Potomac or designer gowns, but Patricia never missed an opportunity to show off she had all that and more. Personally mentoring several college interns a year, she wanted women, especially Black women like herself, to see the heights of her success and know there was a support system in place to enable them to achieve that same success themselves.

"Sorry for the wait," Patricia said. Standing from behind her desk, she walked over to hug Kusum.

"How's Carl doing?"

"He's driving me nuts since he retired!"

"And how are your boys?"

"They're traitors," Patricia said, laughing. "Both starting at American this year."

"We can't all go to Georgetown."

"Thanks for coming in." Patricia motioned for them to sit on a leather couch. "Do you want some water?"

"I want you to drop the small talk and stop fucking around."

"Oh," she said. "It's going to be that type of meeting."

Kusum's nostrils flared as she laid into Patricia about the anonymous quotes promoting her at the expense of Ensign. "Those came from Jamie, didn't they?" Patricia's executive director believed you caught more flies with vinegar than honey.

"Jamie was the first person in this building to suggest it, but I heard it first from several of our biggest donors."

"Do me a favor," Kusum said. "Next time some reporter mentions this garbage, send them to me instead of giving them clickbait."

Patricia sighed. "I'm trying to hold this thing together with Scotch tape. You know how many inquiries my communications team gets daily from reporters wanting a quote on those Bella photos? They're gonna write about something, so why not make it about female empowerment instead of revenge porn?"

Kusum raised an eyebrow. "What do you mean?"

"We're trying to reframe their articles by promoting a vision of this triumvirate of strong women running DC after November. Therese in the White House, you leading Congress, and Bella at the Court."

"And when those reporters ask where that leaves the VP, you tell them Ensign is irrelevant, especially as a white guy from the South in today's Democratic Party."

Patricia shrugged. "I'd like to not tell them anything, but I need a story to distract them with that's just as juicy as the one they want to write, and there isn't much that can compete with 'Supreme Court Justice's nudes leak online.'"

Kusum walked over to a pitcher of water on Patricia's desk, pouring herself a glass.

"Never underestimate Democrats' ability to seize defeat from the jaws of victory," Patricia said. "Nixon got impeached and we lasted a whole four years before electing a Republican who's still lionized for shredding the social safety net in this country. And just a couple years after Brooks is literally exposed as a traitor, Democrats decide to blow another election." Patricia lifted a decorative pillow from the couch as if she meant to throw it before deciding not to. Resignation dripped from her tone. "What did they expect, appointing a whore?"

Kusum gripped her glass so tightly she worried it would break. "What did you just say?"

"I'm not saying I never took a photo like that, but she never heard of a disposable camera? She didn't have the sense to ban her clients from taking pictures like that? You know how it goes—you take every advantage you can get to win a game. And Bella served herself up on a silver platter. It's her own fault."

Kusum's nose touched Patricia's as she whispered her next words. "This isn't a game, Patricia. If I ever see her called that word again in the press, if I see a quote about how Ensign is dumb or Therese needs a better partner, I'm going to assume it came from this office and I'm going to leak our dirty laundry to the *New York Times.*"

Patricia was older and had half a foot on Kusum, but this close, the senator could smell her fear as she backed away. "I guess I know now why people call you a teddy bear."

Kusum blinked. "Excuse me?"

Patricia took a seat behind her desk. "You put on this nice act, but you follow Teddy Roosevelt's advice: speak softly and carry a big stick."

Kusum laughed. "That's actually pretty good. You can leak that to a reporter whenever you want."

Patricia rolled her eyes. "I'm so glad I have your permission."

Such was her anger that Kusum didn't even want to discuss the elections. Walking to the door, she heard Patricia say one last thing. "Careful, Senator. I heard about the impeachment vote. It's a shame you're up for re-election this year. If the vote goes badly, you may be looking for a new job."

Kusum turned to face Patricia, locking eyes with her. "Just worry about whatever it is the DNC does and leave Senate politics to me."

Chapter Eleven

October 21, 2028

Standing at the kitchen counter, kneading pizza dough while her *nonna* made sauce, Bella wished she was back in Maranello. There, no one had known her name. No one had shot at her. She pounded the dough, each punch a futile attempt to turn back the clock.

"You'll break the dough!" *Nonna* said. "*A cosa stai pensando?*"

Bella winced. "I'm thinking about how life was easier in Maranello."

Her grandmother clucked her tongue. "How quickly you forget. You don't want easy."

"What do you mean?"

Her grandma finished cutting onions, throwing them into a blender with tomatoes and garlic and hitting the button. She poured the pinkish mixture into a big pot before adding oil and stirring. "You were tearing your hair out, you were so bored. What no one tells you is that life, if you're succeeding, just gets more complicated."

Bella raised an eyebrow.

"Your life could've been easy. You could've not become a judge. You could've avoided the limelight by refusing the Court nomination. And being single is a lot less complicated than being married. But would you have been happy?"

Bella closed her eyes. What her *nonna* said was true. She didn't regret her past, the choices that'd led her back into Aditya's arms and propelled her to the pinnacle of her career; she regretted people's reactions to her choices, but she'd never be able to control that.

"It's like the dough in your hands," *Nonna* said. "It's best when you stretch it as far as possible, knowing just when to stop so it won't break."

Opening her eyes, Bella felt tears well. "What if I stretch too far and break?"

Grabbing the dough at Bella's side, seeing a few cracks, Grandma Ferrari squeezed them together before tossing the dough in the air and catching it, setting it back on the kitchen table, ready to be baked. "What do those campaign ads always go on about? Kintsugi? Sometimes broken is better."

Bella smiled as her grandma returned to stirring sauce and she moved to stretch more dough out into crusts. Just then, her phone rang with the distinct sound reserved for Senator Raghavan. Washing her hands, she retrieved her cell from her back pocket.

"Senator?"

"Sorry to bother you on a Saturday. How are your grandparents?"

"I'm making pizza with my grandma," Bella said. "You've got grandkids now too, don't you?"

"Asha is about three months old now." The warmth in Kusum's voice spread all the way from DC, but in the next moment, burned out. "...I'll get right to it. I wasn't able to hold off an impeachment vote."

Bella's stomach felt like the blender her grandma used. "I heard a rumor about that." Pacing around the kitchen, she saw her *nonna* stop working to hold her hand, trying to keep her in one place, centered. She let her grandma anchor her. "You promised..."

"I didn't promise anything." Kusum's voice was like a baked pizza, warm and firm. "I said I'd do my best, but unfortunately that wasn't enough."

"...and the photos coming out didn't help..."

Kusum sighed. "I'm going to be with you the whole time. Do an interview on FOX, not with Artie Quiver, but that new girl, Tammy."

Bella dropped the phone in shock.

Her grandma slapped her arm in reproach. "I hope you've paid off that phone. They're too expensive if they break."

Bella rolled her eyes before picking the phone back up. It was nice that *Nonna* could always find the comical amidst the cruel. "Are you crazy?"

"Trust me," Kusum said. "One interview on FOX where you take everything they can throw at you with a smile. It'll project strength and show our enemies you're not ashamed."

"I'm not ashamed!" She felt the warmth of her grandma's arm next to hers. Bella hadn't admitted it to herself before now, but she wasn't ashamed. *Nonna* was right; her life had broken after that night when Karthik had killed her last client, but the pieces made whole again were better than before. She had Aditya now. She'd have a baby soon. She was a fucking Justice of the Supreme Court of the United States. She wasn't embarrassed; she just knew she owed the world nothing. Kaitlin's slogan rang true; kintsugi was a beautiful concept. But Therese was right, too: she'd had enough.

"Think about it," Kusum said, her tone sharp, before hanging up.

"Come, help." *Nonna* made Bella add sauce and cheese to all the pizzas. Made her chop onions so she had an excuse to cry. And when the rest of the meal was ready, when the only thing to do was wait for the oven to finish, she pulled Bella to the couch, lit the fireplace with its crystalline ember bed, and launched into a story. "Did you know my father didn't approve of your *nonno* at first?"

Bella shook her head.

"Dad thought *Nonno* was just interested in my looks, that he'd leave me as soon as I aged."

"*Nonna...*" Bella's whispered, wiping her eyes with a tissue. "What's the point of this?"

"Your *nonno* went to church every single day for a month to prove his devotion. He showed my father that he realized passion doesn't make a marriage. Passion is like ravioli: tasty, but it must be filled with something. Faith and love and respect make delicious fillings that will nourish you for your entire life. They represent a feast you can pass on to others for posterity."

Bella smiled. "It's a nice story, but what does it have to do with me?"

"My father became great friends with your *nonno*. He saw his devotion to something bigger than himself, and that is what I see when I look at you and Aditya."

Bella felt like a deer in headlights.

"You will be able to get through this together. Now, go call your husband for lunch."

———————●————————————————●———————

Bella's grandparents wanted to play a board game over limoncello after dinner. They'd stayed up for hours, late into the night, until *Nonna* caught Aditya stealing cards from *Nonno* while he was asleep on the couch. Sending her grandparents to their room, Bella stood in her bathroom now, preparing for bed. She took her bra off before getting into bed at Aditya's side.

She shook his shoulder. "Something's happened."

Pulling himself up from the mattress, leaning against the headboard, he rubbed the sleep out of his eyes.

"Something happened today."

"Yeah," Aditya said. "*Nonno* actually laughed at my jokes."

Bella's voice dropped to a whisper. "The impeachment vote is happening."

Aditya looked like someone had thrown a bucket of cold water on him. He hugged Bella as if scared the Senate Judiciary Committee would burst into their room right now to steal her from him. Kissing her forehead, he stroked her wavy hair. "Politicians have no souls because they've sold them to the highest bidder."

Bella had shed her tears while talking to her *nonna*; now, only resolve remained. "With Senator Denton as head of Senate Judiciary, the Medulla brothers knew a bargain deal when they saw one. I don't know how, but he's got to be on Gianpaolo's leash."

Aditya nodded. "Whit Pryor is being a bit too vocal about how he'd never slut-shame anyone, even a Supreme Court Justice."

"You think he's involved, too?"

"I met him a couple times when I used to hang around Kaitlin's brother, Chad. And Gianpaolo is funding his Super PAC. I don't believe in coincidences."

Bella nodded. "I'll talk to Kusum tomorrow, see if she can shake anything loose." Turning off the light, Bella hugged her pillow and closed her eyes.

"...there's something else." Aditya turned the light back on. "The adoption agency called…"

"What's wrong?"

"They're gonna drop us."

"What?!" Bella shot up straight.

"It's not final yet, but our background check turned up some significant issues. My status as a former felon. Your…"

"My whoring around." Bella spat the words like venom.

When Aditya started to cry, Bella hugged him. "There's nothing we can do tonight," she said. "Let's just try to get some sleep."

It'd been another hour before Bella had heard Aditya's snores. There was something she could do tonight, he just wouldn't like it. Opening her bedside drawer, she took out a piece of paper with a phone number on it. She'd called the agency weeks ago to request Sadiya's cell. Tiptoeing to the bathroom, she dialed and waited for Sadiya's answer.

"Hello? Who is this?" Even with the time change, it was still past nine in Albuquerque.

"My name is Bella Ferrari."

Bella heard nothing for a moment, and then the cries of a small child.

"God!" Someone shouted, probably Maadhini. "'Diya, who is it? Ask them where they live so I can go kill them; they woke Rukmini!"

"'Dhini, it's Bella Ferrari!"

Bella curled up in the tub, wishing she'd waited until tomorrow. "I'm sorry. This was a mistake…"

"Wait!" Sadiya said. "Why'd you call? I'm putting you on speaker."

"I'm…"

"We know who you are," Sadiya said. "And who you married."

The water wasn't on, but the words left unsaid sent a chill through Bella. "Right." Swallowing, she forced herself to be strong. "We share an adoption agency, New Beginnings."

Sadiya's tone shifted from combative to puzzled. "You're looking to adopt?"

Bella took a deep breath. "The agency gave us your number as a reference weeks ago, but Aditya was too proud to call."

"But now you need our help." Sadiya's tone reverted to combative.

"'Diya...'"

Bella heard some movement and more crying.

"Sorry about that," said a new voice. Maadhini. "Sadiya's always been rude, and having a two-year-old doesn't help."

"I'm sorry," Bella said. "I'm not sure what I hoped to achieve calling you. I just... I have to try everything. I couldn't live with myself otherwise."

Maadhini sighed. "I get it." She stopped for a moment, telling "'diya'" to take Rukmini back to her room.

"That's cute," Bella said. "The pet name. Aditya doesn't believe in them."

Maadhini's smile shined through the phone. "We've called each other that since childhood. 'Diya and 'dhini. Even though we were in each other's lives for decades, we didn't accept our love until we were almost thirty."

"That's like me and Aditya," Bella said.

The warmth in Maadhini's voice vanished. "We're nothing like you and Aditya."

Bella bit her lip. "...I know."

"Aditya's a billionaire. You're a Supreme Court Justice."

"...please..."

"Please what?"

"I'm not gay, and it's true we do come from money, but..."

"Why should Aditya Shetty have a child? What can you say to convince me he deserves that privilege?"

Privilege. Wherever she went, whatever she did, she'd never escape that word. In a world defined by privilege, she'd tried to slip its snares. But you couldn't thrive in this world that way, so instead, now, she leaned in. She told Maadhini everything.

The shame of knowing everyone in the country had seen her vagina. The hurt of not being able to give birth naturally. The disgust of being a political pawn in a presidential election. The fear of being shot at. "I might've committed suicide if not for Aditya," she said. "He's been my anchor, helped me get through the storms."

"I'm sorry you went through that."

Tears slipped down Bella's face. "We've had so much taken

from us. Because of WP, because of circumstance. They say your real life begins the moment you have a kid. We want to start our real lives, now that we know we can build something greater for a child than we had for ourselves."

Bella heard Sadiya join Maadhini again. The child must've fallen back asleep. She heard muffled voices as someone's hand covered the speaker.

Sadiya spoke. "We'll call the agency tomorrow and put in a good word."

The knot in Bella's stomach came undone. "Really?"

"Sometimes there are bad periods in people's lives that cause them to make bad decisions," Maadhini said. "But I have to believe that you are more than your worst moment."

"Thank you." Bella promised herself she'd go to church with *Nonna* tomorrow to pray for Sadiya and Maadhini. Leaving the bathroom, she curled back into bed, hugging Aditya.

"You were in there awhile," he mumbled. "I told you *Nonna*'s sauce is too spicy."

Chapter Twelve

October 24, 2028

Congress loved gridlock until it didn't. It took them a week to introduce the PATRIOT Act, which led to an unprecedented breach of people's privacy. It took them less than two weeks to hold the vote on Justice Ferrari's impeachment, an unprecedented move to remove her from office for the crime of allowing herself to be photographed. Bella offered to come to DC for the vote, telling Senator Raghavan it may sway some votes if members could physically see her, but the senator told her it was a bad idea, reminding her that the whole problem was that members had seen far too much of her already.

The House had gaveled into session yesterday morning and hadn't recessed since. Bella was only the second person ever to face this type of Congressional judgment, and every single one of the 435 members had something to say about it. Members gave speeches ten minutes at a time, sometimes jointly to either praise or condemn the vote.

The final person to talk was Speaker Munroe himself. With his compact frame and a grin the size of the Grand Canyon, he looked like a boxer excited to land a knockout punch.

"I hope this works," Bella whispered.

"If it doesn't," Aditya said, "Kent can start looking for a new job." Aditya held her hand as they sat on their couch at home, watching the proceedings unfold on TV.

"My friends," Kent said, "we are here today because American freedom is worth defending."

Aditya laughed under his breath. "Does he write his own speeches?"

Bella hushed him and turned up the volume. Kent was a misogynistic blowhard, but she couldn't believe he'd be dumb enough to hand Republicans a stunning victory weeks before a presidential election.

"Secretary Lungford said it so elegantly in her joint statement with Mayor Johnson: if freedom doesn't include a person's bodily autonomy, what does it stand for? This is nothing more than a disgusting attempt by some Republicans to body-shame a beautiful woman and try to score cheap political points before an election."

Bella rolled her eyes. "At least he thinks I'm beautiful."

"Would the clerk now please call a vote?"

At ten a.m., the first vote to impeach her was cast by Representative George Adelson (R-NV).

Though the vote was technically supposed to last for fifteen minutes, Kusum informed her last night it'd stay open for as long as it took for each member to make it. More than a hundred members were still in their home districts, including several reliable votes for Bella, so parliamentary procedures would be used to make the fifteen-minute timer last several hours.

"We may as well eat something," Aditya said. He pulled her away to take a walk with her grandparents, as if they had a superhuman power to make her forget what was happening.

They walked by a pet store *Nonna* insisted they enter. Aditya offered to buy her a golden retriever she could take to DC with her whenever Court was in session.

"I may not live there much longer," she said. "Besides, a snake seems more appropriate for that town."

After rebuffing her *nonno*'s attempts to buy her some zuppa inglese and her *nonna*'s efforts to see a movie with them, Aditya gave up and took them back home.

"She can watch," *Nonna* said, pointing to the TV, "but we won't." Her grandparents left Bella and Aditya to binge C-SPAN by themselves.

The vote was 109-95 in favor of impeachment. She knew the

vote would be lopsided since votes were cast alphabetically by last name and most Democrats fell towards the end of the alphabet, but each vote hit her like a brick, whether it was for or against her.

Aditya got up to pour them both a scotch. They drank without speaking, listening to the clerk.

"Mr. Kilgore? Mr. Kilgore: no. Mr. Klane? Mr. Klane: no."

109-97. Even the no votes hurt because they were proof this was her life. Politicians deciding whether or not she could keep doing a job where no one was questioning her competency. She'd be fired for being a woman and a Democrat and confident all at the same time.

"Mr. Korris? Mr. Korris: aye. Mr. Krane? Mr. Krane: no."

Aditya finished his drink, putting his glass down and kissing Bella's forehead as she kept her eyes glued to the screen. "What can I do to convince you to not watch this anymore?"

"If you grow a second head, I might turn away."

Aditya laughed. "Why stop at one? Ravana had ten."

Another hour passed before they even got to the Ts. "Mr. Tykwil? Mr. Tykwil: no." 204-200 in favor. With 218 votes against needed, Bella's eyes threatened to bore a hole into the TV.

At 2:19 p.m., the final votes of the House were cast.

"Mr. Yoshi? Mr. Yoshi: no. Mr. Zeeler? Mr. Zeeler: no." 216-216. A tie.

A tie meant the motion to impeach failed. With the roll call over, all Kent had to do was end the vote. Bella shuddered in relief.

Aditya smirked. "I can't believe Congress did the right thing for once."

Three people hadn't voted, but no one could say they hadn't had the opportunity. Bella moved to turn the TV off when she saw Kent speaking to Rep. Adelson. The man cornered the speaker, taking him away from the floor where the clerk was asking if anyone would like to change their votes before he announced the final count. Bella bit her lip; Munroe was missing his opportunity.

Aditya saw it first, shaking her shoulder and pointing. "Adelson's distracted Kent!"

It was true. Engaged in conversation, Kent wasn't seeing the

Republican bring in the three missing votes.

Bella's heart ripped each time they spoke.

"Mr. Dwyer? Mr. Finley: aye. Mr. Grimley? Mr. Grimley: aye. Mr. Stenson? Mr. Stenson: aye."

219-216. Bella was the first impeached Supreme Court Justice in the history of the Republic. But the humiliation didn't stop there. With her impeachment assured, members raced to change their votes for the congressional record. Plenty had voted against impeachment to seem like team players, but now that she was going down, they had no problem switching their votes for posterity. As the speaker yelled at Adelson, the freshman congressman from Carson City who'd managed to make a fool of the most powerful man in the House of Representatives, Bella went rigid. When it was done, she'd lost 226-209.

Bella didn't answer her phone when Kusum called, but Aditya did. He put it on speaker.

"What the fuck are you guys doing over there?!" Kusum's voice seemed laced with poison.

"Can you tell my grandparents?" Bella said. "I don't want to face them."

Nodding, Aditya kissed her forehead and left the bedroom.

"I can't begin to express my anger and sorrow."

Bella laughed, a mirthless sound. "Try."

"Kent got played."

"No shit."

"He'll lose his speakership over this."

"Or he'll be seen as a visionary leader if the Senate convicts me. The man who defied partisanship to do what he thought was right."

"The press isn't writing that story because everyone knows that's not what happened."

Bella sighed, lying back on her bed. "The truth doesn't matter."

"Don't give up so easily." The grit in Kusum's tone insulted her.

"You think this is easy? The married men who voted for impeachment are going to go home and think of those pictures while they fuck their wives!" Tears fueled by rage and despair consumed her as she lay there, helpless inside. "But that's not the worst part. The worst part is that at some point today the president is going to call me and I'm going to have to apologize for letting him down."

Bella heard Kusum's granddaughter asking for her in the background. "You're with Asha…"

"I talked to the president. He gave me strict instructions."

Bella chewed her hair. "Yeah?"

"He said, 'Kent is a fucking moron. You better make sure conviction fails before Election Day, and let her know I'm proud of her. I want to fight.'"

Closing her eyes, Bella took a deep breath.

"What about it?" Kusum asked. "You ready to fight for your president?"

Opening her eyes, standing up, Bella said yes.

She'd come out of the bedroom twice to let Aditya and her grandparents know she was okay, or at least not suicidal. The next hour was spent talking strategy with Kusum.

Bella was now impeached, but there was still the matter of the Senate. A two-thirds vote by them was needed in order to convict her, to actually remove her from office. There were forty-five Republican senators, and more than two dozen Democrats Kusum thought were on the fence about impeachment. Sixty-nine potential votes to convict, and she'd lose with sixty-seven.

"That assumes all forty-five Republicans vote to convict," Bella said.

"They'd be throwing the election if they didn't," Kusum said. "Doesn't matter what they actually believe."

Bella scrunched her nose in disgust. "Pathetic."

"The good thing is that's true of our side, too," Kusum said. "Doesn't matter what they actually believe. Even if you genuinely disgust some of my guys, they vote for things that disgust them on a weekly basis because it's good for Democrats."

"…why do you work here?"

Kusum laughed. "Because if I didn't, someone less competent with fewer morals would."

After discussing Senate politics, the conversation steered to media strategy.

"You need to do an interview," Kusum said. "If you'd done FOX like I said, we might've won the House vote."

Bella gritted her teeth. "I'm not talking to some guy picturing me naked the whole time."

"The president agrees it'll help."

Walking into the bathroom, Bella splashed water on her face. "Let me think about it."

"Don't think too long," Kusum said. "I gotta schedule this vote before Halloween so my guys have time to campaign ahead of the election."

Bella hung up without responding.

———●—————————————————●———

October 25, 2028

Her fundraiser in Reston, VA done, Therese reverted to thinking about what was at the top of her mind. She'd seen the vote unfold in real time. Her heart had broken for Bella, and for what the action said of the country she hoped to lead. Senator Raghavan had called her after, stating she'd convinced Bella to speak with her. That was where she was headed now, to a clandestine breakfast aboard her campaign plane, one of the last places the two of them could share a meal in peace.

"Thank you," she said to her agent as he opened the door of the black Suburban to let her out on the tarmac at IAD. Bella was already on the plane.

"Good morning, Madame Mayor."

Therese took a seat across from Bella. An aide laid out granola, fruit, and milk on a table between them. Therese sipped her drink. "I'm told milk staves off arthritis."

"Why am I here?"

Therese smiled. "They told me you're not one for small talk. I'm sorry we haven't met sooner." She put her drink down and leaned across the table separating them. "I can't begin to express how sorry I am for what happened."

Bella let Therese take her hand. "We're both too familiar with trauma." She looked around the plane. "This place flies anywhere at your command?"

Therese smiled. "Yeah."

"Want to go to Paris for the next two weeks?"

Therese laughed. "God, yes."

Bella's smile was as wry as the bread. "Kusum said before I make any big decisions, I owe it to you to discuss my... situation."

"And what decisions have you been contemplating?"

Bella popped a strawberry in her mouth. "I told Senator Raghavan I'd fight yesterday. That's what she and the president want... but this morning, I woke up realizing that's selfish."

Therese chewed some pineapple. "You want to resign?"

Bella scoffed. "I don't *want* any of this... but it's bigger than just me, isn't it? I'll resign if it'll make things easier for you. What's selfish is to assume my pride is more important than your election, the good you can do for hundreds of millions of people."

Therese stood up, tugging Bella with her. Walking down the plane, she pointed at drawings taped up behind several seats, given to her by children across the country. "You're right that this is bigger than you." Each drawing had a location written at the bottom: Denver, Madison, Austin. "These were handed to me by mothers around the whole country," Therese said. "Their daughters wanted to share them with the next President of the United States, a woman who finally looked like them, whose candidacy showed them that they could be anything."

They stopped in front of a drawing of the White House, Capitol, and Supreme Court all mashed up next to each other. Outside each building stood stick figures of three women. "It's us. You, me, and Kusum. Three women leading the free world at a time when society would prefer we sit down and shut up."

Bella ran a hand over the art.

"It's not about our pride—it's about theirs. You're a symbol now." Removing the drawing, she handed it to Bella. "Look at this any time you have doubts. It's hard, acknowledging you're more than just one woman now, that you're a symbol, but it's important to understand you represent the dignity of *all* women. Giving up would be abandoning everyone who's been sexually assaulted and harassed before."

Bella blinked.

"That's what women saw: a strong, smart woman assaulted and

harassed for her looks, and a group of old, fat, white men blaming her."

Bella slumped into the nearest seat.

"I haven't forgotten President Begaye's first choice for your seat," Therese said. "Judge Francino. As much as I love the president, he chose a sexual predator first. And not because he's a bad guy, but because that's who the system decided was next in line." Gripping Bella's shoulder, she locked eyes with her. "That means it's time to break the system."

Breakfast lasted another two hours. Therese ignored five calls from Russell and nine from Rebecca. They shared genuine laughter while learning about each other's families and bonded upon realizing that, despite living in Albuquerque for so long, neither of them had ever attended the Balloon Fiesta.

"Next year," Therese said.

Bella smiled. "I hope it's okay for me to say this, Madame Mayor: Jerome would be proud of you."

Therese massaged her neck, letting the quiet grow between them. "...thank you."

Silence permeated the plane before Bella broke it. "Kusum can't possibly be right *all* the time, right?

Therese laughed.

"That's why she arranged all this, huh? You wouldn't convince me to do the interview, but I'd come to that conclusion myself?"

Therese smiled. "She's in a league of her own."

Bella rolled her eyes. "Tell her I'll do it."

"Senator Raghavan's already booked you with Tammy Day for tonight."

Bella laughed. "She was so sure this would work?"

Therese shrugged. "She knows how good she is. It's about time women were rewarded for recognizing that."

●————————————————●

Bella did some breathing exercises Therese had taught her as she waited in Tammy's green room. She'd seen how Tammy interviewed Democrats. Her track record of getting them to give scathing sound bites had brought her show from daytime to prime time within just months of her contract with FOX. *"Pumps and*

Politics," she called it, unafraid to kick up her legs, putting her red pumps on the table during the show. An intimidation tactic, Kusum warned her.

Tammy's assistant opened the door. "On in five."

Bella nodded as the aide left. She'd practiced with *Nonna* and with Kusum, rehearsing a few zingers and memorizing talking points about the latest laws around revenge porn. Walking out to sit at Tammy's side, she held her head high.

"Thanks for coming," Tammy said, holding out her hand. Bella didn't take it.

"On in three... two... one..."

Tammy flashed a fake smile as she announced her guest, telling viewers they'd not only have the chance to listen to Justice Ferrari but also have an opportunity to call in later with their own questions. Bella bit her tongue; she hadn't agreed to that.

Leaning back in her chair, Tammy set her feet on the desk. "My first question isn't about you so much as the Supreme Court. What would you say to people who think your actions tarnish its legitimacy?"

Bella smiled before asking Tammy if she minded taking her shoes off the table because her parents had taught her it was rude, "especially in front of company." Tammy complied, looking like she'd been slapped.

"Can you repeat the question?"

Tammy stammered as Bella leaned back in her chair. Had Tammy thought she'd come to her like a lamb to slaughter?

"Have the photos damaged the Court's legacy?"

Bella ran her tongue over her lips. She was not the lamb but the lion. "I think something like *Plessy v. Ferguson* or *Dobbs v. Jackson* hurts the Court's legacy."

Tammy's eyes shifted to the notes on her desk; Bella suspected she was looking for some hint of what those cases were.

Forcing a giggle, Tammy brushed her hand over Bella's, as if trying to form a bond. "Ignore the cameras for a moment. Just one girlfriend to another, have you asked your colleagues if they've seen you naked?"

Bella rolled her eyes, making sure the camera captured her

displeasure. "You had Judge Francino on your show recently, who we all know was after my job. I'm less concerned with what my colleagues do in the privacy of their homes and more interested in the naked hypocrisy of asking me that question while ignoring the fact that Francino committed sexual assault, and in his workplace, no less."

Tammy's jaw fell.

"Let's get real, Tammy. That's what everyone is witnessing, my sexual assault. And people like you are selling tickets to it for profit. As a woman, as a human being, you should be ashamed."

Tammy played with her hair, whispering something into her microphone. "Great news! My producer says we have viewers already calling in! Let's take a question from voters."

Bella held her breath. She'd never put her faith in the American public, but now it was unavoidable.

The first caller was a male from Alabama. Her stomach was an eight on a seismograph.

"Hey, Tammy, long-time viewer Peter Isca here."

Tammy laughed. "Thank you so much for watching. What's your question?"

"Why wasn't Judge Francino asked about his assault?"

Tammy resembled a deer in highlights. "Um, he didn't get the job, right? And the charges were dropped. So what's the point?"

Dropping the call, she moved to another one, Rachel from Texas, who scolded Tammy for attacking a fellow woman. The next one, Monica from Wisconsin, said her daughter and husband admired Bella for her tenacity. A fourth one, Jeremy from Nebraska, said he hoped Tammy wouldn't become a regular on his "favorite network."

Bella bit her tongue again to keep from laughing. Someone must've whispered in Tammy's mic after that, because next she shifted to a commercial break and her producer thanked Bella for coming in before escorting her off stage. Turning back before leaving, she saw the producer shaking his head at Tammy and handing her a phone.

●————————————————————————●

Kusum was babysitting during Bella's interview. Her three-month-old granddaughter loved tummy time, grabbing at toys in her playpen and laughing at the screen as they watched FOX together. Kusum smirked; her daughter would yell at her later for letting Asha watch TV.

She had other reasons to smirk, too; the interview had gone better than she'd ever expected. Not to mention the phone call she'd received earlier this evening.

Picking Asha up, she was carrying her to bed when the first senator called. "Senator Reese." She nodded as her colleague spoke, changing Asha's diaper at the same time. What was that saying? Politicians and diapers needed to be changed often, and for the same reason. She smiled at Asha as the Democratic senator from Maine told her he was shifting from yes to no on impeachment after discovering how important Bella was as a role model to other women. "Senator, I'm glad you were able to watch. It's like I've always said, Bella's got a once-in-a-generation mind for the Court and it's on all of us to show the nation's young girls they can be more than what society tells them."

After putting her granddaughter to bed, Kusum fielded two other calls from Democratic colleagues wanting to make their new allegiance known.

"Yes," she said, trying to excuse herself from having to speak to Senator Chappell (D-CO) any longer. "I'll be sure to tell the president, and please do give Senator Denton a call for me."

She doubted Chappell could change Denton's mind, but it was worth a shot. He was maybe the only Democratic senator with enough influence to push Republicans from yes to no, and while Democrats could win the impeachment vote on their own, it would be much more impactful to make the victory bipartisan.

Kusum tucked Asha in, closing the door and preparing to call Bella when she received the best call of the night: Senator Clarissa Jansen of Arizona. "Senator?"

A junior Republican filled with ambition, still in her first term, Jansen couldn't be seen associating with a major Democratic leader like Kusum.

Listening to Clarissa, she started pacing around the kitchen. "Thank you for telling me, Senator. That shows real class, and I'll remember it." Kusum did a silent fist pump upon learning that votes she'd written off as solid yes votes were now undecided. If

Kusum secured Denton, he'd bring a half-dozen Democrats and more than a couple Republicans with him. She could limit yes votes to around forty, despite there being forty-five Republicans in the chamber.

Listening to Clarissa, she laughed. "Don't worry, Senator. I won't thank you in public. I wouldn't want to hurt your street rep." Hanging up, she made the second-best call of the night.

Bella picked up on the first ring. "What are you hearing?"

Kusum smiled. "As it turns out, I *can* be right all the time."

Bella laughed. "Therese told you about that, huh?"

Kusum filled her in on the calls she'd had after the interview. Bella said something in response, but Kusum couldn't hear her. "Where are you?"

Static crackled on the line. "Can you hear me now? My grandparents insisted we go celebrate."

"Zuppa inglese?"

"And scotch." Bella chuckled. "*Nonno* thinks he's Aditya's age."

Kusum grinned. "It's good they're with you. I enjoyed meeting them when you got sworn in."

Bella sighed. "They were more present in my childhood than my parents. Especially *Nonna*. She just... gets me."

Kusum nodded. "I hope I have that type of relationship with Asha when she's older. Maybe she'll even be a Justice like you."

Bella paused before continuing. "I'm glad about Jansen, but as long as a prominent Democrat like Denton is voting yes, he's giving other Democrats license to vote yes with him. That'll be the narrative the media pushes, and it'll shift more undecideds to yes."

Kusum bit her lip, eager to tell Bella about the phone call she'd received before the interview. But this had to be done properly if it was going to work. "You just enjoy tonight and let me worry about the media."

She called Kate Caruso next. "Kate, Senator Raghavan." The *Vanity Fair* reporter was working on a write-up of Bella's interview. "How about I give you some more context for your piece? I got an interesting phone call earlier today from Matteo Medulla."

"The billionaire?"

Chapter Thirteen

October 26, 2028

Matteo Medulla had decided to break his brother's heart five days ago. And now, Kusum was reading about the bloody aftermath in *Vanity Fair.*

He'd called her hours after leaving a breakfast with his brother and Senator Denton. Sitting on her couch, Kusum sipped her tea, remembering how Matteo had invited himself to her house. There, in her basement, he'd told her about Gianpaolo's role in Bella's troubles. It was utterly shocking and predictable at the same time. *Man can't get laid, so he decides to rain down hellfire.* A tale as old as time.

Together in Denver, Denton and Gianpaolo had conspired over decades to help each other get rich and powerful by any means necessary. Matteo had stayed quiet out of loyalty, but Bella's humiliation had been a bridge too far.

Kusum had kept Denton's role from Kate—that knowledge could still be leveraged to get his vote against impeachment—but the story she'd woven was still riveting: billionaire brother turns against his own blood to defend a woman's honor. Gianpaolo had paid someone off to get the photos, then Denton had helped him gain access to Congress's servers to distribute the photos and force an impeachment vote ahead of a presidential election. Bella was yet another victim of the misogynistic games of the tech industry's worst actors.

"Why me?" Kusum had asked Matteo.

"Harvey was always going off about how he hated you," he'd said. "I figured that meant you'd be the best person to call."

Kusum smirked. *Vanity Fair*'s story had gone up online about an hour after Gianpaolo and Famóre's CTO had been arrested by the FBI. They'd been playing tennis at their headquarters in Denver when the cops had stripped them of their WP. Kate had ensured she was on-site for the moment, getting a "no comment" from both law enforcement and Famóre's VP of Sales to include in the final sentence of her story.

Now Gianpaolo faced twenty years under a federal revenge-porn statute protecting Bella's right to privacy, and another ten for distributing obscene photos in violation of a person's right to not receive such photos.

As Kusum finished her tea, her phone rang. It was Senator Harvey Denton. Her smile widened. "Good morning, Senator."

"What the fuck did you do?!"

Kusum was demure by nature, but she did admit to the occasional penchant for schadenfreude. "Awful news about Famóre. I know you were close to the company; hard to believe they weren't working with someone on the inside to get those photos distributed in Congress."

Denton gulped. "What do you want?"

"Your vote, and all the others you'd bring along with you."

"Against impeachment?"

"You don't have to mention Gianpaolo," Kusum said. "Just say that you talked it over with your colleagues, with your family. Say Kate's article changed your mind, if you want."

"And Famóre?"

"Matteo is giving up his ownership stake. If it survives, the Medulla brothers won't be around to see it." Kusum smiled. "But I wouldn't sell my shares just yet. Congress has a nasty reputation for engaging in insider trading, and you don't want to do anything to bring that heat on you."

"...you're blackmailing me."

"Yes."

Denton sighed. "Hammond said not to underestimate you."

Kusum laughed. "That's why he's the leader of his party and you're not."

"...okay. You've got my support."

Kusum's voice was as hard and cold as ice. "*Bella's* got your support." She loosened her tone. "Cheer up, Senator, you're about to have an opportunity to show off how valuable you really are. I'm betting you can limit us to forty votes in favor of impeachment. Any lower and I might let you into Senate leadership next term."

She hung up before he could respond. He'd never set foot in Democratic leadership as long as she was Majority Leader, but sometimes people needed false hope.

Chapter Fourteen

October 29, 2028

Therese forgot she was running for president, so engrossing was the U.S. Senate's impeachment vote. After finishing a shower after a rally in Atlanta, she and Russell glued themselves to the TV.

"Mr. Denton? Mr. Denton: no. Ms. Jansen? Ms. Jansen: no."

Hammond and most other Republicans voted for impeachment, but when the clerk closed the roll call it was 32-68 against. Zero Democrats supported impeachment, and thirteen Republicans backed Bella, too: a bipartisan repudiation of Bella's assailants.

A knot released in Therese's gut, unbridled joy released from its prison. She texted the good news to the group chat of moms whose sons had also died of gun violence.

Russell pulled out his laptop and read aloud from Harold Mueller's live blog for the *New York Times.* "Sources tell me that at one point, Senator Raghavan's whip count was 52-48 in favor of impeachment. Still under the threshold for convicting Bella, but above majority support. That would've crippled the final days of the Begaye administration and had sweeping ramifications for Democrats' chances in the upcoming elections."

"They pay Harold the big bucks for that sort of piercing analysis?" Therese asked.

Russell continued. "Such is the breadth of Senator Raghavan's success, especially juxtaposed against Speaker Munroe's failure, that some in the White House are wondering if there's still time to ditch Governor Ensign for her."

Therese smirked. Kusum had told Therese she'd shut down that type of chatter at the DNC. Besides, this was the White House.

"It's gotta be Harmon," Russell said.

Therese nodded. "The vice president's upset he's out of a job come January."

Russell sighed. "Want me to get Rebecca?"

"Yeah. No use letting this lie."

Russell walked down the hall to get her manager.

"Sorry to interrupt your date," Therese said, when Rebecca strolled in.

Rebecca rolled her eyes. "Oh yeah," she said. "Russell walked in on my threesome with Ben & Jerry."

Therese laughed before shifting her tone. "Call Harmon's office for me. As much as I like reading the words 'Raghavan' and 'vice president' together, it's time to stop this."

Rebecca scanned the blog on Russell's laptop as she dialed. Frowning, she handed Therese the phone.

"This is Mayor Johnson. I need to speak with Vice President Harmon."

Rebecca's hands formed into fists as she read the blog. Therese waited. She put her hand over the receiver as Rebecca shouted a four-letter word, hoping Harmon wouldn't hear it.

When Harmon did come to the phone, Therese stepped into the bathroom, closing the door.

"Therese, how can I help you?"

"Mr. Vice President, I read the most interesting thing just now in the *Times*."

"Yeah?"

"I'm sure it was someone on your staff, since I know you wouldn't be so careless, but someone told Harold Mueller there'd been chatter of me swapping out Governor Ensign for Senator Raghavan."

A pause filled the air. "...is that such a bad idea?"

Therese bit her lip, knowing she had to choose her next words carefully. "Mark, it won't do anyone any good to have people questioning my judgment or Governor Ensign's qualifications days before Election Day."

Harmon's tone went cold. "You're talking to the Vice President."

"And you're talking to the next President," Therese said. She wasn't taken seriously by a certain old guard unless she spoke with steel and venom in her mouth, so she looked in the mirror to confirm her nostrils were flaring before she spoke again. "You were a good ally to the president and you've been a strong defender for the country. But let's call a spade a spade if you want to play games: you're a bitter old man who can't understand why he lost to President Begaye eight years ago and why he had to drop out this year before a single vote was cast."

"Hang on," Harmon said. "You think just because you're our nominee and a woman..."

Therese scoffed. "I'd heard the stories about you, but I never believed them until now."

Harmon paused again. "...I shouldn't have said anything about you being a woman." Another pause as the truth sank in for him. No matter if Therese or Kaitlin won, his political life was over: the Democratic Party wasn't going to nominate an old, straight, white male ever again. "What do you need?"

Therese walked back into the room, speaking loud enough for Russell and Rebecca to hear. "I need you to cut this shit out and spread the gospel of the Johnson-Ensign ticket. There aren't going to be any more anonymous hints from 'sources close to the White House' questioning my choice of Ensign over Raghavan for VP. If you speak to a reporter, it's going to be on the record and it's going to be about what great judgment the campaign has shown and how impressed you are with everyone here."

She heard Harmon breathing loudly, and then a "yes, ma'am" before he hung up. Seeing her husband and manager smiling, she asked them what was going on.

"Nothing," Rebecca said. "You're ready to be president."

Chapter Fifteen

October 29, 2028

Kaitlin Lungford was learning a lesson at fifty-seven that most learned by twenty-seven: doing the right thing usually resulted in everyone hating you.

The Party's largest donors had deserted her after she'd released the joint statement. And in the hours since the impeachment vote, she'd ignored not just the press's calls looking for a statement, but also Mirai's. She wasn't eager to speak with her vice-presidential nominee given how it'd gone last time they talked. But when Whit Pryor had texted her this evening, telling her he'd fill her funding gap in exchange for one face-to-face, she'd known she couldn't avoid him. At the rate her campaign was going, she was facing a choice on November 1—of making payroll or pulling all her ads in the swing states.

She'd walked right into his office under the cover of nightfall. "This isn't legal," she said, standing by him as he sat on a couch. "I can't be seen meeting with my Super PAC."

"Feel free to arrest me once you're president," Whit said, "but for that to happen, you'll have to listen to me, first."

Kaitlin looked around at the spartan surroundings. "I would've thought this place would be a lot nicer with the cash you're bringing in."

Whit shrugged. "I spend the money on other stuff."

"Ads and staff?"

"Booze and hookers."

Kaitlin couldn't tell if he was kidding or not. She decided not to ask.

"Today wasn't great," he said.

Kaitlin scoffed. "Understatement of the year."

"It could work for us, though."

Kaitlin raised an eyebrow. "How's that?"

"With the Bella chapter closed, you can shift back to the issues right ahead of Election Day. Talk about rolling back WP legalization, undoing Begaye's crowning achievement. Show conservatives that you're just as much a fighter in politics as you are on the battlefield."

Kaitlin said nothing.

"I bet your polls say the same as mine: down in North Carolina, Nevada. Voters viewed Bella as a distraction, so now you get to reframe the debate right in the nick of time. Come out for a tougher position, or lose."

Kaitlin shook her head. "If that's true, then I'll lose, but I don't think it is. Voters know you can't put the genie back in the bottle. They love watching their WP-fueled sports, eating their WP-coated food, using their WP-engineered products."

Whit stood up. "I can't believe you're so selfish."

"That's rich coming from you. When's the last time you saw your kid?"

Whit gritted his teeth. "If I'm selfish, it's for the good of the country."

Kaitlin laughed, a mirthless sound. "The country needed to see Bella's tits, huh?"

Whit froze.

"I told you I'd tell Melissa what you did," Kaitlin said.

Whit's face went white. "...four million."

"What?"

"I'll wire the money to the RNC right now. That should be enough to keep you on air and make payroll, right?"

Kaitlin's nostrils flared. The son of a bitch was bribing her, but was that so bad? People were counting on her. Olivia needed her. Unwilling to tell him it was okay, she merely nodded. Was this the right thing? She didn't know. But she was keeping her promise to herself to run the campaign her way and she'd be able to make payroll and stay on air doing it. How could that be wrong?

———————•———————•———————

She'd had her security detail drop her off two blocks from Whit's office. Thanking Agent Hanson for opening the door to the Black suburban that'd take her back to her hotel, she saw someone waiting inside the car.

"You're so close."

Seeing her uncle's specter turned her stomach upside down. She grabbed an armrest for support. "Why are you still here?"

"You're a smart woman," he said. "Appreciate how close you are to achieving greatness and just listen to Whit."

Whatever fear she'd felt dissipated upon hearing that advice. Listen to another man? To someone who'd lost everyone he cared about? Who hung on to power because he thought it could fill the hole in his heart?

She replied to her uncle with steel in her voice. "I've always been great, even before joining the military, even without any of this." Long ago, she'd turned down becoming the first female Undersecretary of the Army until her uncle had forced her to take the position. Was that when her life had started morphing into something she didn't like? A father was supposed to advise you, know what was best for you, and make you do it even if you didn't want to in the moment. But Charles wasn't her father...

Arriving at the hotel, she exited the car and closed the door behind her. The ghost followed behind her, but she ignored it the whole way to her room.

Chapter Sixteen

November 1, 2028

Therese's political fortunes were better than ever. Up two in North Carolina. Up three in Nevada. Her pollster had told her months ago she had a ceiling of 277 electoral votes, but the combination of releasing the joint statement and Bella defying all odds in the Senate meant Therese had a shot now of cracking 300. At the Hay-Adams Hotel in DC, everyone wanted a piece of her. Plates for dinner, drinks, and a photo with her didn't go for less than $100,000, and it was $200,000 for the privilege of getting a couple minutes to speak with her at a private reception beforehand.

Rebecca had told her weeks ago how her sister, Claire, had abandoned the campaign. But now that the impeachment ordeal was over and she was up in red states like North Carolina, everyone wanted to buy their way back in. Therese had been thrilled to tell Rebecca she could tell her sister to get lost when she'd offered to buy a table tonight. Gone were the days of having to put her beauty consultant, Erica, on furlough. She'd insisted her entire staff be put up at the luxury hotel tonight. She'd insisted Rebecca and Erica take her room. With its bay windows and Juliet balconies, it was all a bit too much.

Excusing herself to go to the bathroom after an hour of being photographed like a show pony, she met Senator Raghavan in the back entrance to the kitchen.

"Is the senator coming?" Therese asked.

Kusum nodded. "I told him we wanted to thank him for his support of Bella and that it was time for us to plan out his political future."

Therese frowned. "At least that's the truth."

Senator Denton arrived in a tuxedo. "Ladies." He tipped an imaginary top hat. "I'm happy to see you appreciate that no good deed should go unrewarded. We're all getting what we want, huh?"

Therese restrained her impulse to punch him and break loose his flawless teeth. He might've ditched his bolo tie, but the fake aw-shucks manner and drawn-out voice were on full display.

Facing Kusum, he continued. "You hinted there'd be a place for me in Senate leadership days ago, but after thinking it over, I think I can do more good at Treasury."

Kusum smiled. "You do, huh?"

He placed a hand on Therese's shoulder. "The Senate loves confirming its own, and you get an open seat to elevate anyone you want to the most exclusive club in the world."

Therese forced a flat affect. "Governor Minnick would appoint someone."

Harvey smiled. "Don't sell yourself short, Madame Mayor. Suman would pick anyone you wanted."

Kusum stepped between him and Therese. "I agree the U.S. Senate isn't the best place for your talents, Harvey."

Denton chuckled. "What did you have in mind?"

"The Cayman Islands? You could say you want to spend more time with your money."

Harvey's face tightened. "Excuse me?"

"Or perhaps Europe. Retire on the Riviera. Do whatever you want, so long as it isn't part of the U.S. government."

Denton's hands balled into fists. "You promised—"

"I promised nothing." Venom dripped from Kusum's lips. "I told you it was time to explore your political future. Here it is: you've decided to resign to spend more time with your family."

Denton's face shifted from rage to smugness so fast it made Therese dizzy. "...and if I don't? If I pull Harold Mueller from the party right now and tell him Mayor Johnson is just like her son, nothing more than a thug willing to intimidate me?"

Therese moved to slap Harvey, but Kusum beat her to it. He

stepped back, grabbing his cheek.

"Are you out of your fucking mind?!"

"Don't ever mention Jerome again," Senator Raghavan said. "Do anything less than follow my full instructions and Harold Mueller will hear all about how you helped Gianpaolo hack into the Congressional servers to distribute revenge porn." Taking out a folder from her coat, she tossed it at Harvey. The contents spilled out, leaving him to pick them up. His eyes bulged as he scanned the papers.

"I got the emails from Matteo. He recorded the phone calls, too. You can keep that folder; the original is in my office."

Harvey's face turned white. "...why?"

Kusum laughed. "Why?! Because you disgust us."

Harvey pleaded. "You're going to be president. I've got friends across the aisle, Republican votes I can get you on paid family leave, on WP funding..."

Therese scoffed. "You can't promise that."

Denton got on his knees, grabbed Therese's skirt. "There's still the matter of the filibuster. Democrats only have fifty-five seats, probably less after Election Day..."

Therese shoved Denton off. "I don't care if we have forty-nine votes. No offense, Senator Raghavan."

Kusum nodded. "None taken."

"The whole point of having principles is that we stick to them under duress," Therese said. "If we lose, at least we can lose with our heads held high."

Denton stood up, gritting his teeth as he tossed his bow tie to the ground. "You think the two of you will be the only influential people after Election Day? Maybe you've forgotten Speaker Munroe is my hometown friend."

Therese snickered.

"Go ahead and take my Senate seat. I'll sit on a board somewhere, making more money than you've ever seen."

Therese nodded. "I wish you well, Senator."

"Fuck both of you."

The two women collapsed laughing in each other's arms the moment he left, taking a moment for themselves before returning to the party.

Chapter Seventeen

November 6, 2028

Kajal Talwar knew two things tasted delicious if given enough time to simmer: Indian food, and revenge. She'd avoided Whit for over a month, making excuses like how she didn't want to bother him this close to Election Day or how she had to study for the bar. The Whit Pryor she'd read about during the years of President Brooks wouldn't have believed her. Hell, the Whit Pryor of last year might've known something was up. But this one was a drug-addled fuckboi, a far cry from the prim blond who looked as if he'd just walked out of a J. Crew catalog. She doubted he suspected that the whore from LISA had figured out she'd been used to get Bella's photos, or that she intended to even the score tonight.

This time, when he'd called her cell, she'd answered on the first ring. "I'm sorry it's been so long," she'd said. "But I know how important tomorrow is. I wanted to wish you good luck, make tonight something special."

He'd flown her out to Madison, Wisconsin. And now she was naked on the bed as he finished bathing. He'd already fucked her once in the shower, shoving her against a glass door as he dug his nails into her hips and took her from behind. He'd told her to clean up and get a condom while he washed his hair.

Lying back on the bed, she placed the wrapper between her thighs and waited as he walked through the door, toweling off his hair.

"Ready for your treat?" Whit said.

Her eyes followed his as they shifted to the condom laced with unrefined WP.

He sighed as his hand found his member. He stroked it and watched her, remaining where he stood. "Were you with anyone while... while you weren't with me?"

Kajal smiled. "Just one. A woman." His hand moved like a jackhammer. "Does that excite you?"

He was on her like a lion on a gazelle. Ripping open the condom, he'd hardly put it on before thrusting inside her, biting her shoulder. One. Two. Three. His balls slapped against her ass with each motion.

She raked her hands over his chest, embracing his penchant to intertwine pain and pleasure. Whit's eyes twitched as Kajal felt the WP in the condom soaking into his cock. She was becoming wetter, the heat around them palpable. Their hearts beat like boiling kettles about to pop. Grabbing his shoulders, she lifted herself off him, her lips finding his before he could protest. Leaning over his body, allowing him to admire her full chest, she retrieved another condom from her bag. Sitting on her knees, she smiled at him, stroking Whit with one hand as she ripped the wrapper open with her teeth.

Whit's body tensed—with anticipation or fear, she didn't know. "I've never tried two."

Taking his hand, she placed it between her legs and smiled. "More's always better, right?"

He played with her as she bent over and used her mouth to place the condom over his cock. His fingers moved as fast as her head, and she allowed herself to finish. For this to work, her actions had to be natural, lulling him into a false sense of security.

She waited until he was close to the point of no return before stopping, ripping the condom off and sitting on his legs so that her mound was inches from his dripping member.

He grunted in frustration. "Why'd you stop?"

She smoothed her hands over his chest, bending over to suck his nipples before answering. "I told you I wanted to make tonight special. Just like the campaign, drawing out the process makes it so much better at the end." Her head this close to his body, she knew the man's heart wasn't far from bursting.

Leaning backwards to grab a third condom, still sitting atop him, she offered him the best view yet of how eager she was. When she threw the rubber on his chest, he opened it himself, placing it around his cock before grabbing her, shoving himself inside her.

She rode him like it was his last meal, gasping in pleasure as he grabbed her ass and bit her tits, leaving bruises all over her. The marks would work in her favor if she ever ended up before a jury.

"I'm close." He shouted the words, the effects of WP deafening him to reality. She climaxed again, high on her revenge being so close at hand. Bending over, she let him kiss her. He bit her bottom lip until it bled.

"Aagh!" He came with such force that she rolled off him, feeling semen leak out from the broken condom. She saw his eyes bulge as he grabbed his heart and looked for a phone. He barked for her to call 911.

She put her mouth right up to his ear and whispered. "Don't you understand?" she purred. "I'm killing you. And I've got even worse planned for Claire."

Shoving her away, he stood up to grab his phone, only to collapse to the ground. She laughed as he crawled after the fallen phone. "All the girls at LISA said no matter what, never use more than one unrefined rubber." She darted from him as Whit threw up near her feet. "Disgusting." His vomit was black.

Getting dressed, stepping over him, she bent down to her knees to offer one last comment. "Given the world on a silver platter, and still, you wanted more. I don't pity you."

Opening the door, she called LISA to tell them she'd passed the bar. She was quitting.

Chapter Eighteen

November 7, 2028

Election Day. Therese had once had no traditions around it, but now, on the morning of each election, after showering and saying her prayers, she repeated the same words:

"Jerome, Jerome, you are my home.
One day I'll join you, 'til then I'll roam.
What's right is right and what's wrong is wrong,
I'll fight in your name for justice; with you at my side it won't take long."

These mornings were the calm before the storm. She'd have a conference call with Rebecca and her pollster to get an update on turnout in key precincts across the country, but apart from that, she'd go vote and have breakfast with Russell here in Albuquerque. She may even have sex, something her campaign schedule had prevented for weeks.

"Ma'am?"

Her security detail opened the car she was riding in with Russell. It was time to vote.

The walk into the school resembled a red-carpet affair, with journalists shouting over each other to get a quote. "Russell, who are you going to vote for?"

Russell laughed in response.

Another asked what Therese thought of rumors of low turnout among the key Democratic demographic of eighteen- to twenty-four-year-olds.

She stopped at the entrance to John Herrington Elementary School. "Jerome would be twenty-five today if he were alive. Old enough to vote. I hope our youth exercise the right so many of us cannot."

Russell saluted reporters as the pair of them walked through the doors.

John Herrington had been the first Native American to fly in space. The message to students, that they should reach for the stars, wasn't lost on Therese as she filled out her ballot. The Secret Service didn't show her the threats they intercepted, but she knew there were plenty for the first major Black female presidential candidate.

Voting for the other Democrats on her ballot and an initiative to boost library funding, she submitted her ticket and walked towards a woman with bangs who handed her an "I Voted" sticker.

"Madame Mayor, my name is Maadhini."

Therese smiled. "It's nice to meet you."

Maadhini leaned in, whispering. "I'm not supposed to say anything partisan, but I don't think it counts to tell you just how much I admire you."

Therese placed Maadhini's hands in her own. "Thank you."

"My wife and I have a baby girl and I hope I can be half the mom you are. Forgive my presumptuousness, but Jerome would be proud of you."

Therese was grateful for Maadhini's hug, using the opportunity to wipe her tears before facing the press. "God bless you."

Maadhini whispered one last thing before Therese joined her husband outside. When she walked to Russell with a grin on her face, he asked her what was so funny.

"It's a corny joke; I know you hate them."

Russell rolled his eyes. "I do, but let's hear it."

"That woman giving out stickers, she told me if I get anxious tonight during my speech, I should just turn off my nervous system."

Ignoring her "joke" and the shouting of reporters trying to get another comment, Russell took them to the car.

As they drove back home, Therese thought more about what

Maadhini had said, wishing to be half the mother she was. It was something the press, her staff, even Russell didn't understand. She hadn't stopped being a mom when Jerome died, but people had stopped treating her like one. Her favorite part of this whole campaign was being able to mother her staff. Closing her eyes, she thanked God for the blessing of motherhood and Maadhini for the joke that'd keep her from crying tonight, win or lose.

Chapter Nineteen

November 7, 2028

Kaitlin's insides heaved like snakes fighting amongst themselves. They'd set up a war room at the Governor's Mansion in Georgia. The victory party (it was bad luck to call it anything else) would be outside on the lawn. Kaitlin paced in a hallway while Olivia and the rest of her team fielded reports from her staff across the country and spoke with lawyers to file any necessary claims against voter intimidation or fraud.

They'd called North Carolina for her by eleven p.m. Ohio and Florida, too. New Hampshire and Michigan had gone Democratic, but in a surprise to everyone, Wisconsin had just been called for Republicans, and not only had Kaitlin won, but the Democratic senator had lost re-election, too. Kaitlin hated admitting it, but Whit had been right to have put such emphasis on the state.

"Madame Secretary?" Olivia tapped her shoulder. "FOX just called Georgia for you."

Kaitlin sighed with relief; it'd be a pretty lame party if it took place in a state she'd lost. It all came down to Arizona, now. A win there secured the election.

"The governor?" Kaitlin asked.

"She's refusing to leave the residence until there's a verdict."

Just then, Kaitlin's digital director, Vanessa, opened the door. She was crying. "Sorry to interrupt..."

Olivia's skin turned paler than usual. "Arizona?"

Vanessa nodded. "It might take another week to be official;

Maricopa County is always late in counting. But our state director and exit polls paint a clear picture: we lost."

Kaitlin nodded, then leaned her head against the wall. Over a billion dollars spent between her campaign and the Super PAC. Thousands of lives committed to this effort over the last year, eating, breathing, and sleeping in her name. And maybe ten thousand votes had swung it for Therese and decided the fate of the country.

Looking Vanessa in the eyes, she nodded again, thanking her. "I need to see the governor."

Eyes red, Vanessa apologized to her.

"I won't let this drag out," Kaitlin told Olivia. "The country shouldn't have to endure us questioning the legitimacy of the first Black female president."

Olivia hugged her. "I'm proud of you and I'm proud of this campaign. You see Governor Shimizu. I'll handle the staff."

Taking Vanessa's hand, Olivia returned to the war room, leaving Kaitlin to have the second-hardest conversation of her life.

Mirai was alone in her dining room, drinking green tea and eating an anpan. Her face was drawn tight when Kaitlin walked in. "I baked these myself," she said, offering a red bean-filled bun. "I told Ralph I wouldn't wake him until tomorrow morning, and my son wanted to sleep over at his friend's one last time before his world changed. I wanted to be alone when you came to me because I knew what you were going to say."

Kaitlin sighed, a sound that filled the large room. "I'm sorry I let you down."

Mirai stood, nostrils flared. "You were content to lie and steal and bully your way into power until you met me."

Kaitlin shook her head. "It's got nothing to do with you. Uncle Charles's death, Therese's candidacy, it's shown me the importance of change, of leaving something for posterity." She forced herself still as Mirai stepped close enough that she could smell the governor's perfume. "...I'm trying to do better."

Mirai spat venom. "Better for you, but not for the country."

Kaitlin opened her mouth, but no words came out.

"Do you remember that fundraiser in Milwaukee, right after the convention?"

Kaitlin nodded.

"I went to the bathroom at some point, and while I was in the stall, two old ladies entered to touch up their makeup. And you know what they said? That it was smart of you to bring on a skingrafter as VP since it'd make you more appealing to moderates."

Kaitlin grabbed the table, sitting as her knees gave out. "...I'm sorry."

"I don't want your fucking apology!" Mirai picked her cup up, and for a moment Kaitlin thought she'd throw it at her. "That's what the Party is, at its core. We had a chance to do better, but instead, you decided to grow a moral compass. Live with that."

Kaitlin cradled her head in her hands.

"You'll never understand. It was my fault that I ever thought you could."

"You're right," Kaitlin said. She forced herself to look Mirai in the eyes, and held back tears because she knew her feelings were nothing compared to the governor's. "I tried to conduct the campaign with a veneer of decency, but you deserved better. I don't blame you for being mad at me." Standing, she took a bun and bit into it, considering her next words. Swallowing, she held Mirai's hand. "Four years will fly by. You should run for president; I'll endorse you immediately."

Mirai shoved her hand off, looked Kaitlin in the eye. Her face had reddened with fury. "I won't run, I won't do that to my family. But even if I did, your endorsement would be the kiss of death." She left, leaving Kaitlin all alone.

⸻

Therese performed her breathing exercises. Inhale for four seconds, hold for four seconds, exhale for four seconds, repeat. Ignoring protocol, Kaitlin had just called her directly to concede. Bunkered down in a hotel room in Albuquerque, Rebecca had lawyers on standby to fly to Arizona. Therese got to be the one to inform her that wasn't necessary. But before she spoke to her campaign manager, she closed her eyes and spoke to Jerome—the husband and the son. "Thank you."

Opening her eyes, she entered the war room where Rebecca,

Gael, and her pollster were poring over results. Rebecca took one look at her and an understanding passed between them. "For real?!"

Therese smiled with every inch of her body. "For real."

Rebecca jumped on a table, screaming for the whole room to hear. "Everyone, fucking listen!"

The chaos of the room ground to a halt as people closed their laptops and got off their phones. Gael muted the TV, silencing Joy Taylor's commentary on MSNBC.

"I've sounded like a broken record saying it all year, but it now comes with the full force of the law! Because of your hard work, allow me to present President Therese Johnson!"

The room shattered. Her political director, in charge of deploying the moms in her group chat across the country to campaign on her behalf, FaceTimed the group now to pass them the good news. Rebecca's deputy, a man Therese had only met a half dozen times, popped a bottle of champagne. Gael pumped his fist in the air before returning to his laptop, probably generating memes. The mayor of New York, Curtis Levitt, was crying.

"Quiet!" Rebecca's voice pierced through the noise.

Taking her hand, Therese brought her down and climbed onto the table herself.

"First, I want to thank every single one of you. Rebecca's right: I wouldn't be here but for you. And I know what you all sacrificed to do this, putting your lives on hold." The room was silent as a church mouse. "I see my moms on FaceTime." The room laughed as Therese's political director lifted his phone up so Therese could wave at them. "I'm so proud to have every faith represented here. Please join me in prayer." Heads bowed, she quoted chapter two of the Bhagavad Gita to her team.

"The material body is perishable, but the soul is not. And while death is certain, our souls live on so that we can all do our duty."

Raising her head, she saw Russell leaning against the wall at the back of the room. And next to him were her first two loves, as if they'd aged by her side this whole time. Jerome Sr., approaching sixty, having earned every grey hair on his head. And her son, the love of her life, looking every bit as cocky as a twenty-five-year-old in the prime of his life should, grinning, eyes twinkling. She released the breath she'd held since that terrible day Officer Jackson had come to her door, and let Rebecca take her from the room, downstairs, to where she'd deliver a speech to a crowded room, promising a new day for America.

●————————————————————●

Kusum was consoling Senator Rosalina Garcia of Wisconsin when she saw the headline on MSNBC: SECRETARY LUNGFORD CONCEDES TO MAYOR JOHNSON.

"Senator," Kusum said, "I know it's poor comfort, but your vote for Bella did have consequences beyond costing you your seat. I've just been informed Mayor Johnson won." Promising Rosalina she'd see if there was a place for her in a Johnson administration, she hung up and turned back to her own Election Night party at the Mandarin in DC.

Her staff was running their own war room. Though Kusum had won her own re-election by fourteen points, Democrats had lost twenty seats in the House and three seats in the Senate, holding on to razor-thin majorities in both chambers. Still, with President Johnson and Vice President Ensign in office, they'd be poised to enact sweeping change across the country these next two years. Paid family leave. Fully funded efforts to expand WP access. A chance to turn President Begaye's promise of a better future into a reality for posterity.

Five Democrats in the suburbs of Houston and Dallas lost their re-elections after having snuck in on the heels of the country discovering President Brooks's treason. Therese had lost Texas by seven points despite Ensign's governorship, a fact that must've gnawed at the vice president's soul.

As Kusum watched the results come in, one of the Party's largest donors, Elias Johansson, touched her shoulder, interrupting her thoughts. "Something has to be done about Kent."

Kusum nodded. Elias's thoughts would permeate the entire Party's infrastructure before the end of the month. Holding an impeachment vote might've secured Bella's standing, but it'd killed Democratic enthusiasm during the apex of early voting. Kusum had no doubt it'd cost them Wisconsin and Georgia.

"He won't be Speaker in the next session," Kusum said. "Please, keep that between us."

"I'll keep your secrets, but how'll you manage that?"

"Harvey's announcing his retirement this week." She smiled at seeing Elias's eyes widen. Power thrived in darkness, but knowledge needed sunlight. "I think Harvey and Kent should open their own lobbying firm, don't you? Once I let Kent know he doesn't have his best friend in the Senate anymore, it shouldn't be hard to convince him lobbying is a better option for him and his wallet."

Elias chuckled. "You truly are the best in the business."

Kusum laughed. "You're very kind."

"Forgive me, Mr. Johansson." Kusum's chief of staff stepped between them, tapping her watch. "It's after midnight. It'd be a good idea for you to make some remarks to the crowd."

Kusum nodded as she was led to the stage and handed a mic. "Folks, how about President Johnson?" The crowd's applause was muted. "I know we've got cause to be sad tonight, but at the end of the day we've held our Democratic majorities and the White House!" Her smile was infectious, and others started catching it as she went on to rattle off legislative priorities she'd work with the new president to address immediately.

"We've all earned a good night's rest, but tomorrow morning, the first thing I'm going to do is jump on a call with President Begaye and President-Elect Johnson to ensure we have the most impactful hundred days since FDR! God bless you, and may God bless America!"

Leaving the stage, shaking hands with volunteers as she was led to her car, she got out her phone and dialed Therese's number, eager to congratulate her.

Chapter Twenty

November 8, 2028

Bella sighed after getting off the phone with Kusum. They'd known each other eight months, but it might as well have been eight years. Senator Raghavan had informed her Denton was resigning, which meant the Famóre case was falling apart. It hadn't been decided yet, but with Gianpaolo going to jail and Matteo resigning from the company, the Court could focus on the legal issues for posterity instead of some boys' club that said the Medulla brothers had to be protected.

"Who was that?" *Nonno* took his head out of a newspaper as she sat in the kitchen with him while *Nonna* made breakfast.

"Kusum," Bella said.

Nonno smiled. "She must be pleased."

Bella watched him read the front page of the *New York Times*, which detailed Harold Mueller's take on the elections. Accepting a cup of coffee from her *nonna*, she sat at the table and watched Aditya carry out suitcases from their rooms. "I'm glad you're staying another month," she said. "It'll be nice to be together without the election hanging over us."

"We couldn't leave without seeing Puli," *Nonna* said, handing out dishes of fruits and crepes. "You need help with the bags, Aditya?"

Nonno interrupted. "A strong man can't do it alone?"

"Strong men know when to ask for help," Aditya said. "But I'm okay right now."

"I wonder what's for lunch," *Nonno* said.

Nonna slapped his hand as he began eating. "*Patso!* Just started breakfast and already thinking of lunch."

"Nothing crazy about enjoying food," *Nonno* said, helping himself to another crepe.

Aditya smiled. "Don't worry, *Nonno*. Dad is making a feast. Pav bhaji and bhel puri and samosa chaat. He's even bringing in some of his friends from the temple to make dosas."

Bella laughed.

"What's funny?" Aditya asked.

Rather than answer, Bella pulled him back to their room, telling her grandparents she wanted to make sure they hadn't forgotten anything. Once inside, she kissed his lips, running her hands over his sides and through his hair.

Aditya started unzipping his pants. "Okay, I guess we can get a quickie in..."

She slapped his arm. "Idiot." She zipped him back up. "I'm happy, not horny."

He smirked. "Aren't they the same thing?"

She frowned. "I just have to tell you something."

"What is it?"

She bit her bottom lip. "...I contacted Sadiya and Maadhini."

He exhaled. "...it's okay."

Bella's eyebrow raised. "Really?"

"I'd be lying if I said I hadn't battled my fair share of demons this past year. Abhinav. Rakshan. Your past job. *Nonno* saw it as soon as he landed."

Bella touched his knee, seating them on their bed. "I wondered why you started calling him that..."

Aditya chuckled. "We walked around that first day, after I dropped their bags off. He set me straight, told me how a family can overcome anything together, but I have to see us as family before I can draw from that strength."

She smiled. "The men in my life are such drama kings."

Aditya continued. "I understand now that devotion and love don't exist in a vacuum. We need to build community from our loved ones to sustain those emotions, to become stronger than the sum of our parts."

Bella smiled with her entire body, interlacing her fingers in his own. "Come on, Don Juan. I saw you eyeing those crepes; let's get you one before *Nonno* finishes them all."

<hr />

Kaitlin entered her DC office to thunderous applause. Olivia and Emily were there, but also Jake (Communications Director) and Cody (Field Director) and Vinita (Advance Director) with their own staffs. Boxes were scattered across the individual offices as people packed up their things. She smirked—their landlord was going to miss their rent. Two hundred people worked out of this office.

Kaitlin held her hands up, summoning silence. "I'm so proud of each and every one of you, and I hope you don't leave without coming up and giving me a chance to thank you personally. I know you gave up a lot for this opportunity, and I'm sorry to disappoint you."

Vinita shouted from the back. "You didn't disappoint anyone!"

The rest of the room clapped in agreement until Kaitlin again silenced them. "Lunch is on me." The crowd laughed. "There's tacos and burritos outside." More applause. "And I wanted you all to know, I talked to Olivia this morning and the campaign's covering everyone's salaries through December." Kaitlin could hear a pin drop; she thought she saw people crying. "It's not fair to lose and then also be hung out to dry right near the holidays. You need your health insurance, money for gifts. I couldn't win for you, but at least I can do this."

Olivia was the first to break the silence, coming up to hug Kaitlin. Emily followed, and then the others, receiving her embrace and some whispered words. Some laughed, while others cried. Each one came away with a smile, though, lines of determination sketched in their faces. The last one, Miguel, asked her for a letter of recommendation.

Kaitlin hid a wince; she had no idea who Miguel was or what he'd done. "Write out some bullet points for me," she said. "Send them to Olivia and I'll make sure you're taken care of." Smiling, he shook her hand before leaving to join the others at the food truck outside.

"Nice save," Olivia said, alone with her boss.

"You need a letter of rec too?" Kaitlin joked.

Olivia's laugh was mirthless. "The Party will fail without you."

"If one person can bring it down, maybe it doesn't deserve to exist."

Olivia bit her lip. "Call me in four years? Maybe it'll be different with Therese as the incumbent."

Kaitlin chided her. "Madame President to you, to all of us. And if Mirai's to be believed, the Party will change, but it won't be for the better."

Olivia exhaled. "What's next, then?"

Kaitlin smacked her lips. "Long-term? Who knows? Short-term? I owe Vijay a honeymoon."

Olivia smiled. "Where to?"

"Greece, and Paris."

"When?"

Kaitlin smiled with every inch of her body. "Tomorrow."

"No one deserves it more. Thank you, Madame Secretary."

Kaitlin hugged her campaign manager one last time, drawing her tight to whisper in her ear. "You're welcome."

Secretary Lungford stayed for hours with her staff, aware she'd likely never see them again. She played beer pong with Vinita's staff and cornhole with Cody's team and poker with Miguel, who she learned had been tasked with briefing Republican elected officials ahead of making public appearances on her behalf. But finally, it was time to head home to Vijay and pack for their flight tomorrow morning.

Walking to her car, promising some girl named Alex she'd send a gift for her wedding (she was marrying Cody), she got a phone call. It was Therese. "Madame President?"

"Not for another ten weeks," Mayor Johnson said.

Getting into her Suburban, she motioned to Agent Hanson to start driving. "What can I do for you?"

"I don't want to talk about it on the phone. Can you meet me in DC tomorrow night?"

Kaitlin squeezed the phone. She'd been civil for her staff, but she wouldn't mince words in private: Therese had crushed her dreams, left a pain in her gut worse than anytime she'd been shot.

"I leave for my honeymoon tomorrow morning."

"Please," Therese begged. "It's important."

Kaitlin thought she'd break her phone with her grip. "...one meeting. That's all you get."

Hanging up, she knew Vijay would understand: a fact that made her feel worse.

●————————————————————●

November 10, 2028

Kaitlin rolled her eyes as she waited to see the President-Elect. It was technically more than a day since they'd spoken; four a.m. was about the only time of day you could have a private meeting at the Lincoln Memorial. The man's visage, the entire experience of visiting the greatest Republican president, was designed to overwhelm. Walk up eighty-seven steps: the sum of four score and seven. Then encounter thirty-six Greek columns from Colorado, meant to honor each state at the time of Lincoln's death. Inside, the marble of the walls hailed from Tennessee, where Lincoln had been born. Alabama marble adorned the ceiling, some of the best marble in the world. And the statue itself was made from Georgian marble, a reminder that General Sherman had razed Atlanta to the ground. But all these places had marble, and they'd come together now to reunite and build something better than the sum of their parts.

"Madame Secretary?"

Kaitlin heard Therese clomping up the stairs. Turning to face her, she forced a smile. The agents guarding her had changed.

"I'm sorry," Therese said. "These agents have to search you."

Kaitlin nodded, allowing the men to do their job, deducing that Secret Service staff changed once you went from candidate to president-elect.

"All clear," one said, walking to the entrance of the memorial with their colleague.

Looking out across the National Mall, Kaitlin spotted two snipers waiting to cut her down, if needed. Her nostrils flared; what did Therese know of this awesome responsibility?

"Will you walk with me?" Therese said.

Kaitlin let Therese take her hand as they stepped to the North

Chamber, where Lincoln's 2nd inaugural address was carved into the wall.

Therese sighed. "Nearly half the country belonged to the Confederacy at the time of his re-election. You could say he became their leader without their consent."

Kaitlin sneered. "You'd be wrong. They gave their consent when they chose to rebel."

Therese nodded. "I agree."

Kaitlin's nostrils flared. "I didn't come here for a history lesson, Madame President-Elect." Saying each syllable of Therese's new title made her wince. "What do you want?"

Therese motioned for Kaitlin to join her on the south side of the memorial, where she read the Gettysburg Address.

From these honored dead we take increased devotion to that cause for which they gave the last full measure of devotion

Therese sighed. "Family defines us more than anything else. I wasn't lying when I said it at rallies: I wouldn't be running if it wasn't for Jerome's death. He wasn't a solider, but he did give that measure of devotion Lincoln talked about."

Kaitlin's throat tightened. She'd never spoken of Therese's private matters, preferring to keep them just that: private.

"Lincoln's army fought to preserve the Union above all else, and his men knew that wasn't possible without equity in WP distribution. He died before enacting that vision, so you could say Jerome was just another soldier working for Lincoln's dreams."

Kaitlin's mouth thinned. Therese's thinking led down a dangerous road.

Therese broke into a grin. "Of course, the other side can say the same thing. Your uncle is proof of that. I'm sure Senator Lungford saw himself as the executor of Lincoln's will, fighting wars abroad to secure prosperity at home."

Kaitlin scoffed. "My uncle hadn't seen combat for over fifty years when he worked with Brooks, a deserter, to send thousands of my men to their deaths in an illegal war."

Therese's eyes hardened. "And Jerome spent his whole, short life in New York City. But each time a cop kills an unarmed Black man, each time a jury frees them of consequences, that was a shot fired in the longest war our nation's ever fought: an enduring war on justice."

Kaitlin swallowed. "Why did you bring me here?"

"To ask you to be my Secretary of State."

Kaitlin froze. "...what?"

Therese laughed, her eyes twinkling. "You've secured America's interests for decades. You come from institutional royalty. You've been an executive before and the country knows you." Turning serious, Therese narrowed her eyes. "And most importantly: I trust you."

A feather would have knocked her over.

"The joint statement cost you the election," Therese said. "I'll bet you knew that at the time, and you still did it."

Kaitlin bit her lip.

"Wars are never civil and never cold, no matter what we've said in the past." Therese held Kaitlin's hand again. "Help me fix this country, before it's too late."

Walking to the entrance, Kaitlin sat on the steps. Therese joined her. "You know, Lincoln stole his election. His campaign manager didn't have the delegates to secure victory during the convention, so he printed fake tickets and smuggled his own supporters in under cover of darkness." Kaitlin looked up at the black sky above them.

Therese smiled. "That's the American Way. We lie, cheat, and steal for the chance to do something good." Leaning in, she clasped both her hands around Kaitlin's. "It's been a man's world for so long; let's give women a shot."

Kaitlin's stomach churned. In her bones she knew she could do this job, and do it well. But another four years in Washington? Running a major department? Not to mention the travel involved? "I have to talk to Vijay..."

"Of course," Therese said. "When's your flight?"

"Tomorrow. I'll have an answer for you by then."

Kaitlin stood. Therese thanked her and told her agents it was time to go, leaving Kaitlin in the shadow of Lincoln.

Chapter Twenty One

November 10, 2028

Therese's words were like a jackhammer in Kaitlin's mind, digging to break loose a worldview that'd been ingrained in her for decades. *An enduring war on justice.* That was what she'd said. Kaitlin knew it was true, realized now that the war had turned the moment Therese won. Was joining a Johnson administration her opportunity to bring America's longest war to a peaceful end?

She'd gone home and made love to Vijay, an act that'd lessened the blow of telling him after lunch that she needed to leave him one last time. Uncle Charles had haunted her for months on her turf; it was time to visit him on his.

Her campaign had paid for her plane through the end of the week, so she used it one last time to fly to Salt Lake City. Landing at a private hangar near the airport, she rented a car and drove herself to Springville, where her uncle was buried. Standing at his tombstone, she closed her eyes and prayed for his soul. When she opened them, the ghost was floating at her side.

"Hello, Uncle."

"You lost." His gravelly voice was now like water, smooth and rolling, without judgment.

She'd spent the flight knowing what she'd say, had been thinking about it since Therese had left her. "I'm sorry."

He tilted his head so that it touched hers, but she wasn't met with the usual shiver down her spine that made her recoil. Instead, a warmth pulsed through her body, and any speech she'd planned to recite emptied from her mind. "When Matt died and you became my responsibility, all I ever wanted was your happiness, secured through the power of the Lungford name."

A tear ran down Kaitlin's face. "But power and happiness are two different things, and life makes you choose between them. I'm not sorry I lost; I'm sorry I didn't see you trying all these years. And I forgive you... for not being my father."

Charles went silent.

"It wasn't fair to put that pressure on you, but you did shape every inch of who I've become. Including the part of me able to convince a man as good as Vijay to marry me... and a woman as good as Therese to offer me Secretary of State."

Charles's visage charged through his tombstone before returning to her side. "I was a good man, once. Committed to ending the war on justice."

Kaitlin raised her eyebrow.

Charles smiled, half his teeth gone and the other half rotted. "Most in DC know that's the only war that matters. It's why I wrote *A Dark Moon Rises*, to expose the corruption of the Johnson administration and its atrocities, in Vietnam and at home. But then the book was banned and I saw Ford pardon Nixon and I saw Reagan rise amidst Iran-Contra and I realized I was on the losing side of that war. So I joined the other side."

Kaitlin blinked away more tears and sat before her uncle's tombstone.

He hovered above her. "It's fitting that one Johnson administration can finally end a war that began under the previous one."

"You think I should take the job."

"I think you can change things so that future generations don't have to choose between power and happiness."

Kaitlin nodded. "I really did want to win the election. But seeing Therese use the campaign as a platform to honor her son... maybe I can use this job to honor the Lungford name."

"You've decided?"

It was the first time she could remember her uncle expressing uncertainty.

"You taught me to use politics as a weapon, a tool to bring

about change on a global scale. As Secretary of State, that's exactly what I'll do. And the last time this world hears the Lungford name, it'll remember it as an agent of good."

Charles smiled again; a rotten tooth fell to the ground and vanished.

"For the first time, I'm climbing the political ladder because it's something I want to do, not out of some sort of daughterly loyalty to you."

Charles's form touched her again, and the warmth was so painful it threatened to rip her heart in two. Blinking away tears, she whispered her final words to Uncle Charles. "I'm sorry it took me this long, but I know now that you did love me in your own twisted way. And I loved you, too."

When she left the cemetery, her uncle stayed.

•————————————————•

November 11, 2028

Kaitlin called President-Elect Johnson after passing security at IAD and finding a private room. "I'm in, with some conditions."

"Name them." Therese's smile was impossible to miss even over the phone.

Kaitlin wondered how long it'd take her to stop being annoyed at the woman's constant optimism. "I hire my own staff."

"Of course."

"And I'm gone if there's ever even a whiff of press assuming I'm supporting you in 2032."

Therese laughed. "Madame Secretary, I don't even want to think about re-election for another two years."

Kaitlin sighed. "Okay then."

"You at the airport?"

Kaitlin nodded. "Vijay's waiting."

"He's on board with this?"

Kaitlin smiled. "He was on board before I was."

"Well, who'd keep us grounded if not the men in our lives? Have a great trip."

Kaitlin hesitated. "Am I going to see stories about my appointment from Europe?"

Therese laughed again; the sound was infectious. "I'll let the press know I've made my decision but don't want to announce it until I've secured everyone on my senior team."

Kaitlin nodded again. The press would hound some of the obvious candidates for a quote, but since her name wasn't in consideration, she'd be safe. An announcement came down over the loudspeaker; her flight was boarding.

"That's your cue to go," Therese said. "Try to enjoy yourself; it'll be nonstop once you get back."

Smiling, Kaitlin hung up and returned to Vijay's arms.

November 23, 2028

Thanksgiving at the Johnson house always featured a wide cast of characters, and this was the biggest yet. Rebecca. Erica and her boyfriend, Aaron. Aaron's parents, Cassie and Elias (who'd packed food from their diner for the meal). Agents from her security detail. Russell, of course, and Roger from the White House (who was growing on her, though she'd never admit it).

Therese hollered from the kitchen. "It's halftime. Sounds like the men should take over the cooking."

Russell and Roger meandered over from the family room to put the finishing touches on the turkey and stuffing, while Elias handled the sweet potato au gratin and pecan pie he'd made from scratch. Aaron got the mac and cheese and barbecued pork out of the freezer to warm up.

Pouring Cassie and Erica a glass of white wine each as they sat on the couch and prepared to watch the halftime show, Therese paused when her phone rang. Seeing it was Kaitlin, she excused herself to her bedroom. Rebecca moved to join her before Therese waved her off and entered the room alone.

"How was your honeymoon?"

"Great wine, great sex, great sights, but I got only three days I wasn't thinking about the work ahead of us."

Therese threw her head back in laughter. "That's two more days than I expected."

"I read you settled on your heads for the big four."

Therese sighed. The "big four" referred to the departments of State, Treasury, Defense, and Justice. "People will cry murder, and it's definitely a risk with only fifty-two Democrats in the Senate, but I want Curtis as Attorney General."

Kaitlin cleared her throat. "You're lucky you've got me at State instead of in the Senate."

Therese chuckled. "Me and Kusum convinced Manish Nagaraj to come out of retirement."

"Treasury Secretary?" Kaitlin scoffed. "Yeah, that'll do it."

"He's not just a businessman, but a master politician, as well, from his years running the Senate. That on top of him being a minority? There's no one better to help us set up the infrastructure needed to give WP legalization a real chance to succeed."

"I don't disagree," Kaitlin said. "Though he is in his seventies."

"Which is why he's only serving two years to get us set up. He's bringing in this IP lawyer from Eisenhower Blitz as his deputy, Ravi Gandhika."

"A corporate lawyer?" Kaitlin said dubiously. "Doesn't seem your style."

"I gotta give the corporate class something, right? And he knows the legal implications inside out of what we're about to attempt here with Undersecretaries of Drug-Enhanced Commerce. He's got the connections we'll need to make WP public-private partnerships a reality."

"Justice. Treasury. I'm at State. That leaves Defense."

"I picked someone," Therese said, "but I want your sign off."

"Who?"

"Nora Tirabassi."

Kaitlin's silence spoke volumes.

"I thought you'd like her," Therese said. "Female. Lifetime bureaucrat. CIA Director under both Brooks and Begaye."

"And has all the baggage that comes with ensuring American hegemony during the global war for WP. How do you think she'll do under Senate questioning?"

Therese spoke forcefully. "She did just fine during her CIA confirmation hearings." Kaitlin's silence spoke volumes yet again. "What aren't you telling me?"

"...that was before Brooks sold the NOC list."

Therese slumped on her bed.

"Madame President?"

Therese bit her lip. "This is why I need you. I need someone with the intrinsic trust of our law enforcement and intelligence agencies."

"Let me be clear," Kaitlin said. "I'm not saying Tirabassi did anything improper. But you'd have to be pretty fucking incompetent to let anyone walk off with that, even the president."

Therese stood back up, cracking her neck. "Who would you pick?"

Kaitlin answered immediately. "Mason Hsu. He's already gone through the confirmation process as the Defense Department's comptroller, and his mastery of all things China will come in handy."

"Okay," Therese said. "I'll announce it Monday: all four heads."

Kaitlin's voice cracked. "That's it? You're taking my pick?"

Therese laughed again. "Welcome to the big girls' table."

After telling Kaitlin that Rebecca would call her tomorrow with details about scheduling a press conference with all the department heads, Therese wished her and Vijay a happy Thanksgiving before returning to her family.

Chapter Twenty Two

December 13, 2028

Therese had been so naïve to believe being mayor of Albuquerque had prepared her for the invasion of privacy that would come with the presidency. The press rifled through their trash (and inferred from two takeout containers of Chinese food in the same week that she was going to be soft on China and tough on India). A receipt for a $200 gift card to Target (Erica's birthday present) sent the company's stock through the roof. As much as Therese fought the Secret Service to stay in Albuquerque, she'd admitted defeat weeks ago and now moved to Blair House, where every president-elect since Carter had stayed prior to inauguration.

Tonight, though, was her second wedding anniversary, and she demanded privacy. Agent Krueger, lead on her detail, made the arrangements herself, identifying a Taiwanese restaurant small enough to secure, and obscure enough that any passersby could be turned away. Therese chuckled; Mason Hsu would withdraw his name from consideration if he knew she was hosting such an important event at a Taiwanese place. She'd spent hours discussing the issue with Kaitlin and Rebecca, wanting her incoming press secretary to have a good relationship with every Department Secretary, but especially Kaitlin. There'd be no room for error once word got out that Therese and Kaitlin were proposing such a drastic change to Taiwanese relations, but they'd have to keep it under wraps for another five weeks.

Therese and Russell entered the restaurant through a back alley. Though it was named beautifully (A Helping of Hépíng, the Mandarin word for peace), it was about as impressive as a broom closet. Set underneath a nail salon in Chinatown, it had only two tables in the front and half a window. One of the tables was occupied by Agent Krueger and had been moved so that the agent's body blocked Therese from being seen.

"Perfect night out," Russell said, leaning back with his hands behind his head. "Just you, me, and Agent Krueger."

Therese chuckled. "Date nights are gonna look a bit different these next four years."

Russell smiled. "Let's go ahead and make it eight." Ordering them both bubble tea, he tried and failed to use chopsticks to eat some spring rolls.

Therese forgot she was president-elect for the next hour. Agent Kreuger disappeared as she spoke with Russell as if it was their first date, touching hands and laughing and sharing dishes of gua bao and shanghai rice cakes and scallion pancakes. For dessert, they had two slices of pineapple cake (Russell refused to share).

"Luminary is flaming out."

Russell chuckled as Agent Kreuger spoke into her earpiece.

"What?" Therese asked.

"I love your codename."

Therese thanked Kreuger as she stepped into the car that would take them back to Blair House. "You need to pick out your own."

Russell rolled his eyes. "You hemmed me in. I gotta choose something that starts with L now, like yours."

Therese sighed. "It should be Lucky."

Russell smiled. "Hey now, I thought that's what I'll be tonight."

———————●————————————————●———————

December 15, 2028

It'd been two days since Bella had dropped her grandparents off at JFK. She missed them for all the reasons anyone missed loved ones, but on top of that was the silence. There was nothing now to distract her from the call she was expecting any moment, the one where their adoption agency would tell them they'd failed their character test, that they simply weren't the type of people New Beginnings could entrust with a baby. Maadhini and Sadiya had said they'd put in a good word, but Bella's hopes plummeted with each day of not hearing from the agency.

She was pacing around their apartment as Aditya ate ice cream straight from the container like a savage. A phone call broke her reverie.

She answered. "Hello?"

"This is Cassie Nudon. Am I speaking to Mr. and Mrs. Shetty?"

Bella rolled her eyes, thinking about how most people in DC would call them Mr. and Mrs. Ferrari, given her stature. She decided it was easier to agree. "Yes." Covering the phone receiver, snapping her fingers to get Aditya's attention, she moved them to the couch and put the call on speaker.

"Mrs. Shetty, I won't lie, we weren't sure your home would be a safe and nurturing one after hearing about the attempt on your life, your husband's time in jail, not the mention the... other thing."

Bella's heart stilled. "Weren't? Past tense?"

Cassie's voice was light as a feather. "We heard from one of our moms. Two of them, actually."

Aditya stopped shoveling ice cream into his face upon hearing this. "Two?"

"Yes," Cassie said. "Sadiya Murthy and Maadhini Kedilaya seemed to think you'd not just suffice, but thrive as parents. And given your history with Sadiya, especially Mr. Shetty, we took their recommendation seriously."

Bella covered the receiver again as Aditya jumped in the air and pumped his fist before kissing her.

"What happens now?" Bella asked.

"I'll need to send a social worker over to both your places for inspection, and we've got some paperwork to get through. It'll be another few months..."

Bella picked up on the anticipation in Cassie's voice. "...but?"

"We've already received a number of inquiries from expectant mothers. Seems your interview with Tammy Day was well received, Justice Ferrari."

Bella sighed with relief, slumping into the couch. "Thank you."

"I'll email over the forms and let's get you in here tomorrow."

Bella stood upright. "Tomorrow?!"

Cassie chuckled. "There's a particular woman expecting a girl in March I want you to meet."

Bella was too stunned to speak, so Aditya took the phone from her and thanked Cassie before hanging up.

"Tomorrow?"

Aditya smiled, kissing her again. "Life is a lot of waiting with brief interruptions of stunning action."

Bella began pacing, moving around the entire apartment, checking things off with her fingers. "We gotta babyproof two large apartments. We gotta get car seats. Two cribs. Baby food. Diapers!"

Walking to her, Aditya took her hands in his, then forced her to sit at the kitchen table and handed her his ice cream and a spoon. "Eat. You'll feel better."

"Is that your solution for everything?"

Aditya laughed. "It's an amazing thing that's about to happen, the best miracle in the world. Let's enjoy it instead of freaking out. We've got security, friends, family. We'll be okay."

She took a bite of ice cream. Her heart rate slowed and she fought back a smile, not wanting to admit he'd been right about eating making her feel better.

"...there is one thing..." Aditya said.

"What?"

He looked at his shoes. "Cassie said it was a girl... I'd like to name her Deepika... for my mom."

Bella lost her fight against smiling. "That's the best idea I've ever heard."

Aditya kissed her again and a shock went through her system. They stayed on the couch in each other's embrace until they fell asleep together, and the last thought Bella had before passing out was that they'd awaken to a new world, one where anything was possible because their sins didn't have to define them.

Chapter Twenty Three

December 19, 2028

For four days, Bella's head had raced with thoughts of Deepika's upcoming birth and all the things they had to do before then. But tonight's occasion would distract her: a White House wedding. She hadn't expected the invitation, but Anaba Begaye had been insistent.

Their Lyft dropped Bella and Aditya off at the White House Visitor Center. Aditya's tuxedo made him look gallant, while Bella sported a royal blue ballroom gown. Her white heels proved tricky for navigating the snow drifts, so she leaned on Aditya the whole way to the security check-in. In line, they spotted Kaitlin and Vijay.

Bella smiled meekly, tapping her shoulder. "Good evening, Madame Secretary."

Kaitlin took her hand firmly and nodded. "Bella."

Bella cleared her throat. "I never... I never thanked you for..."

Kaitlin waved her hand. "There's no need."

"...but... I..."

"It had nothing to do with you and everything to do with how I wanted to run *my* campaign, live *my* life."

Bella opened her mouth again before closing it.

Aditya broke in to end the awkwardness. "Vijay." Shaking hands, the two men spoke of where their parents hailed from, bonding over their shared roots.

"I've never seen the residence," Bella said. The wedding itself would be in the Rose Garden, steps from the Oval Office, but cocktail hour was in the dining room where President Begaye and his wife, Ajei, ate together each night.

"It's as beautiful or ugly as the current occupant allows," Kaitlin said. "Brooks insisted on the gaudiest decorations: gold chandeliers in each hallway and a blow-up photo of his electoral map in the guest bedroom."

Bella snorted in laughter, prompting a smile from Kaitlin.

"Come on," Kaitlin said, taking Vijay's hand as the pair of couples passed security, "let's see what the president's done."

The Rose Garden was as elegant as ever, with red chrysanthemums and yellow peonies. Per Navajo tradition, turquoise jewelry was laid out for each guest to wear. Senator Hammond's wife set the smallest ring on her finger, making a face as if it was infected. Bella and Kaitlin chose anklets to wear beneath their gowns.

At the entrance to the residence, Secret Service agents took each guest's phone. "No photos allowed," one explained.

Crossing the threshold of the house, Bella spotted Therese and Russell sipping wine by the Truman balcony with Senator Ramachandran while the bride and groom posed inside under a giant dreamcatcher. It was brown and green, with gold and silver at the sides. Underneath was a guestbook and instructions for each visitor to "write your own dreams for us and then put it in this bottle for us to capture forever."

Anaba looked like a princess, clad in a white dress with threaded tassels at the corners. She held a blue blanket around her as she posed for photos. Seeing Bella, she screamed with excitement. "You came!"

Bella smiled. "You look gorgeous. Thank you for inviting me."

Anaba blushed. "Thank you. I wasn't sure you'd come, at first."

"Why?"

"This... year. What you went through. I thought you'd blame me for telling my dad to nominate you in the first place."

Bella patted Anaba's clothed shoulder, feeling the gossamer lace and tassels. "Don't pity anyone their gilded cages. A person can break through the bars any time they please."

Anaba frowned as the photographer snapped a picture. "What do you mean?"

Luther apologized, asking the photographer to try again.

Bella looked Anaba in the eyes. "You have nothing to be sorry for. You made me one of the most powerful people on Earth. If that made my life a little harder, too, then so be it. I wouldn't change anything that happened. You saved me that day."

Bella beamed and held Anaba's hand as the photographer took a second picture, which would undoubtedly come out much better than the first.

To the extent a White House wedding could be toned down, Anaba's was. Filled with Navajo tradition and lacking the usual crowd snapping photos with their phones, all eyes were glued to Anaba's brothers walking down the aisle with her bridesmaids. Then it was her turn, holding the president's hand as she stepped toward Luther.

"Trust in God and in yourselves," President Begaye said, placing his daughter's hand in Luther's before taking his seat at Ajei's side.

———————————•———————————

The vows were beautiful, the ceremony filled with circumstance. Bride and groom arrived wrapped in a blue blanket each, but once married, those were shed and Anaba and Luther were shrouded in a white blanket together. Bella choked back tears as they recited their vows to each other and the world.

The grandest occasion happened after the wedding, after most guests had left. A cocktail hour and a wedding were hassle enough to arrange during a presidential transition and the holidays; Anaba and Luther had insisted on no reception so that overworked and underpaid staffers (not to mention the Secret Service) could go home to be with their families.

"Hang back," Luther said.

Bella stopped walking to the exit. "Me?"

"All of you," he said, pointing to Kaitlin and their spouses. "My wife wants you to come back to the residence."

Inside seemed smaller now that tables were set up in the dining room. Bella, Kaitlin, and Therese sat with Anaba as Luther walked the husbands over to meet President Begaye and his sons.

Kaitlin smirked as a waiter handed out flutes of champagne. "We've had such influence in each other's lives, and yet this is the first time we've all been together."

Therese laughed. "You're right."

Bella sighed. "I told Anaba if I had to do it all over again, I would."

Kaitlin paused before nodding. "Me, too."

Anaba raised an eyebrow.

"On your wedding day of all days," Kaitlin said, "you know there are more important things than winning." She sipped. "I could've won by giving in to the country's worst instincts, but what does that leave for posterity? What does that leave for me?"

Hours were spent playing card games and making inappropriate jokes about each other once drunk, until finally it was time to go.

Anaba stopped Bella as she prepared to leave. "I've decided to go to law school."

Bella smiled. "That's wonderful. You need a letter of recommendation?"

Anaba nodded, hugging Bella when she agreed.

To everyone's surprise, Kaitlin hugged her next. "You worked at a think tank, right? Call the State Department when you're done with your first year. I need interns for our general counsel office."

Closing and opening her eyes, Bella decided to share, too, telling Kaitlin and Therese and this young bride about her own plans for the future, about Deepika Shetty, Jr.

Therese cleared her throat. "No matter what you're faced with, if you can just find the will and grit to keep going, you can find brighter days ahead."

Bella nodded. "To Anaba and Luther."

Anaba responded. "To posterity."

Afterword

All authors have their own distinct style. So here's mine: great storytelling should be able to be summarized in a sentence or two. The story of *Privilege* was "happiness and power are two separate things, and you have to choose." Rakshan and Sadiya started at the same point, as two ill-fated lovers with enough money and education to establish decent lives, young enough to do something meaningful with their considerable resources, and it was their selection between those two choices that defined the rest of their lives. Because you're never too young (or too old!) to determine the rest of your life, that decision is always in front of you.

With *Skingrafters*, you saw that story examined on a microscale, with Maadhini and Aditya. Happiness can be messy at times, but if you're lucky, your life goes on long enough that you come to a time where it seems like you've always been happy. And power? Well, you saw the tradeoffs Aditya made for it throughout the rest of the *WP Saga*.

That brings us to *Posterity*. After decades of sacrifices, of social change on a global scale, what do we leave behind for others? For our children? What do we leave behind in a world that refuses to bend so we have to break it in order to make progress? The story of *Posterity* is that "you are more than your worst moment." These three women, who've been through some of the worst traumas imaginable, all deserved a happy ending. I've tried to give them that, but also one that is realistic for the world they live in. Because that world, the world of the *WP Saga*, is broken.

Ours isn't yet. Ours can still be bent. So let's get to it.

If you liked this book (or if you really hated it and want to tell me why), please leave a review.

www.ingramcontent.com/pod-product-compliance
Lightning Source LLC
Chambersburg PA
CBHW071157020726
47502CB00002B/445